SEEDS 3

Little Dozen Press

SEEDS 3: The Wastes of Winter

Copyright 2023 by Rachel Starr Thomson
Visit the author at www.rachelstarrthomson.com

Published by Little Dozen Press
Fort Erie, Ontario, Canada
www.littledozen.com

Cover design and interior layout by Mercy Hope
Copyright 2023

ISBN: 978-1-927658-71-0

SEEDS 3
The Wastes of Winter
The Chronicles of Kepos Gé, Book 3

by Rachel Starr Thomson

Cast of Characters

The Settlers of Jerusalem Valley

Linette Cole, a new convert to the Tremblers, newly arrived in Jerusalem Valley

John Hopewell, a Trembler

Amos Thatcher, a Trembler

Agatha Moss, a Trembler, widow of Cleveland Moss

Clive Shilling, Puritani

Silas Gromer, Puritani

Smith Foster, Puritani, lately imprisoned in Fort Collins

Sarah Foster, Puritani, his wife

Letty Foster, their daughter

Martin Foster, their son

Samuel Foster, another son

Lila Foster, another daughter

Jonathan Applegate, Puritani, the parson

Corey Sowell, Trembler, a messenger sent for aid

Obadiah Brown, Trembler, a messenger likewise sent

Simon Ferguson, Trembler, a third messenger

Serena Vaquero, a Trembler from Tempestano in the Old World

Jacques de la Croix, an Imitator from the Old World

New Cranwellites

Eben Axel, a former slave

Josiah Axel, his son

Phinehas Cole, Linette's father and Elder of New Cranwell

Beth Cole, Linette's daughter, who is a secret

The Soldiers

Frederick Almon, captain in command of Jerusalem Valley

Thomas Carson, a major who has rebelled against Almon

Matthias Carey, a major who attempted to kill Almon

Paul McIntyre, a young private

THE RIVER PEOPLE OF ANOSCHI PASS
Capenokanickon, chief of the River People
Wetëndeis, his favorite daughter
Anasan, his son
Naamucksha, his nephew
Sanquen, a warrior
Talaman, an older, wise warrior
Machcopoiken, a warrior

AT FORT COLLINS
Ezekiel, an old slave
Anderson, lieutenant in command of the fort

IN THE OLD WORLD
Joseph Crispin, Chief Elder of the Puritani kirk and persecutor of Tremblers
Deacon Adolphus Bure, a servant of the Puritani kirk
Carlos Vaquero, fugitive *conde* of Tempestano and brother to Serena
Massimo Diego, Carlos's captain of the guard and best friend. Goes by "Diego."
Jorges Diego, Diego's little brother
Bettina, their sister
Paulo, her husband
Guenther — a writer works with them on their press
Taddeo Diego, another of Diego's brothers, an apprentice cloth merchant
Caterina Diego, another sister
One-Eyed Driesken, a bandit
Lucaan Feaanstra, a young boatman from the Bog Region of the Western Lowlands
Leeanaert Feeanstra, his brother
Joric Dievoert, a boatman
Jaapje Dievoert, his brother

Prologue

In the Before Time, before anything that is made had yet been made, *Wetëndeis told the women and children in the smoky heart of the longhouse,* the Creator spoke the God Seeds into existence.

There were many God Seeds, so many no one has ever been able to count them. Each one was unique, a thought from the heart of the Creator. Each carried within it the stuff of creation. Some cradled that which would become the elements—wind, fire, water, star. Some were rock, metal, mineral, soil. Some carried the forms of the animals and others of the plants. Some became spirits: the great lights and the shades. And one cradled within its rind and shell and pith the seed that would become Netami and Gahowes, our First Parents and the First Parents of all the Peoples.

The Creator spoke each of these Seeds with great wisdom and care, until they took shape in his cupped hands. And then he planted them in Kepos Gé where they began to grow. Everything formed in the heart of a seed grew to become what it was always meant to be.

The elements burst out of their seeds to find their place in creation. Stone and rock and soil grew until they would grow no more, and become ancient, unchanging except to erode. But the Living Things, all Living Things, bore seed within themselves, and so from that time to this they reproduce themselves after the image born by the God Seed that was their origin. And the Elangomatàk, all People, they carry within themselves too the power to speak seeds as the Creator does, to make words that grow and produce fruit.

But, *Wetëndeis paused, dark eyes snapping as she took in the women and children who hung on her every word,* no creature in this world can do other than be itself. That is why no truly new thing can come into existence, unless the Creator should will it.

"But what about the Machkigen?" a girl of about twelve asked with a shiver. "Aren't they a new thing?"

No, utterly not. Machkigen are not creations of any kind. They are corruptions of creation. They are born of malliku, and malliku is only the twisting of what was once good.

"Then what about the sparrows that look like the leaves?" one of the small boys asked. "The Wise Father says it has changed its feathers to hide itself."

That is true, *Wetëndeis conceded.* The God Seeds contained great wisdom and much ability for change, and every Living Thing to come from them was meant to grow. But no sparrow has ever become a not-sparrow, has it? No sparrow becomes a wolf. No wolf becomes a fish. No fish becomes Elangomatàk.

That is how it has always been, and that is how it always will be.

"But why is it so?" one of the women asked.

It is so because creation cannot create itself. For something new to come into Kepos Gé, the Creator would need to speak a new God Seed.

Part 1
Callings

Chapter 1

November 27, 1642. Below Jerusalem Valley—The New World

Linette Cole held a torch high as she led the others through the darkness of the narrow underground ravine. It cut deep through black rock, its silence palpable. She did not dare light the phosphorescence in her own vines, the bright green tendrils that ran down her neck and arms and over the backs of her hands. She felt as though she had exhausted that gift when she descended through this same pathway yesterday. Without question it had exhausted her, and she could not use it again without time in the sun to regain her strength.

Behind her in grim silence came a small multitude, stretching back far beyond the light of the torch to Sarah Foster's cellar where the path down into the ground began. Never had Jerusalem Valley seen a throng so varied. Soldiers in red military coats eased through the ravine alongside settlers and warriors of the River People. At the back, the River People bore their wounded on stretchers. Linette bit her lip as the ravine began to narrow down till it was hardly more than a tight, narrow cave—a slit leading toward the cavern she remembered so well. She had told them all that the cavern, with its waterfall and pool of water, was unlikely to be there anymore—that they were subjecting the wounded to a difficult journey for no good reason. Like the vineyard she and the Puritani parson, Jonathan Applegate, had discovered under the floorboards of the Trembler meeting house not so long ago, the pool was not entirely of this earth.

But they had insisted. Infected with the poison they called *malliku,* witchcraft, the wounded warriors might not last long before they were consumed body and soul. If the pool was not of this earth, all the more reason to try to reach it before it disappeared.

Jonathan had explained to Linette that the River People thought the pool was something from their stories—a place of healing they called their Sacred Spring. Perhaps it was. That was certainly more than Linette could know.

Behind her, Clive Shilling and John Hopewell walked close behind her, interposing themselves between her and the soldiers. Further back, Jonathan walked amid the River People, holding fast to Letty Foster's hand.

The space in the rock grew narrower, so tight Linette could hear Big John Hopewell trying to squeeze himself through. She imagined the line thinning out, each one coming single file, trying to maneuver the stretchers through the darkness. *Please,* she whispered inwardly. *Let it be there. And let the waters be what they need them to be.*

She strained for the remembered change in the air, the sudden sharpness of water, the sound of it.

And then, suddenly, there it was. She could hear water falling down rock and smell the tang of minerals carried in its stream. It hadn't disappeared. Like the wheatfields growing huge and golden beneath the ground, the spring, too, was still here.

Leading this long procession through the darkness with so much at stake, Linette envied those settlers who were still back amid the wheat, harvesting it with shouts of laughter and tears of joy. Only yesterday they had faced famine, hastened toward its brutal end by Frederick Almon's cruelty. Things had changed quickly.

Perhaps that would happen again.

The path wound around a corner, still heading down, and reached a natural ledge. As Linette descended to it, the scene opened out: water falling into a pool below, and in the pool, some way out, an island that was little more than a large boulder rising from the water. On that rock, she remembered, was a tree—its branches leafed with vivid green fronds.

There was one more sharp descent toward the pool, steep and slick from the spray. Linette used her free hand to brace herself against one side to avoid slipping as she gingerly made her way down.

She reached the sandy, pebbled bit of shore where water gently lapped and raised the torch higher, peering through the darkness. Why couldn't she see the island as clearly as she had last time?

The answer came to her with a sinking feeling. Last time, the tree itself had provided light—its leaves had shone with a pale green light. They had lit this whole cavern.

This time, there was no such light.

There was no such tree.

Or was there? Linette frowned and bit her lip, willing phosphorescence up into her vines, just a little, just enough—there. Light coursed through her and lit up the cavern, and she saw it clearly before she let the light die, her head pounding, her whole body swaying with the effort.

The tree was there. But it was dead. Its leaves were gone, its branches white and skeletal. When she had carried away the seed, the tree had given up its life.

She feared, as she knelt carefully and dipped her hand into the pool's cold water, that the waters would hold no more life in them than the tree now did—that they could do nothing for the sick whose groans she could hear as their bearers laid their stretchers down on the ledge above.

Big John eased himself down beside her. "This is it?" he asked.

She nodded, instinctively reaching out to lay a hand on his arm as she struggled back up to her feet. He let her lean on him without comment, even brought his own hand up to the small of her back to support her. "It isn't what they think. At least, I fear it isn't."

"It's not your fault if the answers don't lie here," John said.

She nodded again, a quick, shallow acknowledgment of words she didn't really believe. So much of what had happened felt like her fault. If she hadn't come here, if she hadn't run away from her father and her life in New Cranwell, perhaps the soldiers would never have come either. Certainly Almon could not have used searching for her as a pretext for oppressing the whole settlement. They had suffered because they refused to give her up, and because she had not given herself up, not until the end.

"Linette," John said quietly, "whatever this place is, whatever the seed you discovered here, you were meant to find it. If you had not done what you did, *everything* you did, it would still be buried. We would still be starving, and the seed would be unfound. Don't believe the lies you hear."

Linette smiled faintly. "Did Herman teach you to read my mind like that?" she asked.

"No," John said with a wink. "But he taught me to be kind about it."

Linette laughed. Others were beginning to arrive, crowding the little beach. John offered Linette his arm, and she gratefully leaned hard on it as they moved to one side. A handful of soldiers fanned out to either side as the Outsiders—the River People—came forward. First were several men, warriors of various ages, accompanying a tall young woman wearing a red cloak. Behind her came a young man with long, loose hair and pale blue vines. In his arms he carried an old man, his father and the young woman's—Capenokanickon, chief of his people.

They were solemn and straight-backed. They spoke not a word, but all three walked into the water, until it came up past their knees, and stopped. The young man with his father in the middle, the woman on their left, an older warrior on their right. Behind them, others filled the beach, inadvertently pushing the soldiers further to the side, and Linette and John with them. The settlers had stayed above. The River People had carried more of their wounded with them and now laid them gently down on the sand. Others waded into the water behind the first three.

The young woman raised her hands. She carried a staff, red feathers and beaded cords tied around its head. She spoke—words Linette didn't understand, but felt down to the core of her were a prayer. The others listened, then joined her, speaking words they all knew.

Finally they waded further into the water, up to their waists. Though the soldiers held torches and some of the River People did as well, they were so far out now they almost disappeared in the darkness of the cavern—bare shadows in the darkness. Linette could still feel the bone-chilling cold from where she stood. Out in the water, she could just see the young man in the middle bending forward as he submerged his wounded chief in the cold, dark water.

She wanted to add a prayer of her own, but no words came. Instead she offered her heart, the empathy and fear in it, and hoped that would be enough.

She didn't know what anyone expected to happen next. If there would be a light, or a change in the water, or some sign of healing. Nothing of the kind happened. Instead, more of the River People took up their human burdens again and carried them into the water, taking them out into the depth and the cold and baptizing them there.

Hoping for healing.

Hoping that some divine power in these waters could heal wounds that were no mere wounds—wounds that were infected with the power to turn a man into a mad, wicked, deformed thing. A *Machkigen*—a thorn.

John nudged her and pointed with his chin toward something happening on the far edge—a sight she didn't expect. A soldier was wading into the water with a man in his arms. This man's lanky arms were looped around the soldier's neck; he wore a simple cotton shirt and trousers. Eben, she remembered. The soldier was Major Thomas Carson. As they approached, the warriors made room for them.

Linette turned away. Tears pricked at her eyes. These were the actions of the hopeful. Or the desperate. *She* had found this place; it seemed she ought to be able to help.

But of course, having brought them here, there was nothing at all she could do more.

First thing that morning, the settlers of Jerusalem Valley had gathered in the Trembler meeting house to hear Linette. Jonathan had spread the word that she needed them, and they had all come except Sarah, who stayed behind to keep an eye on Captain Almon. He could not be left alone—he had been stabbed by one of his own men, perhaps fatally, and was a Machkigen besides.

Linette had thanked them for hiding her, for putting so much on the line for her, and then she had drawn the seed from her pocket and told them all about finding it in a secret pool beneath the ground, and about the golden wheat that grew supernaturally below Sarah's house. And she had told them what she had seen in a dream, or a vision—that Herman Melrose had planted it there, long ago. And now it had come to her, to all of them.

She told them what she knew, though she could not explain to them how she knew it or why the knowledge had been given to her: that it had to be planted again, and not here.

This seed had a purpose, and Herman had failed to fulfill it. He had in fact planted it where it was never meant to be.

"And where," someone eminently practical and a little testy had asked—Clive Shilling, she thought, though she had been so nervous speaking to the entire gathering of settlers that she couldn't remember for sure—"is that?"

She didn't know, she'd told them.

She hoped *they* might know. That in all their years in Jerusalem Valley, bringing the vision of Herman Melrose into the world, the vision of peace and tolerance, unity and freedom, he might have told them about another mission he had yet to fulfill.

But no.

No, no one knew anything.

Crestfallen, Linette had stood in their midst cupping that pebbled, glowing seed in her hands and found that once again, she was not sufficient for the task. Nor apparently could anyone else help her.

Jacques and Serena, the outlanders from the Old World, had been in the very back of the room. She'd thought Serena looked disappointed in her, which was nothing new. Despite having been fugitives together for an uncomfortably long time in Sarah's cellar, Serena still intimidated Linette.

But she was misjudging her, perhaps. After the meeting was over—after Jonathan had also had a chance to address everyone and told them that the Outsiders had helped them and now needed access to the pool under the ground, because they hoped it would heal their wounded of the Machkigen poison—Serena weaved through the crowd to Linette's side and laid a hand on her arm.

"So often, the way is unclear," Serena said. "That is no reason to think you are on the wrong path. The way will become clear when the Fire Within lights it. Not before."

Standing now in the deep shadows of the cavern, feeling the chill of the air and watching as the River People submerged the sick in black waters, Linette chose to be content with a dark path. The seed constituted a calling, she knew that. She had to take it away—to plant it where it was meant to be planted. She did not know why, or when, or how. But to remain here, doing nothing, burying the seed again—that was no option. When she had taken the seed into her hands and felt its warmth and let its light fall over her, something in her had surged up to meet it. And that something was in her now, pushing her to act.

She would not rest again until the task was done.

CHAPTER 2

Frederick Almon lay in a world of fire and torment. Women were tending him. An old woman and several younger ones. The sullen girl who had warned him he might go mad. He couldn't remember her name or who she was, but he hadn't forgotten her words. He kept looking for the other one, the one who had knelt there beside him when he lay dying on the floor. The girl with red-blonde hair like his mother's.

In his fever dreams, it *was* his mother there with him. His mother before her sickness. When she was still good and sweet, when she loved him. Before she changed, and they locked her away and she clawed at the walls and raved and threw a bowl at him and broke it on the wall just beside his face.

He was on fire. He was sure he was on fire. He cried out and tried to run. He had to get away from the flames.

Someone restrained his arms and legs, pushed him down. A cool, clammy cloth pressed against his face. "Shhh," said a woman's voice. "Shhh."

His eyes flicked open. The room wavered like a mirage, but he knew enough to recognize it as the same little room where he had slept on a cot, where another man had gone crazy and died. He tried to strike the woman, shove her away, and run for it.

But someone was still holding him down.

He tried wildly to see who it was, but he couldn't see anyone except the woman, whose face became clearer as he stared up at her. Wrinkles, sagging jowls. An unattractive, aged face.

He licked his parched lips. "Get me out of here," he growled.

Another woman's voice came from the doorway. "Is he still raving?"

The old woman frowned and dabbed at his forehead again. He tried to knock her hands away, but he couldn't move his own. Who was holding him down?

"He's still fighting us," the old woman said. "He can't seem to find peace."

The other woman came into view above him, and he recognized her—sturdy and lean, practical. Sarah Foster. He snarled. Just days ago, Sarah had been defiant and stubborn, opposing him to his face. If he were well, he would put her back in her place.

"He looks worse," she said.

"Maybe if we didn't have him tied down," said the old woman. His heart leaped. Yes! Yes, if they would only let him go free …

Sarah frowned. "I don't like it either, but we can't trust him. You know that, Agatha. We don't know how far gone he may be, and even without the poison working inside him, he was capable of terrible things."

He tried to say something to her, but his tongue was on fire. She had no idea what he was capable of. He could smell smoke; the whole room was hazy. The Messenger was lingering just within his line of sight, staring down at him with utter contempt. Why hadn't *he* helped? Why had he allowed Carey—the rat, the traitor—to stab him?

Thoughts of that moment made him gnash his teeth. They had been under attack. The others had fortified themselves in the anteroom, just beyond the front door, but Carey insisted Almon follow him into the office. It would be safer there. He had shut the door.

Then turned around and put a knife in him.

"You aren't fit to command us," he'd said. "You're a madman and a coward."

The Messenger had been there, leering over Carey's shoulder. He didn't do a thing on Almon's behalf. In fact he had seemed almost supportive of the wretch.

Maybe he had been. Maybe the Messenger had been behind this treachery, just as he'd been behind all of Almon's actions for the last week—if it had even been a week since the Messenger first arrived. He didn't know. He had lost track of the days. Or he had lost track of reality, another voice told him. He had, perhaps, gone mad just as he'd always feared—always known—he one day would. And he might as well accept that.

No. He ground his teeth and strained against the bonds holding him down. His side felt like it would split open. He felt something hot spilling down his ribs.

"He's bleeding," the old woman said sharply. "He's burst the wound."

"Foolish man!" Sarah Foster exclaimed. There was a pause, a few sounds, then Sarah saying "Here"—a moment later, they forced something warm past his lips and down his throat in spite of himself.

After that, everything went mercifully dark.

The women—Agatha Moss, Sarah Foster, and Sarah's daughter Letty—watched silently for a few minutes to make sure the captain was well and truly out. When he did not stir, Agatha raised an eyebrow at Sarah and motioned for needle and thread. Letty handed it to her, and the elderly widow went resolutely to work stitching up the wound in the man's side again.

"Well," Sarah finally said, "we can't keep doing *that.*" Strong herbs were good for many things, but overusing them was dangerous. She knew better than to knock Almon out every time he grew restless, no matter how much she'd like to.

"He is tormented," Agatha said, pulling the thread. "He needs sleep if he's going to recover, and he needs peace if he's going to sleep." She laid a frail and slightly bloodied hand on Almon's forehead. "Creator, set him free."

Agatha stood slowly and stretched her stiff back. Almon was pale and his breathing shallow. In spite of herself, Sarah felt some pity as she looked down on him. With power, he had been terrifying and detestable. Now, weak, perhaps dying, betrayed and stabbed by one of his own men and quickly disavowed by all the others, he was just a lonely and pathetic man.

"It'll be a time before he wakes," Agatha said. "A good time to take a rest ourselves, I'd say." She reached out and locked arms with Letty. Letty seemed surprised at the gesture, but she let Agatha pull her close and steer her out of the room with her hand firmly tucked in the older woman's.

Sarah hid a smile. She knew Letty was meant to think that the elderly widow was leaning on her for strength, but the truth was quite the opposite.

When they had gone, Sarah lowered herself to the floor next to the unconscious captain. She wet the cloth in a bowl of hot water and wiped the sweat away from his face, along with the traces of blood from Agatha's hand—the old woman had transferred it from her stitching when she laid a hand on Almon's head to pray for him. Sarah grimaced, a bitter tang filling her mouth as she looked down at him. Only a day earlier, this man had threatened the lives of her children to force her to betray a friend. That he was now clearly revealed to be ill—possessed of the same strange madness that had once afflicted the young parson, Jonathan Applegate—hardly excused it. Jonathan had been confused and afflicted when the illness took him, and he had tried to fight it. The same could not be said for Frederick Almon.

Sarah wished that the major who had tried to kill the captain had succeeded.

But since he had not, she knew her duty. Care for the sick. Bring the stranger into your house.

The captain's breathing grew a little more even, and he seemed more comfortable. Satisfied that he would sleep for a while, Sarah laid aside the cloth and bowl of water and followed after Agatha and Letty.

When she had gone, Jacques stepped out of the shadows in the corner of the room.

She hadn't seen him, he knew. Nor had Letty. He had not wanted them to see him, and sometimes, what he wanted inexplicably manifested itself in the world.

Agatha had known he was there. He could not hide from the old Trembler's perceptive spirit. But she had said nothing.

He stood with his arms folded, looking down at the smaller man sleeping fitfully, tied to his cot. It was wise of them to restrain him.

Of course, the real threat could not be restrained—not with cords. He could feel the shade's presence like a slight chill in the air. He had forced it to reveal itself once and had no desire to do so again. The creature had taunted him—*"You can do nothing here, Shadowdancer. We will not be driven out. We are coming for you."*

It had been many years since Jacques had heard such a threat. The last time had cost him dearly. For all that he had gained immeasurably in the long run, he did not know if he could bear to pay such a price again.

So why was he here? he asked himself. Why come and stand here and taunt the thing to do what it threatened, to come after him, to attack?

He didn't really know. Perhaps it was just that waiting was such a terrible thing.

He quirked a smile at that. He was starting to think like Serena.

The door creaked open behind him. He didn't have to turn to know it was her. Serena walked into any room like a storm. Her approach shifted the atmosphere.

Almon moaned and twisted his wrists against the ropes holding him down.

"Doesn't sleep soundly, does he?" Serena asked, moving into Jacques's peripheral vision and folding her own arms in imitation of his. She wore a black wool dress and gloves, with a silver-tinged fur cape wrapped around her from shoulders to waist—fox skin, perhaps. Her dark hair hung loose around her shoulders, but she had a fur cap pulled snugly down over her ears and a woolen scarf wrapped around her neck. Now that they'd finally been able to come out of hiding and procure a few things, Serena was undoubtedly the most warmly dressed woman in the entire settlement. And probably still the coldest.

As though to confirm his words, she rubbed her hands together and blew into them. He tried not to laugh. It wasn't her fault she'd been born in a different climate. Or that she *was* a different climate.

"He's dreaming," Jacques said, setting his gaze back on the sick man.

"Not dreaming anything pleasant."

"He's seeing the thing that speaks to him," Jacques said.

"The thing that makes him like this?" Serena said, gesturing with one hand while she kept the other tightly wrapped around herself, trying to hug in whatever warmth was available to her—as though the fire in the hearth were no more effectual than a candle flame. He had tried to tell her a little of what he saw and what it meant. Not everything. But a little.

"I don't understand it," Serena continued. "You say he becomes this because a demon speaks to him. But we can see the poison in his veins. The same poison that infected the parson through a bite, and that infected those warriors because they were wounded by tainted arrows and blades. So which is it? Is he poisoned by poison or poisoned by words?"

"Both," Jacques said. He grimaced, and turned toward her slightly. "Aren't we all. You know, if you would loosen that fur a little, you might feel the heat of the fire."

"As though I would fall for that. I will loosen this fur when spring arrives."

"You might not find spring much more to your liking. I hear it's very wet here."

"Infernal country," she said. But she loosened the fur cape almost imperceptibly.

He was about to ask her why she had come when Frederick Almon groaned, arched his back, and opened his eyes.

They were red. Not bloodshot, not red with strain or fever—but blood-red, red entirely, without iris or pupil, and rapidly darkening to black.

It all happened too quickly. Almon snapped the cords holding him down and flew up. Jacques grabbed Serena and threw her behind him, pushing her toward the door. He heard himself yell "Go!" and turned to follow her even as the man who wasn't a man anymore, the man who was a monster, landed on his back and sank claws into his arms and sank teeth into his neck.

Serena didn't go. Through the pain and panic overtaking him, Jacques heard her scream as though through a whirlwind in his ears—*"Get! Out! By the Father, Son, and Fire Within—go back where you came from!"* He saw her grabbing on to the monster's arm and felt sickening horror as it flung its arm out to knock her away. Its teeth were still in his neck, ripping at his flesh, and his knees buckled. He cried out as he sank to the floor.

This was everything he had feared. It was worse than he had feared. Not only that the creature would be too strong for him, that it would take him as it had threatened, but that it would go after her too—Serena, whom he loved as he loved himself.

But Serena would not be flung aside, and she would not be cowed. Jacques's vision blurred darkly, but he saw her begin to blaze with a fire not of this world. And he heard her speak again, and this time her voice *was* the whirlwind, was all the power of thunder and water and wind: "Go back where you came from!"

Claws and teeth loosened. Jacques heard Almon's breath escape him in a rush, a death song. Serena still burned.

Then he collapsed. He could see nothing more.

On the other side of the world, Joseph Crispin sat up straight in his bed, grasping his chest, his heart pounding beneath his hand. He could see her accusing eyes boring into him, her slender finger pointing at him. She seemed to blaze with glory. He heard her words: *Go back where you came from!*

Throwing off the covers, the big man labored up from his bed. It was cold in this bedchamber, colder than it should be. Tempestano was famed for its mild climate, its comfortable winters. He had dreamed of them while he plotted ways to wrest this palace and province away from Carlos Vaquero. Everything had gone according to his design—well, except for the young count's unfortunate escape. But that would be taken care of soon enough.

No, the bigger problem was that Crispin could not get the face of Carlos's sister out of his head.

Or her voice.

"By the Father, Son, and Fire Within—go back where you came from!"

He flinched. He stalked across the room, grabbed up an iron poker, and thrust it into the coals that lay dimly flickering in the hearth. Such strange dreams. Would that cursed woman ever leave him alone?

A rattling breath across the room interrupted his thoughts. He whirled around, poker high.

Something was there, in the shadows. Just beyond the bed.

But it couldn't be.

"What are you doing here?" he growled.

The shape slowly took form—a familiar form, tall, broad, stocky. His own form, as though looking in a mirror. He hated the shade for choosing to wear his shape; it felt like a mockery. But one couldn't pretend to too much choice when dealing with devils.

"You're supposed to be in the New World," Crispin said.

"I was sent back." Its voice was dry, brittle. Like dead leaves.

Crispin shook and despised himself for it. "By whom?" he asked. He tried to let the anger and contempt in his voice disguise his fear.

"You know whom," the shade said, its voice an insubstantial whisper. "The girl you couldn't kill did this to us."

Crispin groaned and rubbed his forehead between his eyes. A dull ache had begun there and was beginning to grow. How many times would Serena Vaquero stand in his way? Bad enough that the Imitator was still on the scene, alive and uncaptured, and waging war against the shades in Crispin's employ. Now, somehow, Serena had acquired the power to command them too?

"I don't understand why you and your kind are so impotent before them," he said.

The shade rattled lightly, less like breathing and more like something trying to get free. "You should be more judicious with your words," it said. "You might find that one day we are not on your side."

"Nonsense," he snapped. "I am in command here. You don't frighten me. You need what I give you; don't think I don't know that."

"Such a spectacle," the creature said, hissing. "A man who wants power so badly he will ally himself with anything to get it. A man to whom betrayal means nothing."

"And what should it mean?" Crispin said. He could feel the hardness like stone beneath his rib cage, the palpable feeling he knew as resolve and ambition—his true qualities, the traits he had allowed to rise up and choke out everything else he might once have felt. "I am a man who believes in nothing," he reminded the demon. "To one such as I betrayal can have no meaning. One cannot break faith where there is no faith to break."

He turned his back on the thing in the shadows and stared ahead at the fire, still low, still not enough to counter the cold. Of course not, he realized—that cold, clammy chill he felt was the presence of the demon. It stank too; if he paid careful attention to his senses, he could pick up its rotting scent in the air.

Nasty things.

Resolve and ambition. One empowering the other. They had taken him far—from the lowly life of a cobbler's son to the powerful ranks of the kirk, and then higher, to the highest rank of all. And now he had Tempestano. And soon he would have all the princes, and all of the kings, under his thumb. They thought the old order had been bad. He intended to make them all see what a true tyrant could do.

But first, he needed the New World. He needed Jerusalem Valley.

He needed the seed hidden within it.

He had staked a great deal on his plan to kill Herman Melrose and frame Serena for the murder. He still wasn't sure what had gone wrong. And now the Vaquero girl and the Imitator posed a real threat to his plans there. They couldn't find the seed before he did. If they did, they would undoubtedly carry out the purpose Melrose had been too weak to finish.

The purpose that once, so long ago, *he* had been meant to finish.

He raised a hand, thick with golden rings, and waved it in the air. "Get out," he said. "You're a failure. Your presence here sickens me."

He felt without seeing it that the thing was smiling at his back. Then it went, invisibly, and he felt its going like something flittering just over his head and shoulders.

He shivered.

A knock on the door startled him. He jerked his chin up and glared at the door a moment before stalking across the floor and pulling it open.

"What do you want?" he demanded. The man who stood outside was smaller than he, a neatly built figure with a square beard and an earnest expression. He wore nightclothes and carried a candle. "Deacon?" Crispin repeated. "What do you want?"

"I'm sorry," Adolphus Bure said, shaking his head a little. He looked confused—like he had just been awakened from sleepwalking. "I thought I heard something. I thought—I thought something was wrong."

"Clearly you were mistaken," Crispin snapped. He made to close the door in the man's face, then thought better of it. He motioned toward the low, struggling fire and the two chairs on either side of it. "Would you care to sit?" he said. "Clear your head."

Bure nodded, still clearly confused. "Perhaps I should." He entered, then hesitated for a moment, as though sensing something in the air that made him loath to come further. Which was nonsense, of course. The man wasn't sensing anything. The demon was gone, and Bure was dull as a rock besides.

But if he *was* sensing something, better to know it now than have Bure getting ideas without Crispin's knowledge.

Overcoming his hesitation, the deacon tottered forward and lowered himself into the chair. He moved like an old man, Crispin observed, though he wasn't more than fifty and younger than Crispin himself. At night, or in damp, cold weather, he always seemed to age thirty years. He blamed it on joint trouble developed in the Lowland Bogs, where he'd spent his twenties in kirk work—running a mission among the half-savage people there.

When Bure got reminiscing about the old days, which was often—another way in which he was like an old man—he complained of all its hardships, resurrected gossip thirty years obsolete, and blamed all of his current ills on the Bogs. But Crispin never missed the wistfulness in his tone, the almost imperceptible grief for the loss of the past. It wasn't the sort of thing Crispin overlooked—it indicated weakness, something that could be taken advantage of if he ever needed to turn on his righthand man.

Bure laid his candle on the small table beside the chair, then cracked his knuckles and let out a sigh—almost a groan. "Damp in here," he said. "Feels like the old—"

"Yes," Crispin cut him off. He wasn't in the mood for reminiscences. "Now tell me," he said, softening his tone a little. "What did you think you heard?"

Bure shook his head as though he were trying to clear it. "I don't know. Perhaps I dreamed it—a voice. A voice I didn't know. It felt—well, threatening somehow." He shrugged, the look on his face turning from confusion and concern to sheepishness. "Now that we sit here together by the firelight, I think I must have dreamed it."

"Indeed," Crispin said. "You've had so much on your mind lately. Rooting out the Trembler poison, chasing down the runaway count … it's no wonder if your sleep is troubled."

Bure nodded, but he didn't quite look at his superior. Crispin watched him closely, careful to keep his features neutral even as he peered shrewdly at his second-in-command. He didn't like this. It seemed obvious to him that Bure *had* heard the demon somehow, and discerned its nature besides. That shouldn't be possible. Discernment of spirits was not one of this man's gifts, if he had any besides being obsequious. But his showing up here and now with such a story could not be a coincidence.

Had the demon done it purposely? Alerted him to its presence? But why?

"Perhaps it's the Lowlanders troubling me," Bure blurted suddenly. "The ones we imprisoned. It doesn't feel right to me."

"They deliberately aided the count," Crispin said. "An act of sedition in these times."

"According to a one-eyed robber, yes," Bure said, grimacing.

"And more than a dozen of his men who agreed with his witness."

"Brigands and thugs, all of them," Bure said. "And yet they are free while we imprison two men whose only crime seems to have been aiding a stranger in need."

"It should have been *four* men," Crispin reminded him. "Do I need to remind you that your incompetence allowed the other two to break away?"

To his surprise, Bure looked him in the eye. He rested his hands together in his lap, palm to palm. "I'm not sure I'm sorry for that," he said. "It weighs on my conscience, Elder. I confess it to you. It didn't feel right. It still doesn't feel right."

Crispin couldn't entirely prevent his face from showing his surprise. Bure ought not to have a conscience—at least not one that intruded on his work for Crispin. He'd always been easy to lead before.

But these men were Lowlanders, he realized suddenly, and Lowlanders of a particular type. They reminded Bure of the old days. Of the Boggers.

He schooled his features back to pastoral concern and injected a note of solicitousness in his voice. "Do you fear God is displeased with you, brother?" he asked. "Come now. It is the Creator's work we do. You have always known that. Those men aided heretics. We arrested them for the good of their own souls as much as the good of the kirk and society."

"And Diego's family?" Bure said, his eyes just as earnest. He was searching Crispin's face—not accusingly, but genuinely looking to him for comfort and reassurance. "The men we sent after them—that is also the work of God?"

"Diego betrayed us," Crispin said. "He disobeyed our orders, and he lied to our faces. He was told to arrest Carlos Vaquero to answer for his crimes and his heresy, and instead he helped him escape."

"Pardon, Elder," Bure said, lowering his gaze at last and staring at his hands. "But I know the truth—you needn't spare my feelings about it. Diego was ordered to kill Vaquero."

Crispin opened his mouth, but Bure spared him the need to answer, holding up a finger. "I am not questioning the justice of it," he said. "I know full well the young count would have been condemned to death had he come to trial, and a trial would have given the whole matter far too public a face—given the Tremblers another martyr. I know. I remember what happened with Serena as well as you do."

Crispin flushed, but he closed his mouth. Bure went on. "No, I don't question your decision to execute Carlos quietly. And Diego must face whatever punishment for his own crimes is just. It is only that I cannot see why his family must be dragged into it. From what our spies tell us, he has not spoken to them in years."

"Deacon Bure," Crispin said, "if we have learned anything about Diego, it is that his misplaced loyalties run deep. He has no loyalty to us, but he will put his neck on the line for the young count, and why? Because Carlos Vaquero showed him some semblance of friendship in the years Diego served him. How much more do you think his loyalty connects him to his family, even after all these years? If we tug on that line, Diego will respond. And Carlos Vaquero will come with him."

There were parts of the net Crispin didn't mention. Like the fact that Diego's service as a spy and a would-be executioner had not been bought by Crispin, but blackmailed—that Crispin had threatened the very family members he now intended to use to bring Diego home. No, Diego *hadn't* been in touch with them for years. It wasn't because they didn't matter to him. It was because he was trying to keep them safe by staying away from them.

But Bure, who was a good and loyal man but wont to be perturbed, sometimes, by scruples, likely would object. Nor did Crispin bother to explain why he was so sure Carlos Vaquero would come flying to the rescue of Diego's family too. The young count was especially sensitive to family matters. It was Diego's sister Crispin intended to particularly menace, and Carlos *especially* had a thing about sisters.

Not for the first time, Crispin cursed the day he hadn't burned Serena Vaquero at the stake as he'd intended. He had come so close. Arrested her. Tried her. Sentenced her. But before the day arrived when her sentence was to be carried out, it became clear to everyone, Crispin most of all, that the whole thing had been a disaster. Not merely the Tremblers, but all of Tempestano—all the provinces of the Southern Alliance—had been ready to rise in revolt. They'd made Serena a martyr, and she wasn't even dead. To contain the damage, Crispin had cancelled the execution and had Serena thrown into prison in Port Tuscan instead.

Then, with the demons' help, he'd concocted the whole elaborate plan to have her sent to the New World, caught and inadvertently released by that rigid old pharisee Phinehas Cole, framed for the death of Herman Melrose, and then finally—finally—executed after all. His only regret was that he wouldn't be there to see it. Cole would do the job, and then Crispin would remove him too. The plan was ingenious and depended on a great many things falling into place, but the shades insisted it would work.

Except it hadn't. And now Serena was on the loose in the New World with a powerful companion, and they threatened to undo everything Crispin had worked so hard to accomplish.

What could he do now but look to see what lines he still held in his hands, and then begin to pull hard on all of them, until every last one drew its prey to him.

So yes. He would go after Caterina Diego, and Diego would come home. Carlos with him. Crispin would kill the young count and eliminate Tempestano as a threat. Maybe he could even find a way to use all of the resulting tumult to get to Serena again.

"Elder?"

He started, Bure coming into focus in front of his eyes as though he'd just materialized there. He'd been so lost in thought he'd lost track of the man. "Hmmm?" he asked.

"I said, I see the necessity of it. I only wish there were some other way."

Elder Crispin of the Puritani kirk stood and placed a heavy hand on the younger deacon's shoulder. "You've a good heart, Adolphus," he said. "The kirk is blessed to have a man like you serving it. Not much longer now, and the threat in this beautiful land will be truly subdued. Justice and truth will reign here as they do in the north, as they ought to do everywhere. And you will have been a part of it."

Bure ducked his head. "I'm grateful," he said simply.

Crispin patted him on the shoulder. "As am I, to have you by my side. Thank you for checking on me, even if it was only a dream. As you can see, I'm just fine. Now. Let us both get a good night's sleep. We've a big day ahead of us."

Chapter 3

Jerusalem Valley—The New World

Linette and Jonathan had only just returned from belowground and were heading for the governing house when they heard Serena calling for help in a voice that turned the blood in their veins. Linette could not imagine what could do that to Serena, who was always so confident and sure—what could simultaneously fill her voice with panic and tear its very fibers with grief.

She knew as soon as she saw it. Jacques lay bloodied on the ground, convulsing, black and red streaks running beneath the skin of his neck and shoulders, which bore bite marks beneath torn and ragged clothes. Frederick Almon lay beside him, free of his bonds, curled into a fetal position with his eyes wide, his breath heaving.

Serena was kneeling over Jacques, clinging to him and trying desperately to calm the convulsions.

She was also weeping.

Jonathan took in the scene with wide eyes. Almost the moment he and Linette entered the room, Jacques began to come out of the seizure, his body starting to relax. Serena clucked and soothed him as though they were the only two people in the world.

"Almon did this?" Jonathan asked. His hand was on the gnarled club at his waist, a gift to him from the River People.

Serena only nodded.

"He has to die," Jonathan said. He acted immediately, snatching the club free and raising it to deal the captain a killing blow. Serena raised her own hand to block him. She shook her head wearily. "No," she said. "It's left him. He's free. Still sick, but free. Linette, show him."

Linette stared at them both askance for a moment, and Serena gave her the briefest nod that told Linette she recognized her exhaustion—that she saw how it lined her eyes and tugged at her mouth, but that she needed her to overcome it one more time. Linette breathed in deeply, closed her eyes, and lit her vines. The light that shone from her illuminated the network of vines beneath Almon's skin. They were thick and swollen with the poison.

"Not that," Serena said. "Show him the rest."

Linette's light faded a little as she stared at Serena, uncomprehending. It came to her in a flash what the girl meant.

"I can't," she said.

"You can," Serena told her, some of her old confidence back. "You can. Show us. Help us see what is all around us, and what is not."

Linette closed her eyes again, raised both hands, and let the light flood her and flow out of her. She heard gasps of wonder as they all saw what she could see too, what she could see with her spirit even though her eyes were closed. There were shapes all around them, vague figures, some like humans and some like beasts, and others like nothing ever seen on earth—but none hovered near Almon, and none were a threat. Not that sort of threat.

The light winked out, and Linette let out a breath with it. She swayed again, unsteady on her feet.

"You see?" Serena said. "Only the usual. Nothing whispering in his ear. If the creature had still been here, Linette's light would have exposed it."

"Did Jacques do it?" Jonathan asked. "Drive the creature away?"

"No," Serena said. "I did."

"You—" Linette said. "But how?"

Serena smiled sadly. She had Jacques's head in her lap now and was stroking his hair. He wasn't moving. "Let's just say that today, we are all doing things we did not know we could do."

Hope kindled in her eyes as she seemed to really see Linette and Jonathan for the first time. "The spring! Did it—?"

"We don't know," Linette said. "The tree was dead. There was no light, no more seeds. The water was there, but it might have been only a natural spring."

"They submerged all the sick," Jonathan said. "Then wrapped them in warm skins and brought them back to the surface. Agatha Moss is turning the Trembler meeting house into a hospital and tending to them all there, but we don't know yet if the water worked."

Serena nodded and looked back down at Jacques.

"There is hope," Linette said. "The wheat was there. Amos is overseeing while it's harvested. It will feed everyone for the rest of the winter, even if the couriers we sent can't establish trade with the other settlements. If the wheat didn't disappear, maybe the spring will heal them after all."

"Will someone—" Serena seemed to be fighting to gather her thoughts. "Will someone help me take him down to the water?"

Jonathan laid a hand on her shoulder. "Some of the warriors will help."

"And him?" Linette asked, nodding at Almon. "Shouldn't we try to help him too?"

Jonathan tightened his fingers around the club at his waist. But he nodded. "I'll find someone to carry him. His soldiers will help us."

But when they stood by the dark shore again, Linette once more watching over the procession despite how much she ached to lie down and sleep, it was Jonathan himself who stripped to the waist and carried Frederick Almon into the water.

The sight gave her peace.

That night passed slowly, darkly, a waking dream of firelit, shifting shadows as the worried silently tended to the sick. The swollen vines of the worst-afflicted lost something of their inky gorge as the hours passed, and it seemed the sick slept a little easier. Linette, who joined the caretakers in the small hours of the morning after getting a few fitful hours of sleep herself, did not offer to use her phosphorescent light to take a closer look as she moved among the rows of sick and wounded in the meeting house. Nor did anyone ask her to. She was aware that she'd been pushing herself too hard, and others seemed to know it as well. Still, she couldn't help but imagine the other figures she'd seen in that moment of vision, called up at Serena's request—ghostly shapes moving among them, invisible inhabitants of a world that overlay their own. It wasn't exactly a comforting thought, more an expansive one. It made even the murky shadows of the night open out into infinite possibility, infinite mystery.

She had just finished heating more water, then wiping the brow of an unconscious but fevered warrior, when there came a lull in the work. She leaned against the far wall of the meeting house and let out a sigh.

Sarah, who had been tending to someone on the other end of the building, came and leaned against the wall beside her. She said nothing. But her presence was a deeper comfort than Linette could name. It said things were all right between them. And could, yet, be all right with the world.

In the morning, every one of the afflicted seemed to breathe easier.

And not one of them awoke.

Serena sat beside Jacques, reaching over to smooth his hair away from his brow with a regularity that was more for her sake than his. When Linette approached, Serena looked up at her with large brown eyes that harbored uncharacteristic fear. On the far side of the room, a small group of warriors crouched and huddled around their chieftain. Letty Foster stood near them, hovering around the edges of their group. A little apart from all of them, the young boy Josiah Axel sat next to his father, Eben, who lay unconscious on a cot.

"Well," Linette said, dropping her hand into her pocket where the seed sat, weighing down her skirt, "what do we do now? Just wait?"

Serena stared in front of her, her hand still resting near Jacques's brow. The fire that usually filled her seemed to have gone out, leaving an empty hearth.

Linette dropped to a crouch beside them. These two strangers who had come so far to try to help the settlement, to try to help Herman Melrose.

They had come too late, and now perhaps had lost everything. Yet they had accomplished great things for the people of Jerusalem Valley regardless. Jacques had set Jonathan free from the creature that hounded him, giving him the opportunity to be healed. Serena had inspired their resistance against Frederick Almon and helped Linette find the wheat field and the underground pool. Without these two, the seed might still be undiscovered.

She was grateful to them, and her heart ached for their plight.

Serena did not answer her question.

The day passed without any real change. The sleepers continued to sleep. The ease that had come into their breathing, the lack of fitfulness, the lowered fevers and lighter color in their vines—it all held. They were all better than they had been before entering the water, even Almon and Jacques. But they did not get better. And they did not wake up.

Amos and his harvesters finished their work, bringing up the wheat from belowground in huge sheafs and sacks full of oversized heads. The whole settlement got to work threshing, storing, and grinding wheat. Sarah left the makeshift hospital to oversee the baking of bread. The smell of it soon wafted out over the whole settlement, drifting through the cold air along with oven smoke.

A small band of River People left the village to go hunting in the mountains around the valley. They returned late in the afternoon with several brace of fowl and a dozen rabbits, which they set about plucking, skinning, and preparing for everyone to share. The soldiers, under the direction of Thomas Carson, busied themselves making repairs to the Fosters' home. When they had finished, they executed a few maneuvers in the yard of the governing house. Carson dismissed them after half an hour, but they had nowhere to go, and they loitered uncomfortably around the governing house until Carson reappeared from consultation with John Hopewell and Clive Shilling bearing a list of other chores they could do around the settlement—repairs to be made, trees to be felled, newly ground grain to cart from one end of the settlement to the other. With the ground near frozen, there wasn't much they could do, but they accepted anything with gratitude and deployed with obvious relief.

Serena didn't leave Jacques's side. Her faithfulness was matched only by Capenokanickon's children and the small boy, Josiah. Linette noticed him sitting silently and helplessly with his father's lanky left hand between his two small ones. She brought him several slices of Sarah's thick, hot bread, and ventured a smile.

"Can you smell the roasting fowl?" she asked. "The warriors are making a feast for us all."

Josiah nodded but said nothing. He glanced at her from the corner of his eye but otherwise did not turn away from Eben.

"Your father is a brave man," Linette said. "We're all indebted to him for trying to help us."

No response, but she saw his lips tighten.

"He was a good friend to Jacques and Serena on their journey here," Linette continued, just trying to bring some measure of comfort. She meant to finish with, "We'll all do everything we can to help him."

But the boy turned his face suddenly and blurted, "Maybe not."

The words caught her so off guard that for a moment, she had no reply. Stretched out on a straw mattress from Amos's cottage that had been relocated here, Eben slept deeply, the rise and fall of his chest barely perceptible. His complexion was ashy, but the expression on his face was peaceful.

"I don't know what you mean," Linette said.

The boy tore off a bite of bread and chewed it fiercely, muttering through the bite. "Maybe you don't know what you're talking about," he said, and angled away so his back was turned to her.

Licking her lips, Linette stood up slowly and backed away. She didn't want to leave the boy in his anger and pain, but it was clear she wasn't welcome.

Sitting next to Jacques, Serena looked up at her and gave her a slight nod. A hint of perplexity in her expression indicated that she'd heard the boy's words and didn't understand them either.

At least I'm not alone, Linette thought. *For once.*

Checking in with Agatha first to make sure there wasn't some way she could be of service, Linette decided to clear her head before dinner. The entire community intended to feast together—settlers, soldiers, and River People alike, celebrating victory over hunger and the cruel reign of Frederick Almon. They would give thanks and strengthen their odd alliance. And they would pray for the sleepers.

Linette would not take the lead in any of it. That was for Big John to do, and Jonathan Applegate and Major Thomas Carson and whichever of the River People seemed to be leaders in the absence of the chief. She was relieved not to have responsibility, as the seed in her pocket felt like responsibility enough, even if she had no idea how to respond to its nagging presence. And it *did* nag. It tugged at her mind, at her gut, like a deep underlying hunger. It needed to fall into the ground and die, to germinate and grow. And she could feel its need as though it were her own. It felt like having something inside that needed to burst open and flow out, carrying healing with it.

She was sure of that too. The seed carried healing. Planted in the right ground, it *would* be the key to healing the sleepers, even to curing the sickness that afflicted the Machkigen once and for all.

But she couldn't do anything without direction. *Why* hadn't Herman left some kind of instruction? Or a map? Why hadn't he told anyone about the mission he had aborted when he settled in Jerusalem Valley? She had looked up to him so much, ever since she read his columns in the papers back in New Cranwell, and the leaflets of his ideas that others distributed in the streets. She had loved him when she came here, loved him as a daughter loves a father. More than she had ever loved her own father, in fact. She had been gutted with grief when Jonathan, in the grip of the Machkigen madness, had killed him. It was hard to feel angry with Herman now, but she did. Or at the very least, she was confused by his actions. The urgency in this seed was so great. Surely he had felt it too. Why would he abandon something so important, without even a word to anyone about it?

Lost in thought by the time she reached the door of the meeting house and stepped outside, she nearly ran right into Amos. The tall, gangly secretary in deerskin boots and spectacles, a heavy wool coat and black scarf threatening to swallow him alive, took a step back. Then stopped. Essentially trapping her between the door and the bottom of the steps.

"Oh," he said. "I wanted to come looking for you. To bring you this." He held out his gloved hand, revealing a hot biscuit and honey wrapped in cloth. "Sarah sent it for you."

"Thank you," Linette said, taking the cake absently and looking for a way to get around Amos without being too dismissive. He had been her greatest hope for some information about the seed. As Herman's secretary, he had spent hours in private conversation with the man and had access to all of his papers and many of his secrets. But Amos, like everyone else, hadn't known anything. She'd felt the disappointment bitterly, and felt it still, facing him on the steps of the meeting house. She knew it wasn't fair. His face was still bruised from a singlehanded attempt to protect her from Almon's men. He was a good man, and he cared about her.

That, of course, was the other problem. She wasn't just disappointed in Amos. She was also afraid of his attention. She wasn't sure just when he had changed toward her, but it was a complication she didn't want to deal with just now.

"I also," he said, clearing his throat in that awkward way he had, "wondered how you are. That is … are you keeping well?"

She sighed, choosing to stare at the biscuit rather than look at him. "No," she said. "The truth is, I'm worried about them. About, well, everything. And I'm going crazy because there's nothing I can do."

He looked like he wanted to lay a comforting hand on her shoulder, but mercifully, he didn't. She managed a half-smile as she licked a bit of honey off her thumb, grateful to know Sarah had been thinking kindly of her. She lifted the biscuit lamely. "This is good. It was kind of Sarah, and kind of you to bring it. As for me, I think I need to find myself something to keep myself busy. Maybe the soldiers could use a laundress."

This time, to her shock, he *did* reach out and lay a hand on her shoulder. It was less comfort, more command—which could not have surprised her more, really. "There's nothing that needs to be done right now," he said. "You look tired to the bone. You need to rest. If you go and lie down a while before the feast, no one will miss you."

Linette looked back over her shoulder at the door of the meeting house. "Aren't enough of us sleeping?" she asked.

"Linette," he said, treating her name carefully, like a fragile thing, "you've done a great deal already. Rest. I'll come and wake you for the feast."

She shook her head and stepped forward, forcing him to back away so she could descend the stairs. "You don't need to do that," she said. "But you're right. I do need to rest. I will. Thank you, Amos."

The feast that night began in the pale slanting light of early evening. Sarah had insisted that everyone gather in the low-lying yard between the Fosters' farmhouse and the ridge where their barn sat. From her warm kitchen, light poured forth along with the heady smells of baking bread and thick, bubbling stew, made from giblets brought by the River People, thickened with freshly ground flour, festooned with dried thyme and rosemary and other fragrant remnants of summer. In the yard, meat roasted on spits over several large open fires, and the people gathered around them, warming hands and faces against the cold; warming hearts against all of the recent fear and animosity that had separated them.

Linette, whom Amos had roused from a short but deep sleep in spite of her protest, watched Jonathan laughing with Clive Shilling and a young private in a red coat whose name, she remembered, was Paul McIntyre. Letty Foster leaned up against the parson's side, and he wrapped an arm around her shoulder. Sarah burst through the kitchen door once more bearing yet another basket full of hot bread, her cheeks flushed despite the chill in the air. One of Capenokanickon's warriors caught up a loaf and tossed it from hand to hand, blowing it, then threw it with a grin to a friend. Lila, Sarah's younger daughter, followed after her with a tray of biscuits. She had a scarf tied around her head to keep her hair back as she labored in the kitchen. Through the open door, Linette could see Agatha Moss moving around inside, waving a spoon at Sarah's younger son, Samuel—offering a reproof or maybe just making a point.

How simple harmony was, Linette thought. All it took was warmth and bread and the willingness to share them.

Linette was seated on an overturned barrel near the edge of the yard— near the festivities but not in the center of them. She kept her coat pulled tight around her, as the cold still had an edge here. A few figures were missing from the gathering—Amos, Serena, Wetëndeis. Two or three warriors whose names Linette didn't know, though their faces were becoming familiar. And the boy, of course—Josiah. They had opted to stay with the sleepers in the meeting house. Leaving the sick alone was not an option.

The adults among them were both caregivers and guards. No one knew if one of the infected might turn for the worse and become something terrible.

Linette felt a little guilty that Amos wasn't here. She knew he had volunteered for the meeting house just so she could attend the feast. As though he didn't need this as badly as she did. He had done so much, suffered so much. And he had done it all bravely and without complaint. He had come to get her for the feast and then excused himself to tend the sick.

She looked down at her hands, clasping and unclasping in her lap.

Oh, Amos, she thought. *I don't want this from you.*

A small knot of warriors around one of the roasting spits let up a shout of triumph and moved away from the fire, proclaiming that dinner was ready. Some of the settlers cheered. Linette grinned in spite of herself. This was good. This was Herman's vision, realized. More than realized, for he surely had not ever pictured red-coated soldiers and bright-cloaked warriors among his peaceful settlers, sharing bread and laughter. Her smile slipped a little as she wondered if he would have wanted it, or if his vision had limits—if he would have rather the soldiers remained distant and the Outsiders stayed outside.

One voice rose above all the others, and everyone settled into a jocular quiet as John Hopewell slapped his big hands together and called the gathering to order. Despite his somber black Trembler coat, he seemed to shine. "My friends," he said, beaming, "this is truly a good day. A blessed day. *Thou hast prepared a table before me in the presence of mine enemies,* that's what the Book says. *Thou anointest my head with oil; my cup runneth over.* We have all faced grave troubles and common enemies in the days just past. Yes, my red-coated friends, I see those uneasy looks on your faces—you think I may be talking about you. After all, not long ago, many of us might have seen *you* as the enemy."

The gathering remained quiet, more attentive now. And yes, there was a little unease. Linette shifted in place, but she wasn't afraid of what John would say. Herman Melrose couldn't have left a more worthy successor—a man who carried his spirit and his vision and could, just maybe, even enlarge it.

"But we would have been wrong to do so," John continued. "Don't we Tremblers believe that the light of the Fire Within invests all men? And don't you Puritani remind us that our struggle is not against flesh and blood, but against powers and principalities in heavenly places? We've all been through a struggle, brothers and sisters. And by God's good grace, we've *all* come through victorious. Some of us were tempted to forget who we are, or who our real enemies are. But I dare say we've remembered."

He nodded to Anasan and the warriors gathered around him. "You, our brothers from the forest, have been instruments of great grace to us. We're grateful. We're all grateful." He turned and looked to Sarah, who stood framed by her kitchen door, her children arrayed around her—all but Letty, who was still by Jonathan's side. "Sarah Foster, you paid a great price to protect us all. Not only to hide fugitives, but to remind us all of our loyalties and keep us from committing grave sin. And now you open your home to us. We'll none of us forget it."

She nodded, a slight smile playing at her lips. Linette couldn't really read her expression. But she thought it was pleased.

"Now," John said, "let us all pray. And let us remember especially the sleepers, may they awake. And Smith Foster. May he come home to us. And Frederick Almon. May God have mercy on his soul."

Murmurs and spoken responses answered back as everyone in the yard bowed their heads. Linette bowed hers but did not close her eyes, instead staring down at her interlaced fingers.

When the prayer was ended, the tone shifted quickly back to merriment. Clive had brought barrels of cider, which was heated in black kettles over the fires and passed out in wooden tumblers. Linette accepted one handed to her by a shy soldier, and then a chunk of bread dipped in stew, run over to her from the kitchen by Samuel Foster.

It felt strange to eat like this, to fill her belly and feel the warmth on her tongue and filling her from head to foot, without fearing that they would run out. How quickly things could change.

Serena sat by Jacques's side with her mind in turmoil. He slept like death. He might as well be dead, she thought. She might as well have killed him, dragging him across the world like this.

But it wasn't her fault, another part of her argued. She hadn't asked him to come. He'd attached himself to her and her mission without an invitation. Refused to go away. Lied to her so she would trust him and not chase him away, which was, all things considered, a terrible idea. Terrible because she *had* trusted him, which made truth a terrible and risky thing with the power to destroy their friendship. And that had become precious to her above all things.

Thankfully, truth had come out and destroyed nothing.

You still shouldn't have lied, she thought toward the man who lay pale and still on a pallet near the ground in the meeting house. Fire in a small woodstove kept the meeting house warm, but Serena was well bundled in coat and gloves and hat anyway. Strange that it had gotten colder since they came aboveground. Or maybe it just she who had grown colder. She who was losing her fire.

I am like that flare, she had told her brother what seemed like years and years ago. *I caught fire fast and young, and I burn brightly. But I am not meant to burn long in this life. You know this to be true. Don't try to protect me from myself.*

She'd expected to come here and blaze. Become a martyr, at long last, maybe. At the very least, stir up the embers of Herman Melrose's Jerusalem Valley and get everything roaring. It was what she did. Brought revolution and revival. She heard the Fire Within, felt the summons of the Spirit's heat, and acted on what she heard and felt, without much thought and without lingering long to see what might happen next. That was what it meant to live by faith.

She didn't know how to do *this*. Arrive in a place and simply die down to a smolder. Nor did she know how to be so alone. In the Old World, she'd always had her brother, or other Tremblers. She was a fugitive among fugitives, a heroine amid the hounded and hidden. Whatever she was, she was with others. But here, in Jerusalem Valley, it was different.

Here, she simply didn't belong.

Yes, some of the Tremblers knew who she was. Yes, they looked at her with admiration and wonder. But she wasn't one of them, and they didn't need her. Not even Linette, who had spent two weeks hidden in a cellar with her, needed her. Not really. She'd tried to be supportive of the pale redhead, but she didn't really know how to play that role. She felt awkward and stupid in it.

She stared down at Jacques's face. "How could you leave me?" she whispered. "How, after all this time? How could you let them snatch you away? And why couldn't I stop them?"

Tears grew hot and stinging in her eyes. She didn't bother to blink them away. "I know, I sound selfish. I'm not, really. I want you back, for your own sake, not just mine. But I want you back for mine too."

He didn't move. He was barely even breathing. She kept checking to make sure he hadn't stopped entirely, that he hadn't actually ceased living while she sat beside him, unable to do anything for him. If she stared hard, she could just barely make out the rise and fall of his hands, which were folded on his chest.

"Oh God," she said, the hot tears finally falling. "Oh God, don't let him die. Save him, even if I can't be the one who does it. But please, Creator mine, give me *something* to do."

She thought of the seed Linette carried and wished to God it had come to her instead. The seed was a mission, a call. The seed was purpose. Linette had accepted it, even if she didn't know what it meant or what to do next. And Serena envied her more than she would ever admit to anyone out loud.

Someone stirred across the room. For a moment Serena's heart leapt into her throat—she thought it was Almon, the captain. He had been moved out here with the other sleepers after his baptism in the pool. With the … creature … gone, Serena had pushed for that. It shouldn't be necessary to keep him in a separate place, under a separate guard. He was not any more dangerous than these others.

But now, with him moving alone in the dark room—she thought maybe she was wrong.

But then she saw it hadn't been him at all. It was the boy, Josiah, stretching his legs. The sight of him made her feel a little guilty. She knew she'd been wallowing. Letting herself sink into frustration and self-pity. And here was this boy, as faithful as she was or more, watching over the only person he likely had in the entire world. On their journey here together, with Eben leading her and Jacques, she hadn't paid much attention to the boy—although he was a background delight, the energy and curiosity of youth making everything in this vast wilderness of a land seem less threatening and more joyful. He'd romped in the snow and made her less aware of the cold. He was a child, and he'd just been aged too fast.

She caught him looking over toward her, oil light reflecting in his eyes. He looked away just as quickly, a darting glance that told her he didn't want to be seen.

But sometimes we need what we don't want.

"Josiah," she called softly.

The boy looked back toward her, though he kept his shoulders hunched forward over his father, and she thought maybe, just maybe, he would get up and come over to her—but in that moment, Eben lurched up. It was a sudden jerking motion, accompanied by a loud cry, that did not take him all the way up off the pallet but instead let him drop back down with a crash, and then he cried out again and his back arched. Serena was on her feet and running for his side before she could think. The call for help stuck in her throat. Wildly she tried to see into the shadows, to make any invisible threat become clear, but she could neither command the shades to show themselves the way Jacques did nor light up the other side of reality as Linette could. She reached them and instead of trying to help Eben, she grabbed Josiah's skinny shoulders and pulled him away.

He fought her, twisting wildly. She threw an arm across his chest, narrowly stopping him from breaking her grip, and pulled him back, away from the cot and the man who lay on it.

Eben's eyes were open. He stared at the ceiling, unseeing. His eyes had a yellow cast and his mouth was foaming slightly. His convulsions slowed, growing less violent, but his head tossed back and forth on the pallet.

"Linette," he groaned. "No."

"Eben?" Serena asked. "Can you hear me?"

"Pa!" Josiah cried out, bringing his right foot down hard on Serena's.

She let out a yelp but didn't break her hold on the boy. It would take more than being a brat to make her let go.

"No," Eben said again. "No, you've got it all wrong …"

Just as suddenly as his convulsions had begun, they ceased—he lay, now, still as a dead man. But his eyes were still open, still staring, still unseeing. His head had come to rest on its side, and he seemed to stare right at Serena and Josiah.

Linette must have fallen asleep somehow, because she was back in the blackwater pool again. The water was heavy and cold and all around her; she was frozen in it, up to her elbows in the deep cold. It was a dream, it had to be, despite the cold—she must have fallen asleep in the midst of feasting.

A pale green light shimmered on the surface of the water, cast by the living branches of the tree. She was dreaming, she told herself again. Yet she could feel the coldness of the water like iron around her legs, and its weight in her skirt holding her in place.

The sleepers were there.

It took a moment before she realized it, but as soon as she saw them, she knew they'd been there the whole time. They too stood knee-deep in the water, held in the solemnity of this place. Their eyes were open, and they looked toward her earnestly. Jacques stood just a few feet to her left, facing her; Eben was to his right, and Capenokanickon, the aged leader of the River People, to his left. Behind them, the other fallen warriors were arrayed.

They were her friends, yet the sight of them made her want to back away.

Jacques spoke first.

"The seed," he said. "It was a gift from the Creator, meant to be planted for the healing of the world. It might have prevented the Machkigen from ever coming to be, if it had been planted where it was intended. That's why they killed Melrose—they thought the seed would die with him. But it came to you, Linette. You must take it where it has to go."

"What has happened to you?" Linette asked. "Where are we?"

"The waters hold us in dreaming," Jacques said. "If we awake out of sleep, we will succumb again. They keep us safe until the seed is planted and the true waters of healing begin to flow. For now, sleep guards us—it keeps the shades away and quiets the words in our hearts that must not grow."

Linette thought of how Jonathan had explained his madness—that it was caused not merely by the poison that entered his vines, but also by the words of his father long ago, and other lies he had since come to believe. Words, too, were seeds, and some could transform a man in terrible ways.

"But where must the seed be taken?" Linette asked urgently. "I'm willing to carry it, but I don't know where it's meant to go, much less the way to get there."

It almost seemed as though he didn't hear her.

"Do not delay," he told her. "Our sleep will not hold forever. And the threat of the Machkigen grows worse. I fear there are many madmen abroad already."

"But—"

"Do not delay," he repeated, holding her gaze. He looked more serious than she had ever seen him. "The world depends on you."

He faded away. He and Capenokanickon both. The light disappeared with them. It was so dark she didn't know how she knew Eben was still there—but she did. Standing alone, directly across from her, only a few feet away. She felt him like a disturbance in the water.

"Linette," he said. He had a deep voice, with the accent of a man from the low colonies. She thought maybe she could just make out the outline of his body across from her, the slight silver ripple of water as it formed around his torso. She knew a little about him, thanks to Jacques and Serena—they'd met Eben in New Cranwell, and he had led them to Jerusalem Valley, been caught by the army along with them, and put himself at some risk to help them escape in the night. They didn't know much about what had happened to him after that, though Jonathan Applegate had told them some things—Eben had served as a slave in Fort Collins before escaping with the Outsiders and joining the rest of their people—and Jonathan—in the woods.

Linette couldn't begin to imagine why he had come to her, here in this dreamscape.

Or how, if it came to that.

She might have asked him, but he had things of his own to say. "I heard what he said to you, but you can't do it. Not now. You go west with that seed, you'll always regret it when the churchman takes your family down. He knows who you are, you hear me? He'll go after them."

The words were nonsense, yet they made Linette's blood run cold. "What are you talking about?" she said. "You don't know me, or anything about me."

"Hell I don't. You're Phinehas Cole's daughter. The churchman's going after him next. Him and your little girl."

With those words, something in Linette's mind broke. Her head was spinning, the world was spinning, and if Eben kept talking, she couldn't hear him or understand a word he was saying. The darkness, thick before, closed in and smothered her.

Then somehow she was still breathing, she could feel the dead cold of the water more deeply in her bones than before, and his words began to make some kind of sense again.

"… I never wanted anything to do with him, you understand? But what he offered me—that was going to change everything for my boy. You understand. I know you understand. You'd do the same for your child."

How did he know? How could he possibly know?

"Goin' after family, it's what he does. Ask Serena. She knows all about it. I'm sorry I helped him, and me and my boy gonna pay hell for it if I ever wake up again. But you have to know. You have to know what—"

"Linette."

She blinked. Darkness and stillness smothered her, blocked her senses.

She blinked again and the darkness fell away. She was standing by a fire in Sarah's yard, watching the rising heat shimmer in the air. Her fingers were wrapped around a warm tumbler full of steaming cider. She hadn't been sleeping—she'd just *gone* somewhere, somehow, gone into a vision. Jonathan stood facing her, wrapped in a brightly woven blanket of red and blue that must have been given to him by the River People. His expression was curious—perhaps mildly concerned.

"Linette?" he asked again. "Are you all right?"

She was—no, she wasn't. Her hands started to shake so violently that hot cider spilled over the lip of the tumbler and burned her hands. She sucked in her breath, and Letty Foster reached over and took the tumbler from her. "Here, let me," she said. "Do you need to sit down?"

"I—no," Linette said. "Where is Eben?"

"Eben Axel?" Jonathan asked. "He's in the meeting house, with the other sleepers."

She knew that, of course. She had already turned from the fire before Jonathan answered, gathering up her skirts to run. She hardly heard Jonathan and Letty calling after her. She could only think of one thing.

Her child.

Her little girl.

Beth.

She tore across the empty farm fields toward the meeting house, dashing the back of her hand against the tears that formed as the cold stung her eyes. She ran from the gathering at the Fosters' house, from the fires and the warmth. Back to the meeting house and Eben and the past. Every pounding step on the cold earth hollowed her out more inside.

She burst into the meeting house, out of breath. Two pairs of wide eyes greeted her. Serena and Josiah, both of them hovering over Eben. Serena's hands were stretched out over the man's body as though she had just been touching him a moment before.

"Is he awake?" Linette asked, hope jumping into her throat before Serena shook her dark head, killing it.

"What do you know about him?" Linette asked, crossing the floor quickly. She knelt down across from Serena and stared into Eben's still, ashen face. Willing him to wake up and talk to her again.

"Linette, what's happened?"

"What do you know about this man?"

"That his son is right here," Serena said. Her voice was low, deliberately calming. Linette recalled herself and nodded, forcing herself to breathe more slowly, to catch her breath. For the boy's sake. She closed her eyes to will control into her limbs and emotions, then looked up at Serena again. In the dim light of the meeting house, Serena looked stricken. She was putting on an act for the boy just as much as Linette was.

"He spoke to me," Linette said just as Serena told her, "He was having a fit a moment ago."

They stared at each other.

"I saw him in a dream," Linette said. "A waking dream. Or didn't *see* him … not exactly … it was dark. He told me …"

She stopped herself and looked away from Serena, over to the boy.

Josiah Axel squatted beside his father's head, perched like a bird next to Serena. He was small for his age, thin and lanky, but with an expression in his light brown eyes that was too old for him. She saw the same expression in the way his mouth pulled as he waited for her to talk, like an old man's.

"Maybe we shouldn't talk here," she said.

"I can hear it," Josiah said. "I got a right to hear it."

Serena laid a hand on his shoulder. He tried to shrug it away, but he was too close to her, and the gesture seemed halfhearted anyway. She left it there.

"He knows things about Crispin," Linette said. "He said—he said he was working with him? That Crispin made him some kind of deal."

Serena stared at her, uncomprehending. Then she went suddenly, terribly pale. "Oh, God," she whispered.

"And he said Crispin is going after my … my family," Linette said. "My father. He said that's what he does, that I should ask *you* about it."

Serena almost smiled at that. "It is what he does," she said. "Uses families against each other. He tried to use me to force my brother's hand more than once. To force him to give up his lands. To betray the Tremblers. He wouldn't do it, though. My Carlos."

"Why would he go after my father?" Linette said. "They're on the same side."

"Crispin is on no one's side," Serena said. "Only his own."

Linette reached into her skirt pocket and fumbled with the seed for a moment before pulling it out. She stretched out her hand.

"You have to take this," she said.

Serena's eyes widened, and she looked shocked for the third time since Linette had burst into the room. "What are you talking about?" she said. "This is yours. Your calling."

Linette shook her head. "I can't. Eben said if I go west, Crispin will go after them. Or he's going after them anyway, and I have to warn them. I don't know. It didn't last long, the vision."

"Crispin is a liar," Serena said. She was still pale—if anything, she looked more torn and stricken now than she had earlier. The seed cast a wan light as Linette held it out to her, throwing a green pallor on Serena's skin, but she did not reach out to take it. "The creatures he works with are liars. Devils, some call them—you know what that word means? Slanderer. You can't believe everything he said."

"You callin' my pa a devil?" Josiah cut in, pulling away from Serena's hand on his shoulder.

"No, no," she said. "Not him. But who knows what Crispin said to him."

Linette shook her head. "Eben knows things," she said. "About me. Things he couldn't know unless Crispin told him. Maybe the threat is empty, but I can't risk that." The seed was getting heavy in her hand as she held it out. She shook it a little. "Please, take the seed. Keep it, plant it, if you can find the place where it needs to be planted. I can't."

"Linette …"

"*Take* it."

Serena stared hard at her for a moment, and something in her expression set. She reached out and took the seed. Linette almost wept with relief.

She pulled her hand back, and a feeling of loss hit her in the chest so strongly it knocked her breath away. The pull she'd felt inside, the nagging feeling like a tide, nearly turned her stomach inside out.

"We're going to talk about this," Serena said. Then she turned and looked at the boy. She settled back on the floor, folding her arms in a way that said she was settling in for a long time. "Josiah. What do you know about all this?"

"Don't know nothin'," Josiah said. He didn't meet Serena's gaze.

"If your father came to Linette in a *dream* to tell her, in the middle of the day, he doesn't want it kept secret anymore. It's all right. We won't be angry with you, or with him. Tell us. Why did your father help Jacques and me escape New Cranwell?"

"He only tol' me what he tol' you," Josiah said. Still not meeting her eyes, or looking up at Linette either. "He wanted to come out here, to Jerusalem Valley. Needed your help gettin' here without no one stoppin' us."

"The help of two fugitives on the run," Serena said.

Josiah squirmed a little, but his expression was angry. "White fugitives. My pa a free man, but anybody stop us travelin' alone, they try to send us back south and ain't nobody gonna say nothin' to 'em. You better than nothin' even if you trouble."

"And he just happened to find us?" Serena said. She breathed out a long, heavy sigh. "He was working for Crispin. I should have seen it. I don't know why I didn't. Maybe if I had …" Her gaze drifted across the room, to where Jacques lay unconscious, motionless—hardly breathing. A casualty of a war none of them really understood.

The sight of Jacques reminded Linette that he had spoken to her too, before Eben did. What had he said?

"Do not delay. The world depends on you."

She felt the stirring again, the pull of the seed. No, she decided in that moment. She was doing the right thing. The world could not depend on her. Much better that it depend on Serena.

Serena, who had never let anyone down.

CHAPTER 4

Harbortown, Angleland—The Old World

Despite the cold, Carlos stayed above decks for the entire passage from the Western Lowlands to the misty islands across the rough, choppy channel. They left in the evening and sailed through the night, a journey of some sixteen hours. The sun was rising behind them, casting its light on Angleland's winter-grey shores, when the island came into view.

The sailors skillfully guided the ship into port. Carlos stayed at his position, silent and thoughtful, as the ship's mast became just one more among a forest of masts, its curved wooden hull one among hundreds of its kind. Even early in the morning, the harbor stirred with activity. This was one of the great trade ports of the west—a place where some men traded their souls for wealth, while others pursued fruitless adventures and still others simply pursued a day's work and a day's pay. Fog drifted amid the ships and the men at work on the docks. Here and there, rays of golden morning sun broke through the pervasive grey. It looked warm, even if he was too spray-soaked and the air too cold to allow for real warmth.

Diego appeared at his side, blowing into his hands. "Sleep has nothing to offer you, I assume?"

"I couldn't have slept if I tried."

"Which you didn't. It would be wise to shore yourself up before going into conference with the Angle King," Diego said.

"There will be time," Carlos said. "We can't go straight to court; better to announce ourselves properly. I don't like it belowdecks. It's too dark."

Diego nodded with a slight roll of his eyes, but he didn't argue. The Vaquero siblings had their quirks, but they'd earned them. At least, that was what Carlos hoped he thought.

Diego had paid for passage before they boarded the ship. They had few things to collect, so it only took them minutes to disembark once the ship had properly tied in and the gangplank was lowered.

It had been years, Carlos thought, since he wandered these docks, this harbor. Another lifetime. He had been so young then, just a boy accompanying his father on a diplomatic mission meant to open up new trade opportunities for Tempestano. He had disliked the cold then too, been bowled over by the pomp and show of the royal court, paid more attention to the raciness of the younger men and the lure of the best pubs and private clubs than he did to anything his father tried to teach him, and accidentally missed the opportunity to meet King Aldous. He'd been out drinking with one of his new friends and ended the night hung over, failing to wake up and join his father as he was supposed to.

Years later, Serena had met the king alongside Herman Melrose, the Trembler visionary. It was *that* connection Carlos hoped to renew now—the friendship and support Aldous had given to Melrose and his Tremblers. If the Angle King remembered Serena, so much the better. He probably did. She always made an impression. There was little chance he would remember Carlos's short time in his country.

He and Diego made their way up the streets from the docks. Their eventful journey here had left them without much money in hand, but they had enough to hail a cab, and once they had reached the better part of town, Carlos had no trouble using his name and title to access plenty of credit. Soon he and Diego were outfitted in new, well-tailored clothes; their purses full of coin on loan from a banker who had known Carlos's father well; their stomachs full of a fine, warm meal; and a coach and driver enlisted to take them inland to the capital. The trip would take the better part of three days, during which Carlos would make up for the time on the ship and get some sleep.

That was his plan, in any case. And as it turned out, it worked better than he expected. All the stress of the last several weeks seemed to cave in on him at once, and seated in the privacy of a coach with Diego to watch over him, he crumpled under its weight and fell so soundly asleep that he hardly registered most of the trip. He was blurrily aware of stopping at an inn each night and Diego forcing more food and ale down him, and then it was back to the rumble of the coach and the bliss of sleep. He blessed the roadmakers of Angleland, who kept the island's thoroughfares in such good repair. It was a beautiful land and a green one much of the year, but now it was mostly greyed out in rain and fog, trees and moss dormant for the winter, and he welcomed the clouds like an extra layer of oblivion.

When his head finally really cleared again, he was seated across from Diego in a private study, a fire briskly snapping in the hearth. He had rented a house in Loren, the capital, as befitted a man of his station. He sat at a small desk with a pen in his hand, writing a letter to the king to announce his presence in the city. Diego was looking out the window with a frown.

"What's troubling you?" Carlos asked. It was amazing how much less troubled he felt after sleeping for several days straight. Diego had been right—he really did need rest.

"Something isn't right here," Diego said.

Unease stirred in Carlos's chest. "What do you mean?"

"Did you notice the mood in the streets when we arrived? Or the inns on the way here? The people seem apprehensive. Like they're expecting something bad to happen."

"They're Angle men," Carlos said. "They always expect something bad to happen." Even so, his fingers tightened a little on the pen, and he looked down to make sure he hadn't smudged his handwriting. He hadn't—the words stood out crisp and clean on the page. Carlos Vaquero, Count of Tempestano, son of Favaro Vaquero, requesting an audience with Aldous, king of Angleland, to whom he owes his most grateful and illustrious respects.

He sounded flippant, but he wasn't really dismissing Diego's caution. He knew better than that.

Diego sat up a little straighter, suddenly, moving a curtain aside for a clearer view of the street below. "Something is happening," he said.

Carlos dropped his pen in its inkwell and joined Diego. He was right—a crowd was gathering in the street. They seemed to be congregating around a man dressed in the king's livery—a crier, Carlos realized. Diego stood and threw the window open in the same moment.

They both heard the words together, as clear as any trumpet.

"The king is dead!" the crier called out. "Hear it, everyone! King Aldous, Aldous the Great, is dead!"

"No." The word escaped Carlos's lips without his bidding. The world that had sat so heavily on him throughout the ship's passage suddenly came back, pushing him down into his seat at the desk. Aldous dead? How? Why? He *couldn't* be dead—Carlos was counting on his support to help him take his homeland. "No, how can that be?"

Diego gave him a concerned look, then left the room without a word. He returned in less than an hour. "The king was ill," he said. "For several weeks, apparently—long enough for word to spread throughout the country."

"But … now what?" Carlos said. "What does this mean for us?"

"It means we have to win the favor of a new king," Diego said. "His son, Henry, will take the throne. At least there is no question of a troubled succession this time." He met Carlos's eyes. "We can hope Henry shares his father's affinity for religious dissidents."

Absently, Carlos's fingers reached up and brushed the talisman he wore hidden beneath his shirt—a gift from the Sacramenti in their hidden mountain fortress. He doubted Henry's favor would extend *that* far; the break between Puritani and Sacramenti had been especially bitter and bloody on this island. By comparison, asking for grace for the Tremblers seemed a very small beneficence.

"You'll need to rewrite that letter," Diego said, glancing down at the abandoned parchment on the desk.

Carlos nodded. "Express my condolences, and my regret. Who would have imagined that my first appearance here since my foolish youth would be to attend a funeral?"

"Do you have the list we talked about?" Diego asked. "I'm ready to go and find you friends."

Carlos nodded and reached into the desk, where he'd put a second piece of parchment in the drawer. This one was finished, and required far less of a creative touch—it was a list of names he remembered from his father's contacts. Some of them had even made their way to Tempestano over the years, or had stayed in touch by correspondence, and Carlos could claim to know them in his own right. The list was short—fewer than ten—and none of them were close confidants, but all were people of position and means who could be expected to invite Carlos into their homes while he was in the city.

He grimaced. He hated politicking nearly as much as he hated the foppery and cattiness of the court. As a younger man his response had been to flee into foolishness and vice. He'd grown rather more serious since then.

He closed his eyes as the years seemed to pass before him—years in which his initial resistance to the Trembler movement and its embodiment in Herman Melrose gave way to intrigue, then to a sort of terrified and wonderful assent as Serena took up the cause as her own. Those early days of fear and fascination gave way to heartache and pain, hounding and death and persecution. He felt the terror of Serena's arrest and trial. His shoulders bowed with the weight of loss, his father's death, and the burden of becoming the Tremblers' protector. He felt the heat of the burning tavern in Tempestano, when Diego had betrayed him such a short time ago and Crispin had massacred so many of his friends.

People he had given so much to keep safe.

The boy he had once been, light-headed with wine and young women, was a fool. But he had to confess he missed him a little. He missed his optimism and the simple pleasure he took in things.

He reached up again and fingered the talisman. A finely carved loaf of bread. The symbol of one crushed and remade, broken to become bread for others.

Diego laid a hand on his shoulder as he picked up the list and scanned it. "I'll take word to them all," he said. "At least the king's death will give you something to talk about."

With Beth's fate burning in her breast—and concern for her father growing as well, the more she thought about it—Linette took little time to determine what she had to do. She could not make her way through the forests herself. She had to leave Jerusalem Valley the same way she had come to it—escorted by the army.

So, with the gathering at the Fosters winding down and everyone sated and happy, she sought out Major Thomas Carson and begged an audience with him. She put it to him as plainly as she could: she had to return to New Cranwell, and she had to do it now. She begged him to escort her.

"It's a poor time to travel," Carson told her. "The river may be frozen in places; it makes passage long and hard. There's little food and the cold itself is a hardship and a danger. But I'll take you. There's only one thing you should know. Captain Almon is coming with us."

Linette blanched. "Why move a wounded man if the season is so inhospitable?" she asked. As though it were concern for Almon that motivated her, and not fear of him—and fear that he would slow them down, and she wouldn't reach New Cranwell in time.

She didn't even know what she was racing, and yet the fear of losing the race was more than she could bear.

"Because what happened here leaves us all open to charges of insurrection when our superiors learn of it," Carson said, "and I am determined to invite the questions and face them myself, without 'help' from my superior at the fort, whom I do not trust. Taking Almon to New Cranwell will give an opportunity for everything to be settled without his involvement."

"Lieutenant Anderson?" Linette asked.

"As I said," Carson said. "A man I do not trust. I will gather a small group. We will escort you and take Almon with us for care and examination. Carey too."

Linette looked down and nodded. She wanted to protest—traveling with not just one but two criminals was certainly not what she'd had in mind—but she was not in any real position to do so. She should be praising the Creator on high that Carson was willing to entertain her request at all. And she felt a measure of comfort knowing that he would be part of the group to escort her back. A tall, broad-shouldered man with thinning blond hair and a strong, square jaw, he had secretly helped the settlers as best he could while Almon was still ruling the valley. There was something solid and comforting about him. His hands were big and calloused, strong hands. At the ends of his coat sleeves, she could just see the tips of vines, blue in color with a deep purple sheen. He was wearing a thick gold band—a wedding ring.

She caught herself noticing that, caught herself looking, and looked back up with a blush that she hoped he didn't see. She felt a slight sense of loss and berated herself for it.

None of that. She hadn't come here to find a man. Why should she feel anything at all at the knowledge that this one was taken?

"I'll give the orders to prepare," Carson said. "And appoint a successor. We'll leave tomorrow."

Linette nodded again. Part of her cried out, *So soon?* Another part of her couldn't leave soon enough.

Yet, as she stepped outside again, back into the cold, grey dim as dusk fell over the valley, the knowledge of loss drove her breath from her lungs. She looked out over the silhouettes of the settlement as it sank into the night—the apple trees, the scattered rooftops, the barren fields and twisting lines of smoke. From here, she could see lights in a few windows.

This place had almost been home.

She couldn't let the melancholy drown her. She shoved it down and back, turning the acute pain into an ache in her bones.

She went to tell Sarah she was leaving.

Standing in the shadows of the governing house, too hesitant to call her name, Amos watched her go.

PART 2
GOING

CHAPTER 5

In her little shingled cottage, Linette finished packing her things. It wasn't much—just a bundle of blankets, clothes, and extra boots, tied up with twine to be easy to carry on her back. Sarah had helped her with it. It wasn't likely that she'd have to carry it at all; the contingent to New Cranwell was made up of fourteen soldiers, and they would do the hard work and treat her like a lady.

Sarah had come to Linette's cottage and let herself in an hour earlier. She'd hardly spoken a word, just helped her pack, stoked the stove, cooked a pot of grains and handed a bowl to Linette with a spoon and a look that commanded her to eat. She folded her arms and leaned against the wall while Linette obeyed.

Finally she said, "The others will be gone by now. They were leaving before sunrise."

Linette nodded.

"I understand," Sarah said. "If I had a daughter in danger, I would do the same."

Linette nodded again.

"You'll come back," Sarah said. Her voice was strained. Tight. "Won't you?"

At that, Linette swallowed hard. She tried to look her friend in the face but found that she couldn't. "I don't know," she said.

"You belong here," Sarah said.

"Do I? Now? It was always about the seed, Sarah," Linette said. "I was always supposed to find it. And I gave it up. I gave it to Serena."

"That doesn't mean you're done here."

"I left New Cranwell because I wanted to run away," Linette said. "From the past. From who I used to be. But it seems I can't run. I'm going back now because I *can't* leave the past behind. Not while Beth is alive. Not while my father is elder in New Cranwell, and both our sins still find us out. I tried to leave it all behind and start a new life, become someone different. Instead, I'm just going back to face it all again. Maybe that was what I should have always done. I was a fool to think things could change."

"It seems to me," Sarah said quietly, "that the woman going back to New Cranwell is not the same woman who left it. So things *have* changed. You've changed." She hesitated, and Linette glanced up at her. Sarah was looking away, toward the far corner of the house. "You've changed, and you've changed us. Changed me. Changed all of us. You *do* belong here, Linette. You always will."

She smiled crookedly, and Linette sensed how hard it had been for practical, no-nonsense Sarah to get those words out. She laid a sturdy hand on Linette's shoulder. "Come back to us," Sarah said. "When your work is done, come back home."

A sharp, military rap on the door spared Linette the need to find words in response. She blinked back tears and stood. She and Sarah nodded at each other, and Sarah opened the door. Paul McIntyre, the young private with thick brown hair, stood in uniform in the morning light.

"I've come to fetch you, ma'am," he said. "The major says it's time to go."

Wordlessly, Sarah picked up Linette's bundle and hoisted it onto her own back. "I'll carry it to the dock for you," she said.

As they followed Paul toward the dock where the small contingent of soldiers waited to begin their trek downriver, other figures melted out of the morning shadows and joined them. Sarah's children, Lila and Letty hand in hand, the boys hanging back a little. Agatha Moss and John Hopewell came from the direction of the Trembler meeting house, where Linette imagined they had been praying and watching over the sleepers. Other settlers had already gathered around the soldiers. As they approached, each one sought out Linette's eyes. They nodded solemnly or shook her hand. Agatha let out of a sob and pulled her into a tight embrace.

"God go with you, child," she said in Linette's ear. "Don't give up listening. Don't give up hearing. The Fire Within will never leave you if you don't give up heeding."

Linette nodded and pulled herself free, only to be engulfed in another warm, strong hug. Big John.

"You've done us good," he said. "Herman would be proud."

Those words almost broke her, even as they flooded her with warmth. No one *should* be proud of her. She wasn't. She was giving up, wasn't she? Or at the very least, giving in—to the tidal pull of the past.

Major Carson stepped up and nodded curtly to Linette. "If you're ready, ma'am," he said. "We'll be off." Behind him, two soldiers stood by a stretcher containing the warmly bundled figure of Frederick Almon. Four others stood around Matthias Carey, dressed not in regimental colors but in simple clothing provided by the settlers, with his hands manacled. He kept his eyes up and glared at everyone around him. She shivered—she wasn't sure if she was more afraid of the chained man or the sleeping one. But she understood Carson's insistence on bringing them, and she was glad they wouldn't be left here for the settlers to manage.

Carson gave an order, and the men fell into formation—several out front, then the stretcher and Carey, and the rest bringing up the rear. Linette walked toward the back with Paul McIntyre by her side. Just like that, they began to move out. Following the river. One foot after another, her own feet taking her away from the life she had dreamed of and nearly possessed.

Then she heard the sound of footsteps jogging up behind them, and turned to see Amos Thatcher, in deerskin and furs and a black Trembler coat, catching up to them. He wore a pair of snowshoes strapped to his back along with a long rifle, and a pouch of ammunition at his waist. He fell in beside Linette, and the soldiers didn't say a word in protest.

"Amos, what are you …?"

"I'm going with you," he said. "I'm sorry I'm late."

"But … are you sure the major …"

"He knows," Amos said. "I talked to him yesterday. You need someone who knows the woods in winter."

She wanted to say, "But *you,* Amos?" Despite the fact that the gangly secretary had largely grown up in Jerusalem Valley, he had always seemed like the least likely of all the settlers to be on the frontier. He was bookish and gawky, gifted with ledgers and penmanship. There was a reason he had served as Herman Melrose's secretary and not as the local trapper.

Moreover, he made Linette acutely uncomfortable. He hadn't always. Not long ago, she'd seen him as a harmless friend. But lately he'd been look-ing at her in a particular intense way, and during the recent persecution, he had gone to great lengths to protect her and Sarah's family. He didn't seem harmless anymore, and she didn't know how to feel about it. Deep down, she'd counted that as one of the very few blessings of leaving the valley—that she wouldn't have to deal with whatever was happening with Amos.

She was not happy that he was coming along.

But she tried hard not to show it.

As they moved along the level ground, the low, half-frozen river on their right and the valley to their left with the grey, mist-shrouded moun-tains sweeping up beyond, leaving the settlers to wave and look after them and finally begin to dissipate, Amos stepped up close beside Linette and said, "'Look after the growing things, Amos.' That's what I heard in my ear. That's what I'm doing, but I don't expect anything from you. I want you to know that. I'm your friend, Linette, no matter what else may be or may come. I'll see you safe to New Cranwell, I promise."

She dared a look up at him, a brief glance into his brown eyes. "Thank you," she said.

They marched on in silence. There were trees up ahead—a tangle that would soon hide them. Linette paused and looked back.

Most of the settlers had gone. But Sarah and her family still stood by the dock, arms around one another. Lit up in the dawn. Linette raised her hand one last time.

But it seemed they didn't see. Sarah turned and walked away. Her chil-dren followed.

Winters in Tempestano were famously mild. A little chill, a little damp, but with afternoons of streaming sunlight and vineyards that never entirely retreated into dormancy. The days were not as long as they were in the summer, of course, but no one minded that—shorter days made for longer evenings spent in taverns or around family hearths, singing, storytelling, finding warmth in friend and fireside.

Deep underground, in a perpetually cold and dripping dungeon cell, none of that warmth ever settled in.

Lucaan Feeanstra, the youngest son of Leeanaert Feeanstra the Older and beloved brother of Leeanaert Feeanstra the Younger, had spent much of his life in cold and dripping environs. The Boglands, where he'd grown up, were rarely anything but damp. The dungeon, though, lacked everything that made cold and dripping places tolerable. Lucaan was a son of his people, whose hearts were all hearth fire, whose spirits were the best of tavern songs. He did not regret having helped the strangers fight against One-Eyed Driesken in the Lowlands, where he lived, but he did chafe against the injustice of what had happened since. How was it that assisting men to recover a young captive from a notorious bandit should put him and his brother and friends in the position of enemies of kirk and state? That they should in fact be plucked out of *their* state entirely and brought here, to some wine-drunk, too-warm place, and then—as Leeanaert had complained—not even be allowed to enjoy it?

Lucaan and Leeanaert—the latter of whom had been released several days ago—had been promised a trial but never given one. They had been arrested by command of Joseph Crispin, High Elder of the Puritani kirk, and it seemed no one was in any hurry to question his whims.

High Elder. Lucaan snorted at the thought. What sort of nonsense was that? Was not the very idea of a single human leader over the Creator's kirk the principal idea against which the Puritani had rebelled in the Wars? Was not the heart of their beliefs a fundamental equality between men under

God, and a separation between the powers of religion and the power of the sword?

Perhaps not. Perhaps he was naïve to think so, or simply too boggish. He'd been told his people were not so much the heart of the Puritani movement (as they liked to think themselves) as its far-flung fringe. Leeanaert would roll his eyes and say he didn't know why Lucaan worried himself about all this, anyway—did he think himself a kirkman? Or a trouble-stirrer like the Tremblers, who, it was rumored, hid in this land of Tempestano like rats in a ship?

No, of course not, Lucaan would say. He would fall silent with a sheepish smile while his brother elbowed him over a tankard of ale and froth sloshed down and ran over his hands. Jaapje and Joric would raise their glasses and start up a song. But Lucaan would keep thinking, keep troubling himself about Crispin and the kirk and the loss of ideals worth dying for. Ideals like freedom and autonomy, conscience and the right to do what was best. Lucaan always thought more deeply than his brother or his friends— worried more, dreamed more, cared more.

He would feel a little unseen as his brother and his friends roared out their song, as they began stomping on the floor and starting up a dance. He would feel misunderstood despite his brother's great affection and love, and the deep devotion Lucaan felt in return. He'd always felt a little that way.

Right now, alone in a dungeon in Tempestano, he would give anything to feel overlooked by people who loved him.

Somewhere close by, there came the creak and clang of doors opening, then footsteps down the corridor toward his cell. Lucaan sat up straight. It wouldn't be Leeanaert; they had agreed he should leave Tempestano immediately when he was released. But it might be his unexpected friend.

It was. The older man, short and square, appeared with a lantern in his hand and sat down, as usual, on the chair just outside the ground. He set the lantern beside him and dug into his cloak, pulling out a loaf of bread and handing it through the bars. Lucaan gratefully stood, hunched—the ceiling in the cell, carved out of rock, was too low for him to stand up to his full six feet—and accepted it.

"Thank you," he said simply.

"I'm sorry I can't do more," Deacon Bure told him.

"Have you word from my brother?"

"Gone," Bure said. "He headed back to the Lowlands two days ago, as I advised. With luck you will be out in a day or two as well, and you'll be able to catch up to him on the road. It wasn't easy to convince him to do what you agreed to and go—but I'm glad he listened. I'm glad you both did. I don't want to see you hurt more than necessary. Crispin has no real quarrel with you. He simply wanted to make you an example. You shouldn't have helped the fugitive *conde.*"

"So you've said," Lucaan said. "But it seems to me, and it did so seem to all of us, that if a stranger comes into your town and is clearly outnumbered, outsmarted, and outgunned, it is only the right and manly thing to do to help him."

Bure groaned a little, in the way he did. Lucaan had quickly figured out what that groan meant—that the deacon fully agreed with him; thought him, in fact, wise beyond his years, and was growingly convinced that his own life was a sham and a shame. The groan meant *Yes, it is the only manly thing to do, and I won't do it and don't do it, so what am I? Not a man.*

Lucaan liked the deacon. He'd wrestled some with the man's complicity with Crispin, but he'd decided in the end to count him a friend, no matter what things he might have done or helped to do that he rightly regretted now. All were sinners, and all could change. What man didn't have regrets?

For Adolphus Bure, it clearly helped to air some of those regrets. So Lucaan invited him to do so. "Have you had any success finding your man?" he asked. He suspected he knew the answer. If Crispin and Bure had found the fugitive count, lord of this dungeon, who had surely fled to safe grounds somewhere far west of here, Bure would not have been able to hide the crushing weight of his own self-condemnation.

The stout man shook his head, his face falling half into shadow as he did. But his brow lowered and he looked more troubled than ever. "He has gone to Angleland, where we can't reach him," he said.

"Why so sad, then?" Lucaan asked. Bure looked up with evident surprise.

"Come," Lucaan said. "You don't really want to catch him."

Bure huffed, an affronted sound, but didn't argue. A moment later he grew morose again and said, "I believe our cause is right. I only wish the elder's methods weren't so ruthless. I'm an old man, Lucaan. I've lost my taste for this sort of hunting." He grew quiet and said, almost under his breath, "The poor girl."

Lucaan sat up straighter, reflexively tearing the loaf of bread in his hands. "What's that now?" he asked.

"It's all too much," Bure said. "So much intrigue. Politics. I miss the old mission days, when it was all about preaching and reaching the lost. None of this unsavory work of rooting out dissenters."

"What girl?" Lucaan asked.

"There are layers, you see," Bure said. He wasn't looking at Lucaan, more looking off into the distance—trying to explain things to himself. "Political delicacy. Things we can't just come out and *do,* not in some places. It wasn't so long ago, Crispin used to keep the count in line by threatening his sister. Serena. Nearly hounded her to her death. She's gone now. Fled across the ocean." He frowned. "The elder thought he could control her there too, but she got away."

Lucaan was not following any of this, except that it made him slightly more impatient for Bure to break out of Crispin's net. He would, eventually. He was clearly a good man under all his "layers," and he was clearly in the throes of conscience. Crisis would pull his head above water soon enough.

"Serena is the girl you mentioned a minute ago?" Lucaan asked.

"No," Bure said with a heavy sigh. "There's another one. Carlos isn't alone, you see. He's traveling with his old captain of the guard. The man was in our employ for a long time—a spy. But he broke free too." He sounded wistful. "Just like Serena. Diego is his name. Massimo Diego. He has brothers and sisters. Two of them not so far from here. Crispin used them to keep Diego in line, same as he used Serena to control Carlos. It's effective. Threaten the weak."

His voice trailed off. Again Lucaan could see the wrestling in his eyes. If Leeanart were here, he would reach through the bars and hit Bure, hard, in the head, to help the right side win the wrestling match. But Lucaan couldn't reach, and besides, it seemed not the best way to help, given that he was already a prisoner for less than assaulting a deacon of the kirk.

Bure came back to himself. "So now that Diego has rebelled, Crispin will hurt his sister. Word will reach Diego, and he and Carlos will come back, before they're ready. Then the elder will spring his trap. It will work. There's little doubt of that. So I say—that poor girl. Just a pawn in the elder's plans."

"She lives near here, you say?" Lucaan asked.

"Two days' ride. To the south. She's a cook; her brother apprentices with a cloth merchant. Taddeo Diego is the boy's name."

"And the girl's?"

"Caterina."

Lucaan leaned back against the wall. The name called up an image of a lovely girl, persecuted and hunted down by Crispin's ungodly forces. He imagined himself flying to her rescue, beating back Crispin's soldiers, and standing at last battered but triumphant. She would look at him with shining eyes, and he would feel love welling up in his heart. He would fall to one knee and ask for her hand, and she would receive his proposal with tears of joy.

Just a daydream, of course. Lucaan well knew that he was in no position to bring any girl home with him. His wandering, adventuring lifestyle with his brother would not fit a wife, and he was a long way off from saving the money he needed to go back to the Boglands and buy a patch of land with a house, as he'd long desired to do. The brothers had no inheritance. Most of their old family possessions had been seized from their grandfather during the Wars, and Leeanaert the Older had lost what little remained to hardship and debt.

So no. Dreams of a wife and family and a hearth of his own would have to wait.

Of course, that didn't rule out being of service to someone in trouble.

"What does she look like?" he asked.

Bure looked over at him, seeing to notice him for the first time in the conversation. "I don't know. I've never seen her. What are you thinking?"

"Nothing," Lucaan said. "Nothing at all."

"You shouldn't get involved," Bure said. "I shouldn't have told you anything."

"What have you told me?" Lucaan asked. "Nothing. Hardly anything. Anyway, I am a prisoner. What can I do?" He shifted uncomfortably. The image in his head hadn't faded. "Has Crispin already moved against her?"

"He sent men south several days ago. You should not get involved, Lucaan."

Lucaan waved a hand in the air. He wasn't going to get involved. Helping Caterina was a daydream, nothing more. He was going to head for the Lowlands and meet Leeanaert on the road, as they had agreed. They would journey back toward the coast and look for their friends. "My home is north and west of here."

That night he lay wide awake in his cell and thought long and deeply about the Puritani kirk of his day and the way Crispin was leading it. He thought of the freedom his fathers had fought for and the abomination of twisting that freedom into license to hunt and to kill. He thought of his brother, and his father, and what they would do in his situation. Lucaan had never been the leader of the family. When Leeanaert the Older died, his elder son took the lead, and Lucaan followed. He was happy there, in Leeanaert's shadow, for Leeanaert's shadow fell in pleasant places. Lucaan could always know that following his brother, he was doing right. He was on the side of truth and justice. Their adventures, their fistfights, their hardworking days on the river all tended to glory and virtue. Someday he hoped it would lead him home, where he could settle with a family of his own, but he was content for that day to be somewhere far off.

But now?

What if the time had come to cast his own shadow?

Two days later, when Lucaan was released from the dungeon with a stern lecture from a representative of the elder, an official warning about the company he kept, and a small bag of coin snuck to him by Deacon Bure to help him on his way, he went first to a tavern seeking word from his brother. It wasn't hard to find: Leeanaert had left word of his route and told Lucaan to come and find him.

Instead, Lucaan had a message written up and sent ahead of his brother on a ship. It said he would come home.

But not yet.

First, he had to go south.

South of Tempestano—The Old World

Caterina Diego, Bure had said, was two days' ride to the south. But Lucaan was not a rider, given to days on horseback, so he did not seek out a horse. Like his brother and friends, he was a boatman. So he borrowed a boat.

It was a small boat, little more than a skiff with a sail. He liked the look of it—it would be fast, easily maneuvered, easy to fly downriver. He felt a little guilty borrowing it, as there was no time or opportunity to discuss it with the owner, but he did leave almost the entire bag of coin from Bure nestled beneath the post where the boat had been tied. He left a note, too, written by the same helpful tavernkeeper who penned his letter to Leeanaert. He promised to bring the boat back, or, barring that, to replace it. He hated to take it, but he did not have time to spare.

And indeed, once he had set the raft floating downriver and guided her skillfully out beyond the docks into the morning, where the sun shone on the water and the cold and bracing wind blew, it took Lucaan very little time at all to fly. His little craft fairly skimmed the top of the water, his sail full, golden hair blowing behind him. He wore leather breeches and a sheepskin vest that kept him warm, with a heavy wool cloak over it all. His vines, bright red in color like his brother's, contracted against the cold, pulling his muscles tight. He exulted in the feeling of speed, purpose—of being alive.

The journey south—faster and more direct than it would have been on horseback—changed the landscape more than he expected for such a short distance. The river cut inland, winding through lands that were both sheltered from the sea and close enough to it to be warmed by thermal currents coming from the south. The landscape grew greener and warmer by the hour. He marveled at it. Sure this was nothing like winter in the Western Lowlands, or before that, in the Bogs.

He worried some over his brother and hoped he had made the right choice to leave him. He knew Leeanaert was likely lagging along the road, waiting for Lucaan to catch up with him. He had only agreed to leave town alone because Bure pressed so hard, urging both brothers to get out of Tempestano as soon as they could and court no further trouble. Lucaan had seen the sense of it and joined in encouraging Leeanaert to leave. He told his brother that he would not be far behind.

Except that now, of course, he would. Still he knew that Leeanaert would support his choice. The brothers had always been inseparable, yet they knew themselves to be in service to a higher cause. Freedom for them was freedom to find the right and do it. Adventure was duty and obligation. It was why they had helped Carlos Vaquero, the runaway count of Tempestano. And it was why Lucaan would help Caterina Diego.

That, and he couldn't get his imagined image of her out of his mind.

The wind carried Lucaan through the day and all through the dark, starry night. He kept his little ship pointing south until he reached his destination in the early morning hours. He tied off in a small village harbor and made his way up into the riverside streets. Fishermen and farmers were up early, the former headed to the river, the latter headed to their fields. Lucaan asked around and found his way further into town until he stood in the doorway of a weaver's shop, hat in hand, early morning sunlight spilling over the wooden floor from the open door behind him, and said to the young man who stood amid bolts of cloth, framed by a large loom— "Diego? Taddeo Diego?"

"That's me," the young man said, his back turned to Lucaan. He lit an oil lamp, then another and another, their warm light bringing out the colors of the cloth around him—mostly dark purple and green, their shades alternating between shadowy and jewel-like in the glow of sun or lamplight. Lucaan had intruded before he finished opening shop. Done with the lamps, Taddeo turned to face him, smoothing his simple waistcoat with his hands. He was a small man, wiry, with dark hair and a furtive expression. His features were much like those of the older Diego, who traveled with Carlos Vaquero. But his hair was thicker, and he was clean-shaven, with carefully tapered sideburns framing his jaw. His eyes were bright and intelligent, and he openly scrutinized Lucaan.

"You've come far," he said. "But I don't know you. Why are you looking for me?"

"I met your brothers," Lucaan said. "Two of them."

Something in Taddeo's eyes sharpened, but he didn't react. Lucaan went on. "They were traveling west together with a companion in some trouble, and got themselves in more. The long of it is, my friends and I helped them out of it, and I just now got out of prison for my good deed."

"Prison where?" Taddeo asked. "Not here."

Lucaan motioned with his head, as though jerking it north explained everything. "In Tempestano."

"And that's the long of it?"

"It seems it was more the short." Lucaan took a step forward and lowered his voice, leaning forward. "It's not why I came, to tell you all that. I came to warn you: Crispin is coming after your sister."

At that, Taddeo paled. He looked around him, as though suddenly worried that enemies might be hidden amidst the bolts of cloth and bags of undyed wool, or lurking behind the looms that crowded the shop. But the shop was empty and still, save for dust motes floating in the rays of sunlight.

"What are you talking about?" Taddeo asked. He took a step toward Lucaan and lowered his own voice, matching him. "How could you even know this?"

"The elder has a secondhand man," Lucaan said, "one who is plagued by second thoughts. He told me while I was still in the prison. Felt bad about it, see. He thinks Crispin is doing wrong, but he can't get up the guts to make him stop."

"I don't know how anyone could make Crispin stop," Taddeo muttered. "Tell me everything. What do you know?"

"The elder knows you and your sister live here. He sent men on horseback several days ago—maybe four." Lucaan frowned. "They should already be here. I didn't think I would warn you in time. Unless the elder's men are very slow, or as conflicted as the deacon."

Taddeo almost smiled at that. "I don't think we can count on such luck," he said. "They may have been here. This is a small village, but busy. Men come in and out all the time, doing trade along the river."

"But if they came here, they would have sought you out."

"Maybe not," Taddeo said. "Not if they asked around and found out that Caterina is already gone. I wish I could say that the locals would have told me if someone was looking for us, but we're not from here, and the people of this place are not free with their trust."

This was good news, and heartening for that, but it also left Lucaan at a loose end. So he asked, "But, already gone? Where did she go?"

Taddeo seemed amused, although Lucaan could perceive worry in his eyes as well. "If you think I'm going to tell you that, you presume I am very free with *my* trust. Which I am not, for reasons I'm sure you can understand."

"But why would she leave?" Lucaan asked.

"I think I've told you more than you have a right to know already," Taddeo said. "Caterina is not here. If the elder's men have been here, they are gone already, and no harm done. I would assume you are one of the elder's spies, here to pose as a friend and learn her whereabouts, but you seem so artless that it's hard to believe that. Even so, I'm not going to tell you any more. I hope you understand."

Lucaan shook his windblown head slowly. "Sure, I do," he said. "What kind of devil's work is it this elder does, that families have to run from him in fear, and keep their secrets from strangers who want to help?" He lifted his eyes quickly, meeting Taddeo's again, and assured him—"I *do* understand. Only it's a sorry thing when a man or a woman is hounded for helping his friend. That's what all this is … because your brother stands by the count of Tempestano." He reached out and clapped a hand on Taddeo's shoulder. "Take some heart that you do not stand alone. Now, I'm going to find out where your sister's gone so I can go and make sure the elder's men haven't found her. But I won't ask you to help me. I know you can't do that. You're a good man to protect your family."

He turned to go, and warm sunlight splashed across his feet and into his face.

"Wait," Taddeo said.

Lucaan turned back. Taddeo was eyeing him strangely. "Why are you getting involved?" the young man asked. "You don't have to."

"My brother Leeanaert, he told me once, 'Lucaan, some men do great grand things and they change the world. Others just see where help is needed, and they do something. You and me are that kind, men who do what needs done.' Who could have thought that a man would tell me, while I sat in a prison cell, about you and your sister and the trouble that's seeking you? But he did. So I know that I'm bound to lend my hand."

He turned again. This time Taddeo didn't call him back. Lucaan walked out into the sunshine and went in search of breakfast.

Chapter 6

The Court of the Angle King—The Old World

The funeral of the Angle King was a solemn and portentous affair, taking a week in all—five days in which the king's scented and powdered body lay in state in a large, domed chapel, while people traveled from all over the island to see him. Light filtered in through gold-paned windows, falling over the body in its splendid coffin surrounded by tall lit candles. Dressed in white, servants of the kirk hovered around the edges of the room, tending to the candles and keeping order among the guests, some of whom wept loudly or flailed with grief. Filigreed vines and flowers climbed the interior of the dome, a rich, golden tapestry that grew thicker as it branched and arced overhead, every branch coming together at last to form a massive carved bouquet in the center.

On the sixth day, thousands of people crammed themselves into the cathedral where kirk men and courtiers spoke at length about the virtues and accomplishments of the dead man, and choirs sang prayers from morning into the late afternoon. Carlos and Diego, who had made an uncomfortable visit to the coffin, stood in the pews in the middle of the cathedral along with other noblemen of middling importance and their attendants. The truly powerful and important took up the front, and lesser individuals packed into the back. Carlos was stiffly dressed and even more stiffly behaved, doing his best to look interested and appropriately sorrowful even when his mind was days ahead and many miles away. He had managed to meet with a few of his father's old friends, who shared meals with him and asked veiled questions. Trust did not flow freely on either side, and Carlos knew his hosts were getting the measure of him even as he was of them. But no one he'd met with had the clout he needed—the ability to get the ear of the crown prince at such a time as this. He had sent his condolences directly to the prince, of course, along with the announcement of his presence in Angleland, but had received nothing back except an acknowledge of receipt from Henry's chief steward. As was to be expected, really. The men who stood on either side of Carlos and Diego now, packed into the pews of the kirk as music fell all around them, were not precisely friends and allies, but they were at least known. It was worth something.

On the seventh day, the king was buried, and Carlos got the closest to Henry that he'd managed all this time—close enough to see the man's face. Henry was not a young man anymore; he had passed forty some time ago. But he had always been hale and lusty in his approach to life—one who liked his ale and the hunt a far sight better than he did the administrative work of a king or even the more refined pleasures of court life. Nor had he ever struck Carlos as a schemer.

During a reception in a large palace courtyard after the burial, Carlos turned away from a painfully vapid conversation with a long-lashed young woman in a dress that was far too low-cut to be appropriate for the occasion and caught a glimpse of the crown prince standing with several of his advisors only six feet away. Carlos had a clear view of the prince's expression. Henry did not look bowed down with grief or alight with ambition. His expression was somber and ready—and unexpectedly approachable. Carlos felt an urge to dash through the crowd and address Henry directly, etiquette be damned. He knew better than to think that would go well, and restrained himself. A moment later, the prince and his retinue moved in the opposite direction.

"*Surely* you think so?" the woman asked. She batted her long eyelashes up at him, and Carlos realized she was waiting for an answer.

"I'm sorry," he said. He reached down, took her by the shoulders, and kindly but firmly moved her aside. "I didn't hear a word you just said, and I'm afraid I can't stay to hear you repeat it. Excuse me, please, with my apologies."

He strode off, leaving her behind—gaping after him and most likely growing red. He felt bad, but he couldn't waste his time here being drawn into conversation with every eligible daughter who had been introduced to him over the last week. He spotted Diego talking with several men in uniform and veered toward him, narrowly avoiding two more women who were intently coming his way. He recognized them; they had spent seventy-five agonizing minutes asking him questions about his estate at an evening reception the day before. He couldn't remember their names and wanted nothing more than to avoid a repeat of the conversation.

He should have known that showing up here as he had, a handsome young count from the Southern Countries without wife or women in his retinue, would be assumed to be looking for one in the court of the Angle King. In fact, most of his father's old friends had quietly presumed that to be Carlos's reason for visiting, and had probably spread the word. Certainly it seemed that every other person at court wanted to introduce him to some pretty young thing. He was half-tempted to invent a fiancée just to quell their enthusiasm.

Diego turned his head and spotted Carlos coming his way. He raised a hand in greeting, and Carlos quickened his pace—but before he reached his friend, something drew his eye, and his steps faltered. Twenty feet away, partly blocked by the flounced skirts and lace-trimmed coats of the courtiers, another man was sitting on the edge of an ornate fountain, never minding that spray from its gushing flow wet his hair and shoulders. He was watching Carlos intently.

And with a start, Carlos recognized him.

He raised a finger to Diego with an apologetic glance and then turned abruptly and headed to the fountain.

The man didn't get up. Carlos seated himself on the rounded marble beside him and let the fountain spray wet his coat and tickle the back of his neck. The man nodded in recognition.

"Hello, John," Carlos said.

"It's been some years," John Worthington answered. He shifted a little, turning so he could get a look at Carlos beside him. "You look different. Grown up at last."

Carlos smiled sadly. "It happens to all of us, I suppose."

"It doesn't," John said with a shake of his head. He gestured slightly toward the crowd, thickly packed, forming small islands where people stood and talked with one another and swirling eddies where they broke free and looked for more advantageous partners. "Fully half of these have never grown up, especially the women. They're still playing the same old games."

Carlos tried not to stare at his old friend. John Worthington had the same handsome jawline and perceptive eyes he'd had as a dashing young rogue. His hair was thick and curly, falling around his head profusely. His vines were dark green, and on the right, they came over his ear and followed his cheekbone, resting lightly near the edge of his mouth. Except for the left side of his face, where his ear was gone and much of his skin had burned away, where the edge of his cheek looked pulled and discolored from skin grafts and where his vines were black and lifeless, he might have seemed unchanged from those years—physically. In every other way, John had never been the same since the accident.

Carlos had been there that night. It had scared him sober for the rest of the visit to Angleland, and for much of his life after that. It had made him more open to the things Serena said, and to the serious, gentle prodding of Herman Melrose when he asked after the health of Carlos's soul. It had in fact been the catalyst to Carlos's finally realizing that life was more than a game and that he needed to take his place in it. He was thankful, but he had never stopped feeling a twinge of shame when he thought of his old friend.

He'd been grateful to know John had survived, but not brave enough to stay by his side through the long and painful recovery. And he had not written or visited him since.

"There was a time," John said, pointing to the young woman Carlos had snubbed—who was now blushing and batting her eyes at a young nobleman in uniform—"when a girl like that would have appealed mightily to us both. I saw you set her aside just now, which tells me your heart is taken up by another."

"Not by a woman," Carlos said.

"I didn't say that. I did not even suggest it. You've grown serious, Carlos Vaquero, I see it in your eyes. And I'm glad to know it."

"Don't you miss your younger days?" Carlos asked.

John smiled—an odd smile, stretched out of its normal proportions by the tight skin on the left side of his face. "No," he said. "I heard about that bad business with Serena. Is she all right?"

"I don't know," Carlos said. "She's gone to the New World. I can only hope and pray she's found her feet. But that bad business is why I'm here, John. Crispin has seized Tempestano. I need the crown prince's help to get it back."

John raised both thick eyebrows. "Do you now?" he asked.

"I'd hoped to renew our old alliance with King Aldous," Carlos said. "You can see for yourself how well I timed it."

"I'd say your timing is impeccable," John told him, "seeing as Crispin will be here by tomorrow."

Carlos nearly catapulted off the side of the fountain. On his feet, he turned to John, trying to temper his body language so as not to draw so much attention. "What?"

"Did you think the High Elder of the Puritani kirk would allow a new king to be crowned without his presence?" John said. "Of course he's coming here."

"Then my timing is terrible," Carlos whispered loudly. "Crispin will have the prince's ear before I ever get close to him."

John waved to him to sit back down and waited until he did so before resuming, looking mildly annoyed at Carlos's show. "Not necessarily," he said. "You are assuming Henry welcomes the elder's presence, which I would wager he does not. Relations between Angleland and the continent have been unsettled for years, as you well know, and Crispin is beginning to get a reputation for power grabbing. He is coming here, yes, but I suspect Henry is in a mood to resist."

"Then I'd like to help that mood along, if I can," Carlos said.

John smiled again. "There's the spirit. Tell me, does Crispin know you're here?"

"Not as far as I know," Carlos said. "He tried to have me killed, John. I escaped him and fled here. I assume he pursued, but if all went well, my man and I covered our tracks well enough."

John whistled, a low sound that was entirely out of place in the finery and foppery surrounding them in the courtyard. For that matter, everything about the man seemed out of place, now that Carlos looked more closely at him—his clothes were well tailored, but they were simple, made of wool, more like something a tradesman would wear than a courtier, especially at an event like this one.

Carlos dropped his voice even lower. "Have you become a Trembler, John?"

His old friend shook his shaggy head. "Nothing so radical as that," he said. "But have I become religious? Oh yes. Facing death and disfigurement in the prime of your life and the depth of your sin will do that to you. Do you know, when I finally came out of all those months of agony and delirium, I discovered I was going to be a father by one of those tavern wenches we frequented. She was told to dispose of the baby, but she wouldn't do it. The truly terrible thing is, our worlds were so far apart, I might never have known about it. She'd never even have gotten word to me except my father was a man of conscience. Here we were, crossing that gulf between worlds whenever we wanted so we could drink and carouse and feel like men, and the women on the other side could never have done the same if they were in the most dire need."

"But she found you?" Carlos asked. "Your father got you word?"

"He did," John said, nodding firmly. "So I married her. Nine years, it's been. I can't bring her to court. The scorn is too much for her, and she can't keep her head up or hold her own in a conversation. I can't talk to her of books or philosophy or even religion; she doesn't care about any of it. She still steals my silver and hides it away, like she thinks I'm going to banish her one of these cold nights and she'll need it to sustain her on the streets."

Carlos didn't really know what to say. "I'm sorry," he said.

"Don't be," John said. "Our son is a delight. His mother is a trial, most often. But I had to marry her. Because I did, I'm healing. If I hadn't, I think I would still be in torment. And do you know, sometimes, she delights me too."

Carlos fell quiet. At last he said, "I'm sorry I wasn't there for you. I was … afraid."

"Think nothing of it. You were just a boy. We both were."

"I should have been a man."

"You became one, in time. That's good enough for me." John clapped a hand on Carlos's shoulder. "Anyone would have been afraid, Carlos. Creator knows I was. Now. Tell me about Tempestano, and what you need. And then we will go and talk to the prince."

Carlos nearly jumped to his feet again. "We … what?"

John chuckled. "I didn't mention that, did I? I have Henry's ear. I'll take you to meet with him. This is not a good time, as I'm sure you can imagine, but in a time like this, you are not the only one who needs allies."

Carlos lingered at the reception for another thirty minutes after John had gone, thinking that perhaps there would be something more to be gained by rubbing elbows with the king's court—the crown prince's court, now—but eventually his impatience won out. He found some excuse to pull Diego out of conversation with his compatriots, and the two men called a carriage and returned home to the townhouse Carlos had rented. He was paying for a small household staff as well—a necessity, if they were to be taken seriously while they were here—and his valet had a bright fire and spiced, steaming mugs of rum waiting for them. Carlos blessed him while he paced the study and told Diego everything.

Diego listened with pursed lips. He wasn't so sure as John had been that the new king would oppose Crispin, even quietly—but if anything, that only made the need to see Henry more urgent. Crispin was coming whether they liked it or not, and with the change in regime, alliances might turn. The crown prince might want nothing to do with the High Elder, or he might be impressed by the power Crispin had amassed on the continent and decide to strengthen ties with him.

They needed to reach the king-to-be and speak with him before Crispin arrived. If Carlos was going to take back his seat of authority, it was essential that he do it now. And besides, someone needed to speak for the Tremblers.

"And you believe this man, that he can get us an audience with the prince?"

"He wouldn't lie," Carlos said. "It's a good sign, Diego, if the prince has taken John into his confidence. It speaks as well for his character as it did for Aldous that he favored Herman Melrose."

"From what you said earlier, when you knew him, the young lord was a rake."

"Trust me," Carlos said. "If you'd seen him, talked to him, you wouldn't doubt him. What happened to him was terrible. It changed us both—but him most of all, I think. You should have seen him—sitting there dressed like a Trembler, just watching the whole affair, not even dipping his toes into all that peacockery."

"You envy him," Diego said with a smirk.

"I'm here to strengthen alliances, not to gossip and strut. You know that." Carlos allowed himself a small smile at his own expense. "At least you can talk with the guards and the military men. I am a magnet for eligible young women and their vainglorious young brothers. I looked and felt ridiculous today, Diego. I suppose that means I've grown."

Diego laughed, his craggy face transforming with a hearty smile. "From vainglory to valor," he said, still smiling but sincere. "It's a long road you've walked so far. And now it will take us to the footstool of a king."

CHAPTER 7

Wilderness West of Jerusalem Valley, The New World

Smith Foster woke before dawn. Despite his heavy winter coat and boots, and the threadbare woolen blanket Ezekiel had smuggled out of the fort, his feet were numb from the cold and his torso ached where Anderson had stabbed a knife between his ribs. Sleep was a fitful, torturous thing, and he wasn't sure it was better than being awake.

It was necessary, though. He needed whatever rest he could get if they were going to make it all the way home.

Grunting as he struggled to sit up, he looked through the dim light across the embers of their fire and shuffled the grey woolen blanket higher around his shoulders, trying to cut off the cold that sliced at his neck and slid down his collar. He missed Sarah's red scarf. Before Anderson had soaked it with Smith's own blood and sent it to the valley as a warning to Smith's faithful wife, Smith had formed a habit of wrapping it around his hands and praying for her and their children.

Across the fire, one of his companions stirred. His bulky form and hunched shoulders marked him as Premislav, the former army commander who had been exposed as a dissenter and possible spy. The sky was lightening steadily, and Smith could see the white cloud of Premislav's breath.

Behind him came the shuffle of feet in the forest, Ezekiel returning to the fire after keeping watch. The old black man moved stiffly in the cold. He came into view and hunched over the fire, poking at the embers with a stick and drawing an encouraging flare before feeding the fire with kindling he'd gathered in the predawn stillness.

It had been two days since Ezekiel released Premislav and Smith from the prison at Fort Collins and led them out into the wilderness. Two days of tracing their way through a numbingly cold, forested wilderness, trying to follow the river while staying well out of sight. Smith was a farmer, not a woodsman, but he'd lived on the frontier long enough to know some things about covering their tracks. It did him little good. His companions were not at all versed in the ways of the wilderness, and with Smith and Premislav both nursing injuries, it was all they could do to walk steadily onward— forget stealth and secrecy. Ezekiel was an old man with aching joints who had spent most of his life in the confines of Fort Collins and places like it. If anyone chose to chase them, they would not be difficult to find.

Even so, two days had passed, and they had not been caught and returned to the fort. They had not even heard sounds of pursuit.

Smith moved toward the fire, soaking up its increasing warmth, and cradled his arm against his wounded side. It was a little bitter, to think he mattered enough to Anderson to stab and threaten, but not enough to chase out into the cold. Or else he was just fooling himself, and Anderson's men would be along at any moment—easily tracking and outpacing the fugitives and swooping in to arrest them again.

Premislav had propped himself up across from Smith. He stared across the thin cloud of smoke that rose from Ezekiel's damp kindling. His eyes were dark and intelligent in a bruised, heavily jowled face. The soldiers had beaten him badly, and his breathing labored in the morning air. Ezekiel sat down beside him and drew a pouch out from under his too-thin coat and a pan from amongst his small bundle of things. He pulled a handful of corn from the pouch, threw it into the pan, and held it over the fire. As they parched, the kernels began to shift and swell, and a few jumped in the pan.

Ezekiel said nothing as he finished cooking, just pulled the pan off the fire and tipped some of the hot corn into Premislav's cupped hands. Then he stood and stumped across to the other side, and Smith held out his own hands and accepted the offering gladly. He blew on the corn and shuffled it from hand to hand before nibbling at the kernels.

As the sun continued its wan winter climb, Smith lifted his eyes, following the subdued red-brown of the pines to their grey-green needled boughs above. A light dusting of snow lay on the branches. Beyond the trees, pale purple mountains rose to the north, climbing up from the river valley. They seemed barren and forlorn this morning. An owl hooted nearby, sounding the last call of the night.

When they had finished eating, all three men got to their feet and began to bundle their things—Premislav and Smith rolled their grey blankets to carry on their shoulders, while Ezekiel packed up his cooking pan and corn and tied everything into a single burden for his back. He shouldered it without complaint, shaded his eyes as though the newly risen sun was too bright for him, and looked east. "Reckon we'll make it nearly there today," he said.

Smith merely grunted in response. He was less optimistic—he hated to think how slow they'd been walking, and surely Anderson would be on their heels at any moment.

Premislav, who ordinarily might have been the most garrulous of the three, seemed to be struck dumb by the cold. It was his way every morning, Smith had realized after sharing a prison cell and now a trail with him. The commander's tongue would loosen as more hours added themselves to the day.

With his blanket arranged, Smith stamped out the fire regretfully. He picked up the long bough he'd been using as a walking stick and, as had become habit, led the way.

It was to his home they were returning. His path to pick out for the others. His story they had joined, for better or for worse.

Not for the first time, as the three began their slow trek up through the forest, Smith wondered if he'd done the right thing by going with Ezekiel. He had refused to break out earlier, when he could have done so easily with the River People. But that was before Anderson stabbed him and showed just how far he would go to use Smith against Sarah and the rest of the Jerusalem Valley settlement—before he'd realized that he wasn't helping them by staying a prisoner, as he'd originally thought. He'd thought it would be best for everyone if he just submitted, tried to keep the peace. He had been wrong. But he wasn't sure if this was so much better. What now, if they didn't reach the valley before Anderson could catch them?

What now, if they *did?*

The ground where they walked sloped upward, through channels between the rock filled with snow and dead leaves. The day grew brighter but not discernably warmer, though Smith felt a light sweat beneath his clothes as he pushed himself forward.

Without warning, Premislav barked, "Get down!"

Smith reacted instantly, falling into a low crouch. He turned to see that Ezekiel had done the same. Premislav, armed with a flintlock pistol Ezekiel had managed to steal from the fort, was still on his feet, sharp eyes sweeping their surroundings. Smith had heard and seen nothing, but he strained now to sense whatever had put Premislav on alert.

With a startling clatter, four large birds burst up from one of the cuts nearby. They beat their tremendous wings and rose until they had broken from the trees and went into a slow, circular glide.

Vultures.

Premislav slowly lowered his gun while Smith, his heart thundering in his ears, got back to his feet and approached the cut.

He found himself looking down at a human body, and one he knew.

Stomach sinking, he took in the grisly sight a little at a time, and closed his eyes with a sigh of fear and grief.

The man's name was Corey Sowell. He was younger than Smith by about ten years. When Smith had last seen him, he was heading into the wilderness on a mission to find other settlements that might trade with Jerusalem Valley for food.

He opened his eyes again, all but unseeing as his mind tried to work out what had happened. Had Corey simply lost his footing out here—fallen into the small defile, hit his head on the rock, been overtaken by the cold? It was clear he had been here some time—he was half-covered with snow, even after the tugging of the vultures had pulled him partly out.

Premislav approached. He seemed like he might lay a hand on Smith's shoulder, but he refrained.

"Someone you knew?" the commander asked.

Smith nodded. "One of ours. He went out scouting for us not two weeks ago."

Premislav surveyed the body without flinching. Ezekiel came up behind them both, looked down, and said quietly, "Lord have mercy."

"Whatever did that had a murderous streak in it," Premislav said. He didn't specify *that*; didn't put words to the torn-out throat and the wounded face. "It killed just to kill, not to eat. Vultures did the rest."

"Have mercy on us all," Ezekiel repeated.

Smith swallowed back gorge and turned away. He wanted to lead them on, just to walk on out of this place until the body was far behind. He couldn't, of course. They had to bury Corey, or at least to cover his body with rocks or deadfall—they didn't have tools to dig, and the ground was half-frozen besides. They couldn't leave a good man just lying there.

Premislav had already turned away. Ezekiel had not—he was staring, or praying, unable to tear his eyes off the body in the snow. But before Smith could say aught to either of them, he heard something moving.

He raised a hand. The other two saw and understood; Premislav froze where he stood, and Ezekiel lifted only his eyes, silent and still.

Some instinct, deeper than his senses, told Smith they needed to move. He scouted a quiet pathway, a little deer trail clear of debris that led up to a boulder half-covered with roots from a steep limestone bluff. There was room to shelter there, with no chance of being attacked from behind. Signaling for the others to keep silence and follow him, Smith led the way. All three backed up against the bluff and beneath the roots, with the boulder mostly hiding them. They hunkered down and stayed quiet, scanning the trees beyond. Premislav held his pistol at the ready.

For a few heartbeats there was nothing, and then they all heard it—the sound of something moving nearby. Smith, peering over Premislav's shoulder, stopped breathing.

He saw motion before he could make it out—a strange, rolling, forward movement, like something lurching forward and then back again. It was large but lean, not a deer—its presence was too predatory for that. At first Smith thought it was a wolf.

Then it moved out of the tangle of branches and into a clear patch where Smith could see it. He strangled a gasp. It wasn't a wolf, this thing that crawled on all fours, stopped, sat back on its hind legs, then moved forward again.

It was a man.

Or it had been.

It wore the remnants of buckskin and a torn, bloodied wool cloak. Its hair was long and black; its skin dark from long days in the sun. It might have been one of Capenokanickon's kin, once. Now its arms were covered with green scales. Its eyes were yellow, and its shoulders were strangely over-sized and hunched. It scanned the clearing where it sat, and a forked tongue lolled from its mouth and pulled back in between fangs.

Machkigen.

Despite the remnants of its humanity, the creature resembled a man less than it did the bear Jonathan had once faced—the one whose poi-soned scratches seemed to effect the parson's own awful transformation. Of course, Linette and Jacques had saved the young preacher long before his state ever reached anything so horrifying as this.

Smith tried not to breathe. Behind and before him, Ezekiel and Premis-lav did the same. The commander held his pistol steady, and Smith tensed every muscle, ready to run. Or leap to the commander's aid. Or grab a fallen bough and beat the creature with all his strength.

Whatever presented itself to do, he prayed he would be ready to do it.

The creature had shifted back on its haunches again and sat with head erect, still, like a wolf scenting air. Slowly, it turned its gaze toward the body of Corey Sowell, but it didn't move. Smith had no doubt the creature had killed Corey. Why it lingered here now, he wasn't sure.

Once more, the creature turned its head—this time in their direction.

Smith's legs burned from crouching, and he resisted the urge to throw himself out of the hiding spot and attack first. But he didn't have to.

The creature whipped its head around, then turned, crouching so its fingers rested splayed on the ground and its shoulders aimed forward. A moment later they all heard what had distracted it. Someone was coming through the woods, and they weren't coming quietly.

The creature hissed. Smith caught a glimpse of red through the trees.

Anderson's men come at last.

Premislav turned his head slightly and nodded at both Smith and Ezekiel. He didn't have to speak; his meaning was clear. *Time to go.*

The creature sprinted suddenly forward, lost in the trees, headed for the soldiers. Shouts and musket fire followed a moment later.

Premislav bolted from the hiding place, Smith and Ezekiel spilling out after him. Smith led the way off the path, away from the river, deeper into the woods. They ignored the sounds of a fight behind them and forsook the body of Corey Sowell, confined to a shallow and snowy grave.

Maybe, if the soldiers came out of this altercation alive, they would bury him.

Smith hardly had a moment to care.

Wetëndeis, Capenokanickon's tall and most favored daughter, often dreamed.

Because she also interpreted her dreams, and her interpretations proved wise and prescient, she was held in honor among all of her people and not only by her father, who had adored her from the moment she was born.

She dreamed today, as she sat by a fire in the small encampment made by her people in the valley where the settlers lived. She sat with her palms angled up, fingers loose, eyes closed; her long staff with its red feathers resting across her knees.

In her dream, a great wolf approached her. Its fur was black and grizzled silver; it regarded her with ancient eyes and dipped its head.

She inclined hers in return. In the dream a scarlet tanager, her namesake, sat on her shoulder and ruffled its deep red feathers and black wings.

Wetëndeis spoke first. "You have come far, brother," she said.

The wolf answered her, "I come to ask for your help."

That it spoke did not surprise her at all. That it begged her for help did. For that was its tone—it pleaded. It was not a tone she would have associated with this creature of great strength, stealth, and power.

"What do you need that we can give you?" she asked. She could feel the calming weight of the staff across her knees. The bird on her shoulder whistled.

"See, creation suffers," the wolf answered. "The thorns overgrow the ground. They pull us down and we cannot loose ourselves from their grip."

As the wolf spoke, she became aware of a tangled thicket behind it, deep and high as a forest, dark and twisted as a nest of serpents. Thorns grew as long as her staff; diseased, darkened sap dripped from their ends. They had overrun the ground and were dragging it down, pulling creation into darkness. A foul stench, of rot without remedy, drifted from the thicket.

"We cannot heal this," the wolf repeated. "You, O Flame of Spring, must help us. You and your family must bring back the glory of the world before the thorns consume us all."

Wetëndeis blinked, and she sat awake by the fire, watching smoke drift lazily up against a darkening sky, watching flames lick at the wood.

"But how?" she asked aloud, though no one stood near to answer. Nor would anyone likely have known what to say.

Across from the fire, her father lay bundled in furs and blankets, silent on a cot of aspen and fir. He remained in his deep, uncanny sleep. His white hair and tattooed cheekbones marked him as uncommonly wise.

If only he could sit and talk with her now.

A commotion drew her attention away from the flames. Someone was approaching the settlement's governing house from the direction of the river. Settlers who had been keeping watch gathered to meet him, and several of the warriors stood from their place in the encampment and loped toward the gathering.

She looked solemnly down at her father once more, then stood, pushing herself up with her staff, and went to hear for herself what had happened.

She did not know the man. He wore buckskin leggings and a long leather coat lined with fur. His face was pale and his eyes bloodshot as though he'd not slept in many days.

He spoke fast, and his voice shook.

"They're gone," he said, seeming to repeat himself. "They're all gone,

John. All dead."

John Hopewell, for now the leader of the settlement, fought back tears of grief, but the emotion that filled his large and heavy frame was fear.

"Was it—"

"It was Outsiders. They massacred the entire settlement. I searched for survivors. They're all dead."

The man looked up, seeming to notice the warriors for the first time. His eyes rested briefly on Wetëndeis before returning to John. He lowered his voice, but they could still hear him.

"There's no question about it. They died from hatchet wounds; there were arrows, footprints."

"It wasn't these," John said, nodding to the warriors. He opened an arm in a gesture that said Capenokanickon's River People should draw closer, that they were welcomed here.

Talaman, whose hair was long and grey, stepped into the circle indicated by John Hopewell. "Other tribes have come to these mountains," he said. "We too were attacked only days ago. Many of the enemy were no longer human. They were Machkigen. Thorns."

The emissary paled even further, if that were possible. "It wasn't any beast that did it. I tell you the killers were human."

Wetëndeis exchanged a glance with her brother Anasan, who said, "There are many two-legged Machkigen in the forests. The sickness you brought with you has spread."

The emissary looked at John as though seeking confirmation. Hopewell nodded his big head. "It's true, Simon."

The scout eyed the River People with a look that said he was not too happy to see them there. But he said only, "I see a lot has happened since we left. Have the others returned?"

John shook his head, slowly. Troubled. "Not yet."

Wetëndeis thought, but did not say, that if there were other scouts in the woods, traversing the forest paths alone, they were in danger. The settler-men should send a party out to look for them. She trusted they were wise enough to come to that conclusion on their own.

In her heart she saw a great black-and-silver wolf and heard him say, *You, O Flame of Spring, must help us. You and your family must bring back the glory of the world before the thorns consume us all.*

The scout was eyeing them warily again, and she turned away suddenly, annoyed. Naamucksha, her cousin, said in the language of the River People, "They should send men out to look for their scouts. They may need help."

"I know," she told him. "But they can manage their own affairs."

"We came here to help them."

"Then they can ask for our help."

She looked over her shoulder, back at John Hopewell. He was talking in a low voice to the scout, and both had turned and drifted further away from the River People. It was like they didn't even know they had allies.

When she and Anasan had lived with the colonials in New Cranwell as children, she had often felt this way. She and her brother had many things to offer the newcomers to this land, but they were never asked. Wetëndeis and Anasan had enjoyed learning new things, but she grew tired of being unseen, and they missed home. So eventually they left. When they arrived in the village on the other side of Anoschi Pass and settled down at Cape-nokanickon's fire, he just looked at them with his seeing eyes, grunted once, and said nothing. They were home. They were welcome. They did not leave again.

Not until Wetëndeis and Naamucksha went into the west to seek their allies among the tribes beyond the mountains.

They had found Machkigen instead.

It troubled her that the thorns existed so far to the west. She believed what all her people believed: this poison had come with the settlers. But then how it had it spread out so far, leagues beyond the boundaries of the furthest colonial settlements? The white men rarely sent even scouts past the mountains. Perhaps the beasts had carried it. Beasts like the wolf in her dream, but devoured and transformed by the poison that rooted within.

The crowd around Hopewell and the newcomer swelled as more of the Jerusalem Valley settlers became aware of his return. Wetëndeis watched their faces grow ashen as they heard the news. She heard the words *massacre* and *Machkigen* floating on the wind.

Naamucksha, beside her, folded his muscular arms and waited.

Wetëndeis smiled a little when Jonathan Applegate elbowed his way into the small, tightly packed crowd and asked what was going on. He had traded his buckskin to dress like a settler again, but he'd neglected to wash off a little of the red warpaint from his neck and the corner of his jaw. It took Jonathan only minutes to hear the news and step away from the others to wave the River People forward—to invite them into the circle.

"You believe it was the Machkigen?" Jonathan asked them.

"Who else would come here to destroy a settlement?" Naamucksha asked. "The tribes have no reason to break their peace. The Machkigen hunger for power and bloodshed."

"Then we need to know where they are," Jonathan said. "And how many, and what they'll do next. If they're killing settlers, Jerusalem Valley could be next. Will your people help us search the forest?"

John Hopewell nodded, seconding Jonathan's request. "We will send some of our men with you."

"I'll go myself," Jonathan said. He put a hand to forestall John's objection. "I need to see for myself what's happening out there. Besides, we still have two scouts out there, do we not? Corey Sowell and Obadiah Brown. They might be in trouble."

Naamucksha answered for the River People. "We came here to help you," he said. "We will go."

John Hopewell's eyes bespoke true gratitude, and Wetëndeis found that she had to lower hers. Her father had fallen in battle with the Machkigen because he was protecting her. The war party that attacked her people in the woods on the way to Jerusalem Valley had tried to carry her off with them. She knew why—she had refused a great warrior in the west. She had shamed him, without even consulting with her own father to know his will in the matter. Some part of her feared that all of this was her fault.

Naamucksha leaned close to her and said, "You did not do this, Wetëndeis. What you did in the west was right."

Flame of Spring, said the wolf.

You and your family must help us.

Flame of the Dawn, her father loved to call her.

The thought of her father straightened her back and lifted her head. Capenokanickon lay in the strange sleep brought by the healing waters. She hoped and prayed the sleepers would awaken and be healed, but for now they were helpless. If an attack came, they would die.

Her fingers tightened around her staff.

They would not die. No matter what happened, she and the others would protect them.

CHAPTER

8

Heavy snow blanketed the river valley as Linette and the soldiers followed the Mescahannec on its long journey toward the sea. Tall pines and heavy-laden firs grew in thick clusters, scenting the cold air. Oaks and aspens lined the river, bereft of their leaves. It was a different world in winter, Linette thought.

Their first night on the trail, it snowed again, deepening the snow, deepening the stillness.

Amos stayed close by Linette. Now and again they exchanged a few words, but mostly they all marched in silence. They moved at a steady pace. Linette thought Carson was watching her, deliberately measuring the soldiers' pace so they wouldn't tire her out. She felt guilty and grateful at once. She hated to slow them down, but she couldn't give more than she was already giving.

They formed a loose column as they marched. Carson kept Linette near the front, just behind him. Just behind her, soldiers carried Frederick Almon on a stretcher. He tossed fitfully, making the job harder. Behind him, Carey walked with his hands bound, under heavy guard. It was strange, after hiding so long from these men, to walk freely in front of them now—free, and yet surrounded by enemies, leaving the home she wanted more than anything.

She wrestled with the feeling that she had no more place, no more purpose. She'd given that up with the seed. She thought again of Serena and assured herself, yet again, that it was for the best. Linette had never been worthy to do whatever it was Herman wanted her to do. The seed had come to her, but it wasn't *for* her. It couldn't be. All that had happened, the voice she'd heard of the Fire Within, the hidden places she had uncovered beneath the ground, it was all so that Serena could come and take the seed and carry on the work. And Linette could go back and do what she always should have done—accept who she was and the consequences of her past actions.

Frederick Almon and Matthias Carey were living reminders of that. The soldiers in colonial red were reminders of it. These were the kind of men who surrounded her father in New Cranwell, who had surrounded her all of her life growing up. They had been sent to find her and bring her home. And in a strange way, they had succeeded.

As she trudged on, walking in the footsteps of the men before her where the snow was already packed down, the world seemed to narrow to a single pathway through the snow and the shadows. She lost sight of the sky and the trees and the river, of Amos in her periphery and Paul McIntyre scouting the edges of the column beyond him. She wanted to lift her head but did not. There was only one way to go, and the miles oppressed her.

That night they made camp on a sheltered cove of the river. Amos watched her with concern as she made her bed by the fire. She noticed his attention, and for once, she didn't mind it. With so many strangers surrounding her, she admitted to herself that she was glad he had come.

Thomas Carson approached her before she lay down. She pulled the heavy woolen blankets over her knees as he spoke.

"I'm sorry we can't offer more in the way of comfort," he said. "The open trail is hardly a place for a woman. But if you find yourself lacking anything, do let me know."

"I have all I need, Major," she answered. "Thank you." She managed a wan half-smile at him. His presence too, tall and manly and broad-shouldered, gave her some comfort.

"You're very brave," he told her. "Not many would stand the hardships so well."

"Your men are standing them," Linette said. "And I imagine the women of Jerusalem Valley have endured far worse. But thank you."

Carson nodded and moved off to inspect his men. Amos drew a little closer, crouching down as though she were a shy animal he was trying not to frighten. He glanced up at the thick grey clouds gathering in the gloomy evening sky.

"It may snow again," he said.

"As long as it doesn't slow us down too much," Linette said. She sighed and pulled the wool blankets up over her shoulders. Worry for Beth gnawed at her.

Amos surveyed her. "It will be all right," he said. "We'll get there in time."

She nodded. But her heart said, *You don't know that.*

Amos curled up nearby and went to sleep. Linette lay beneath the heavy blankets and stared into the fire until sleep finally won out over the cold and pulled her under too.

At the edge of the camp, something stirred in the realm beyond sight. It inched toward Frederick Almon and whispered his name.

Linette woke in the light before sunrise.

Something was wrong.

It took her a moment to realize what. Her eyes struggled to make out what she was looking at in the dim light.

Frederick Almon was seated on the other side of the fire. He sat perfectly straight, with an ease in his bearing that said his injuries were somehow healed. He was sharpening a knife on a whetstone. The ropes that had bound him lay in pieces at his feet. He had cut his own bonds somehow.

He looked at her and saw her staring.

He smiled—a wolfish, teeth-baring smile that filled her with fear.

She jolted upright, scrambling back to put more distance between them, and yelled.

Soldiers stirred from their own beds around the fire, and a few saw what she saw and jumped up, voicing their consternation. Next to Almon, Matthias Carey struggled upright, blankets falling away from his still-bound hands. Almon turned to him and snarled.

"You bastard," Carey spat out. "What—"

He had no chance to finish. Almon plunged his knife into Carey's gut and pushed it to the hilt. As the bigger man gasped and choked, Almon twisted the knife and then shoved him hard. Carey fell onto his back and writhed in the snow.

Linette couldn't tear her eyes away. Her mouth fought to form words, but there were none. Almon turned his eyes on her again, and she thought he would come for her next.

He didn't get the chance. Carson's men were already on him, wrestling the knife away. Truth be told, Almon didn't seem to fight them. A soldier grabbed each of his arms, and Thomas Carson, still half-asleep and clapping his hands against the cold, staggered to confront him. He took in the scene with evident disbelief, then reached down and pulled up Almon's shirt to expose the knife wound that should be there.

It wasn't. Where it had been, a mass of woody tissue had knit itself solidly together.

"Incredible," someone said. Linette got to her feet, helped up by Paul McIntyre, who kept staring at the grisly scene even as he lent her his hand.

"I didn't think that was possible," another of the men said. "I've heard stories of wounds healing like that, but I thought they were just legends."

Almon grinned. There was no joy in that grin, no goodness. Something inhuman glowered in his eyes. "You can call me the chosen one then," he said.

"What do you think you've done?" Carson asked. His voice shook as his gaze rested on Carey, whose struggles had stilled. The big man took a last labored breath and went still.

"Never fear, Major," Almon said. "You can tell them it was self-defense."

He looked at Linette again, and her body seized with fear. Carson saw the look, frowned, and moved between them, shielding Linette and blocking Almon's gaze. He nodded to his men. "Put him in manacles," he said. "Chains, not rope. Double guard. Watch his eyes. If you see anything strange, sound the alarm."

He didn't have to come out and say it. The sudden healing, the sudden strength, the sudden calm—all suggested Almon's illness had come back.

Amos Thatcher moved to Linette's side.

"Are you all right?" he asked quietly. But his eyes were on Almon.

"Yes," she said. "Don't worry about me." She gave him a quick smile, trying to reassure him, but his expression remained grave.

No one in the camp would rest again. They ate a hurried breakfast, then put out their fires and moved on within the hour.

Linette feared they were taking a demon to New Cranwell.

Serena took a rare break from Jacques's side to go out and see off the small scouting parties appointed by John Hopewell and the River People. Word of Simon Ferguson's return had spread quickly, along with the terrible news he brought—that he had reached another settlement but found its people massacred, their bodies lying out to decompose slowly in the cold. He said it had been the work of Outsiders, tribal people; the River People insisted the attackers were Machkigen, or under the sway of those who were. Serena was inclined to believe them, though the very idea was terrifying.

No one really had to say it: if there were enemies on the warpath, Jerusalem Valley might be next. So they would send out small scouting parties to find the marauders, count them, discern their intentions. And perhaps to find the other two scouts who had left Jerusalem Valley in search of trading partners, and escort them safely home.

The seed Linette had pressed into Serena's hands was tucked safely into the inner lining of her woolen dress. She didn't know what to do with it, but at the very least she could keep it safe.

As long as they weren't all murdered, of course.

The scouting parties were mostly warriors of the River People, with one or two settlers. Jonathan Applegate went with one. Letty Foster hung around the edge of the group, looking worried. Clive Shilling volunteered to go with another. Watching them arm themselves and say their good-byes, Serena remembered a vision she'd had of this valley surrounded by wolves—thousands of them, yellow-eyed and hungry. Not for the first time, she wondered how Crispin had managed to poison a place that should have been so far from his reach.

Across the clearing, the boy Josiah Axel crept out of the meeting house and came close enough to see and hear what was going on. The sight of him brought back the terrible revelation Linette had given her—that Eben had been working for Crispin.

Serena had thought long and hard about that, as she sat by Jacques's side in the dim meeting house, Eben breathing slowly nearby and Josiah hovering around him.

Crispin had intended to frame Serena and Jacques for the murder of Herman Melrose. But he could only do that if he knew someone would kill the governor. He could only *know* that if he'd sent someone.

Jonathan had done it, of course; Jonathan in his maddened Machkigen state. That Crispin's wishes could be carried out half a world away, so far from his apparent influence, had made Serena think he had powers beyond comprehension.

But no. No, all he'd had were the usual powers—intimidation, money, and too much control over the lives of others. He must have sent his instructions with the captain of the *Ventarrón*. It hadn't been an accident that Eben and Josiah encountered Jacques imprisoned on the ship, or that they freed him and then helped him rescue Serena from Elder Cole. Eben had been acting on Crispin's directives the whole time. He needed to reach Jerusalem Valley, with Jacques and Serena, not so that he could make a new life for himself and his son as he claimed. He needed to go there so he could murder Melrose and make it look like Serena and Jacques had done it.

Eben was the assassin. He always had been.

But something had changed. At the last minute he had abandoned the quest Crispin gave him and instead aided Serena and Jacques. She wondered when he had changed his mind, and why.

She wished she could ask him.

Instead she crossed the clearing and stood near Josiah. He moved closer to her. She wanted to put an arm around his thin shoulders and draw him near, but she knew he wouldn't want her to. Not in front of all these warriors, all these men. The boy didn't know anything substantial, she was convinced of that. He wasn't so naïve that he didn't know his father had been dishonest with them, but he wasn't privy to Crispin's plans.

Whatever Eben had done, for good or for ill, of one thing Serena was certain—he'd done it for his son.

And so she felt the need to protect the boy like she protected the seed in the lining of her dress. His father was asleep. Like Jacques. Asleep, wounded, unable to protect those they loved.

So she would do it.

She would stand for them, no matter what it took.

For the first time since coming to this valley, she felt as though she might have a clear purpose.

The scouting parties finished their preparations. Heads bowed as John Hopewell said a prayer over them. Then Talaman, the eldest of the River People, stretched out his hands and chanted a blessing of his own. Letty had moved closer, taken Jonathan's hand. She clung to it, their fingers entwined, as the words of both men fell over them like a protecting veil.

Then they moved out. The mingled settlers and warriors watched them go. Serena regarded Wetëndeis, the chief's daughter, who stood tall and somber in her deep red cloak as the men departed. Then she ducked her head and returned wordlessly to the nearby encampment where her father slept. Originally, Capenokanickon had lain in the meeting house with the other sleepers. But the River People had moved him, saying he would be more comfortable in a shelter of their own. It had taken them little time to erect shelters in the midst of the valley, made of reed mats and skins laid over bowed saplings.

Despite how strange and frightening Serena had initially found the Outsiders—and despite the fact that they had never spoken to each other—she felt a kinship with Wetëndeis. How could she not? They both kept the same lonely, terrible vigil.

Josiah shifted away suddenly. "I'm goin' in," he announced.

He trudged back to the meeting house without another word. The rest of the crowd was dispersing as well. Serena lingered a moment longer, looking after the scouting parties. Two made their way toward Anoschi Pass, another two went downriver.

Protect them, Fire Within, she prayed.

Keep us all.

Jonathan Applegate had decided to join Anasan, Naamucksha, and Sanquen in scouting the western slopes beyond Anoschi Pass. The four fell into a punishing pace, led by Naamucksha. Sanquen brought up the rear, perhaps to make sure Jonathan wouldn't lag behind. But there wasn't much danger of that. As exhausting as the previous days and weeks had been, the prospect of more Machkigen warriors in these woods, preparing a large-scale attack, killed off any fatigue and charged him with purpose and with fear.

The pass led them high into the snowy mountains. Rather than descending toward Capenokanickon's summer village, though, they pushed north, higher into the slopes, following the mountain range. Another group would explore the bottomlands and hardwood forests around the river. They intended to get a bird's-eye view.

"The band that attacked us before," Jonathan asked Naamucksha as they paused to drink from a running stream, breaking through a thin sheath of ice to get to the water below. "Why did they go after Wetëndeis?"

Naamucksha took a moment to answer. He crouched by the stream and looked into the distance, scanning the piney woods as he spoke. "The Machkigen in the west were different from the animals. Even different from you. They were more sane, and honored by others. Some of the councils raised them up to be warriors and leaders. Some are even chiefs."

A shadow passed over his face as he remembered what he had seen. "The tribes in the west are forming alliances. They fear the white men will keep coming and pushing them out of their lands. They want to push back. One of the chiefs wished Wetëndeis to marry his greatest warrior so that Capenokanickon will be allied with them. But the warrior is a Machkigen. She refused him."

Jonathan tried to imagine the scene. "I can't imagine they took that well."

Naamucksha grunted. "They made us prisoners. We escaped. But I did not think they would come after us."

"The River People are not such a great tribe," Anasan said. "That they should care so much for an alliance."

"It is not the alliance, I think. It is pride. The warrior did not like having his ugly nose tweaked by a woman."

Naamucksha stood and stretched. Then, without another word, he jogged back up into the pines, leaving the stream behind. Jonathan picked up his musket and followed.

They heard the cry just as they crested a ridge. It was high and strained, the cry of a man in pain.

They froze, Naamucksha holding out a hand to bar the others from surging forward. Then slowly, as one, they crept to the edge of the ridge and looked down.

Below, rising from the pines, a column of smoke signaled the presence of someone—or someones—encamped in the trees. The cry came again, this time tapering sharply into a scream.

Someone was being tortured.

Jonathan tightened his grip on his musket and shifted his position so all four could meet one another's eyes. Signing rapidly, Naamucksha signaled for each of them to take a different path down the ridge. They would surround the camp. They nodded and split four ways.

Jonathan took a brushy switchback down to the trees, staying low and covered. His every sense stood on edge. The scream came again, and his legs moved faster almost without his bidding them to. The brush blurred around him as he sped his descent. At the bottom, he found himself pushing through heavily drifted snow toward the smoke and the sound.

A bloodcurdling shriek sounded, then stopped.

The silence it left behind was worse than the screams had been.

Jonathan's blood rushed in his ears as he halted his forward motion, gripping his gun tightly, suddenly aware that he was too much in the open.

The trees had given way to a clearing scattered with limestone formations, and bare branches had opened to a pale and clouded sky. If anyone was watching, they had a clear view of him—and a clear shot.

The first arrow nicked his ear the moment he realized it.

His ear stinging, he dived for the ground as two more arrows whizzed overhead. Just as suddenly, the air split on every side with war whoops and yells, the screams of battle. He recognized the voices of his friends, under attack. And warriors poured out from the trees toward him. There were a dozen or more, coming from all sides.

This was a trap.

Jonathan pushed himself back to his feet and fired his musket at the nearest warrior. There was no time for careful aim, but the man fell. He threw the musket aside and snatched his hunting knife from his belt, slashing at a second warrior who was nearly upon him. His knife cut across the man's face and neck before it glanced away from his collarbone, throwing off the attack just enough for Jonathan to pull back and this time plunge his knife into the man's stomach and then kick him away. A third man was on him from behind. A blade sliced through his shoulder blade. The pain stole Jonathan's breath; he tried to turn, but he was moving too slowly. Then he heard someone shout his name, and the warrior went down with an arrow in his back. Jonathan saw across the clearing to where Sanquen stepped out of the pines, bow and arrow in his hands.

The next moment Sanquen fell. Behind him stood a large warrior painted green and white, holding a bloody axe. Even at this distance, Jonathan could see that the man's bare chest and shoulders were a mass of hard green scales. He wore a furred bearskin like a cloak and grinned at Jonathan with murder in his eyes.

Swallowing grief and pain, Jonathan ducked as another attacker flew at him. This time he saw the unnatural yellow glint in the warrior's eyes. The man's momentum carried him too far, and he stumbled, giving Jonathan room to get behind him. Jonathan wrenched a tomahawk from the man's belt and used it to dispatch him.

But more warriors were coming. They were almost there, filling the air with bloodcurdling yells.

Jonathan turned and ran.

He made for the trees, toward the column of smoke and the camp. Maybe there would be more enemies there, but at least there was cover. And maybe somehow he could still rescue whoever had screamed, whoever needed rescuing.

The same moment he reached the tree line, he saw Naamucksha to his right, aiming his bow at the oncoming enemy. He had a bare moment to wonder where Anasan was when Naamucksha loosed an arrow and another of the attackers fell. A second was nearly on Jonathan's heels. He ducked and weaved suddenly, putting a slender chestnut between him and the warrior, who found himself snagged and tangled in the tree's lower branches. Jonathan threw his tomahawk into the man's chest.

More whoops and screams. To the side, Naamucksha was down, wrestling with an attacker on the ground. Three more men were rushing straight at Jonathan, and screams on all sides told him he was about to overrun. Fear flooded him.

Deep within him, something surged and boiled. A darkness, black like pitch. It rolled in his gut and pushed out through his vines. His shoulders heaved; his skin seemed to stretch.

No.

No, this couldn't be happening.

He stared at his hands. His skin buckled, his bones strained. His fingernails stretched into claws. His yellow-green vines were turning black.

But he was supposed to be free. The waters below the earth had washed him clean; the light had cleansed him. Even Wetëndeis had told him the poison was gone.

For some reason the warriors had not yet reached him. He was hardly aware of it. All his attention now was inward, on his own transformation, his stark and awful fear.

The thing inside surged again, pushing outward. He thought his vines would split open and let it out.

No!

Screwing his eyes tightly shut, he tried to force calm through his body and mind. His breathing sped up, his heart racing. The water. The light. He forced his mind back to the waters that had cleansed him. He forced it back to the voice that had spoken to him there, of love and of grace. Hyperventilating, tears streaming down his face, he heard his own heart cry out—*Please, help me!*

He fell, spilling onto his face in the snow. Every muscle in his body spasmed and then went rigid.

He lay still.

He opened his eyes as his breath began to slow. He was still human. Lying on his back, he raised his hands in front of his face. His vines had gone back to their normal bright yellow-green. He was human. He was himself. He was saved.

Footsteps pounded his direction. Before he could react, Anasan grabbed him under his arms and hauled him to his feet. His friend's hands were sticky with blood. When Jonathan was standing on his own, Anasan took his own tomahawk in hand again and gestured for Jonathan to follow him.

He did. The three men who had been rushing toward him when his transformation began were dead on the ground. Anasan and Jonathan ran, crouching low, and Naamucksha fell in beside them. His face was battered and bloody, but he was alive. They were all alive.

Alive and still human.

Moving swiftly, the three wove their way through the trees, going deeper into the forest. The smell of smoke tinged the air. Blue tendrils drifting among the high branches told them the camp was near.

Naamucksha stopped suddenly and ducked low behind a line of granite boulders. Jonathan and Anasan followed. They sat side by side, their backs against the rock, breathing, listening.

The forest was still. They could hear no one coming after them.

The attack had been swift and sudden. But perhaps now it was over.

They remained where they were for some time, silent granite lending them their strength. Blood trickled down the side of Jonathan's neck from his nicked ear and glistened on Naamucksha's face from the split skin around his left eye. Anasan stared at the branches overhead in silence. Jonathan remembered the sight of Sanquen falling, and helpless anger welled up in his chest. The surge of emotion scared him. He tensed against it, against the visceral fear, lest it build into something more than emotion and pulse through his veins, through his vines, turn him into the thing he feared.

It did not. Instead it simply knotted in his chest and built up behind his eyes as tears that he could not afford to let fall.

He knew the others shared his grief. They sat and felt it together.

Finally the squawk of a bird somewhere nearby broke the stillness. The trees rustled where a small animal moved through their branches. A pair of squirrels, abroad on this winter's day, began to natter at each other.

The sounds were a sign—they could breathe easy. The enemy was gone, or at least no longer creeping through the forest.

Anasan stood first. Stiff and sore, Jonathan struggled up after him. His shoulder cried out in protest. He would have to take careful stock of himself later, discover if he'd been wounded in any other way. For now they just needed to move.

Of their mission, they had succeeded in this much: they knew there were enemies in the forest, with a will to attack. They knew the enemy were Machkigen, or at least numbered Machkigen among them. But they needed to know more. They still knew nothing about the enemy's numbers or their ultimate intentions. So far, the only intention they'd been able to discern was an impulse to kill.

They didn't talk about where to go or what to do. They just moved, one or the other taking the lead. Through the trees, through the boulders and rocky ground formations, following the dying scent of smoke.

They stepped into the camp without a word.

It had been abandoned some time ago. A dead man sat near the smoldering fire, tied to a tree. Jonathan let his eyes flicker over the man before looking away. He couldn't bear to look too closely, but he recognized the clothing as belonging to one of the settlers—not, he thought, from Jerusalem Valley. He might have come from the settlement Simon Ferguson had visited.

There were others, though.

There were thirty or so. Mostly tied to one another in small clusters, seated or lying on the ground, silent, still, all dead from what Jonathan could see.

Then Naamucksha dropped to his knees and began to wail—a long cry, deliberately subdued. He could not afford to cry out his grief to the heavens. But he scooped a body into his arms as he lamented, and Jonathan pulled in a sharp breath and held it in, feeling it knife through his chest.

Naamucksha held a child dressed in furs. A child of the River People. As though his eyes had just been opened, Jonathan realized that many of the dead in the clearing were River People—some of those whom Capenokan-ickon had sent west to their winter home.

Anasan fell to his knees beside Jonathan. He made no sound, but every line of his body gathered grief and offered it as a sacrifice.

Whatever would come next, there would be no turning away from what had happened here.

Jonathan closed his eyes, suddenly wearier than he could possibly say.

They could not bury the dead. There was no time, and every moment they stayed here, they risked the enemy returning and discovering them.

Naamucksha held the child close to his chest as his wailing turned to a chant. He sang over her, kissed her, and laid her back on the earth.

Then he stood, nodded to Jonathan and Anasan, and pointed north, back up the ridge. "We go," he said.

Hours later, they reached the heights of the ridge. It was late afternoon, and the light was already beginning to fail and fall into dusk.

It was dark enough that they could see the fires burning below, small spots of orange light scattered amongst limestone-rimmed clearings and along streams that meandered through the valleys. There were not dozens of enemy warriors filling these woods.

There were hundreds.

It was all they needed to see.

CHAPTER 9

Smith Foster knelt by a cold stream, filling a canteen with water. Evening was falling fast around him. He had not ceased to be on edge since they found the body of Corey Sowell and witnessed the inhuman creature crawling through the woods the day before, but it did seem they had escaped the danger. Fired by the things they'd seen, they all moved a little faster now. They were making good progress toward home. Or at least, he hoped they were—that they weren't instead hopelessly lost.

He chided himself for worrying. How lost could they be? They had managed to stay somewhat close to the river—close enough to hear it from time to time, still on their right where it should be. And the mountains formed vaguely familiar outlines to the north and east, telling Smith they were headed in the direction of Anoschi Pass. They would make it. They would get home, they would warn the people of what they'd seen in the woods, and Smith would hug his children and kiss his wife again.

He was telling himself this when a man in a tattered red military coat staggered out of the woods and said, "Please, help me."

It was all he got out before his knees buckled and he fell forward, half into the stream. Smith was on his feet instantly, instinctively moving forward to catch the man and haul him out of the water. Blood matted his hair from a wound above his right temple. His clothes were torn and filthy.

Too surprised to call for help, Smith maneuvered one shoulder under the man's arm and wrapped his arm around his back, pushing him upright.

Then he half-carried, half-pulled him out of the stream and staggered with him toward their small camp. The canteen stayed by the stream, abandoned for the moment.

Ezekiel saw them coming. Eyes opening wide, he jumped up, looking unsure whether Smith needed help or defending. He decided quickly, shoving his pack aside to make room by the fire and darting to the soldier's side to lend him another arm and shoulder. Together, he and Smith angled the man to the place Ezekiel had cleared and gently sat him down.

The soldier moaned. He was conscious, though barely. Ezekiel quickly dabbed a cloth in water from his own canteen and began to dab the man's face, washing away the blood and exposing the wound. Though it was dusk and the fire cast more shadows than light, Smith could see that the injury wasn't as bad as it had first seemed.

"Water," the man croaked. Ezekiel acted immediately, setting his daubing cloth aside and putting the canteen to the soldier's lips. He drank gratefully, then his head nodded, chin dipping to his chest. He seemed to fall asleep.

"Here," Smith said, grabbing his blankets and laying them out beside the fire. "Lay him down."

Ezekiel did so, carefully lowering the man's head and shoulders as he slumped down. He groaned and his eyes fluttered, as though he were trying to wake.

"Rest," Smith told him. "You're safe."

The soldier made a protesting sound. Premislav stumped out of the woods beyond the fire, pistol in hand. He'd been keeping watch, but he must have heard the soldier's arrival.

"What's happening here?" he asked.

"Commander," the soldier croaked.

Recognition lit Premislav's face, and he moved stiffly to Smith's side and bent over the soldier, touching his fingertips to the man's face.

"I know you," he said. "Klein, isn't it?"

The ghost of a smile flickered over the soldier's face. He was young, Smith thought. Thick dark hair and thin blue vines framed a handsome face with a square jaw and blue eyes. But his skin was pale and clammy, and the bloody wound on his head still seeped.

"Move aside now," Ezekiel instructed. Smith and Premislav did as he said, and Ezekiel began carefully cleaning blood and dirt from the wound. He'd pulled a bundle of clean rags from his pack, to serve first to cleanse the wound and then to bandage it.

Smith's mind worried over the circumstances of the young man's appearance. He must have been tracking them—why else would a soldier be in the woods so close to them? But then what had attacked and wounded him? Was it the creature they'd seen around Corey Sowell's body? Was this soldier one of those who had come upon it in the woods? It was hard to imagine that the beast could have done so much damage as to wound this soldier and split him off from his fellows. Smith had assumed they would dispatch it quickly—they were fully armed, and from the glimpse he'd caught of the men in the woods, he'd assumed there were at least six of them.

Branches suddenly snapped and tangled beyond the fire. Footsteps broke the crust of undisturbed snow. Smith looked up and his breath stopped in his throat.

An enormous wolf stood at the edge of the clearing, staring back at them. It was twice the size it should have been. Its shoulders and neck were scaled. Yellow eyes burned, as though with fever. Its mouth opened, revealing dripping fangs.

Premislav moved slowly in front of the others. The wolf's stance was crouched, still—ready to leap. Premislav had time for only one shot. He couldn't afford to miss, or to wound the creature but leave it mobile and angry.

The wolf's breath steamed and gathered in the chill air. Smith was aware of his own stance—his hand stretched out protectively over the wounded man, toward Ezekiel, who was still and frozen. Smith's mind raced as he tried to map out some kind of plan, to prepare somehow for what would happen if Premislav missed and the wolf leaped.

The muscles in the creature's neck and shoulders bunched. It sprang.

Premislav's pistol cracked.

A sharp whir in the air warned Smith to duck an instant before a long, feathered arrow buried itself in the wolf's shoulder. A second followed, piercing the creature's head between the eyes and driving deep into its skull. A third took it in the right leg.

The wolf fell. Its momentum carried it almost into Premislav, who jumped out of the way. Before Smith could react, four Outsiders spilled out of the woods and crossed the clearing, tomahawks and knives in hand. They went to work quickly dispatching the wolf for good.

The Machkigen, Smith reminded himself. *Thorn.* That beast was no mere animal of the forest.

After the Outsiders came a familiar face, dressed in leggings and a long woolen coat and carrying a musket. Clive Shilling, one of Jerusalem Valley's Puritani congregation.

Smith wanted to weep with relief. Instead, he merely grasped his friend's arm and nodded his thanks. Clive returned the grip.

"It is right good to see you alive and well," Clive said.

"You couldn't have chosen better timing," Smith said.

Premislav, his face spattered with the wolf's blood—it had a dark, greenish cast that turned Smith's stomach—stalked up to the men.

"One of your countrymen, I take it?" he asked.

"Clive Shilling," Smith said. "Clive, this is Commander Principio Premislav. He's a friend. And Ezekiel—also a friend, and the reason we're in these woods and not in prison in Fort Collins, for what that is worth."

Clive looked troubled. "Freedom is worth a great deal," he said. "I think we've all been recently reminded of that."

Ezekiel stood, and Clive shook his hand. "Smith is a good man and our governor," he said. "We're obliged to you for releasing him."

Premislav glanced to the side, where the four Outsiders stood over the wolf's twisted corpse. Then he looked down at the young soldier.

"That's one danger dispatched," he said. "The last one for a while, we can hope."

But the soldier, his face paler than ever against the white bandages, shook his head. "No," he said, "no. There are others. Many others."

The soldier's name was Rob Klein. He seemed eager to tell them his first name. He was a major by rank, but out here that didn't matter so much as being human—or that was how Smith understood it, anyhow. His story didn't take long to tell. A dozen soldiers had left the fort to recapture Smith and the others as soon as they discovered they were gone—perhaps four hours after their escape. They would have caught up with them the same day, but only six or seven miles from the fort, they'd been attacked by Outsiders.

"They weren't right," Rob told them. "Their eyes weren't right, the way they moved. They were like—like that wolf."

He'd seemed afraid to say it, like the Outsiders would be offended or Premislav would reprimand him for talking crazy. But none of the small band acted surprised, and Smith simply told him, "Keep talking, lad. We believe you."

"We were separated in the attack," Rob continued. He was half-sitting up now, leaning on a rock and some blankets Ezekiel had given him. "Myself and four others stayed together. I don't know what happened to the rest. We tried to find them, but there were more of the enemy in the woods. We had no choice but to stay quiet and try to find some kind of high ground. But—"

Tears filled his eyes, and he looked ashamed.

"It's all right, boy," Premislav said. "There's no shame in grieving."

"We were set upon again," Rob said. "I ran, tried to get where the trees could cover me and I could turn and fight. The others didn't follow me. I thought the enemy would come after me, but they didn't. I didn't mean to run away—to abandon them. I just meant to find better ground for a fight."

Smith nodded. Machcopoiken, one of the Outsiders who had come with Clive, said in a heavy accent, "Me, I would have done the same."

Rob didn't respond, but he looked grateful as he continued. "I went back, but they were all dead. I thought the enemy were gone, but one was still there—hiding in the trees. He leaped out at me with a club. We fought, and I killed him."

Machcopoiken nodded. He looked proud—like he'd known the boy had it in him.

Premislav grunted. "That how you got that head wound?"

"I think so," Rob told him. "To tell you the truth, it's not all clear to me what happened. Or when."

"Do you know how long you've been wandering in the woods?" Premislav asked.

Rob flushed. "No."

"Hit hard," Machcopoiken said. He tapped his own temple. "Make head like water."

"Did you get any sense of how many of them there are? These enemies?"

Rob shook his head gingerly, wincing as he did. "They seemed to be everywhere. I'm surprised you haven't encountered them."

Premislav raised an eyebrow. "So am I, now that you put it like that."

"One good thing we can tell you," Smith said. "We saw the other soldiers—the ones you were separated from, unless I miss my guess. They nearly caught up to us, but they encountered another ... thing. One that used to be a man but is not any longer. We left them to face it alone, but there was only one of it, and many of them. I don't think they were in real danger."

"Unlike us," Premislav said. "We need to get out of these woods." He turned to Clive and the Outsiders. "Gentlemen, you tell us that you came seeking to learn what was happening out here. Have you learned enough to satisfy you?"

"No," Clive said with a grunt. "Enough to satisfy me would mean numbers and real knowledge of their plans. All we know is the woods are full of them, and they're attacking anyone they encounter. That's not news I want to take home."

"You go," Machcopoiken said. "Lead back to the valley. Get help for him." He nodded at Rob. "We stay here, learn more."

Clive nodded. "It's probably for the best. I only hope our return to Jerusalem Valley doesn't lead the enemy there."

"They may have been following us already," Premislav said. "That may be why we haven't been attacked. Then again, perhaps that gives them too much credit for staying unseen and undetected. Those we *have* encountered haven't seemed especially stealthy. But it doesn't matter. The settlers need to be warned, and this young man needs better care than we can give him in the woods. Anyway, Jerusalem Valley is not hidden. If they don't already know where it is, it won't take them long to find it—with or without us."

CHAPTER 10

Jacques de la Croix, man of the cross, knelt.

The stone floor of the chapel was cold beneath his knees. The smooth wooden pew on which he leaned, hands pressed together in prayer and resting lightly on the wood, was carved of dark oak and beautiful. The talisman he wore around his neck matched it—bread, the symbol of the Creator broken and given.

On all sides, Jacques was surrounded by men wearing long black robes over leather armor, like his. They chanted their prayers together, voices raised as one.

We lift our eyes to the mountains, whence cometh our help.

Our help cometh from the Lord, who made heaven and earth.

He will not suffer our foot to be moved; he that keepeth his own will not slumber.

He that keepeth his own seed shall neither slumber nor sleep.

The Lord is thy keeper: the Lord is thy shade upon thy right hand.

The sun shall not smite thee by day, nor the moon by night.

The Lord shall preserve thee from all evil: he shall preserve thy soul.

The Lord shall preserve thy going out and thy coming in

from this time forth, and even for evermore.

Jacques's own voice sounded strange in his ears.

It seemed to him that he oughtn't to be able to give voice to prayer or to anything else. Something had happened to him, hadn't it?

The deep, warm chant of men's voices rumbled in his chest. He glanced to the side and spotted a man dressed in white on the other side of the chapel. His body was small and frail, almost shriveled; his crutches lay on the stone before him. He prostrated himself, and Jacques's heart stirred with loyalty and affection and inspiration.

There was no natural light in this chapel, carved out deep in the heart of a mountain. Only candles burning and the glow of oil lamps hung from the vaulted ceiling. Yet Jacques knew it was early morning, and all the men gathered here were soon to rise and go forth on a mission of great importance.

How did he know that?

How was he even here?

Something about this—something wasn't right. *Something had happened. Something had stolen his voice. He shouldn't be here, shouldn't be …*

Awake.

He shouldn't be awake.

He was sleeping.

So this must be a dream. And yet the stones beneath his knees were cold. The wood beneath his hands was smooth and shining with the light of the oil lamps. The smell of incense hung heavy in the air. Moreover, he had been here before. He had lived this moment. It was a memory.

The chanting swelled, then tapered into silence. Their prayers finished, they rose and wordlessly left the chapel one by one. A few stayed behind, still kneeling in prayer, including their leader in white. Jacques remained on his knees till most had gone, then rose and followed them out. His path took him through halls carved into the mountain and outside, onto a terrace where the sun, newly risen over the sea, shone brilliantly and washed the world in light.

Jacques blinked into the morning. The beauty of it made his chest ache.

Next to him, one of the men who had exited alongside him turned and seized his arm. "Well met, compadre!" he exclaimed. "It has been some time since I saw you last."

"Indeed it has," Jacques answered in some confusion. He said the words naturally—he was sure he had said them before, when this scene first played out. But his mind queried why he was here, how he was here. If this was a dream, which it had to be, how could it feel so *real?*

"I am told you are going to the Boglands," the man continued. "That's well. There's great need for men like you in that low, stinking country." He lowered his voice in conspiratorial fashion. "Take it from one who served three years there, your happiest moment will be when you leave. But then, you have always had the better taste for adversity and the better attitude of obedience besides. Maybe you will make better use of it than I."

Jacques smiled and began to give some answer when his attention was drawn beyond the man to the wall of rock behind him. It was moving—shimmering, then dissolving, like a fall of water. Someone stood beyond it, a young woman, small and dark-haired, a face he recognized—but for a moment he didn't know why. The sunshine, the mountain, the friend who still gripped his arm near the elbow, these were real and present and right. The girl on the other side of the veil was not.

But then it was all gone. He was standing in darkness, in a place that was no place. In front of him, the air shimmed and stirred like a curtain of water shot through with gold, and Serena was on the other side.

Serena. Of course he knew her. He needed to get back to her …

She was pacing the wooden floor of a rough-hewn structure, praying and clearly distraught. He said her name and tried to reach for her, but she did not react. She couldn't see him, couldn't hear him. With a start, he realized that *he* was lying on a low cot at her feet—lying as still as death. Her clear distress had something to do with him.

"*Why,*" she protested, "can I do nothing? Why can I chase off a demon and then *nothing?* I am trapped here! We are trapped! Why have you left us like this?"

She was talking to God, Jacques realized. He was merely eavesdropping. He wasn't certain if she was praying out loud or if he was somehow hearing her thoughts. But the fire of her words didn't surprise him. Serena had always been fire.

She flung out a hand toward him, as though he were a damning exhibit in a trial. "He is your servant, and he lies there, helpless, practically dead. And I need him. I *need* him. We all do. I know you sent me here, for some reason, but whatever you want me to do, I can't do it alone."

"You don't have to," Jacques told her. "I'm here. I'm not dead, and I can see you."

But she couldn't see him. She couldn't hear him.

She stopped her pacing abruptly. "Fire Within," she said simply, "you have never led me wrong. But this time I question your judgment."

Jacques almost laughed. It was so like Serena.

The door to the meeting house banged open. She spun to face the open door and the flood of light. So did Jacques. The big form of John Hopewell stood in the doorway, one hand still on the door.

"Serena," John said. "You're wanted outside."

Serena stumbled out of the gloom of the meeting house, brow knitted. Who—

The hand that raised to greet her was the last she expected. Principio Premislav, looking gaunt, bruised, and utterly worse for wear.

"Commander!" she said. Four other men were with him. One, a young soldier Serena did not recognize, leaned heavily on Premislav's shoulder. Another, whom Serena likewise had never seen before, was an aging black man carrying a bundle of blankets, pots and pans, and various goods on his back. His whole body seemed to shrink shyly away from the gathering of settlers that was even now pulling together around them, but his eyes were kind and courageous. The third, Serena had seen only once, and then briefly—Smith Foster. The fourth was Clive Shilling, returned from his explorations—but without the Outsiders who had accompanied him, Serena noted.

A cry from across the clearing drew their attention, and Sarah Foster came running. She reached them, tears of joy anointing her face. Smith, weeping now without shame, picked up his wife and swung her around as though it were just the two of them. Sarah's children came after, gathering around. Josiah Axel slipped out of the meeting house just then and moved to the side of the old man, who smiled and laid a hand on the boy's head.

Smith kissed Sarah long and deeply, and Serena looked away with a smile that she just couldn't help.

"I'm glad to see you're well," Commander Premislav told her.

"I wish I could say the same for you," she answered. "You have looked better."

Premislav grunted. "I've earned it, I assure you. Now, this young man needs food and water and somewhere to lie down and recover. He hit his head rather hard and it's all I can do to keep his body and soul attached."

Serena gestured to the meeting house. "He's not the only one. He might as well come join the rest in our poor little hospital."

She eyed the young man curiously, and he nodded to her—an act that made his eyes swim alarmingly. "I'm Rob Klein, ma'am," he said. "From Fort Collins, of late. I'm obliged to you."

"Don't be," Serena said. "None of this is my doing. I am just a stranger in a strange land." Nevertheless she turned toward the meeting house steps and beckoned for Premislav to follow her with his human cargo. The settlers had all brought blankets and boughs and rough-hewn box frames to the meeting house; she could make up another bed easily enough. At least this patient was awake. It would make a nice change to have one who could answer back. She felt a pang of guilt the moment she thought it, but she shoved that aside and led the men in, taking them toward the back of the long room, past the cots of sleepers. When they reached the far end she began to throw spruce boughs into an empty box frame, ready to have a thick feather tick and a layer of blankets placed on top of them to make a bed.

Premislav waited, propping the young soldier up, and looked gravely around him at the sleepers. He paused with his gaze on Jacques's still form.

"Well," he said. "That's very bad. Do I dare ask what happened here?"

"Poison," Serena said. "They fought Machkigen, most of them. They were badly wounded. Jacques is different—he was attacked by the former captain. Almon."

She watched the young soldier closely as she said that, but he didn't react to Almon's name—though he had already gone a little more ashen at the mention of Machkigen. Ashen, but not surprised.

"We were afraid their wounds would fester and turn them into thorns, so we took them and washed them in the spring." Serena paused. Clearly she had lost them. "Never mind that," she said. "We tended to them, and they fell asleep. They seem better, but they don't wake. What about you?" she asked Rob. "What happened to you?"

To her surprise, his eyes welled up with tears. She felt instantly chagrined—he likely felt embarrassed by crying in front of her, but his head wound seemed to have rendered him childlike. "We were in the woods, my company and me," he said. "Trying to track down the commander and the others who escaped. It was nothing personal, you see. Just following orders."

She nodded in what she hoped was an encouraging way, and he went on. "We were set upon by those things, whatever you called them—Outsiders, but not just Outsiders. They killed all the others. I fought and killed one, and I must have been hit in the head."

Momentary alarm filled Serena, though she tried not to show it. She scanned the young man's body, looking for tears, bite wounds, claw marks, blood. Anything that could have transmitted the poison. To her relief, she saw none. His overall appearance was haggard, and the bandages wrapped around his head were bloody, but he didn't seem torn or fevered.

Premislav caught the look on her face and the quick scan and seemed to understand it. "From the looks of the wound on his head, he bounced it off a rock," he told her. "Nothing to fear, I think."

The words must have sunk in to the young man's mind, because he turned even paler. "You don't think I'm—"

"No, I don't," Serena said. "But we'll keep an eye on you. If you start to run a fever, we'll … well, we'll try to help you." It was the best she could promise. If the young man began to show evidence of infection, they would carry him down to the waters and dunk him same as everyone else. If he fell into a deep sleep it would be a loss of company, but at least he wouldn't turn into a monster and die.

At least not yet. She reminded herself that they didn't really know what would happen to these men—Jacques, and Eben, and Capenokanickon and the rest of the wounded Outsiders. Maybe all they had done was slow the inevitable. Maybe they would lose them all yet.

No. She shoved that idea down somewhere deep where she could keep smothering it until it couldn't rise. Jacques would be all right. He had to be.

She thought of the seed in her pocket and wished heartily that she had some idea what to do with it.

Premislav shook his big head as he looked down at Jacques with something akin to mourning. "This is a bad business," he said. "Very bad. A man like him—one of his—he shouldn't be taken out like this."

Serena eyed Premislav carefully as she laid the last of the blankets down and then signaled for the commander to maneuver Rob into place. She wondered how she'd missed it so long—the truth that Premislav was Sacramenti. She wondered why the Fire Within had never shown her, throughout all their long association.

Maybe because it hadn't mattered, she thought. Rob let out a relieved sigh as blankets and pillow welcomed his battered body, and he lay back. Premislav had been an unexpected ally through her worst times, a man who officially worked for her enemy but unofficially showed her kindness and even help. Did she really need to know anything more about him?

Now, even though others in the settlement knew what Jacques was—he had flat-out told Linette and Sarah Foster, much to Serena's shock—it felt as though she and Premislav shared a secret, as well as sharing history. It was a surprisingly nice feeling. Deprived of all other friends and relations, she was glad he was here.

"I confess," she told him quietly, "I have felt lost him without him. I leaned on him all the way here, and now I can't even help him."

"Keep faith," Premislav told her. He looked across the cot and Rob's prone, happily sighing form. "The Creator brought you both here. He has some reason for it. And you said it yourself, he's not dead—just sleeping. There's hope yet."

Serena nodded, swallowing a lump in her throat. She tore her eyes away from Jacques and met Premislav's. "And you?" she asked. "What are you doing here?"

"Almon sent me to the fort in chains," he said. "I got out, thanks to that slave you saw with us. He let me and the settler out of our cell. We came back here seeking for shelter. And to warn you of monster men in the woods. But it would seem you already know. What did you call them?"

"Machkigen," Serena said. "It's an Outsider word. It means 'thorns.'"

Premislav grunted. "Fitting," he said. Then he raised a large, bruised hand to his forehead and rubbed it. "Now, I don't mean to seem overly greedy. But I could use a drink, and a good meal, and a bed."

Serena smiled. "You shall have them," she said.

Outside, Smith reported what they had seen in the woods. He kept one arm tightly wrapped around Sarah's shoulders; she leaned into him as though she never intended to move away again. Their children hovered around them like anxious birds. Ezekiel had seated himself on a sizable rock a few feet away, and Josiah stood behind him, quiet and listening.

When he had made clear the threat, Smith turned with some effort and gestured to Ezekiel. "This man put himself on the line to get the commander and me out of there," he said. "I assured him there was a place for him in Jerusalem Valley."

"Indeed there is," Big John said. "We're indebted to you. Smith is the best of us."

Letty Foster, Smith and Sarah's oldest daughter, bit her lip. "Simon Ferguson came back," she told Smith.

He frowned and looked at John.

"No good news, I'm afraid," John told him. "The contrary, in fact. He found a settlement, but they'd been killed by Outsiders. We put two and two together and guessed their attackers were Machkigen." He grimaced, as though the word itself felt strange and distasteful in his mouth. "What you've said makes that all the more likely. From what Simon said, it was a massacre."

"Jonathan went to scout the pass and the woods beyond," Letty said.

"He and some others. They feel we need to know the size of the danger."

"Only right, of course," Smith said.

"And they thought the others might need help getting back. Corey and Obadiah."

Smith blanched at that. His voice gentling and strained, he said, "I'm afraid Corey won't be coming home. We found him in the woods. It was—well, the same as what you've said. It was Machkigen."

Letty swallowed hard. Smith reached out a big hand and laid his rough palm against his daughter's cheek. He didn't say *Jonathan will be all right.* But he assured her of it all the same, despite not really knowing. Despite knowing that if Jonathan was out in the woods, he might be facing enemies more terrifying than they'd ever imagined.

At least Jonathan himself was no longer one of those enemies. There was mercy even in these harsh days.

The sun, which was low when Smith and the others returned to the valley, had disappeared behind the mountains. The remaining light reflected blue off the snow. The moon hovered above them, ready for the coming of darkness. Smith turned and faced the way they had come, troubled. He drew Sarah even closer with one arm and gathered Letty to himself with the other.

"What is it, Smith?" Sarah asked. "What's wrong?"

"I don't like to think of what's out there," Smith said. "I pray we didn't lead anything to you."

Somewhere in the valley, a dog barked.

The sound seemed sharp and out of place. Belatedly Smith and the others realized that the valley had fallen deathly silent. Even in winter, nightfall should have brought stirrings with it. The ghostly passing of owls' wings; the faint crunch of creatures moving through the snow. But there was nothing.

Only the dog, barking more loudly now and more insistently, a clarion. A warning.

Premislav stepped onto the front steps of the meeting house and shouted, "There, in the trees! Arm yourselves or flee!"

He pulled his own reloaded flintlock pistol from his belt and fired it about the same time anyone else saw what he was shouting about. Branches exploded at his shot, sending splinters of wood everywhere, and a loud, hideous whine answered as a wolf easily the size of a pony leapt to one side, exposing itself to open view. As it did, three more left the trees, baring dripping, enormous fangs.

The clearing erupted in screams and shouts as settlers scattered. Sarah simultaneously pulled her daughters to her and pushed them toward shelter in the governing house, Agatha Moss coming just after them with John Hopewell shielding her. One or two Outsiders who had been in the clearing when Smith and the others arrived brandished tomahawks and yelled, sending their distinctive war whoops into the air. Answering yells came from the Outsider encampment not far away, and more warriors rushed to join the fight.

The wolves had followed Smith and the others to the valley.

The great wolf scanned the clearing with its yellow eyes. It lit on the settlers scattering in every direction, unarmed men and women running for cover. It rested on the few brave men who stood facing it with weapons drawn, their faces pale, their jaws set. It saw the running forms of others coming, blades and bows in hand. Its fellows, first two, then four, leapt into the clearing ahead of it. Some went down, yelping, under a rain of arrows and smoking musket fire. The great wolf itself skirted the action and went for a dark, yawning hole in the side of the whitewashed, plank-board building. It was driven by a gnawing hunger in its gut and the prodding of whispering voices in its ears. Voices that had lodged in its consciousness and driven it for days, even as its form grew and changed and scaled over.

Deep inside, something in the wolf whined and cringed like a whipped pup. But it could hardly hear itself. The voices in its ears urged it forward into the doorway. Urged it through, into the close, dark interior where the air was cloyed with the smells of blood and sweat and smoke. Bodies lay on cots, wounded and asleep.

Kill them all, whispered the voices in the wolf's head.

Growling low in its throat, it stepped forward on massive, clawed paws.

But someone stood in its way.

The wolf lifted its massive head to take in the sight of a small woman, wearing a simple woolen dress trimmed with fur. She stood with her hands outstretched, though they were empty—weaponless. But her eyes blazed as she faced the wolf.

"No further," she said.

The wolf did not understand. But the voices in its head did. They hissed and screeched in protest against her.

The wolf stepped forward, crouching lower, growling more loudly. It bared its teeth against her.

"Get back," she said. Behind her, the wolf caught sight of a boy and an older man in the shadows. Both were crouched, poised to help her if they could. But what could any of them do? They had no weapons, nothing with which to fight.

The wolf lunged. The woman stood her ground. She flung out one hand and shouted, "Out! By the Holy Name, out!"

The wolf arrested its own forward motion and fell back, writhing, as all the voices in its head screamed. One tore away like a leaf from a branch and crumbled into the air, shrieking.

The wolf growled and lurched forward again, but again the woman flung out a hand and commanded "Go back where you came from!" and again a voice tore away, shrieked, and vanished in the air like smoke.

Confusion racked the wolf. Its mind rioted; its stomach twisted and kicked. Baring all its teeth, it tried again to attack the woman, to quiet its mind by silencing her. Hunger and fear drove it, as sharp and demanding as anything it had ever felt. But she stood over the sleepers like a mother over her young and refused the wolf access.

"*All* of you, go!"

The great wolf fell to the floorboards with a howl. As it did, there was a crash and a splintering as two more wolves dove through the windows of the meeting house, shattering the thin glass panes. They landed on the floor and bounded for the sleepers without pause. The woman turned, eyes wide in horror as one of the wolves tore out a sleeper's throat.

"No!" she screamed. She spread her arms wide. And the red vines that grew through her shoulders and arms and into her hands, that rose up her spine and curled around her collarbone, the vines that came from within her heart, grew. They stretched out from her small frame and then shot upward and outward, expanding like a forest grown in an instant. They filled the meeting house, shaping tangled latticework thickets over the sleepers, wrapping around the wolves' necks and yanking them back, away from the helpless men who lay on their cots unaware that death flew over their heads. Vines wrapped around the great wolf's legs and around its neck and held it fast.

And the woman cried out, "By the Father, Son, and Fire Within, go!"

A thousand screams deafened the great wolf as the voices tore away, one after the other, whirling and twisting in the air, rushing together like a funnel cloud, lifting into the air. The woman was on her knees now, arms still outspread, vines extending from her in every direction. One hand reached forward as though she would grasp her invisible enemies and hurl them from the earth forever.

The man and the boy found their feet and rushed to her side, ducking and dodging through the tangle of vines with their eyes wide. They knelt on either side of her as she convulsed with sheer effort—but she did not collapse. The vines held, tightening around the wolves, thickening around the men they protected. The voices shrieked even louder and suddenly, with a rush so loud it roared, they whirled into one and departed, blowing a hole through the roof as they went.

Moonlight poured in.

The woman let out a breath and fell forward, gasping. The old man caught her shoulders and lowered her gently to the floor. The vines snapped away from her body, releasing her to fall.

The great wolf whined.

Its body was shrinking. The scales fell away, leaving bald patches of skin. Its fear faded, its hunger changed. The puppy inside of it trembled, and suddenly the red vines wrapped around it felt not like constriction, not like a trap, but like comfort.

Serena half-knelt, half-lay on the floor, exhausted and grieved but triumphant. She had lost one of the men in her charge, one of Capenokanickon's brave warriors. But Jacques, whom she could just see in her line of vision, was alive. The others were all alive. She had done as she promised and protected them.

Jacques was in the Boglands.

Of all the country called the Lowlands, the Bogs were lowest lying of all. They were home to a people who had barely risen above barbarism in all their centuries of existence there. While the rest of the world embraced civilization, building cities and cathedrals and well-maintained roads, the Boglands stank, steamed, and wreathed their people in persistent fog and damp. Their excuses for roads wound along eel-like stretches of solid ground or topped manmade dikes. Their towns and villages huddled on small islands of forested soil and small, poorly tilled patches of farmland. But the Boglanders were a cheery people, in sharp contrast to their surroundings, who knew the value of a family hearth, a tankard of ale, and a rousing song.

Jacques liked them.

He was doomed, as usual, to be unknown by them. He lived and worked in their midst, plying a cobbler's trade. He went to worship with them in their Puritani kirks and attended the Bogland's unlikely theological school—unlikely because it was located in a heathen backwater and yet had earned a reputation as one of the best places on the continent for an aspiring divine to distinguish himself—where he played the part of a poor student. He sometimes sat and drank with them in their alehouses. But they did not know him, for he did not let himself be known.

The tasks he carried out as an Imitator were important, Jacques knew. They were worth any number of sacrifices. And the role he played here was especially important—the man he shadowed, whose story he was watching and learning, mattered more than most. He knew this to his core.

But still, this need to remain unknown and hidden—it was the hardest thing he did. Here in the Boglands, where human companionship seemed more vital and real than it did in many more civilized places, it was especially difficult. It was lonely, and it necessitated a kind of lie. He struggled to reconcile this with his faith that what he did was right.

Hands wrapped around a cold pint of beer, he looked down pensively at the foam that rested atop it. The light was dim in the tavern; it was late, and fire and lantern light only did so much to cut the night shadows. Students sat all around him, most deep in heady discussion or hot debate. No one sat with Jacques or talked to him. He looked at his own hands, analyzed their form, their long fingers and fine bones, the white skin that had grown gradually tougher as a cobbler's tools calloused them.

These hands are yours, he said, falling into his habit of silent prayer. *Use them, Almighty. Work your works through me.*

One voice rose above the others, belligerent in its tones though its topic was ostensibly holy, and Jacques looked up—taking advantage of this opportunity to openly scrutinize his charge.

The man he had come to the Boglands to watch was older than most in the room—in his late thirties or early forties, a good seventeen or eighteen or perhaps even twenty years older than Jacques. He was large, meatily built, though not corpulent. He had a thick head of curling brown hair and a way of speaking that arrested attention and convinced almost before others realized they were being persuaded. He was a student despite his age, like the friend seated beside him, who at this moment took a drink of ale with an amused expression as the younger men around them erupted in a mix of hearty amens and heartier protests. A few pounded the table with their mugs. Joseph Crispin, the cause of it all, raised his own glass with a pleased grin and then downed it heartily.

Crispin was Jacques's first long-term assignment. He had been shadowing him since before he arrived in the Boglands, though it was doubtful whether Crispin had ever noticed him. Jacques had a genius for remaining unseen if he wanted to. That was why he'd been given this job.

Watching them, Jacques turned his attention back to Crispin's friend. He was a large man also, though a little shorter and a little wider in the shoulders. In contrast to Crispin's garrulous personality, he was generally thoughtful and pensive. He was an older student, like Crispin, which might be why the two had attached to each other. Both men might have been teachers by their age, except they had spent years still serving in the armed forces after the war against the Sacramenti—trying to bring peace as they had once wrought violence.

Jacques took a slow sip of his beer. It was golden, rich. He wondered if his father had ever fought these men. If either of them might have had a hand in killing him. Who could know? The war had done untold damage to tens of thousands. His father had fallen on some Lowland field. No one knew exactly where or even when. Jacques knew only that he had never come home, and that the general under whom his father served sent his mother a letter thanking her for her sacrifice and enclosing his father's wedding ring. Another soldier had taken it off him, then died himself at some later battle before he got a chance to deliver it. So all the details of Jacques's father's death were lost with him, lost in a chain of death and ignorance.

It was bitter, not knowing.

More bitter, in some ways, than death itself.

Crispin's friend intrigued Jacques. He seemed like a man with secrets, or at least secret thoughts—musings and perhaps beliefs that were deeper than he was willing to share with his fellow students, young and boisterous as they were.

In another life—if Jacques had been, for example, the simple cobbler he claimed to be—he would have tried to befriend Herman Melrose and ask him outright what thoughts he harbored. If he read the man aright, they could be friends, the real kind.

But he could not be so bold. Could not draw attention to himself. Could not share his own thoughts, his own heart, or his purpose here.

So he simply sat in the corner and drank alone, watching Joseph Crispin and Herman Melrose as they held forth amidst a sea of younger and less wise men.

"Anyway, the old don is no longer with us and so can have no more to say in the matter," Crispin said, occasioning laughter from those around him—though Herman, Jacques noted, did not laugh. He seemed troubled, a trouble that deepened into a frown when Crispin said, "Lucky stodge—positioned in Wärtersburg. He'll be feasting at princely tables there."

"Yes, for better or for worse," Herman said. His tone was almost caustic, which surprised Jacques. He wasn't a bitter man, but it was clear the prospects of which they spoke tasted foul in his mouth. "And he'll be having princely ears and princely power."

Crispin smiled indulgently and clapped a warm hand on his friend's shoulder. "Come, now, Melrose," he said. "I know you don't approve of the way the world works, but it *is* the way the world works. Think of all the good the old man can do with a princely ear, if he doesn't shy away from using it."

"You're right, I don't like it," Herman said. He bent forward a little over his ale, shifting in his seat so he withdrew from Crispin's friendly touch. "Wärtersburg was a bloody enough princedom on its own. Did we learn nothing during the wars, that we have to go on fanning the flames of enmity?"

Crispin's eyes sparkled. "But enemies are important," he said. "Doesn't the Book itself teach us to imprecate our enemies? Without enemies, what do we have to unite us? To keep our feet on holy paths and our minds in holy places?" His tone was jocular, sarcastic—and yet Jacques knew all too well how much sincerity might lie beneath his words. Crispin raised a glass to his fellows with a wink. "To enemies," he said. "Long may they plague us! And may God send more of our long-spoken and most-honored dons to bury them with words and leave us in peace."

The others laughed and drank to the toast, but Herman only frowned and folded more deeply in on himself.

The night grew long, and the students began to go. Some staggered their way out, arms around each other, drunken and dissipated. Most were more sober and went their way to sleep or to study. Crispin and Herman left late, pulling on their coats side by side and talking in low tones. Jacques had nearly become one with the shadows as he waited. No one noticed him as he slipped out of his corner booth and followed after them, his ears sharp.

They paused in the doorway just before stepping out into the damp cold of the night. Jacques likewise stopped, sinking back into the darkness of a small alcove. Even as he did, the air in the tavern shimmered—he seemed to sense something beyond it. Some other place. Some danger, sudden and keen. Without warning his heart pounded and his head rushed, and he staggered backward … and then it was all gone. He was still in the tavern. Thankfully it didn't seem that he had given himself away by gasping in fear.

The voices of the men he followed rumbled. "You joke freely, and I envy your light heart. But I worry, Joseph. What's to stop us from becoming just like them? If we use power this way, who's to say we won't become the very thing we rose up against?"

"You worry too much, my friend," Crispin said. Unlike earlier, his tone now was sincere. Caring. "We have the Book to guide us, to keep our feet on the straight and narrow. And I was not entirely joking about the place enemies may play. Our Creator uses them to sanctify us too, does he not? As he uses all things?"

Herman reached out a hand for the door and stopped abruptly. He turned. "Joseph, I've heard of a new thing. A new kirk … a people called Luminari. They say that when they meet, the Fire Within comes to men and enlightens them directly—from *within,* not just from the teachings of dons and elders. They say that he comes as a tangible presence in their meetings and makes men tremble."

"I've heard of this too," Crispin said, sounding a little perturbed. "Tremblers, some call them."

"They are mocked by all who hear of them, but I confess that I'm intrigued. I came here to seek the Creator because my heart was bruised and empty after all our years at war. I've had enough of enmity, Joseph; I am hungry for life. But you know as well as I do that *life* does not well describe our studies here."

"You mean that they are the only dry thing in the Boglands," Crispin said with a laugh. "With our dear don off to Wärtersburg, we may hope that will improve. There may yet be water in these rocks. We study a Book, and history and philosophy and rhetoric. Surely neither of us expected every moment to be an overflowing fountain. We study because we have hope that as we do, truth will sink into the cracks of our lives and take root down there. Have patience, friend."

Melrose sounded a little encouraged when he spoke again. But he was not ready to let it go. "Yes," he said. "Yes, you're right. But Joseph, what if what's said of the Luminari is true? What if, in simple faith, they have found something we've overlooked in our theologies and our histories and our science?" He hesitated only a moment. "I've not just heard of Tremblers, Joseph; I've met some. They intrigue me. And they've invited me to a meeting. I mean to go. Will you come with me?"

Crispin was not quick to answer. Then: "The Puritani elders view them with some suspicion. I think trouble will come of this movement."

"Be that as it may, I mean to go and see for myself what they do."

"Then I will go with you, friend. For the sake of our friendship alone."

There was a smile in Herman's response. "Thank you," he said. "I am glad."

Chapter 11

Serena knelt on the floor of the Trembler meeting house, leaning forward on her hands, and stared at the destruction she had wrought. Red vines filled the entire length of the building, twisted around rafters and the remnants of shattered windows, branching out in protective clusters over the sleepers, and holding the wolves fast. They had detached from her when her work was done, and their ragged ends retracted and drew back into her skin.

There were three wolves—the huge one Serena had faced, now smaller, and the two that had burst in through the windows. One had a bloodied muzzle from its kill. Serena swallowed back a cry of shock and grief as the sight replayed in front of her eyes.

"Ezekiel," she choked out. "Ezekiel, the body ..."

She nodded toward the dead man. The movement made the whole world spin around her. She barely had enough strength or equilibrium to keep herself from falling over.

She didn't know how she'd done what she did. Only that with the wolves threatening those she had sworn to protect, she had reached deep within herself and discovered the power to keep her promise.

Ezekiel needed to be told nothing more. Patting her once on the shoulder and arm before letting go of her, he crossed the room and maneuvered around the vines to arrange the dead man's arms across his chest and pull a blanket up over his face.

Serena didn't even know the warrior's name. She had never seen him conscious—he'd been one of Capenokanickon's fallen, brought here wounded after an attack in the woods. But she keenly felt her failure to save him.

"Glory all," Josiah Axel said, crouching on the other side of her lest she suddenly slump sideways and need to be propped up. "I ain't seen nothin' like that in all my days. Never even heard tell of it."

"Neither have I," Serena managed to say. Her throat felt like sandpaper, and her voice came out in a croak. She'd done it for him. For him and for his father, and for Jacques.

"Come here, boy," Ezekiel said. "Help me clean up." He seemed to intuit that Serena needed a minute alone.

Josiah left her reluctantly and went to help clean up the carnage. He skirted the trussed wolves. Serena stared at them. The vines she'd wrapped around the animals didn't seem to be in any danger of bursting. The wolves were hardly fighting. Their whines filled the air, and Serena became aware suddenly of more noise outside, of howls and shouts and musket fire.

The door burst open. John Hopewell and Premislav pushed through the door accompanied by four warriors. They stopped short.

"What in God's name …" Premislav began.

"Serena did it," Ezekiel said. Josiah, excitedly, said something in the River People tongue. As though jolted into action, the warriors rushed forward, brandishing their tomahawks to slay the bound wolves. Serena felt a strange inner protest but said nothing to stop them. Of course they needed to kill the creatures.

She said nothing, but Wetëndeis did.

The chief's daughter had appeared in the doorway right after the warriors entered. She held out her hand and said something sharply in her own language. It halted the warriors on their bloody errand. They looked warily at her, and one of them asked a question. She answered, then drew a knife and moved toward the first wolf, the one across from Serena.

Everyone in the room held their breath.

She stood over the wolf in its tangle of vines, looking into its eyes. It looked back at her. Serena saw intelligence there—and pleading.

Wetëndeis knelt and put her knife to the vines, cutting through them and snapping them away.

The moment it was free enough to move, the wolf twisted itself onto its feet with a whine and shook itself free from the last of the net. It licked its jaws and peered at Serena for a long, breathtaking moment. Then it looked at Wetëndeis again.

She held her knife ready to defend herself. The warriors were poised to rush to her defense.

But the wolf made a long, high sound, and it bowed at Wetëndeis's feet.

Serena could hardly breathe. It was holy, this moment. This redemption.

Her eyes not leaving the wolf, Wetëndeis held up her hand and motioned to the warriors. They went to work quickly, cutting the other wolves free. They too twisted free from the vines and jumped onto their feet, then crept forward and bowed in deference. And in gratitude.

Serena glanced over at the others. Ezekiel and Josiah's eyes were wide.

Wetëndeis turned to Serena. "You drove the tormenting spirits away," she said. "They thank you."

Serena didn't ask how Wetëndeis knew this. But she said, "They're welcome."

Sheer exhaustion overwhelmed her, and she nearly fell forward.

Wetëndeis looked away toward the open door of the meeting house. Outside in the moonlight, people were milling in confusion, but it seemed the attack was over.

Serena reached up a hand to Premislav, who had stalked across the floor toward her. "Help me up," she said. "I need to lie down."

"Once again, Miss Vaquero," he said as he obeyed, "you have surprised me."

Jonathan returned in the morning, with Anasan and Naamucksha. All three were pale and bloodied. The entire community came together to hear their report—settlers and River People alike. Serena, still feeling as though she had gutted herself and poured out every ounce of life in her body, sat propped up by Josiah. She'd wanted them to meet in the Trembler meeting house, out of some stubborn idea that Jacques could hear them even though he was asleep, but there wasn't room. They met in the clearing outside instead, and left the door of the meeting house open. Anyway, the vines with which she had filled it were still clinging stubbornly to every part of the interior and refused to be easily cleared away.

The news was quick and bad. There were at least a hundred warriors in the woods, outfitted for war and coming their way. Many of their number were Machkigen.

No one had to be told what this meant. It was bad enough to face maddened and hungry wolves. Human beings were another story entirely.

Letty Foster wrung her hands while she listened. She gazed at Jonathan with an adoration that made Serena's heart ache, especially because Jonathan seemed strangely determined to keep some distance between himself and the young woman.

Wetëndeis sat like a queen on a rock with her staff in hand, surrounded by wolves. Warriors stood all around her, armed and painted. Serena got the feeling they already knew what had to be done and were just waiting for the settlers to come to the same conclusion.

"So we've all heard it," Clive Shilling said when the other scouts had finished. "I fear Obadiah Brown is likely dead, and the settlement he tried to reach along with him. Our enemies are everywhere and closing in. We can't defend this place effectively. If we stay here, we're as good as finished."

"You're telling us to abandon the valley?" Agatha Moss said, her voice quavering. "Where would we go?"

Silas Gromer grunted from where he leaned on a pair of crutches. "Fort Collins," he said. "It's built to be defended. It's our only hope."

"But Smith just *came* from Fort Collins!" Sarah burst out. "They held him prisoner; they sent Almon here! They're as much our enemies as these Machkigen."

"Peace, Sarah," Smith said. "Aye, the men at the fort are no friends of ours. But they're not merciless killers. Not monsters. I don't want to go back there, but maybe we were only meant to escape so we could come here and help warn you."

Rob Klein, who sat on the ground near Smith with his head swathed in bandages, blinked up at everyone and said, "The fort? We should go to the fort. It's … safe there."

But Serena was shaking her head. She knew two things with cold certainty. First, that Silas was right—the settlers needed to go to the fort. And second, that she could not go, nor could she take Jacques there. The soldiers had received orders from New Cranwell to place her and Jacques under arrest, so almost certainly they knew that both had implicit death sentences hanging over their heads. The other settlers might be placed under arrest if they went to the fort. But she and Jacques might well be executed.

Even if she was willing to risk it for herself, she wouldn't put Jacques in that position. Not after she'd just given everything she had to save him.

She couldn't imagine what alternative she had. Stay here with Jacques, alone in the meeting house, and wait for the Machkigen to find them?

Fire Within, what now?

While she was distracted by her thoughts, the discussion carried on without her. Big John Hopewell was in the lead now, agreeing that the settlers had little choice but to go to the fort. More concerning was whether they would make it the twenty miles there without being met and massacred on the way.

"We will go with you," Naamucksha said. "We will protect you. Then we go our own way."

John turned, surprised. "I assumed you would come with us all the way," he said. "Take shelter with us in the fort. Surely you are in as much danger here as we are."

The warrior shook his head. "Some of us will stay with you behind walls, maybe. But most will not. We will go and find allies. Not all the People have turned to thorns. Some will fight with us."

John looked confused. Anasan said, "In the west are many more People. Some move west, like our families, going to our wintering grounds. Others are always there. We will seek out more warriors and come back to fight these Machkigen."

"And we will take water from the sacred spring," Wetëndeis announced. "We will take healing with us."

Serena blurted the words out before she could stop them. "I'll go with you," she said.

All eyes turned to look at her, and her face burned. "And so will Jacques." She almost held her breath, waiting for them to say they could not carry a paralyzed man with them. But they seemed to understand, and Wetëndeis nodded. She gestured toward the wolves. "You will help us heal the animals," she said. "Maybe even the men. The People will help us when they see."

Serena nodded even as a wave of nausea washed over her. She couldn't imagine helping anyone again—but she *had* proven more than once that the whispering shades would flee at her command, just as they had at Jacques's. Once she regained some strength, maybe she could help somehow.

"But first we will take you settler-men to the fort," Naamucksha concluded.

"What if the soldiers won't take us in?" Sarah asked. But the protest had gone out of her voice. She sounded resigned to the inevitable.

"They won't have much choice," Smith said. "If we show up on their doorstep, they'll have to give us entrance. Even if they send us all straight to prison, we'll still be behind thick walls and earthworks, with all their guns to guard us from attack. But don't worry—" he bent and kissed the top of his youngest daughter's head. "I don't think they'll find imprisoning us all practical."

John Hopewell clapped his big hands. "We have work to do," he announced, "and not much time to do it. We'll pack up all the food stores we can and carry them with us. I want every gun, hatchet, and tool in our possession to come along—we must be as armed as we can be. I'll not ask any man or woman among us to do violence to a fellow human being, but we may face more of the demon animals in the woods, and we can hardly ask our warrior friends to do all the fighting for us. We'll load our horses with supplies."

"When do we leave?" Silas asked.

John looked at the sun, already high in the sky. "At first light tomorrow," he said. "Daylight won't see us all the way there today, and I don't want us to spend a night on the trail if we can help it. But tonight, no one stays in their homes. Gather here. We'll fortify the meeting house and governing house as best we can and keep watch over one another till morning."

A general murmur of agreement rose, and the settlers began to disperse—going off in small groups to do what John had commanded. Serena noted that although John had refused to be elected governor after Melrose—nominating Smith for that role—he'd taken up the mantle of leadership all the same. It was good, Serena thought. Smith had enough to worry about looking after his family. She watched as they departed for their home and farm—Smith with his arm still firmly around Sarah; their sons, Martin and Samuel, flanking them; Letty and Lila trailing just behind.

Letty paused and looked back plaintively at Jonathan, but he didn't respond to her, and after a moment she turned and trudged after her parents.

A wolf seated at Wetëndeis's feet opened its mouth and yawned, showing off fearsome teeth. The reality of what she'd just agreed to do crashed down on Serena like a fall of rock, and she fought back panic.

She must have leaned a little harder on Josiah, because the boy shifted his weight suddenly to keep his balance.

"I'm sorry," she murmured. Was that her voice, sounding so pitifully weak?

"You really gonna go with them?" Josiah asked. He pointed his chin at the mix of warriors and wolves.

"I believe I am," Serena said.

She could hardly credit her own words.

Chapter 12

Portafiela, The Southern Provinces, The Old World

Caterina Diego stood in a bookshop in the small port city near the sea, only half paying attention to the children nearby. Sunlight poured through the harbor across the cobblestones of the town, turning the streets gold and gleaming. She leafed through the pages of the book in her hand, wishing for time and freedom to lose herself in it.

Alas, those were luxuries she did not have.

Outside, one of the children yelled. His tone was angry, and Caterina hurriedly shelved the book and rushed outside. The older brother had the younger one by his shirt collar and was pounding him about the shoulders while the younger boy threw punches at his brother's gut. She shouldn't have left them unsupervised this long.

She strode into their midst and pushed the boys apart with some effort. Her long, dark red braid fell over her shoulder as she did. They scratched and flailed at her arms, and the older one turned an angry glare on her and said, "Get your hands off me."

Caterina stepped back slightly but kept her hand pressing against his shoulder for a moment until she could be certain he wasn't going to lunge around her and start pounding on his brother again. He straightened to his tallest twelve-year-old height, turned away from her, and muttered, "Meddling cow."

Caterina ignored him, instead turning to the younger brother, who glared back at her just as angrily—though with a little less scorn. His nose was bleeding, and he'd wiped it on the back of his hand—smearing blood across his face and onto his clothes. Hang it all. She was going to pay for that. Their little sister lingered nearby, watching with wide eyes. She clutched a handful of pretty weeds in one hand and had pressed herself against the bookshop wall while her brothers went at each other. Caterina sighed and reached out a hand to her. "It's all right, Amelia," she said. "They're not going to fight anymore." *For the moment, anyway.*

"It's time we went home," Caterina announced. She thought with regret of the book she'd abandoned. She'd hoped to get a few more pages in before her responsibilities drew her away.

"Yes, let's go home, so you can explain how *that* happened to him on *your* watch," the older son, Nico, said smugly. He pointed at his brother and laughed as he spoke. "You look like someone pulled you out of a manure pile."

Daniel, the younger brother, did look worse for wear. Their brief tussle had smeared him with dirt and planted a leaf or two in his hair, and his nose was still bleeding. Caterina thought of her own brothers and wished Diego were there to teach the horrible little bully a lesson. But a pang of guilt struck her too. Nico was right; this was her fault. She shouldn't have left them alone.

Nico led the way home. He knew he had nothing to fear. Any blame to be had would fall squarely on Caterina, as it always did. She'd taken a post as nanny, not as a whipping girl; but in this household, it amounted to much the same thing.

Amelia slipped her little hand into Caterina's as they walked and held it tightly. She sniffled.

Their walk up the streets of the town took them into the richer precincts high on the hill. They arrived at an ornate manor house, its gates and elaborate doors gleaming with bronze and architectural flourishes.

The gate guard opened to them and surveyed the motley crew with a raised eyebrow. "You're late," he said. "And in trouble, it would seem."

Caterina cursed inwardly, suddenly realizing how low the sun had gone in the sky. She *was* late. How long had she been lost in that book? Apparently this day was only capable of getting worse.

The boys' tutor appeared in the yard and called for them. "Amelia, go to your room," he said. "Caterina, you're wanted inside."

Twenty minutes later—they kept her waiting purposely, she knew—Caterina stood in the main hall with her head bowed and her hands clasped in front of her while her mistress rained invective on her head. Caterina was negligent, stupid, and evil-minded, a worthless, low-born girl who wasn't worth a quarter of what she was paid. If Amelia didn't like her so much, they would have thrown her out in the street months ago to earn her living in the only way pretty but useless young women could find to do. The master, who was lounging to the side on a luxurious velvet couch, sipped a glass of wine and watched with evident amusement.

Caterina responded to the diatribe by keeping her eyes down, muttering "Yes ma'am" at appropriate intervals, and wishing she could shield herself from the master's eyes. She didn't like how he looked at her at the best of times. It was worse when his wife was berating her like this.

A slight stir of movement to her left drew Caterina's attention, and she turned her head almost imperceptibly. Nico and Amelia were there, shadows in a doorway—the latter wide-eyed and clutching a doll, the former smug, with arms crossed across his chest. Of Daniel there was no sign. That wasn't surprising. The middle child had no interest in her. To Amelia she was a mother figure; to Nico, she was an unfortunate path to superiority and power. Like father, like son.

The mistress finished, finally. For a parting blow she said, "I'm docking your pay this month. If you wish to receive full wages next time, bring my sons home without their faces bloodied."

Caterina just nodded. There was no point in protesting, and short wages were better than none. Anyway, it was fair. She should have stayed closer to her charges.

It was after dark when Caterina made her way home to the small apartment near the waterfront where she lived. Torches burning outside of taverns and light from the inside of small homes and shops sparkled off the black waters of the harbor. The air smelled of fish and rank refuse. It was a rough neighborhood, and she passed through it with care, but she preferred it to living in the master's house. Besides, for every drunken sailor and stevedore who staggered through these streets after dark, there was a decent-minded tavernkeeper or shop man who kept an eye out for her.

As she made her way through the shadows, she thought again of her brothers. Of Diego and the letter he'd sent, telling her and Taddeo to leave their home of two years and hide somewhere new. They were in danger, he'd said. But Taddeo hadn't been willing to flee. His apprenticeship was too promising and too close to his heart. He'd brought her here, found her a job, and left her.

Likely he would not be happy to know she'd deserted the servants' quarters at the manor house and taken up residence here instead, but he wasn't here. As far as she was concerned, he'd forfeited his right to say where she lived.

Skirting the waterfront, Caterina passed a well-lit inn where the smells of stew and ale mixed with the rank scent of the water. Music and the noise of laughter and brawling spilled into the street along with a group of men, whose steps lurched and rolled as though they were on the deck of a ship. She hung back and let them pass, singing loudly. She was nearly home— only another block up the street.

She hurried her steps as she approached the bookkeeper's shop with its small apartment on the side, eager to be home, to lock the door behind her and breathe deeply and let the day roll off her shoulders.

She spotted the men hiding in the shadows around the shop just in time. Instinctively, she knew they were waiting for her.

She froze for a bare second. The threat she and her siblings had spent years dodging was finally here.

She turned and ran.

They followed. One called out for her to stop—a conciliatory tone, meant to comfort her, to tell her there was nothing wrong. She knew better. Heart in her throat, she pushed herself into a new burst of speed and ran back toward the tavern. Maybe she could lose herself in the crowd, or some of her neighbors would come to her aid.

A hundred feet ahead of her, two more men stepped into the street and began closing in on her.

The water was to her left, blocking any escape. To her right, a dark alley led—somewhere. She knew these streets, though not as well as she should have—she spent far too much time with her nose in a book rather than paying attention to her surroundings, just as Bettina had always reprimanded her for. Still, it was likely she knew these streets better than the men giving chase did. Praying no one was waiting there to ambush her, she ducked into the alley and ran a zigzag pattern, going from one alleyway to another, one dark hole to the next. By instinct she found the florist's shop with its outside stairs leading up to a rooftop garden, and she took them two at a time. She could still hear the men chasing, but she hoped they were far enough back, and it was dark enough, that they didn't see her ascent.

As she bolted up the stairs, heart pounding, her head demanded to know why. Why these men were here. Why they were after *her*. Why her brother wrote her letters telling her to flee place after place, town after town, terrible job after terrible job.

If she had been a different kind of young woman, she might have considered simply putting a stop to all of it by refusing to have anything to do with Diego. Surely there was some way she could distance herself from him effectively enough—could, when it came right down to it, betray him.

But she wasn't that kind of woman, and she didn't consider it. She just kept taking steps two at a time, racing through the darkness with the black waters sparkling below, until she reached the roof garden and realized she'd cornered herself. She could hide here, but if they found her, there was nowhere to go unless she wanted to leap off the roof.

The garden was made up mostly of tall, fragrant hydrangeas and thick, low-growing cedar. She ducked behind a row of flowers and stopped, eyeing the end of the row where the parapet was the height of her knee. Moonlight glimmered off something on the next roof over. It wasn't too far. Maybe, she thought, she could make the jump if she had to.

Or maybe she had escaped them, and all she needed to do now was keep still.

She held her breath, trying to be silent, though her heart seemed to be pounding loudly enough for the sound to reach the street.

Footsteps on the stairs. They were coming.

She ducked lower, holding her breath again, as the men appeared on the roof and fanned out, searching the rows. Six of them. They were going to find her. She might have been able to dodge them if there had only been one or two, but with so many, someone would see her if she moved.

She closed her eyes. This was it. The moment she'd been running from for years, ever since Diego and Taddeo got her and Bettina out of the hidden convent where they'd spent their teen years. And she still didn't know why she had to run.

The men moved from row to row slowly, prowling, cat-footed. As though they thought she might be some kind of threat.

"Come out, girl," one said in a thickly accented voice. "We know you're here." She glanced to the side again, to the end of the row where the parapet loomed. How bad would it be if she were caught? Would it be worse than making the jump—and missing?

"You can't hide," he said again. "It's time to stop running."

She didn't know what this was about, why they were here or why they wanted her. She *did* know that if they caught her, it would hurt Diego somehow. It would put him in danger.

She jumped to her feet and ran for the edge of the roof with all her might.

The men shouted as she took off, and they lurched into a run. But they were at the other end of the rows, and she was fast. She reached the parapet, leaped up, and pushed herself off with every ounce of momentum she had. Her body arced out over the darkness, and she reached for the next roof in desperation.

It was too far. She wasn't going to make it. She would fall to the broken, cobbled alleyway below.

But someone from the roof above grabbed her arm just above the elbow and pulled her toward him. Her own energy propelled her forward. Wild with relief and terror, she landed in a heap on the other roof.

"Get up," he said. He was already helping her as he said it, pulling her to her feet and pushing her behind him. He held a pistol in his hand, and he fired it at the men pursuing her with a flash of light and a loud boom. It had been his gun barrel the moonlight reflected off, she realized. She had no time or light for a good look at him, but as lead balls flew toward them in answer, she got an impression of tawny hair and muscular arms. Those arms wrapped around her waist and pulled her down, his body shielding her. An instant later the pistol fire was over and he was pulling her up yet again and running with her, hand in hand, toward the stairs that led away from this second roof. The sounds of shouts and cursing followed them.

"Who are you?" she managed to ask as they raced down the stairs. He pushed her up against the side of the alley as he again covered her, this time peering around the corner and looking both ways before grabbing her hand again and dashing out into the street.

"I'm called Lucaan," he said. "I'll explain later."

"What are you doing here?" she exclaimed as they ran toward the docks.

"Rescuing you," he said.

This much was obvious. Yet it confused her immensely. For years, Caterina had expected that someday men might appear and threaten her—abduct her, arrest her, something. She had been given good reason to expect this. She had not expected a rescuer.

In her confusion she hardly noticed where they were going until they ran the length of a dock and then jumped across the gap in the water to the deck of a small boat. She made to protest, but he put a finger to his lips. She could see it in the moonlight. He hunkered down and gestured for her to do the same. She complied.

They crouched side by side in the gently rocking boat and watched as men poured out of the alley onto the waterfront street. There were more than six now—there must have been others on the ground. Amid the lights of the waterfront, they seemed to take shape out of the shadows and then melt back into them again. One gave orders, and they spread out in all directions. Searching.

Caterina swallowed a whimper. Suddenly the thought of allowing herself to be captured was unthinkable.

Diego, she thought. *What did you get yourself into?*

Beside her, the young man Lucaan crouched like a lion. Golden strength exuded from him.

"There!" someone shouted. Then they were pounding down the dock toward the little boat.

Lucaan stood very suddenly and brandished something—a club. He leaped forward at the same moment the first man reached them, catching him off guard and knocking him into the water with a loud splash. The second man was on him in a moment, jumping onto his back and wrapping a thick arm around Lucaan's throat. Caterina cast about wildly and spotted a wooden anchor. She picked it up and jumped off the side of the boat, clutching the anchor in both hands, and drove it into the back of the man's head as hard as she could. He released Lucaan and fell to the dock with a yell and a spasm. Lucaan whirled around, grabbed Caterina's hand again, and leaped back into the boat. He ran its length, then jumped onto a dock on its other side—and from there to another boat. Panting for breath, she strove just to keep up with him.

The boats were small, but they rocked and knocked against each other. They were making it too easy for the brigands to find them.

Without warning, Lucaan slipped over the side of the boat into the water and pulled her in after him.

She had the presence of mind to go in smoothly, without making a splash, but terror filled her as she did. The shock of cold, stinking water seized her. She couldn't swim.

Maybe he knew it from the frantic way she clung to him in the water, but he shook his golden head at her and pulled her head close to his. He said, so quietly she could hardly hear him although he spoke directly into her ear, "Hold on to me. I have you. But not so tight. I can't swim when you hold so tight."

Swallowing hard, she forced herself to loosen her grip and relax her body. His strong arms stroked through the water, pulling her along with him. He swam quietly, assuredly. She willed herself to remain still and easy, to trust his strength.

They moved through the shadows between the glimmering lights and swam beneath a pier. Lucaan grabbed on to one of the thick, low pillars and disentangled Caterina from his neck so she could do the same. Clinging to the wood, she breathed a little easier. Overhead, footsteps pounded along the pier, along with shouts. Someone paused just overheard; she could hear him cursing to himself.

It was dark beneath the pier, but she turned to look at Lucaan and their eyes met—lit just enough by the moonlight reflecting off the water. He smiled. There was a sparkle in his eyes that didn't come from the moon.

Was he *enjoying* this?

More than that—was she?

The man overhead moved off. A few more footsteps sounded, heading back to land now. Boats were still rocking in the harbor, splashing and disturbing the water. But one by one, things grew still.

Caterina felt heavy and numb with cold. As the last voices finally receded and the sounds of disturbance died away, exhaustion hit her so hard she began to tremble. Lucaan inclined his head as if to say "let's go." But she couldn't pry her fingers loose from the pile.

He seemed to understand. He reached up and covered her right hand with his until she felt her fingers relax just a little, and he took her hand and lowered it, pulling it back around his neck. Shivering, she let go with the other hand on her own, getting a loose grip on him again. He swam them out from the pier and over to a rope ladder that extended down into the water. He didn't speak—but he communicated somehow nevertheless, because she knew what he wanted her to do. She grabbed on to the bottom of the ladder and waited while he climbed up slowly, looking every way, ensuring the way was clear. Then he reached a hand back down, took hers, and helped her climb up.

Cold and shock set in earnestly now, and she shivered violently. He wrapped an arm around her shoulders, a gesture which seemed natural and giving even though he was a strange man and she was a young woman who should probably shove him away and slap him. She didn't. She needed his warmth, and anyway, he'd played one role and one only from the moment he appeared—that of protector. She couldn't stop trusting him now.

He spoke, and she caught his curious accent—Lowlander, she thought, but there was something unusual in it too, something more specifically regional.

"You can't go home," he said. "They'll be waiting."

She nodded. "I know." She managed to lift a finger and point down the street toward the tavern. "Friends," she said through chattering teeth. "They'll help us."

"Are you sure?" he asked. "Those men may have asked about you."

It was an awful thought—that someone in the neighborhood might turn her in for money. But the tavernkeeper and his wife would not. She was as sure of that as anything. They were staunchly against bullying and oppression of all kinds; they would not hand her over to a gang of thugs even if they were offered the price of the tavern to do it.

They kept to the shadows as they headed toward the tavern. Halfway there she took the lead, guiding Lucaan around the back and inside through a service door.

An hour later they sat by a fire in an upstairs room. Both were dressed in dry, warm clothes, gifts from the tavernkeeper's wife. Not everything they wore matched, but it all fit well enough. Lucaan wore various pieces of clothing left behind by overnight lodgers who left too drunk to remember their things. Caterina wore a skirt and underthings gifted to her by the housewife, who was about her size, with a man's shirt and coat—again, left behind by errant guests.

Holding a mug of steaming cider tightly in her hands and all but leaning into the fire's warmth, Caterina tried to hold just as tightly to the moment—the comfort, the heat, the few touches of familiarity in this room. She didn't want to leave. But they had to, of course. *As soon as we're dry,* Lucaan had said. *We should not stay the night.*

She thought with regret of little Amelia. It tore at her conscience not to say goodbye. But who knew what trouble she might bring on her employers if she stayed?

It occurred to her suddenly—and awfully—that the thugs might well have gone to the manor house after they failed to find her at home. Her dockside neighbors might not sell her out, but her employers would not hesitate.

Deliberately, she was not looking at Lucaan. Partly this was because she wanted to hold to the illusion of homey sameness for a few more minutes. Lucaan was not homey, and he was not like anything in her life before now. Partly it was because she was afraid if she looked at him she would look a little too long and a little closely, and she didn't want to be caught at it.

"We should go," he said.

She nodded. He was right. She ventured a glance over at him. His bright blue eyes were a little anxious and keenly sympathetic. His vines were bright red and gleamed in the firelight. He was young, no older than she was—early twenties—and he exuded youthful strength and vitality, but with a quiet wisdom that she found powerfully attractive.

Who was she kidding? She found everything about him powerfully attractive. She was at once excited by the idea that he would be accompanying her to some safer place and appalled by it.

They had spoken to each other very little in the last hour. There was too much fussing and bustling from the tavernkeeper's wife; hurried changes of clothes, rushed and whispered explanations. And Caterina needed silence to say goodbye to this place, and Lucaan seemed to understand.

But now she stood, finished her last swallow of cider, and nodded. "Yes," she said. "We should."

He smiled, and she went weak at the knees. Harm it all. Was she going to be a fainting female this whole trip to—well, wherever they were going?

"Where are we going?" she asked, the question coming out tentative and soft.

"Somewhere as far from Crispin's men as I can take you," he said. "At first, just away from here. Then, you can decide. To your family, maybe?"

Her mind raced. To whom—Paulo and Bettina? No, she couldn't go there; she didn't want to endanger them. There were reasons they had all split up in the first place. Taddeo? She didn't want to ruin the life he had worked so hard for. Diego. She should go to Diego, on whose behalf she was in trouble in the first place. He could find her somewhere to hide. But since trouble had erupted on his behalf, she doubted very much he was in Tempestano anymore.

There had to be some way to find him.

So she nodded. "My brother Diego," she said. "He can help us. But I don't know where he is."

To her surprise, Lucaan smiled again. "I might," he said. "I saw him not so long ago. My brother and I helped him win a fight."

He opened the door and gestured gallantly for her to go first. Looking curiously at him—was he going to leave that story just hanging?—she passed through.

Chapter 13

They started the conversation again once they were well down the road in the darkness, outside Portafiela by several miles. They rode—Caterina used her last month's wages, meant for rent, to buy them two small but hardy-looking horses from the tavern's stable. The tavernkeepers had done her a favor again, for the horses were surely worth more than she was able to pay for them. Her mistress had docked her pay last month too, for some imagined slight complained about by her sons.

Really, Caterina thought, well bundled against the chilly air, with the horse moving rhythmically beneath her and Lucaan's intriguing company by her side, this was not so bad. It wasn't like she was leaving behind some glamorous and successful life.

"How in the world did you find me?" she asked. "Who are you? And you saw my brother? Where—" she stopped and laughed. "I'm sorry. This has all happened very fast, and I don't know where to start."

"My name is Lucaan," he said. "Lucaan Feeanstra, son of Leeanaert Feeanstra the Older. I come from the Boglands in the north. I met your brother on the road from Tempestano to the Western Sea. He was traveling with his friend, the young lord of Tempestano."

"Go on," Caterina said.

"They were in disguise," Lucaan said. "Trying to hide from the likes of the men who came after you. The lord is in some trouble and your brother helped him escape. When we met them—my brother and I, that is, and our friends beside us—they had run into trouble with local bandits, so we helped them beat them. Your brother and the young lord got away." He made a sound that she interpreted, in the dark, as a verbal grimace. "But then the kirkman came to town and started asking around."

"Joseph Crispin?" Caterina asked. Lucaan had said his name earlier—but she hadn't really needed him to. What exactly Diego was in the middle of, she did not know. She *did* know that Crispin was their enemy, and always had been. The hawkish churchman best known for hunting down dissenters was no friend to her family.

"The very same," Lucaan said. "Someone in the town fingered my brother and me and our good friends, and we were arrested. They took me and Leeanaert to Tempestano and kept us a while. I learned there about you and the danger you are in, so when I got out, I came to find you."

"How did you arrive at exactly the right time?" Caterina asked. "How did you get on that roof?"

"For the timing I can only thank the good Creator," Lucaan said, "for he must have guided my steps. For the roof—I saw the chase but did not know where you were, so I thought if I went high, I could get a view of the streets. I got there, and there you were. So we must thank the Creator again."

"We must indeed," Caterina said, her heart strangely warming. She glanced down at her hands, at the faint light on the backs of them, on the saddle and the arc of her horse's neck. "I don't think I've thanked you," she said. "You may know more than I do about why those men are after me. Diego has kept his distance for years. He writes from time to time, to warn us to move, to hide. I don't know exactly why. To protect us, he doesn't tell us. But I know you saved me from something tonight. And likely my whole family with me. I don't know how we can repay you."

"You were in need," Lucaan said simply. "No payment is necessary."

He sounded oddly restrained, like he wanted to say something else. She wanted to hear it—nearly asked him outright to state it. But she didn't.

"And besides," he finished, sounding oddly embarrassed, "to love our neighbor is all our duty."

They rode another hour, or perhaps two, following the road. Caterina breathed easier the more miles fell away behind them. The night grew darker, and finally Lucaan whistled to her to stop. She reined her horse to draw up slowly alongside him, and he reached out and took the reins from her hand.

"Do you see that barn, yonder?" he asked.

She thought she did—that she could make out a faint outline of a roof, across a field to her left. Lucaan must have eyes like a cat to have spotted it.

"I think it's a good place to get some sleep," he told her.

They turned the horses off the road, and the animals quickened their pace across the field—perhaps recognizing that they were about to be rested and fed. They dismounted in the darkness, grateful for the scrap of moonlight that made it possible to see some of what they were doing. Lucaan led the horses into the barn while Caterina went in search of water. She pushed the wide back door open soundlessly and found a pump and trough inside the barnyard, with a rusted old bucket handy—she wouldn't have seen it, but she nearly tripped on it on her way to the pump, banging her shins and sending the bucket clanging away.

The pump hadn't been used in quite some time, and it took effort to get the handle unstuck and the water flowing—but she gave it all her might, and soon cold, clear water was splashing into the bucket she'd set inside the trough. She carried it inside, careful not to splash too much water over the edges, and handed it to Lucaan, who was rubbing down the horses. He took it gratefully and offered a drink to his horse first, standing patiently while it drank long and deep. Caterina moved to her own mount and patted its neck. "Don't worry, girl," she said. "Your turn next."

"Your brother was going to Angleland," Lucaan said casually. "If you still want to go to him, I will take you there."

"Angleland!" she exclaimed. "So far!" The island nation might as well be a world away. What was Diego doing there?

"They went there seeking allies," Lucaan said, as though he read her mind. "Crispin is not so powerful in the islands. I think it would be a good place for you."

"I was thinking," Caterina said, "maybe I could just hide again. I can find some other city, get another job. That's what Diego always asked us to do."

Lucaan finished watering one horse and turned to give the little remaining water to the other. "To me it seems that things have changed for your brother," he said. "Hiding may not be so possible. If you are with him, you can't be used against him."

"But it's so far," she said again, flushing. "I can't ask you to go all that way with me."

As she said the words, longing burst inside her chest. She shoved it down.

He set the bucket down and turned toward her. She couldn't make out his expression in the gloom, but she read his stance aright. There was something stern and straight about it. "Forgive me," he said. "But under the circumstances, you can't ask me to leave you alone. Those men will come after you again. I will see you safely settled before I leave you."

"Are you not giving me any choice?" she asked. The longing tried to come up again, and she forced it into submission. It was wild and unidentified, and she could not set it free.

He paused. When he spoke again he sounded properly chagrined. "You always have a choice," he said. "But please don't ask me to leave."

She ran her fingers through her horse's rough mane. "I don't want you to," she said quietly. "I just … don't know how to accept your help."

He was smiling; she could hear that in his voice. "It is not hard," he said. "You just say, 'Lucaan, you're a brave and handsome man. Thank you for your help.'"

She couldn't help laughing. "Don't push it," she said. "But I do thank you for your help. And I accept it." She picked up the empty water bucket. "I'll go refill this."

Her thoughts warred with each other as she made her way back out of the shadowy barn. She thought of Diego, of far-off Angleland, and of threats in the darkness. But mostly she thought of Lucaan, and the thoughts made her blush, and they made the deepest part of her ache.

She worked the pump handle again until the water poured out, hitting the bucket in cold spurts and splashing her clothes. Her mind wandered back to the earlier chase. She lowered the pump handle, and the water stopped flowing and settled. Suddenly the surrounding field and the patches of woodland beyond it seemed not to be empty, but brooding and full—maybe full of threats.

She tried to shake off the spike of fear as she scanned her surroundings and listened into the silence. She could hear an owl hooting somewhere in the darkness, and a shiver of dry grass—was something moving out there, or was it just the wind?

Lucaan wouldn't have let her come out here alone if he thought they'd been followed. She swallowed back the heavy feeling of foreboding and picked up the bucket. It seemed heavier this time. She carried it by its handle, and it bumped against her shins, reminding her that she'd hit and bruised them earlier. She winced and bit her lip. Rejoining Lucaan, she handed the bucket over without a word.

"Come," he said when he'd finished with the horses. He closed them into their stalls with a few final pats and words of encouragement, then gestured for Caterina to follow him. "We can sleep in the loft. There is straw up there, not too dirty. I looked."

Nervous that they might disturb some animal sleeping in the straw—it had clearly been some time since anyone made use of this barn—Caterina followed Lucaan up a ladder of boards nailed into the barn wall and through an open trapdoor. He gave her a hand clearing the door and scrambling up onto the loft floor. The boards sank and creaked under her feet alarmingly, but Lucaan was right—the loft was full of inviting piles of straw, and the air—though dusty—smelled sweet.

"You can sleep here," he said, leading the way toward a particularly inviting pile of straw. "I'll take that one over there."

She followed him, wondering why this straw seemed so clean and so new when the barn itself gave the impression of dilapidation and abandonment. Well, except for—

She stopped. "Lucaan," she said. "No one has been here in a long time, isn't that right?"

"So it seems to me," he agreed, turning toward her and taking another step backward toward the pile of straw.

"Then why were the hinges so well oiled?" she said.

"What are you talking about?" he asked. "I could hardly get the stalls to open, they were so rusted."

"The pump too," she said. "No one had used it in ages. But the barn door, the one to the backyard, opened like a dream. No sound. No trouble with it at all."

Lucaan spread his hands and shrugged. "Maybe somebody has been coming here for something other than farming," he said.

The loft floor chose that moment to fall out. She heard the floorboards beneath Lucaan snap and crack and threw herself forward without even thinking about it, trying to grab him and pull him away. She only succeeded in widening the collapse. The rotted floor dropped away beneath their feet and they plunged down—arms around each other, somehow—and landed on their backs in something hard, slippery, and shifting.

Blinking up at the dark hole above them, Caterina lay stunned and fighting for the breath that had been knocked out of her. She didn't know if anything hurt—she didn't think so, not too badly. Lucaan's arm was around her shoulders. With his other hand, he reached beneath them and pulled up a handful of—paper?

There was an old window somewhere above them, and it let in enough moonlight that Caterina could see they were lying in a large bin, and it was full of what appeared to be printed leaflets, stacked together and bound. Their fall had broken some of the twine and caused a top layer of leaflets to slide loose. The bin was full enough, or shallow enough, that they were near the top—the rim only extended about six inches above them.

Lucaan tried to sit up, but the leaflets shifting away beneath him made it difficult. He let go of Caterina and grabbed the rim with both arms, hoisting himself up so he could look over the edge. He jumped over the edge, leaving her behind. He disappeared from view—apparently the bin was a little taller than a man's height.

"Come, I'll help you down," he said.

Still struggling to get her breath back, she reached up for the rim and fought to straighten up despite the slipping, sliding surface beneath her. She peered over to see Lucaan standing below, holding up his hands like she was a child and he would catch her.

"Just one moment," she told him, and looked back down at the mass of paper gleaming dull yellow in the moonlight. She grabbed up several handfuls of the leaflets and stuffed them into the pockets of her skirt and coat. Then she grabbed on to the rim with both hands, swung a leg over, and scrambled down. Lucaan caught her waist when she was halfway and helped her with a soft landing.

She brushed a long strand of red hair out of her eyes. "Well," she said. "That was unexpected. Are you all right?"

"Are *you?*"

"I'm fine." She eyed him carefully. He seemed unhurt. "Answer my question?"

"I'm not hurt," he said. "Just a little embarrassed to have fallen through a floor in front of you. It smarts a surprising amount."

She laughed. "Well, let that pain go," she said. "There should be no embarrassment between friends. And I fell through the floor too, if you didn't notice."

She pulled a leaflet out of her pocket and did her best to straighten it. "Do you have a light?" she asked.

Obligingly, he pulled a tinderbox from his pocket and quickly struck up a single flame. He held it up so she could see.

Her breath caught. What she saw was so unexpected that she laughed out loud again—this time an incredulous burst.

"What is it?" he asked.

She held up the paper toward him, but it occurred to her suddenly that he might not be able to read. She'd been taught by monks in their mountain hideaway, but literacy was not a universal skill. "It's my brother-in-law," she said. "Paulo. He's a printer—he printed this." She laughed again. "It's Diego's story. Or rather, it's Carlos's story—the young lord he travels with."

She flipped the pages of the leaflet, skimming the long, carefully printed columns of text. "It's meant to rouse sympathy for him and expose the wrongs Crispin has done."

She quieted as she quickly read bits here and there, catching pieces of story that turned her stomach but were not enough to dampen the sudden exhilaration she felt. "This can't be coincidence," she said. "The Creator led us here, Lucaan. Whoever is using this barn must be a sympathizer with us. Spreading the word. They won't mind if we take some of these papers and help them spread it as we go. We can take Carlos's story everywhere between here and Angleland."

She held up the leaflet in one hand and grabbed another handful out of her coat pocket, all but shaking them in Lucaan's face. She didn't just have to run—to hide and flee from enemies she didn't understand like a fox gone to ground. She could help Diego fight his battle. *They* could help.

Lucaan seemed a little slower to grasp the implications—or if he did, he wasn't quite as excited about them. "You want to take these with us?" he said.

"Yes, as many as we can carry. We can spread them everywhere."

"It will leave a trail," he said. "It will tell Crispin's men how to find us."

"They won't know it's us," Caterina said, but even as she said it, she knew he was right—they would be inviting trouble. "We'll just have to move faster than they do." Her tone pleaded with him to understand. "I don't just want to hide," she said. "I've been hiding all my life."

He nodded slowly. "It's a good work. My brother would have suggested it. My friends too. You talk like an adventuring boatman."

She understood that as a compliment and flushed with pleasure.

He smiled at her. "We will do it!" he said. "Of course we will do it. But we will have to move very quickly."

"I can do it," she answered. "I won't slow us down."

CHAPTER
14

Carlos and Diego stood dressed in their finest attire, humbled even so by the opulence of the small study where they waited for the crown prince to arrive. John Worthington, simply and humbly clothed, waited with them. They were nervous and sweating. He was calm as a sheltered bay. Somehow, with the coronation scheduled for later in the day, John had managed to get them an audience. It wasn't ideal, trying to present their cause in the midst of so much busyness and personal upheaval on the future king's part. But they had to speak with him before Crispin did.

Henry entered the room without fanfare and immediately dismissed the attendants who followed him. They bowed and retreated swiftly, closing the door behind them. A big man, tall and broad shouldered with a full beard and piercing grey eyes, Henry carried himself like the king he was. His vines were golden. He wore a rich red doublet and a gold jerkin trimmed with ermine. A ceremonial sword hung at his side, but Carlos didn't doubt he knew how to use it.

Without waiting for them to make obeisance, Henry strode across the study, popped the top of a crystal decanter, and began pouring glasses of rich whiskey. He gestured for his guests to take them before taking a sip of his own.

"Ah," he said. "That's better. A man could suffocate on a day like today. Now, I needn't tell you I don't have much time. What is this about?"

Suddenly panicked, Carlos looked to John—who, thankfully, was ready to speak. "You know Carlos Vaquero," he said. "His associate, Captain Diego."

"Of Tempestano, yes," Henry said. He raised his glass to John. "You did inform me when you asked for this meeting."

A hint of a smile passed over John's lips, but he didn't give vent to his humor. "They are here because they have been wronged, and they need an ally."

He nodded to Carlos, who tried mightily to remain in control of himself. So much rode on this meeting—but he couldn't let himself be afraid of what would happen if Henry did not take their side.

"I have been unlawfully deposed," he said. "The province that is rightfully mine has been annexed by my enemies through conniving and murderous means. I wish to reclaim it before the change of governance can become more permanent, but I need allies. Your father was a friend to my uncle and to many of our friends. I hoped I could ask him to back me. I am sorry for your loss, my prince—but I hope I can ask the same of you."

"Unlawfully deposed?" Henry said, frowning. "Murderous means? And who is the powerful thief who has wrested your earldom away from you?"

"None other than Joseph Crispin," Diego said darkly. "You are familiar with the Vaquero family's long history with dissenters, and also with Crispin's increasing program of persecution against them. He massacred a group of Tremblers sheltering in Carlos's lands and arrested him for helping them. He ordered him summarily executed—I know this, because I was working for Crispin, to my shame. I was able to get Carlos away without Crispin knowing it, though he may know it now."

Henry listened with the glass of whiskey held still in his hand. He glanced from man to man and sucked his teeth when Diego had finished. "I am no admirer of the High Elder, nor do I support his policies," he said. "I sympathize with you heartily. But surely you can see that I can't take a public position on your side. Too many factions in my court would support Crispin, and I can't afford to begin my reign by making enemies. Things have been uneasy between us and the mainland far too long as it is. Much has changed since you were last here, young count. We do not have the luxury of being quite so independent as my father was."

"If you pander to those factions," John said gently, "you may find that Crispin ends up holding your puppet strings. He is trying to consolidate power everywhere. Don't imagine that you are not already in his sights."

"That is true enough, but I have an answer to it already," Henry said. His attention seemed to have shifted away from Carlos and Diego entirely. "I have been meaning to tell you. Our kirk, of course, is not attached to that of the mainland. I need a High Elder of my own—a man to oversee religion in this island whose integrity I can trust absolutely. You're it, John. I am appointing you head of the Puritani kirk of Angleland. In fact I want you to set the crown on my head tonight."

John looked stunned, but he nodded slowly. That was good enough for Henry, who turned back to his visitors. "I can't give you an answer now," he said. "As you can see, I will already be making Crispin angry tonight. Wisdom would probably dictate I attempt to placate him after I've rubbed his nose in the dust. I'm sorry I can't pledge my help. But I wish you the best in taking back your lands."

"*If* we take them back," Diego said. He seemed angry. "Without allies, it may be impossible."

"Nothing is really impossible," Henry said. He swirled the whiskey in his glass and tossed his head back, draining it all and thunking the heavy glass back down on the table. He winked. "I know enough of the Vaquero family to know they always find a way."

He nodded to them all. "A good afternoon to you," he said. "I hope you will be there to celebrate with me tonight."

He left them all looking after him. Carlos's face burned. All this way, all this effort—for what?

"So that's it then," Diego said. "We've accomplished nothing by coming here."

"I wouldn't say that." John had been leaning against a tall side table throughout the meeting; he straightened himself now, a movement that seemed to cost him something as his darkened vines pulled at the puckered skin of his face and left arm. "I will do all I can to help you, and I don't think you should write Henry off just yet. You got his ear before Crispin did. Now give him some time."

"We don't have time," Carlos said. "Every hour we spend here and not in Tempestano is an hour that our ability to go back slips further away."

"Is it?" John asked. "Or are you speaking out of fear and impatience? Maybe you have all the time you need, friend."

He placed a hand on Carlos's story. "Come to the coronation tonight," he said. "Let Crispin see you here, see that you are still a friend to the Angle King. That will make a statement of its own. Henry says he cannot take sides, but he has invited you personally—that will say something publicly, and he knows it."

That evening, Carlos stepped into the candlelit cathedral and caught his breath at the beauty of it.

Chandeliers blazing with light hung from soaring ceilings overhead. Row upon row of tall gold and white candles flanked the long rectangular nave like angels, reflecting off the white and gold marble of the floor. Choirs sang as the guests filed in, filling the cathedral with heavenly music. Stylized vines, leaves, and flowers, carefully wrought in delicate gold, worked their way up every wall and surrounded every stained-glass window. More were carved into the backs of the gleaming wooden pews.

Having entered this otherworldly place, Carlos took a moment to pray for the new king of Angleland and for the success of his own mission.

Diego gave him a minute before urging him forward. Then, to both their surprise, a steward intercepted them and led them to a seat of honor near the front. They would have an unobstructed view of the king in his splendor. And many, Crispin included, would have a clear view of them.

On the other side of the aisle, the corpulent cleric was even now seating himself amidst a small flock of deacons and attendants. All wore ornate robes proclaiming their position and importance. Crispin carried a symbolic staff, curled at the end. Facing his enemy, who had not yet spotted him, Carlos felt like the air had suddenly gone out of the room, and he could hardly breathe. He didn't know if it was hatred he felt, or fear, or anger, or something else completely. But he trembled.

Diego lightly touched his arm. "Sit," he whispered.

Carlos couldn't tear his eyes away from Crispin. Their last encounters played out in his mind—Crispin's overbearing arrival in Tempestano, his insistence on Carlos's hospitality, his presiding over the massacre of the Tremblers. Philippe and Elsa. Their children.

"Sit," Diego said again, more insistently. Carlos snapped back to the present. All around him, people were being seated. He was drawing attention to himself.

He sat.

The ceremony began with a flourish of trumpets and a grand procession. Henry was resplendent in gold and white. Ranks of attendants displayed wealth and power in their bearing and their dress. John Worthington still dressed simply, but now in white, not his customary drab colors; and he carried a staff much like Crispin's, but less ornate.

When they had passed up the aisle, Crispin caught sight of Carlos for the first time. Carlos happened to be looking his way, and he caught his eye: he saw the High Elder flush with displeasure and nearly rise from his seat. Crispin caught himself and remained where he was, but not without glowering threats at Carlos.

There was nothing at all the High Elder could do to him—not here, not now. They were seated as equals under Henry's beneficence. The realization that he was invulnerable to attack made Carlos feel suddenly better than he had in months.

At the reception after the coronation, they came face to face.

Each held a glass of wine in his hand. The elder smiled smugly and raised his glass, inclining his head slightly. "Imagine my surprise to see you here, *Conde*," he said. "You are far from home."

"For reasons you well know," Carlos said. "But not for long, I hope."

Even as he said it, he wondered if he was being a fool. But Crispin was clearly discomfited by his presence here, no matter how he tried to cover it up. Carlos wanted very badly to keep him off balance. So Henry hadn't promised to help him. Crispin didn't need to know that.

"There are some who would say you don't belong here," Crispin said. He paused to sip his wine. "These are dangerous times, Conde; there are enemies everywhere among us. I am distressed that you so often choose to side with them."

Carlos did his best not to give in to his rising anger. "And where would you say I belong?" he asked.

"I should think that obvious," Crispin said. "It is a hard thing, is it not, when criminals are allowed to run free instead of being locked away where they cannot work their harm?"

"Locking me away would be a mercy," Carlos said, seething. His voice was low; he had no wish to draw attention, but neither could he walk away from the conversation. "You ordered me killed."

Crispin ignored the statement and acted offended. "Why do you assume I am talking about you?" he asked. "I am merely commenting on the sad disarray of our society at this moment. But since you bring it up, yes, I fear there are too many in prisons whom we would better see dead, where they can't work their witchery and confusion any longer." His eyes glittered dangerously. "It's not a mercy to let disease run rampant, my young count. Better to burn it out before it can spread."

Crispin was deliberately baiting him, and yet it was all Carlos could do not to haul back and hammer the man's smug face with his fist. This man had murdered his friends. This man had sentenced Serena to burn at the stake. This man fanned the flames of enmity, fear, and prejudice across the civilized world. That *he* was not imprisoned, or dead, was the worst injustice of all.

"Be careful, Conde," Crispin said. "You look ready to do something you'll regret."

In that very moment the band struck up a dance, and the skirling music drowned out conversation as crowds of courtiers flocked into lines and patterns on the floor. Carlos and Crispin were pushed back toward the edge of the room. One of the insufferable young women Carlos had met during his stay in Loren smiled at him and half-covered her face with her fan, sending a clear and provocative invitation. He should answer it, he knew. He should leave Crispin behind and insult him by dancing and flirting as though the High Elder were not even there. But he couldn't do it. He opened his mouth to reengage the conversation at higher volume when a powerful arm around his shoulder stopped him.

It was Henry.

Joseph Crispin reddened at the sight of the newly crowned king extending such an obvious sign of friendship and favor to the young count.

"Ah, Elder," the king said. "You know my friend Carlos Vaquero, do you not? I trust you are both enjoying the courtesy of my house. But you look unhappy, and I can't have that on the day of my crowning. Whatever dismal business you are thinking of, I command you to cease thinking of it and enjoy my hospitality more heartily. Now, young conde, come with me."

Henry steered Carlos away without waiting for a word of protest. Nor did Carlos have one to give. He was too surprised and flustered to say anything at all.

"He is baiting you," Henry said in a low voice. "If you want to get the upper hand, you cannot let him do that."

Carlos glanced back at Crispin in spite of himself. The High Elder was nearly purple with rage. But even as Henry continued to steer Carlos away, a messenger approached Joseph Crispin and whispered something in his ear. The elder's countenance changed immediately—he smiled. The sight struck fear in Carlos's heart.

"He's up to no good," Carlos said. "Something is wrong—whatever that man just said to him—"

"I realize you have many good reasons to hold Elder Crispin in the deepest suspicion and doubt," Henry said, finally releasing Carlos's arm and neatly sidestepping a row of dancers who almost blundered into them. Henry had led them onto the edge of the dance floor. "But right now he is just a guest, as are you."

Carlos caught sight of Diego on the other side of the dancers. He nodded to the king, afraid he was being irreparably rude to this most powerful of his friends, but unable to shake the image of Crispin's smile from his mind. "Thank you, your majesty," he said. "You honor me with your attention."

"But you disagree with me and want to be released from my company," Henry said with a laugh. He waved his royal hand, heavily jeweled rings flashing, gold vines wrapped around his fingers. "Worry not, Conde; I don't take offense. Go pursue whatever you must, but don't bait the High Elder of the mainland Puritani into a fight at my party."

Carlos bowed his head. "Your grace," he said, and then, grateful, wove his way through the dancers on the floor to Diego's side. He scanned the crowd as he approached, picking out the messenger who had spoken to Crispin. He was hovering near a long table heavy with sweets and other delicacies.

"Do you see that man by the table?" Carlos asked, not bothering with a greeting. "The one dressed in purple livery."

"I see him," Diego said.

"He spoke to Crispin just now. I would give a great deal to know what he said to him."

Diego nodded. "Are you giving me an excuse to leave this party?"

Carlos glanced at his friend, finally. Diego looked overdressed and over-heated, his face flushed and his bearing stiff. "Do you want one?" he asked.

"I have never been happy in high society," Diego told him. "The pretension is so thick you could choke on it. All except your friend Worthington and perhaps the new king himself."

"It's not all *that* bad," Carlos said, but he couldn't help smiling. "We've other friends at court."

"Yes, but we usually have the pleasure of taking them one by one. Not stuffed into a banqueting hall like too many fish in a barrel." Diego clapped a hand to Carlos's shoulder. He picked out the same silly young woman from the crowd—she had somehow positioned herself to eye Carlos again—and nodded toward her. "I'll follow the messenger out and see what I can learn. It seems you have more important things to attend to. The women of the court aren't going to flirt with themselves." To Carlos's consternation, the woman saw Diego's nod and began to meander toward him.

From across the hall, the king saw it too. He raised his hand in a mock salute and loudly laughed. Carlos straightened his shoulders and turned to speak cordially to the woman, and Diego patted him once on the back and then slipped away.

Diego stepped gladly into the cool, damp air in the stable yard. The scent of horses and hay, mud and carriage leather braced him and made him feel as though he'd returned to the world from some kind of feverish dream. Court life with all its luxuries and leisures was, to many men, the pinnacle of existence. To Diego it had always seemed unreal.

The messenger who had spoken with Crispin did not seem to be in any particular hurry as he retrieved his horse and made his way out of the yard. Diego followed him on foot, keeping well back so the man would not spot him. They left the palace precincts and wound down the city streets toward a noisy, populated area. Many were out celebrating the coronation in the streets.

The man tied his horse outside a popular pub and went in. Diego followed, entering a wash of noise and laughter within the pub's smoky interior. Huge platters of pork and bread were passed around while tankards of ale splashed amid shouts of "All hail the king!" Judging from the general mood, Henry was popular among the common folk. The messenger pushed back his hood, rolled up his sleeves, and joined right in.

Diego edged his way through the crowd and put an arm around the man's shoulder, raising his other hand for the barkeep. "Here!" he called. "Give this man what he wants, on me!"

The messenger turned, surprised—but not at all displeased. He seemed an ordinary man, not the skulking kind of schemer Crispin often kept around him. He might have been forty years old, probably a husband and a father. But Diego noted weariness around his eyes.

"Thank you, friend," the messenger said. "To what do I owe this generosity?"

"Nothing at all, except for the king's coronation," Diego answered. "This is a happy night for all."

"You're not from here," the man said—but again, he seemed genuinely curious, not suspicious. "Come with the guests from the Southlands, did you?"

The implication caught Diego off guard—but of course, it would seem to this man that he had come as part of Crispin's retinue. A very helpful seeming, that.

"I did," Diego said with a half-smile. It wasn't untrue. "That's why I picked you out. I saw you talking to the High Elder at the party up on the hill."

The messenger flushed a little. He looked like a man with a bad taste in his mouth who didn't want to spit it out for fear of giving offense.

"He's a powerful man, the Elder," the messenger said. "It were a stroke of luck I was sent here on a night like tonight—I'm not from Loren, you see. I come from the outlying towns. The Elder has business everywhere, as I suppose you know, and I was sent to bring him word of some of it. A lucky thing, a lucky thing."

But he didn't look like he felt lucky. So when his drink arrived, Diego encouraged him to drink deep—and quickly bought him another when he'd finished. The more the revelry around them roared, growing louder and looser, the more the messenger seemed to sink into unhappiness.

When he'd downed three of the big tankards, Diego said casually, "A shame to bring such evil tidings on a night like this, isn't it? And you a decent man."

The messenger banged his fist on the bar. "Damn right," he blurted. "Damn right. We should all be celebrating! We should be drinking and happy! And I have to think about ruins and … burning. Damn schemes."

Diego leaned forward a little, bringing his ear closer and lowering his voice. "What ruins? What burning?"

The man immediately withdrew a little, casting Diego a suspicious glare. "That in't for you to know."

"I mean no harm by it," Diego said. "You and me, we are servants of powerful men. We go where we're told and do what we're told to do. I know, friend. I know all about it."

He tightened his grip on his own tankard of ale—which he'd barely sipped while his companion lost himself in drink. "I tell you, one time, I was told to march out with Crispin's soldiers and roust a nest of dissenters," he said. "I did it too. They killed them all. They were good people."

He was taking a chance, but his instincts told him it would work. His voice cracked. He didn't like to talk about what he'd done—but it was the reason he was here now. Risking so much, even his own family, to oppose

Crispin. "Good people, women and children too. But it didn't make any difference. The soldiers just killed them and burned the place. A tavern like this one."

The messenger shook his head woefully and drained the last of his ale. Diego immediately signaled for another, and the barkeep was quick to comply. The messenger eagerly grabbed up the new tankard, clutching it like life. "It were no tavern this time," he said, "nothing so decent. What do you think—they was meeting in a cave, down in the old coal mines. Set it all up with their charms and their superstitions. Gave me the willies, it did."

Diego's blood ran cold. "Who were they?" he asked quietly. But he already knew the answer.

"Nest of Sacramenti rebels," the man said. "Been there who knows how long. Elder's men found them this time, though. Burned the place out, like you said. Killed a lot of them, I think."

Diego swallowed hard. It was bad enough when it was Tremblers. But Sacramenti … his own people …

"The High Elder ordered the attack?" he asked.

"Seems so," the man said. "I don't rightly know it all, but some of his men came through a few days before, and when the deed was done they sent me off to report it." He shook his head again. "It's a bad business, I say. Excuse me—I don't mean to speak against your master or your fellowmen neither. But it's a bad business, this turning people on each other. It weren't soldiers did the burning and looting here, it were villagers. Some of my wife's kin. Some of mine. Did they do it for fear? For greed? I don't know."

Diego stood abruptly. He patted his new friend on the shoulder. "Drink deep, friend," he said. "And safe travels home. Between you and me—maybe get out of the elder's employ."

The man nodded as though Diego had said something incredibly wise. Tears appeared in his eyes. "Maybe I'll do that," he said. "Maybe so."

Diego left the tavern deeply troubled. Carlos had been right to send him after the man. It bode trouble if the High Elder was sowing the same kind of enmity and persecution here that he was in the mainland—and without Henry's awareness, apparently. On the other hand, when he learned of it, the new king might be more likely to make a public alliance with Carlos.

The High Elder's behavior was certainly provocation enough. Diego would seek out John Worthington first thing in the morning and tell him what he'd learned.

Rather than go back to the palace, Diego turned down a side street and began the walk to the house Carlos had rented. It wasn't too far—the courtier neighborhoods were all clustered around the palace precincts. The streets were unusually busy. With the night growing later, more and more carriages and cabs clattered over the cobblestones as they drew their lords and ladies home. Drunks and other revelers were happy, and there was little sense of threat in the air. Diego allowed himself to get a little lost in thought.

So he was surprised by the man waiting for him on the steps. He caught sight of him only an instant before the man reached out of the shadows by the door and grabbed his arm.

"Peace," the man said as Diego reached for his knife. "I mean you no harm."

He stepped forward a little, into the light from the streetlamps. To Diego's surprise, he recognized him. He'd met this man in Tempestano.

Adolphus Bure, a deacon of the Puritani kirk and one of Crispin's closest associates.

What in the world—

"I thought it safer to come myself than to trust to a messenger," Bure said in a rushed whisper—as though anyone could hear him. "I don't trust them, any of them."

"What do you want?" Diego asked. His eyes were filled with visions of the massacre in Tempestano. This man had been there. He had ridden beside Crispin.

"I want to talk to you, and to the young lord," Bure said.

"Talk," Diego said.

"To *both* of you," Bure insisted. He looked both ways as though he expected someone to sneak up on them. But the streets were the same cheerful, unthreatening mix they had been all night.

"I can't talk here," he said. "Not now. But tomorrow. Meet me under the Palace Bridge at midmorning tomorrow. The Elder is meeting with others; I can get away. Both of you come."

"Why should we?" Diego asked. "You're here now; you can talk to me. I won't put the young lord in danger."

"I don't know you," Bure said. "Forgive me. You've betrayed your lord before, I know. And you've betrayed the High Elder. I want to talk to both of you."

Angry, Diego bit back a retort. He couldn't deny what the man said, as much as he wanted to—but he *did* deny the implications of it.

"What is this about?" he asked again. "You may not trust me, but I have no reason at all to trust you. Give me a reason we should come to you tomorrow."

The deacon dropped his voice so low that Diego could barely hear him. "Because I took a risk in coming here tonight," he said. "And I know things. Things you need to know. Things the king of Angleland needs to know. I'm tired of all this, Captain. I'm tired of being part of it. I want to talk. Tell the conde I know things about his sister. I know things about yours too."

Diego grabbed the man's arm and squeezed hard enough to cut off his circulation. "What about my sister?" he asked.

The man yelped and tried to pull his arm away, to no avail. "Let me go," he said. "Let me go or this deal is off."

Diego released him immediately. "Tell me what's going on."

"Tomorrow," Bure said, brushing himself off with an attempt at decorum. "Tomorrow under the bridge. You and the conde, or I say nothing." To Diego's surprise, the deacon met his eyes with an intense stare. "I thought I was serving God, Captain. I thought it was all justified because it was done for the right reasons. But I begin to see differently, and I'm tired of it. Come to the bridge, and I'll tell you everything."

He left, disappearing in the reveling crowds. Diego watched him go with his head spinning. He wasn't sure how the encounter had turned so quickly—how he'd gone from having the upper hand to having little choice but to do as the deacon said.

But he was fooling himself. He'd been the stronger, the more apt to be violent. That didn't give him the upper hand.

It was after midnight when Carlos left the coronation party. He was a little unsteady on his feet—too much wine over the course of the night, too much perfume in the air, too much rich food swimming in his stomach while music and dancing overwhelmed his remaining senses. He wished Diego had come back but was not surprised he hadn't.

What had been the point of all this, anyway? Showing friendship to Henry, he supposed—but for what? The king wasn't going to help him take back Tempestano. He was a pleasant, friendly, wealthy man, and he would probably give Carlos a permanent place in his court if he asked for it. But he wasn't going to ally himself against the High Elder, who had been at the party all night long and talked to every last truly important person in the room.

Carlos, by contrast, had been the target of young women and a few wise old friends who rescued him from time to time. He had no real influence and no real respect.

"Carlos," a voice said, interrupting his exit. He paused on the marble steps leaving the place and turned. John Worthington made his way down the steps toward him, staff in hand. He leaned on it a little, letting it support him.

"It was good that you were here," Worthington said. "Don't be discouraged. The king will come around. Come back tomorrow, show your face at court again—don't let your cause slip his majesty's mind. I will talk to him again. Crispin may have overplayed his hand tonight—he was trying too hard to make allies. Henry won't like that."

Carlos nodded. Outside, the air cleared his head a little. So did John's unwavering sobriety and friendship. Perhaps things weren't as hopeless as they seemed.

"I feel so far from home," Carlos said. "I'm here, dancing and eating and drinking, and my people are under influences I don't even know. What's happening in Tempestano tonight? Who rules? Who is safe, who is in danger? I don't even know."

"You didn't abandon them," John said. He seemed to understand. "You came here to seek out help on their behalf. I'll do all I can to see that you succeed. Take heart. You're closer than you think."

Swallowing a lump in his throat, Carlos nodded. Serena's voice, strangely silent of late, spoke out of his memory. *Hang on to hope, Carlos. As long as the Fire burns, there is always hope.*

CHAPTER 15

The Wilderness—The New World

Major Carson gave orders to pack up and move out a few hours after dawn. He'd allowed a longer than usual period of rest, which Linette received with thanks despite her misgivings. It had been an oppressively cold night, and she had not slept well. She helped with chores around the camp—carrying buckets of water from a nearby spring, cooking up a brace of white rabbits brought in by one of the soldiers—with gratitude for the chance to move and do something productive that wasn't marching.

They had been walking for days. At night they kept warm enough to stay alive by virtue of their furs and blankets and campfires, and on especially cold nights some of the men heaped up snow around them to serve as sheltering walls. Even so, Linette worried about frostbite in her feet and hands and was convinced she would never be fully warm again. She didn't light her vines, though they would have afforded a little warmth if she had. The sunlight was too slanting and scarce to reenergize her effectively; she would weaken herself too much for the journey.

Fear drove her onward nevertheless. There was no question of turning back when her daughter needed her.

As they trudged down the white and silent trails of the river valley, Linette noticed whispers and anxious glances among some of the men.

Amos wasn't far. She beckoned him over. He carried a long musket in his hands.

"Is something wrong?" she asked him.

"Nothing too serious," he said. "We're being tailed by a pack of wolves." He saw the alarm on her face and hastened to add, "They're being cautious, hanging back. They're *just* wolves. We should be all right."

Linette nodded, wishing she hadn't asked. She knew wolves were smart, that they were unlikely to attack while the odds were against them—and a whole column of soldiers constituted very bad odds. At night, the wolves wouldn't come too near fire. But she understood better now why the column had compacted a little. No one wanted to be seen as a straggler who would be easy to pick off.

Just a few men ahead of her, Almon walked in shackles. He was still on his feet, still miraculously strong and healthy again. Too bad they couldn't put *him* in the back and let the wolves get him, she thought. She rebuked herself for the thought immediately. Almon was still a man. She should want him to be saved, not slaughtered.

Not for the first time, she breathed a word of thanks that New Cranwell was not much more than a week's journey along the river. They were halfway there already, or at least they should be.

A few hours later, one of the soldiers fired a musket in the air. Warning the wolves to stay back.

Once, Linette thought she saw a splash of grey fur along a rocky ridge to their left.

She must have sped up her pace without realizing it, because suddenly she was walking alongside Almon. He glanced over at her. She tried to ignore him.

"You remind me of my mother, you know," he said.

The words were so unexpected Linette nearly tripped over her feet. The soldiers before and behind Almon looked interested but said nothing.

"You look like her," he continued. "She had hair like yours. Eyes like yours. Sometimes in my fevers I thought you *were* her."

She didn't even know why she asked. Did she feel some pressure, out here in the wilderness, to make polite conversation? "What happened to her?"

He grinned. The grin was wolfish, grim and frightening. "She went mad. My whole childhood, she was going mad. She was like an animal. Everyone talked about it. Everyone looked at me like I would be next. Do you know what that kind of shame is? You spend your whole life trying to rise above it. Wanting people to see something else in you. But all they see is your crazy mother, writing on the walls, clawing at her own face, throwing things at you."

Linette forced herself to look at him. "I—I'm sorry."

He bared his teeth again, but this time there was no hint of a smile in it. "I hated my mother. She hated me."

I'm sure that's not true, Linette wanted to say. Why? Why defend him, even to himself? Because maybe, if he thought someone had loved him, he wouldn't be so unhinged now?

Or because she was afraid to see her daughter. Afraid of how Beth would react to her. What kind of mother gave her child up?

Another musket crack came from behind them, and Amos jogged up beside her, casting a threatening glance at Frederick Almon as he did. Once again Linette felt gratitude and warmth at his presence. Out here, he didn't seem like the gawkish secretary of Jerusalem Valley. He felt like a frontiers-man, and a friend.

"Nothing to worry about," Amos said. "It's just a warning."

The Boglands, Somewhere in Time—The Old World

The Tremblers met in a dusty, disused storehouse. It contained none of the trappings of a traditional kirk: no pews, no pulpit, no candles or stained glass. Old, empty barrels had to be rolled out of the way; crates were pushed together to make seats for those who couldn't stand or sit on the floor. The air was stale, and mouse droppings rimmed some of the cor-ners. A small but dedicated cleaning crew had tried to scrub it up, but the space was large and the dust so persistent they could only do so much. As a result, the floor in the center of the room was so clean it gleamed in patches, and the crates were free of cobwebs and layers of dirt, but the corners and far edges and high ceiling rafters still bore all the marks of neglect.

In the electrified *feeling* that charged the room, none of this mattered.

There were easily two hundred people crammed into the storehouse, perhaps three. Many were on their faces, weeping. Others trembled violently and cried aloud, wringing their hats in their hands. Others held their hands high and poured forth words of worship and praise. Some sang. Some prayed. Some were silent.

All were in the grip of the feeling—whatever it was.

Jacques had never seen anything like it. Neither, he thought, had the two students who edged their way cautiously into the room, not far from him. Both seemed troubled. Herman looked intrigued as well—perhaps hopeful. Crispin's expression was more guarded.

Rather than follow them here, Jacques had obtained information about the meeting and gone ahead. They would not likely notice him this way.

They spotted open seats toward the front—if "front" really applied in a gathering like this. There was a wooden rail stretched across the far end of the rectangular space where many people were kneeling in prayer, and three men who might have been preachers paced on the other side of it, speaking their prayers aloud. They were dressed simply, as were most of the people gathered here. There were not many strong, not many wealthy. These were mostly simple folk—craftsmen and tradesmen, farmers. Men and women mingled near the front, though toward the back of the room, they had separated into different sides.

Jacques couldn't hear Melrose and Crispin speaking to one another, though he saw them leaning close and whispering. They seemed to be arguing. But he was too far to make out the sound, especially in this din, and—

Wait.

The air seemed to move, to shift around him. His surroundings grew dimmer, and he realized something with a sense of shock: He was not here. He had never been here.

This had never happened to him.

He had learned of Melrose and Crispin's intention to attend a Trembler meeting, had even found out where it would take place, but he had chosen not to go there himself.

He did not understand this. But it seemed to him that if he were not here—not really—then the laws of noise and distance should not apply. He should be able to hear them.

And so he could.

"We should go," Crispin said. "This is madness."

"But is it?" Herman said. "Can't you *feel* it, Joseph? There's a power here. Almost as if the Son himself walks in our midst."

Crispin crossed his arms and looked unhappily around him. "The only thing I feel is overworked emotion. They're pushing themselves into a frenzy. That's not God, Herman."

"Let us just stay a little while," Herman said. "It can't hurt us to pray. And I would like to hear the preachers."

Joseph Crispin heaved a sigh. Once again Jacques's world shifted—jarringly this time. Looking at the tall, broad student beside Herman, he expected to see evil. He expected the sigh to be one of mockery or anger. But it was neither. Crispin seemed genuinely uncomfortable, yet at the same time, genuinely tolerant of his friend.

And when he bowed his head, folded his hands on his knees, and started to pray in the midst of the Tremblers, Crispin seemed *real.*

This image, held alongside one he knew well—the image of a scheming, power-hungry hypocrite—threatened to fracture Jacques's mind.

In that place of tension, as two sides of his mind seemed to move farther and farther from one another, he heard a woman's familiar voice say, *"And still you sleep on. We could use you awake, you know. I could use your advice." She sighed.* He strained to see her, as his surroundings grew dimmer, cast in dark, shadowy tones. Jacques sensed cold, a flurry of movement—people speaking to each other, packing, getting ready to move. She was right there, just beyond sight—but he couldn't push through the darkness to make her image come clear.

The darkness blinked away. He sat on a wooden crate in a packed-out, noisy room, under rafters thick with dust and cobwebs.

One of the preachers was holding forth at the front of the room, behind the altar rail. He held a book in his hands and thumped it as he spoke. His voice rose above other noise; many in the room were still praying aloud or weeping. In his frustration, Jacques stood—as though he could propel himself back to that other world, where the woman needed him. Where *many* needed him. He couldn't remember why, or who they were or where, but he knew that he needed to return to them.

In the periphery of his vision, invisible figures swathed in white moved. Beyond them were others, waiting with outstretched claws and hands, hollow and leaf-like. Shades … *demons* …

That world too disappeared, and Jacques was fully back in the storehouse with its Trembler meeting. His mind reeled as he tried to grasp just how many parallel realities he was experiencing at once.

Then it all numbed away. He was back. He was … here. He was on his feet, but no one paid him any mind. What before had seemed chaotic now seemed like a rhythmic swell, a rise and fall of prayer that wove together like a song. Even the words of the preacher beat in time with it.

Time had passed. Melrose and Crispin were at the makeshift altar rail. Melrose was on his knees, tears streaming down his face.

Crispin lay prostrate on the floor, trembling. His hands were outstretched in front of him.

Reality grew porous again. Jacques saw the figures in white, standing and kneeling along the length of Crispin's body, tending to him, guarding him. He saw them without seeing them, the way one might see a wisp of cloud passing over the moon.

The Trembler gathering did not break up for days. Nor did Crispin get up from the floor.

In his outstretched hands, a seed began to grow.

Jacques heard the words spoken to Crispin's spirit as surely as if they thundered in the air: *This seed is for the healing of your soul and for many. Take it to the New World and plant it in the place that I will show you.*

At last Crispin rose. His whole body trembled; tears had washed his face till he seemed transfigured. In Trembler fashion, he shared aloud the words he had heard in his heart.

The others confirmed it and praised and worshiped the Creator.

Herman Melrose stood next to his friend, trembling and shining like a man newly washed clean. He beamed with pride and awe at Crispin's words and the task he had been given—a task that had literally manifested in his hands.

Overcome, Jacques, too, worshiped.

Jerusalem Valley—The New World

While the settlers packed, Serena took a hunting knife and went into the meeting house to cut away the vines. Several of the warriors helped her—or rather, she helped them. She was still too weak and exhausted to do much, but she refused just to sit and watch while everyone else had work to do. The vines clung to every knot of wood and crack in the walls and floor. They curled around rafters and windows, pulling the frames away from the wall. They formed an intricate web, especially thick and intricate over the sleepers, whom they protected.

Serena shook her head. She didn't know whether to be proud or appalled. She'd saved lives, there was no doubt about it. But she didn't understand how—she only remembered reaching inside herself for some way to protect the sleepers, to protect Jacques and Eben and Josiah as she'd promised. And she'd made an incredible mess.

She only lasted ten minutes before she had to sit down and take a break. She positioned herself next to Jacques, as usual. She spoke to him a little, got no response, and pulled the seed out of her pocket and cupped it in her hands.

Linette's seed.

It was about the size of a small pinecone, encased in a hard green rind. It fit neatly into the palm of her hand. It glowed slightly, giving off a pale green light. Serena gazed at it like it might give up its secrets if she did.

It gave up nothing.

Nothing at all.

The warriors hacked at vines around her, pulling them down and bundling them up to be removed from the room. The settlers would pack in here tonight, sharing the space with Serena and the sleepers. Who knew if it was really safer that way—maybe all they were doing was creating a convenient target for their enemies. But they could hope for strength in numbers.

Serena ran her thumb over the bumpy surface of the seed. Drawing up what little strength she could access, she put the seed back in her pocket, stood swaying to her feet, and went back to hacking at vines. So much power, and so little at the same time. She could dismiss shades with a command, stop wolves in their tracks, fill a whole building with vines. Yet she couldn't wake the sleepers or unlock the mystery she held in her hands.

If this is a joke, she told the Fire Within, *I don't think it's funny.*

The Fire made no answer.

That night she sat sleeping against the wall in the corner. Jacques slept near her, and Eben Axel beside him. Josiah curled up next to Serena and fell asleep with his head on her shoulder. Other settlers packed into the space, and last of all came the Outsiders. They stood guard at the door. Serena caught a fleeting glimpse of the wolves prowling outside—keeping their own kind of watch. She shivered.

No Machkigen came to trouble them that night. But Serena hardly slept. She passed the night in the warm, crowded haze of the room, seeing the strange crowd gathered there as through a glass darkly.

They set out at first light as promised, joined by other settlers and River People from the governing house. They formed a loose column. The River People and wolves went first, disappearing into the woods ahead of them— but Serena knew they wouldn't be far. Led by Naamucksha, they went ahead to scout the path and keep it safe. Then came some of the armed Puritani, then settlers with their belongings bundled and packed onto horses, mules, and a few cows. Wetëndeis and some of the warriors had gone into the woods before dawn and come back with sapling poles they used to construct litters for the sleepers. Some could be carried, others pulled behind the animals. Jacques was loaded onto a litter behind John Hopewell's mule while Serena stood by, fretting. Jonathan's little dog, Rusty, darted around, running between litters and through clusters of people, until Jonathan whistled and called him over.

Another group of River People brought up the rear. These would stay closer to the column.

Ezekiel, wearing a warm coat and boots that Big John had given him, held the mule's lead. He patted the animal on the neck and looked over at Serena with concern. She gave him a wan smile.

"I'm all right," she said. "Or I will be." She muttered the last, but he heard her. Like her, he hadn't slept much the night before. He'd been sitting on the other side of Eben, and he and Serena were well aware of each other all night. They'd formed a silent bond, sitting company with their backs against the wall.

"What do *you* think of all this?" she asked him, suddenly ashamed that she hadn't asked him earlier.

He clapped his gloved hands together against the cold. "I think I can't rightly believe I'm headin' back to the fort not days after leavin' it. There aren't words for some kinds of foolery. But we don't have much choice now, do we?"

He glanced over at Josiah, who was nearby, hovering around his father—who was being carried between two of the settlers.

"Just concerns me for the boy, that's all," he continued. "They freedmen, Eben and Josiah. But the fort didn't observe that distinction before. Seems hard to take them back. Don't want to see them back in bondage."

"And you?" Serena asked gently. "Aren't you going back to slavery?"

Ezekiel sighed. "The right question might be whether I ever left it. I had a few days free in the woods, chased by soldiers and those monsters. Maybe that's as close as I get."

"Talk to John Hopewell," Serena said. "He'll speak for you—all of you. He'll take your part with the soldiers."

Ezekiel wheezed something that might have been a laugh. "Sure," he said. "If they leave him free himself and don't just throw him behind bars." He shook his greying head. "Don't worry about me, miss."

The column began to move. Serena turned and looked up the river valley with deep trepidation. The clouds overhead were steel-grey. She could see the breath of her friends rising in the air. As the mule jerked into a start, she stretched out her hand to steady the litter where Jacques lay bundled in blankets and furs, still and silent.

They hadn't gone a mile before Ezekiel handed the mule's lead to Josiah and silently fell back to Serena's side. He gave her an arm to lean on, and she did so gratefully. They walked like that for a little while, then Ezekiel said quietly, "Best you ride."

"But the mule is already pulling Jacques."

"Me and Josiah will carry him," Ezekiel said. "Won't we, boy?"

Josiah nodded, standing as tall as he could.

Serena doubted Josiah's ability to carry Jacques far, even if he did have the energy of youth to make up for his small stature and strength. But she could only nod in return. If she kept trying to walk, she was going to collapse into the snow. Whatever exactly she had done to protect the sleepers back in the meeting house, it had drained more of her strength than she'd realized.

Hoisted onto the mule's bare back, riding precariously with both hands clenched in the animal's mane, she had a clearer view of the valley and the brave column struggling up the river. The River People carried skins full of water they had collected from the spring beneath the Fosters' farm. Wetëndeis's wolves loped near the head of the column, making the animals further back nervous. The Fosters were just ahead of the mule, and Sarah looked back and gave Serena a smile that was meant to encourage her.

It didn't work, not really. Sarah looked exhausted and fearful. They all did.

It wasn't a good choice, going to the fort.

But it was the only one they had.

The Wilderness—The New World

It had been hours since the soldiers last fired a musket to scare back wolves.

Now, a different threat loomed. Clouds, so grey they were almost black, rose in the sky beyond the conifers like a wall. Linette had long since lost track of the time, but she knew it was getting too dark, too fast. A storm built ahead of them, swallowing the sun.

Carson called his men to a halt and fell back to speak in whispers with a few of his men. He spotted Amos and waved him over, apparently asking his opinion about something.

Good idea, Linette thought. Amos might not look much like a frontiersman, but he'd lived out here for years. He knew things about reading skies—reading winter—that the soldiers didn't.

Carson nodded, and a few of the voices grew a bit louder. It seemed they were reaching some kind of consensus.

A few feet ahead of her, Frederick Almon had his head tipped back and was staring up at the gathering darkness. He was making a noise, she realized—a low keening sound that made her skin crawl.

"We're going to camp," Amos said, walking toward her. "Wait out this storm."

She turned to meet him. Then a roaring wind like nothing she had ever heard or felt bore through the line without warning, carrying snow with it. She lost sight of Amos as he disappeared behind a wall of white. Everything went dark as night, and a deafening crack split the air as a bolt of lightning knifed into the ground near Linette's feet. The air crackled and the energy of the strike picked her up and threw her back. She hit the ground hard, breath driven from her lungs, and fought to get back to her feet amid the howling, swirling, blinding darkness.

"Amos!" she screamed.

There was nothing. No answer. She couldn't hear him—or anyone—or see them. She was blind and deaf in the roar. Wind slammed against her, pushing her back again, off her feet. Helpless, she curled up on the ground, hands over her ears, and tried to block out the storm.

But no. She had to find Amos, or Carson, and get to shelter. Staying exposed was death. She thought she heard horses whinnying in terror, but they had no horses. It was only the wind—or creation itself crying out.

Forcing herself onto her feet, Linette raised one arm in front of her face to try to keep the blinding snow out of her eyes, and she staggered in the direction she thought she'd come.

"Amos!" she cried out again. There was no answer. Taking one staggering step after another, Linette kept pushing on. She brushed up against something and reached out for it in the endless white. Her hand found the rough surface of rock. She ducked down and felt her way forward until the rock gave way and a small patch of darkness opened in the storm—she'd found some kind of shelter. She got down to her knees and crawled into it. It wasn't a cave—just a shallow cleft in the rock with enough space for her to get inside. Instantly, things grew quieter. She could still see and hear the storm raging, but she was out of it.

Deafening thunder cracked, shaking the earth. Another bolt of lightning struck, this time illuminating a tall, needled tree in the darkness. Snow swirled around it in a rising funnel. Linette covered her ears and tried just to keep her heart beating. She'd never felt such primal fear.

The light disappeared into darkness and snow, leaving the shape of the tree and the rock overhead etched across her vision. Where were Amos and the others? Had that first blast of lightning—

She shook her head. She couldn't consider that Amos could have been hit—killed in a freak storm. The thought ached inside her with a strength that she allowed herself to acknowledge but had no time to interrogate.

Thunder cracked again. Dirt and clumps of snow showered down in front of her. She pulled her knees closer to her chest and ached wordlessly for rescue. She wanted to pray, but she couldn't choke words out.

From some moment in the past she heard words, in her father's voice, or maybe in Sarah's. *He found him in a desert land, and in the waste howling wilderness.*

Her lips formed one word: "Please."

She had no way of knowing how much time passed. In the roar of the blizzard, time had no meaning. Form and direction ceased to exist. It was the end of the world, with only thunder and lightning to speak into the void and give it shape.

The thunder ceased; lightning no longer split the night. The roar died down, but the wind still blew and the snow still came down. Linette wrapped herself more tightly in her cloak and leaned back against the earthen hollow where she had burrowed beneath the rock. Roots tickled her cheek, an improbable sign of life down here, even if the life they supported was dormant.

Her whole body felt heavy, and her eyes closed on their own.

She wasn't sure what woke her. But she shifted and opened her eyes, looking out on a wall of white. She wasn't buried—the position of the rock had caused the snow to go around her, so she looked out on a hollow in the snow, beyond which snowdrifts rose to three or four feet. She could see the tops of fir trees out beyond, and past them, a blue sky.

Had she slept through the night? Or was it still the same day?

Stillness hallowed everything. She pushed herself forward and crawled out of the hole, struggling to her feet and relieved that she could move and her legs would hold her—that she wasn't frozen solid. The rock and snow all around had insulated her from the worst of the wind and cold.

Straightening, she looked out over the deep snowdrifts. A white rabbit, standing atop the snow on its wide, furred feet, looked back at her, ears and nose twitching. It watched her for a moment before bounding away. Something else moved in the trees beyond. She stood stock-still, trying to make out what it was. There—grey fur.

Wolves.

Heart pounding, she didn't move. A large grey wolf moved to the edge of the trees and stared back at her. Its ears cocked forward and its eyes fixed on her. She *couldn't* have moved even if she wanted to.

Others moved in the trees behind it. The whole pack was here. She didn't have a gun, only a small knife tucked at her waist.

Still she couldn't seem to pray. Nothing except that one word, and she couldn't voice it—couldn't pull it up any higher than the depths of her heart. *Please.*

She had abandoned the Creator's mission for her.

Why should he help her now?

The wolf opened its mouth and panted, showing off sharp teeth and a long red tongue. Then it tossed its head and bounded away. The other wolves followed.

She let out the breath she hadn't known she was holding.

After waiting an interminably long time, Linette cautiously pushed her way forward through the deep drifts toward the higher ground where the trees were. She needed to find the river—that was her best bet of finding the others. She didn't consciously admit to herself that she might not find them, but she knew deep down that she had to find the river either way. Following it would take her to the sea and New Cranwell, with or without her escort. Failing to find it, and follow it, would mean being lost out here. And that meant death.

The woods were full of wolf tracks in the fresh-fallen snow, and the drifts formed in waves and patterns around the trees, rising in high peaks and troughing in lower pathways where it was easier to walk. Linette followed a trough a short way as it wound through the forest, moving toward a lighter patch of sky where she hoped the trees might thin out and lead down toward the riverbed. But she stopped after climbing a short ridge and realizing it was an illusion—the light simply came through a patch of deciduous trees barren of leaves, not from an opening. She was going deeper into the woods.

A bare rock invited her to sit, so she did, blinking away tears of frustration and fear. Crying would do no good for her or for anyone. And why was she crying, anyway? Because she was lost, because she was alone?

They were bitter tears, and stubborn. They kept falling.

Then a man said, "There you are."

Her head jerked up, and her eyes fixed on the figure leaning with one hand against an elm tree, just across a thick patch of snow.

Her heart sank.

It was Frederick Almon.

He made her way toward her with some effort, the knee-deep snow slowing his steps. His hands were free of his shackles, and he swung them from side to side as he propelled himself toward her.

She wanted to turn and run. But she couldn't move.

Surely any human company out here was better than none.

She didn't believe that.

There was a feverish cast to his eyes as he crossed the clearing and reached the rock where she sat, but he seemed lucid—and relatively human. Maybe she imagined the look she saw there; maybe it was only exertion. He gazed down at her with an expression she couldn't read.

He had a pistol at his belt.

"Where did you get that?" she asked.

He glanced down as though confused. "Oh, this?" he asked, drawing the pistol and waving it in the air. He grinned. "One of the soldiers gave it to me."

That was undoubtedly true. No one else out here was armed. But Linette strongly doubted the gun had been given willingly.

She stood stiffly. "What do you want?"

He waved the gun again, a motion that was deliberately cavalier. "The same thing you do—a path out of this damned wilderness. New Cranwell calls. Shall we head home?"

She eyed him warily. Everything in her told her to turn and run. But she couldn't. She didn't have a chance out here alone. Together, they were more likely to find the others—or be found—*and* more likely to regain the path. Since God wasn't answering her prayers, it seemed she would be forced to make a deal with the devil.

He made it through the snow and climbed onto the sturdier ground beside her, tucking the pistol back into his belt. Maybe she could find some opportunity to get it away from him. She didn't know how to shoot, but even so hers were the safer hands. Waving for her to follow, he led off in the direction she'd come. He seemed confident that he knew where he was going. She didn't share his confidence—but she really had no choice but to share his company.

Grimly, she followed him.

Chapter 16

The Boglands, Somewhere in Time—The Old World

Herman Melrose and Joseph Crispin did not return to seminary for nine full days. They spent most of that time immersed in the Trembler gathering. When the gathering occasionally dispersed—giving way to the desperate need of its attendees for rest and food of a less spiritual kind—they went back to their dormitory but avoided encountering their fellow students and did not return to class.

Jacques shadowed them. It was impossible, what he did—he simply followed them, entered their rooms, listened to them. They neither saw nor heard him. And in his strangely detached moments, he knew that was because he wasn't really there. He had never done this, had never seen these men in such intimate moments.

He was sleeping, he reminded himself in one of his more aware moments. This was a dream.

Nevertheless, all of it had really happened. He who had been called Shadowdancer was a Timewalker now.

The room they shared was simple—two sparse wooden bedframes with straw mattresses on either side of the room; a desk crammed against the end wall between them, a small table with only one chair near the door. A high window, small and square, let in some light from above the desk.

Seven days in, Crispin lay on his bed, knees up, hands and head propped against the headboard. The seed lay on the desk beside his head. He was staring ahead, contemplating things unseen.

"You were right," he said for the thousandth time. "You were so right. It's like nothing I've ever felt, Herman. Like nothing I've ever imagined." His eyes filled with tears—again. "How could we be content with so much wood, hay, and stubble? How, when there is such *Fire* in the Creator?"

Herman, sitting at the table with his hands on his knees, smiled at his friend. He seemed a little more anchored in the present, but his countenance too had changed. He wasn't the same man who had gone into the Trembler meeting hopeful and a little afraid. He was a man whose hopes had been fulfilled and whose fears had been burned away. He held up a cloth bag with a loaf of bread and a small hunk of cheese. "Come," he said. "Eat. You're still flesh and blood, no matter how it feels."

Crispin closed his eyes and breathed out, but he grinned. "Impossible. There's nothing left of me but flame."

He got up after another moment and joined Herman for their small repast. When they had finished they went back into the night, heading back to the Trembler gathering. Once they had left the school grounds well behind, they sang together as they walked.

On the tenth day, they returned to school.

Jacques sat in the back of their classroom, so he saw them come in and thread their way to their desks.

"And so the prodigals have returned!" their professor boomed from the front of the room. "I thought you must have left us and taken ship for the New World, but some of your fellows assured me you occasionally came back at night."

His tone, gregarious at first, gained a sudden edge. "You will stay after class and speak with me."

"Yes sir," Herman said. Crispin reddened but said nothing. His master glared at him. "You are sitting here only by my grace," he said. "I am well within my rights to dismiss you for good. Or do you think it's some light thing to be admitted as a student here?"

"No sir," Crispin muttered. He didn't meet the man's eyes, but his face flushed again and he blurted, "But sir, what we have experienced!"

"I know what you've experienced," the professor said. "You experienced heresy and human foolishness—a demonic farce, if not a front for the Sacramenti."

Crispin looked up, eyes flashing. "It's not so," he said. "We've experienced the Creator's very Fire."

"Another word," his master answered, "and I will dismiss you for good. Do you understand me?"

When class was over, both men stayed behind. They were silent while their master berated them. He turned to asking questions, which Herman answered with complete honesty—though he didn't volunteer any details beyond what he was directly asked. Crispin stayed silent. His manner had turned sullen.

The meeting ended in a stalemate. The professor expressed what great hopes he had for them both. They were gifted, he said, and serious minded. Men who ought to become great and influential pastors in the Puritani kirk. The devil would dearly love to turn them away from the path to which they had been called. If they returned to the heretics, he would be forced to dismiss them from the seminary for good. But he would not relish doing it.

Halfway back to the dorm, Crispin took the seed from his pocket and said, "I should leave. I should go to the sea and take ship for the New World at once."

"It's a bad time of year," Herman said. "You won't find anyone to take you until the weather changes. Stay, friend, and make the most of the opportunity here. I know how you feel; I feel it too. But education will benefit us both, no matter what our ultimate calling."

"I don't want it," Crispin said. "Lessons are so much gravel in my mouth."

Herman lay a hand on his friend's shoulder. "I know," he said. "Wait out the winter. Take ship in the spring."

"And stay away from the Trembler meetings? Do what he commanded us to do? How can we, when we know what riches are there?"

"He said we would be thrown out if we were caught returning to the Tremblers," Herman said. He gave a wry smile. "So we shall have to be more careful not to be caught."

Weeks passed. Both men quickly realized they were being watched constantly. They settled back into their studies—even Crispin.

In the fourth week, Herman left the seminary property after dark. He came back early in the morning, his face glowing. Crispin, hunched over his studies, looked up and nodded to him when he came in. The expression on his face was wistful.

But he didn't do the same.

Spring came, cold but bright. Mud, always so prevalent in the Boglands, grew thicker as ice melted. It made the air pungent with rot and new life. Students tramped through soft earth and dead leaves uncovered by melted snow. It stuck to their boots and flecked their pantlegs.

It was graduation day at the seminary.

Ships had begun leaving for the New World earlier in the spring, but Joseph Crispin had not gone.

In truth, he had not been back to the Trembler meetings either. As time went by, he spoke of his experience there less and less, and took to holding forth in the tavern again, garnering the admiration of the younger students. Herman didn't join him in this, and he seemed saddened by it.

They'd spoken on their way to convocation. Herman was uncharacteristically pushy, wanting to know when Crispin intended to sail. Crispin, as had become his habit lately, was short and evasive in his answers. He still carried the seed—he'd sewn it into the lining of his coat. But it had been a long time since he'd talked of going to the New World.

Jacques watched and listened to them but without any sense of his own location in the scene. Always before he had been standing near a door or sitting on a bench or hiding in a corner. Now he seemed to be a part of the air—nothing and nowhere, yet present. This struck him as naggingly strange because for once, he was sure he was *supposed* to be here somewhere. He had after all spent time in the Boglands, following these two men and watching them; he had been really present in the tavern, he had sometimes really infiltrated the seminary rooms. He was sure he had been at their convocation, though he couldn't remember what had happened there. Or rather, what was about to happen.

They reached the large, solidly built chapel where exercises were to take place. Their fellow students, dressed in robes, buzzed happily. They had worked hard. They had reached the end of their journey. Today they would be laureled with the coveted pieces of parchment that would declare them educated divines.

Their professor, standing in the doorway of the chapel, saw the two coming and jerked his head toward a smaller door to the left. "Herman," he said.

Frowning, Herman shared a puzzled look with Crispin before obediently stepping to the door. His professor ushered him inside.

It was a small, undecorated reading room, empty of people. The professor clasped his hands behind him and looked sternly down at his student— a difficult thing to do, given Herman's size, but the professor shared his height and build and had the weight of authority behind him.

"You may stay for the celebration if you wish, but I think it only fair to tell you that you will receive nothing today. The chancellor has declared you *excommunicare* from this body; all rights and privileges of a student of this school are closed to you."

Herman looked stunned. "But I don't understand."

"You should. Do you think we don't know that you've continued to go off and join yourself with the enemy? With those dissenters who so threaten our holy kirk?"

Herman's expression clouded. "They threaten nothing," he said. "They simply seek to worship the Creator and hear his voice."

"As do you?" the professor asked.

Herman didn't answer, and his teacher glowered at him. "Your silence is answer enough. I hoped you would see the light as your friend appears to have done and return to the fold without disciplinary action. But you didn't, and we cannot in good conscience license you to pastor any Puritani flock. I'm sorry, Herman, but you've brought this on yourself."

Herman nodded slowly. He seemed almost numb. When he spoke, his voice was measured. "You've been aware for some time of where I was going.

You took my tuition gladly enough."

"And educated you for it," the professor said. "You can't complain that we haven't given you what you paid for. You have everything but credentials, and I hope it will do your soul some good. Now. If I were you I would go, rather than endure public questions and shame when you alone are not awarded a diploma."

Herman nodded again. He had leaned back against a small table; now he stood up straight, though he looked as though something heavy sat upon his shoulders. He paused on his way out the door. "Thank you for warning me," he said.

Crispin was waiting for him outside. His black robes billowed around him in a stiff spring breeze; laughter and shouts rose from the students beyond, who were standing in cheerful clusters around the chapel yard, teasing and congratulating one another.

"What was that about?" Crispin asked.

"I've been dismissed from the school," Herman told him. "They won't award me a diploma."

Crispin's face fell. "Oh, my friend."

Herman shrugged like he could make the weight go away. "Their recognition should not matter."

"But it does," Crispin said. His tone was heated. "It does. You've worked for it. You've paid for it. And you're a better educated man than any other in this yard, for you've thought and prayed and read more than any of us. Besides, without credentials—how will you teach? How will you—"

"I won't," Herman said. "But perhaps I should not have expected that I could teach or pastor in a Puritani kirk. I've been too deeply changed."

Crispin set a sympathetic hand on his friend's shoulder, but he seemed to be searching for words. Finally he said, "Perhaps it's not too late. If we go together to the chancellor, make an appeal—"

Herman barked a laugh. "What appeal? He'll question me about the Tremblers, and I'll tell him what I know: that I hear and feel the Fire Within, and I live and move and have my being in him. And then he will congratulate himself for throwing me out."

"But …" Crispin paused and lowered his voice. "My friend, think about what you're doing. Think about all you're throwing away."

"Think about what I've gained," Herman said. He looked sharply at Crispin. "I'm not so sure it's me who's throwing something away. What about you, Joseph? What about the seed you carry? What about your own experience of the Fire?"

Crispin waved his other hand. "It was like nothing I'd ever felt," he said. "I'm glad I felt it—glad I experienced the enthusiasm the Tremblers carry. I don't agree with the elders that they're a danger; when I'm in some position of power, I'll speak up for them. But after all, it was just a feeling."

"You would not have said that three months ago. Three months ago I had to stop you from trying to board a ship in the dead of winter to obey that 'feeling.'"

"You were a good friend to me, preventing me from acting on that impulse."

"Was I? I'm beginning to think I made a terrible mistake. Have you fallen away, Joseph?"

Crispin's eyes flashed. "Fallen away from what? From feelings of devotion? From meeting with enthusiasts? I'm still devoted, Herman. The meetings would have taken too much time away from my studies, and besides—"

"They might have gotten you thrown out," Herman said. Bitterness edged his voice. "Like me."

"I'll speak for you," Crispin said. "I'll argue that they should give you what you're due."

"And you'll tell them the Tremblers are nothing but foolish peasants in the grip of enthusiasm," Herman said. "You'll imply that I only go because I wish to see for myself how the common man desires to worship. That it's all just harmless curiosity."

"I didn't say any of that."

"But it's the only way you could help me. Make them think that you too have been carried away by Tremblerism, and you'll risk your own laurels."

Crispin looked down. "They've already awarded me a place," he mumbled.

"What?" A new note of hurt crept into Herman's voice.

"They asked me three days ago if I would take it. It's a worthy place in the Midlands, a place of influence. I can do a great deal of good there."

Herman nodded. "I see." He reached out and took his friend's hand, then shook it formally. "I wish you all the best," he said. "I think it's better that I don't stay. I don't want to cast a shadow on your joy."

"Come now," Crispin said. "Don't be like this."

"Like what? Like I'm unhappy when my friend turns his back on what he knows is true? When he turns his back on the call of God?"

Crispin's face went red. "You go too far," he said.

"And you aren't going far enough," Herman said. "So you'll go to the Midlands. And that seed? Will it go with you? Sewn up in your jacket? Is that where you were told to plant it?"

Crispin was shaking his head, growing angry now. "Don't tell *me* what I heard," he said. "I was carried away. Overwhelmed by all the—the noise, and the feel in that place. I was hungry and emotional. I don't know what I heard."

"Let me remind you. 'Take this seed to the New World and plant it in the place that I will show you.' Those are the words to which we all bore witness."

"They are the words to which you all gave assent when I spoke them," Crispin snapped. "In an overheated, overcrowded, overwrought atmosphere. I thought then that the words came from the Creator. I'm not so sure now, and I don't know what gives all the rest of you the power to judge one way or another. Certainly I'm not beholden to the Tremblers of the Bogs, or to you. My body and my life are my own."

"But that seed isn't," Herman said.

"It came from me," Crispin said. "It grew from my heart."

"It was a gift from the Fire Within," Herman said.

"And it was given to *me*. I will decide what to do with it. And when." He cooled his voice with some effort, taking on a more conciliatory tone. "Listen, Herman, I'm not saying I won't go. Of course I'll go. Even if that voice was my imagination, it was stronger than anything I've ever heard. I'll go once I've settled into my new position. I'll convince them to spare me for a time. Surely my new congregation will be able to muster up enough missionary zeal to send me off for a few months. But I have dreamed of this for so long. I dreamed of it when we fought, and when we slept in open fields with the bloody wind after battle blowing over our heads. I dreamed of it when we prayed and talked together. You and I both did."

Herman swallowed hard. "I know."

"You may think me cavalier for treating the seed so lightly," Crispin said. "But what about you? What are you throwing away? How many decades of hope, how many years of study? How long has it been since you were convinced the Creator was calling you into the ministry? And now you throw all of that aside?"

"The Fire Within is burning in me," Herman said. "I can't deny it. Not even for this."

He didn't say, *Not even for you.*

The chapel doors swung open; the pupils were called inside. Organ music spilled out, triumphant and inviting.

Crispin turned to go. He took one last look back.

"Goodbye, old friend," Herman said.

It would be years before their paths crossed again.

Mescahannec River, West of Jerusalem Valley—The New World

The whispers began at the front of the line and burned straight back like flame down a fuse; they reached Serena in a flurry of action. Letty brought the news; her parents and brothers were already leading their animals off the trail toward the woods.

"There are Machkigen ahead," she said. "The scouts saw signs of them. They say we're too exposed by the water."

Serena nodded, wishing there was something she could do. Instead she sat atop her bony mule and tried not to fall off as Letty took the mule's lead and pulled the animal after the others. *Machkigen.* Fear gripped her as tightly as she clung to the mule's stiff mane. It had been too much to hope that they could make it to the fort without coming near the enemy. She knew that. She'd hoped for it anyway.

Under cover of the trees, the column of travelers formed up more tightly. Few people said a word, though some whispers continued to run up and down their lines. Serena caught snatches of it and figured out the rest. They had not come into contact with the Machkigen, simply seen signs of them. It was best to keep pressing forward. The woods would slow them but also keep them hidden.

Serena turned and looked behind them, catching sight of some of the River People slipping through the trees. The warriors were arranging themselves in a protective formation around the settlers, both acting as scouts on all sides and also putting themselves first in case of any attack. They still unnerved her, but her old fear of them had given way to gratitude. They didn't have to be here. They could have abandoned the settlers to deal with their own problems, and no one would have blamed them. Instead they were risking their lives to help.

She caught sight of wolves, too, running alongside them.

They moved forward, urged on by the River People on all sides. Despite the trees and the uneven footing, they picked up their pace. The light in the woods was low; the sun had come down a fair way in the sky; and the forest blocked its thin rays. In the whispers that flitted through the group, Serena caught the idea that the fort was only three more miles ahead. Behind her, Ezekiel and Josiah grunted as they bore their burden over rough ground. Ahead, Smith and his boys held muskets and tomahawks in hand.

Behind them all, two warriors came at a run and burst through the trees. Anasan, Capenokanickon's son, held a spear high and shouted with all his strength: *"Run!"*

It all happened so quickly Serena hardly had time to understand it. Other River People took up the cry, sending the command through the column: "Run! Go! Run for the fort!" Even as they did, Anasan turned his back on the group and dropped to one knee, aiming his spear for the trees. Others took their places beside him, forming a line bristling with spears and arrows, facing the coming attack. Wetëndeis joined them, and her wolves coalesced from the trees, snarling and snapping, lining up beside and between the warriors.

The mule fidgeted and bucked; Serena hardly held on. Ezekiel, wild-eyed, looked every way and seemed on the verge of dropping the stretcher where Jacques lay.

"Go!" Serena yelled at him. "Get to the fort!"

Her heart smote her. What kind of orders was she giving them—an old man and a boy, carrying a paralyzed man. They couldn't run. They could barely keep up a steady walk.

But Ezekiel nodded sharply to the boy behind him, and both adjusted their grip on the stretcher and jogged after the other settlers, who were breaking into confused clusters, some surging forward, some freezing where they stood. Several animals were abandoned as their owners dropped their leads and obeyed the urging of the River People to flee.

Jonathan Applegate stood conflicted and frozen in place. He looked toward the line of warriors forming at the rear, and his jaw worked. He held a tomahawk in one hand and a pistol in the other. He moved to join them.

But Smith Foster stopped him with a hand on his chest and a stern shake of his head. "We need you," he said.

Jonathan opened his mouth to protest, but no word came out. He stood another moment, visually torn. Then he sheathed the tomahawk in its leather holster, grabbed Letty by the hand, and ran with her and the Fosters. They left their animals behind.

Watching his choice somehow made Serena's for her. She slipped off the mule before it could kick her off—and stumbled toward the rear.

She took a knee next to Wetëndeis, who acknowledged her presence with a wordless nod. A short spear lay on the ground next to Capenokanickon's daughter; instead of a weapon, she held a waterskin in her hands, her fingers ready to loose the leather ties that held it closed at the neck. Serena raised her empty hands, fingers outstretched.

They faced into the implacable forest.

The first of the enemy burst into view. A huge dog, its fur red and patched with scales, bounded toward them. Behind it, two men in green warpaint charged straight toward their line.

Serena fixed her eyes on the bounding dog, pushed her hands forward, and yelled, "Out, creature of the dark!"

At the same moment, Wetëndeis dipped her hand into the skin and came up with a handful of water that she flung at the beast, which was nearly on them. The dog went down, and Wetëndeis leapt up and ran toward the warriors, throwing handfuls of water into the face of one even as he engaged Anasan spear to spear. The spear shafts cracked against each other, the man's painted face twisted as the water hit it, and he sputtered and staggered back in confusion. Serena, too weak to get on her feet and throw herself into the melee, stretched out her hands toward the man and did the only thing she knew how to do—she addressed another shade and commanded it to go.

As she did, the scene before her eyes seemed to waver. She saw, as through the surface of water, glowing eyes glaring back at her from a dark and shriveled face. The thing drew back—but then she realized there were more of them.

Many more of them.

Serena blinked despite herself, and the vision vanished. But only the vision. The shades, she knew, were still there. Surrounding, menacing, and hating her and her little band of defenders with every fiber of their being.

More warriors were coming out of the woods, all of them showing telltale signs of the terrible disease that turned men into monsters. Anasan and the other warriors cut them down with spear and arrow and grappled with those men they couldn't stop. One bowled a warrior entirely over, and Wetëndeis—still throwing water everywhere she could—in desperation upended her entire skin on the man's head.

He spluttered, shook, spasmed away from Anasan—and let out a long, shuddering breath. He lay still.

Serena kept pointing and trying to cast the spirits away, but her voice was hoarse and she didn't know if she was reaching them. She couldn't tell if the monsters fighting them were doing so under the power of the demons or out of their own volition. Was it possible to release men who didn't want to be set free?

Out of water, Wetëndeis had snatched up her spear and fought alongside the men now.

Serena shook her head. What kind of crazy woman used healing water as a *weapon?*

A brave one, she decided, and one with faith.

The attack ended almost as soon as it had begun. Some of the enemy lay fallen; others had retreated into the woods. Panting, bloodied, the warriors stood with their weapons in hand, scanning the edge of the forest for more. Serena still knelt behind them—even charged with the adrenaline of battle, she hadn't managed to get to her feet.

Slowly, Wetëndeis edged back to the Machkigen she'd felled and nudged him with her toe. He grunted—like a man snoring deeply—but didn't move.

She whistled through her teeth. "It's not good enough," she said. "He's asleep. What happens when he wakes up?"

She looked down at the empty waterskin on the ground near him and shook her head. Serena read frustration in the lines of her body, in the tone of her voice.

"The sacred spring should have power to heal, not just cast into sleep. Something has weakened the water."

As though she herself were waking up, Serena said slowly, "Or else it needs something to feed the spring."

Wetëndeis looked at her and waited.

"Something like this?" Serena said, and pulled the seed out of her pocket. She held it up, its faint green glow making the air around it shimmer.

Wetëndeis waited.

This wasn't the place for a conversation like this. It certainly wasn't the time. But the idea had hold of Serena, and it wouldn't let go. And the River People, tense, ready for another attack, listened.

"It was growing in the water, on an island. Linette said it had to be planted again, somewhere else. And I've seen a place—in my dreams, in visions. A lake with an island. The sound of thunder or of … of drums."

"The New Creation Place," Wetëndeis said.

Serena turned and stared at her. "What?"

"I have seen this place too," Wetëndeis said. "And we know it, from our stories. When Creator made the world, the air was filled with the music of drums and the beat of Creator's heart. In the New Creation Place, they can still be heard."

"Then that is where the seed must go," Serena said. "I'm sure of it. If we plant it there, healing will come. Something strong enough to counteract all of this death and disease. All of this madness." She looked at them pleadingly. "It's a real place? Not just a dream?"

What kind of question was she asking—she, whose whole life had been staked on the things she heard with her inner ears and saw with the eyes of her heart? What did it even mean to ask whether something was "real," when her dreams were the most real things she knew?

But Wetëndeis answered simply, "It is in the west. My father took me there when I was a child."

"Can you take me there?" Serena asked.

The question was broader than the woman who stood looking back at her. It encompassed Anasan as well, and the others—this small band of people who had already given so much to save their neighbors.

And to save their own world, Serena realized. The home they loved. The wolves and the animals. Each other, most of all.

"We will take you," Anasan said. "But first we must keep our promise to the settlers. We must find allies to fight the Machkigen."

As though she could see them, as though she carried them within her, Serena felt the flight of the settlers with every beat of her heart. She felt their struggle to carry the sleepers, their breathless fear, their relentless push through the woods and the snow toward Fort Collins and safety.

And she heard Jacques speaking to her from somewhere beyond sight, beyond hearing.

"Serena, nothing matters more than this. You must give your all to preserve the seed—not the one that Linette entrusted to you only, but the seed of the people of the valley. They too have been entrusted to you. Don't abandon them."

"But how can I help them?" she asked. "I have always been driven by pas-

sion, but passion escapes me now. I don't know what to do or how to do it. I don't even know who I am, here, in this place. I'm carrying a seed that belongs to someone else and fighting to realize a dream that has nothing to do with me."

"This isn't about passion," Jacques said. "It's about duty."

"But I'm not like you," Serena said. "I'm a new thing in a New World, and I don't know how to act or be or—"

"You are not a new thing," Jacques said. "What has been birthed in you is old, Serena, very old. You stand in an ancient line. Be faithful to it."

"But I'm not like you," she protested again.

"You are," he said. She could feel his eyes gazing at her, strangely ancient in their own way, kind, but unrelenting. "You are."

"Come!" a voice in the real world said urgently. "We must go!"

The voice jolted Serena back to the present even as strong arms reached for her and Anasan hoisted her onto his back like a child. Wolves circled around his feet. Wetëndeis nodded as though she were pleased by the sight.

The other warriors peeled out of the clearing first, running after the settlers. Anasan loped after them.

If Serena had been given a mandate—*don't abandon those entrusted to you*—she knew with sudden and bracing clarity that she did not carry it alone.

Chapter 17

Loren—The Old World

The air beneath the Palace Bridge in midmorning was damp and foul smelling. Diego waited with his arms crossed, trying to contain his own nervous energy. He had come early, insisting that Carlos join him later, once he'd had time to make sure it wasn't a trap. He stood in the shadows and the muck at the edge of the city, looking across the river toward the manicured palace grounds on the other side. He knew the deacon wouldn't come from there—the man wasn't going to wade through the river to reach him; he'd cross the bridge and double back. But his gaze kept wandering there regardless. The palace represented all they had come here for: the seat of power, the hope of help.

Maybe now they would finally get it.

Or maybe they were about to be betrayed.

He heard the deacon coming before he saw him—he might have been Crispin's crony for years, but he hadn't mastered stealth. Diego turned slowly to regard the man as he stumbled down the riverbank toward the base of the stone abutment where they were to meet. Bure had wrapped himself in a cloak that flapped behind him as he came. Diego scanned the bank behind him—they were alone.

Bure reached him, out of breath, and alarm filled his broad features. "Where is the conde?" he asked. "I told you both to come."

"He'll be here," Diego said. "We felt it best to be cautious. You can understand."

Bure nodded and rubbed the top of his head. "I can," he said. "I can. Forgive me. I'm nervous."

Diego found the man's lack of guile disarming. For the first time, he started to thinking that meeting with him had been a good idea.

"Will he come soon?" Bure asked, eyes darting from side to side.

"He will," Diego said. "Once I've signaled him."

Casually, he stepped out from beneath the shadow of the bridge and took a small mirror from his pocket. He angled it to catch the sun, causing it to flash three times, then tucked it back into his pocket and took his place against the abutment once more.

Minutes later, Carlos stepped off the bridge and made his way down the slope. He joined the other two and wrinkled his nose against the smell. He greeted Bure with a nod—no words. Diego could see the tension in his friend's whole body. The last time these men had seen each other was at the massacre in Tempestano.

Bure seemed to make the same connection. He ducked his head in shame and said, "My lord. Please accept my great sorrow."

"Did you know?" Carlos asked.

Bure looked up at him, questioning. The young lord's eyes flashed back.

"Did you know what he intended to do? That he had ordered his soldiers to kill the Tremblers when he found them?"

"I—" Bure swallowed. "I could have guessed it. I won't waste time trying to defend myself. I have spent years convincing myself I was doing God's work. I can't do it anymore. Crispin has to be stopped."

"Why tell us this?" Diego asked.

Bure looked suddenly eager. "You have the new king's ear, do you not? You can gain his help. Tell him what I tell you. Crispin is not invincible no matter what he thinks. If King Henry will oppose him, others can be convinced to do so as well. Others in the South, especially—if you will lead them."

He reached for a satchel over his shoulder and opened it, displaying a collection of rolled parchments, some of them sealed. "Letters," he said. "Proof that what I say is true."

"And what do you say?" Diego asked. "What do you want us to tell Henry?"

"Tell him that Crispin intends to bring him under his control," Bure said. "He'll do it by stirring up hatred and dissent in Angleland. He's doing it already. Months ago, when he knew the old king was ailing, he spent spies to find Sacramenti enclaves and resurrect old fear and resentment of them. He primed villages all over this island to erupt in violence just after Henry took the throne."

Diego nodded slowly. "It's already happening," he said. "I learned of just such a conflict last night. But what good does that do for Crispin?"

"Plenty," Bure said, the shame in his face giving way to anger. "This is how he works, always. If he can find nests of dissenters—Tremblers or Sacramenti—he can easily convince the people that they are being plotted against. That dissent means conspiracy and betrayal. He can accuse the local kirk authorities—your friend John Worthington—of complicity, or at least of being too weak to do anything about the 'problem.' He sends his own men in to strengthen the local resistance, and then he takes over. All the time, he preys on the fears of the people to give himself more influence with them. Eventually he becomes so powerful not even the civic leaders can stand against him. You know this for yourself."

Carlos nodded. It was what had happened in Tempestano.

"The more he grinds dissenters under his heel, the more they resist and grow. The more numerous and passionate they become, the more the local people fear them and believe the rumors Crispin spreads. It all gives him more power. He doesn't create enmity or fear. He just feeds it, and then feeds off it."

A foul taste was growing in Diego's mouth. Pressed, he might have described Crispin's rise to power in just this way. It was no secret that the High Elder commanded the respect and resources he did precisely because he had enemies—*because* there were people for him to fight and keep under, according to the will of the people. The princes could not refuse to help him without risking rebellion and unrest in their precincts. But hearing it all described as so baldly deliberate—even intentionally manufactured—made him sick. It wasn't a game Crispin played. Real lives had been ruined and lost.

"Tell the prince—the king, I mean—that Crispin fears him. This island has always been too independent. He is working hard to undermine Henry. In the New World too. Show the king these letters; they will confirm everything. If Henry can act now, cut off the unrest before it spreads too far, he may be able to turn it all back on the High Elder's head."

"What about the New World?" Carlos asked. "You told Diego you knew something about Serena. Does this have to do with her?"

Bure's face darkened, and his voice lowered. "What is happening in the New World is evil such as I've never seen," he said. "I am more ashamed than I can tell you to have been part of it." He looked from Carlos to Diego, as though weighing whether to go on—whether he could trust these men with what he had to say.

"He sent Serena to the New World," Bure said. "She didn't know it—it was a plot, carefully calculated. He sent an Imitator with her. He intended to have Herman Melrose murdered and frame them both for it, then see that they were executed before they could ever return to tell their stories. He wants to undermine the existing government and kirk in New Cranwell, too—make room for more direct control on his part."

Carlos was pale, but he didn't look surprised. Crispin had told him as much himself.

"His plan was insane," Carlos said. "He couldn't possibly control so much from across the sea."

"I thought so too, but now I fear he has succeeded. He knows human nature better than you can imagine. He knows how to manipulate it. And he must have had an agent already in the New World, someone who would intercept Serena and the Imitator on their way to Melrose's settlement and infiltrate their company—then kill Melrose on Crispin's orders. But that isn't the worst of it."

"What do you mean?" Carlos pushed. "What could be worse?"

"Serena is not the first person he sent to the New World," Bure said. He seemed to be trying to speak through something thick and heavy.

"This other agent—"

"Not him." Bure cut Diego off. He struggled for words. "I don't know how to tell you what I mean. I don't know how to describe it. And I don't know why it took me so long to see the evil for what it is. Without that boatman …"

"Just say it, man," Diego said.

But Carlos held up a hand. "Wait, boatman? What boatman?"

"The one who helped you in the Lowlands," Bure said, sounding miserable. "The one who went after your sister. Not yours—" he cut off Carlos with a raised hand and nodded at Diego. "Yours."

If Diego had felt sympathy for the man, it was gone now. It took all his self-control not to grab the hapless deacon by the folds of his cloak, shove him against the stone wall of the abutment, and threaten to choke the news out of him.

Bure shook his head from side to side, like a much older man might when in the grip of confusion. "I'm sorry," he said. "I'm not making sense."

"That's right," Diego said. "You're not. Start over. What's this about a boatman?"

"When we discovered that you had escaped," another nod at Carlos, "we sent men after you. They picked up your trail, and Crispin followed you personally. We tracked you to a town where a one-eyed brigand told us you had passed through. According to him, he recognized something was amiss and tried to bring you in to the authorities, but a group of boatmen stopped him and helped you escape."

"That's true," Carlos said. "Some of it."

"We arrested the boatmen," Brule said. "Two of them slipped our grasp somehow, but we brought the other two back to Tempestano for … for questioning. They didn't know much. Crispin had them beaten and put in the stocks for a public shaming. He might have kept them in prison longer, but for what? Their other two friends were making a fuss, and we didn't have good legal grounds to hold them. He finally let the older one go, but he kept the younger one longer … Lucaan."

"I remember him," Carlos said. The phrase seemed to pain Bure. Perhaps it was because it underscored how little the boatmen actually *had* known Carlos or even helped him—that they'd suffered for principle more than relationship.

"He was a good man," Bure said. "*Is* a good man. Young, but better than many who are his seniors. He reminded me of my own youth, when I worked missions in the Boglands. I took to visiting him in the jail. I thought I could comfort him. Give him some hope. He was really so young, and I knew Crispin wouldn't hold him much longer."

He shrugged—like he was attempting to stand up straighter but failed in the attempt. "He was a good listener. I didn't mean to tell him so much. But I was questioning. What we did to him, to his brother, it was wrong. What we did to you was wrong. I've worked so hard to justify it all for such a long time. I didn't want to keep doing it. So I told him … things. I told him about you, about why we were chasing you. I told him that Crispin had other holds on you, and that if we didn't find you, other innocents might get hurt. I mentioned your brother and sister." Here he nodded to Diego. "I knew Crispin might threaten them. Then he *really* surprised me. He wanted to know where they were." The ghost of a smile crossed his face. "He wanted to help them. I think he half-convinced himself he was in love with your sister."

Diego turned red. He wasn't sure how to respond to any of this. Bure saved him the need by turning back to Carlos. "But all of that, it's not anything compared to what he did. What he sent over there."

In contrast to Diego, Carlos's tone was gentle. He might have sensed that the man was on the verge of breaking down. "You're not making sense again," he said. "Tell us what you saw."

Bure shook his head again, more slowly this time. "He—he poisoned a man," he said. "A prisoner. I don't know what he gave him. Where he got it. But he covered a knife with it—it was black and sticky, like tar. Like blood maybe. He stabbed the man with it. And the prisoner started to … to change."

Diego's anger drained away. His heartbeat seemed to slow as he wrestled to understand what he was being told.

"He was going mad, but it was more than that," Bure said. "He talked to himself, got angry. Got violent. And he was changing. Growing. His vines turned color. He was becoming something not … not human." He swallowed. "Something monstrous. Crispin put him on a boat and sent him to the New World. Locked in the hold. The captain had orders to take him to the frontier and let him go out there."

"And did he?" Diego asked.

Bure shuddered. "I assume he did. The ship reached the New World. It was left in the docks. The captain never returned to it."

"Never?" Carlos asked. "How long ago was that?"

"Two years now," Bure said. "We were alerted about the ship after eight months had passed."

"Why would he do that?" Carlos asked. "Why would he release some kind of madman?"

"It's not the man he cared about releasing," Bure said. "Judging from how the disease progressed, I doubt very much he lived more than another year. It wasn't the man, it was the poison. He sent him out to spread it."

"On the frontier?"

"It's a good place to experiment," Bure said. "If the poison takes, and spreads on its own, it will create the kind of conditions that usher Crispin into power. All he needs to do is take ship to the colonies and step into a position of authority when he arrives. If something goes wrong—well, it's far away. He never needs to involve himself or admit any connection to what's happening."

"He sent Serena there," Carlos said. "To a place where there are … monsters."

Bure nodded miserably. "He doesn't need all of his plans to come to pass. Just one or two will advance his purposes well enough. If Serena isn't executed, maybe a monster will kill her."

"Why?" Carlos spat out. "Why does he hate her so much?"

"Isn't that obvious?" Bure's question seemed genuine. He blinked. "He's afraid of her. Deathly afraid. He always has been."

"So what do we do?" Carlos asked.

Bure shoved his satchel of letters toward him. "Take these to the king. Take them to John Worthington. Show them how deeply Crispin has wormed his way into matters here, how hard he's working to undermine them, to make them vulnerable so he can control them. They need to know he's an enemy. He's *their* enemy. If they will believe it, maybe others will too.

Then go home. Take your throne back. Don't let him keep you out. Don't let him threaten you, no matter if he *does* have his family, no matter if—"

"Stop," Diego said. "Does he have my family? Has he gone after my brother and sister?"

Bure's expression twisted. "Yes," he said. "That is, I don't know if he's found them. He went looking. That's when I knew. I knew it had to stop. I couldn't let it all happen again—all of this abusing innocents to create a conflict no one wants but him."

Carlos looked at Diego with an expression that was more anguished than anything else. But for Diego, pieces were falling into place. In all his years of ostensibly working for Crispin, and secretly trying to oppose him, he'd never understood what the man really *wanted.* He'd never understood how the High Elder could think that manipulating leaders and persecuting dissenters could lead to anything but chaos.

Now, finally, he saw it.

Chaos was exactly what Crispin wanted.

Outside Fort Collins—The New World

The dash to Fort Collins felt like the kind of nightmare where you try to run with all your might, but with every step you take, you bog down and go slower and slower.

Jonathan ran the entire way like a sheepdog: worrying the edges of their group, herding strays, doubling back to the end of the line. His lungs screamed for air and his sides split, but he kept running. He spelled off those who were carrying the sleepers and even put Agatha Moss on his back for a little while and ran with her. John Hopewell saw him, took over, and set Jonathan loose to double around to the back again and make sure no one was being left behind.

When they'd broken into a run on the warriors' command, they'd been able to hear the sound of a battle behind them as the River People stood off against the Machkigen. Now, Jonathan didn't know if he could still hear it or if it was just his imagination.

They had three miles to go. Just three. None of them were conditioned to run, but they were driven by fear and the absolute necessity of life or death.

When they broke out of the woods into the clearing that looked across to Fort Collins, Jonathan nearly cheered. And nearly collapsed, both at once.

Everyone had staggered to an uncertain halt. The fort sat atop a ridge, with a high embankment overlooking the river. On every other side, deep, wide trenches had been dug around the fort, making it impossible to rush. A palisade of tall, sharpened logs formed a stockade around the fort, with only a few doors in or out. It was their refuge, their one place of safety. But they weren't sure how to get inside.

The last of the settlers staggered out of the trees and joined the panting, wheezing group. Letty Foster came up beside Jonathan and took his arm. She clung to it. He looked down at her, stricken with shame. She wasn't looking at him—she was staring straight ahead with fierce determination. She was going to get inside those walls.

And she was going to do it *with* him.

He'd been cruel to her, he knew that. He'd hardly spoken to her since coming back from the scouting mission. They'd had little time as it was since everything had started to go wrong; they were separated throughout the army's occupation of Jerusalem Valley, and before then, Jonathan's illness had kept them apart—in heart and mind, if not in physical proximity. Letty had stayed by his side through his worst days, he knew that.

But that was the problem now. He'd thought he was cured. Now he knew he wasn't. Not completely.

He loved Letty. He wanted to marry her. Wanted it more than anything.

But how could he, if fear or anger could turn him into a Machkigen again?

He couldn't tell her that, here and now. Nor could he break her heart by shaking her off his arm. So he let her cling, and he reached over to cover her hand with his own. He squeezed her fingers gently and said, "We're almost there."

The main gate into the fort was on the front side, facing the river. A path led up the embankment to the gate. Guard towers on either side looked down on it. John Hopewell waved with his big arm, beckoning the settlers to follow him through the woods toward the river so they could pick up the path.

Letty started forward first, tugging Jonathan along with her. He didn't resist.

But after a moment she stopped, looking back and frowning. Smith was hanging back. Sarah clung to her husband's arm in a mirror image of Letty and Jonathan, and their other children were clustered around them. They all looked stricken.

Jonathan's first thought was that Smith was refusing to go to the fort after all. He'd been a prisoner here and escaped. There was nothing stopping Anderson from clapping him right back in irons, and surely none of them wanted that. But then he realized their attention wasn't on Smith. It was on someone else standing near them.

Ezekiel, the old slave who had been carrying Jacques all this way.

While the settlers followed John, Ezekiel had planted himself on the earth and refused to take another a step forward. Two others stood by him: Premislav, the Old World commander who had been imprisoned with Smith; and the young boy Josiah.

Josiah and Ezekiel had been carrying Jacques together. Now his stretcher lay on the ground, and they had taken a step back. Jonathan surmised that they'd asked Smith and his family to carry him.

"We can't leave you out here," Smith said as Jonathan and Letty approached. "The risk is just too great. You'll be found and slaughtered."

"Maybe so," Ezekiel said. "But my life ended a long time ago, when I buried my sons in that ditch there. I got a new life when I left. If it's short, it's short. Now I've brought this man all the way here for you. I go no further." He gestured at Jacques. "I hate to send him in with you. The soldiers know him, and they might kill him. But he don't stand a chance out here."

"I'll protect him," Jonathan said. A lump was growing in his throat. "I owe him my life. I'll see to it that he's not harmed."

Letty tightened her grip on his arm. There might be no way for him to keep that promise. He might be endangering his own life by making it—he certainly endangered his freedom. If the soldiers decided that his loyalty amounted to conspiring with Imitators against the Puritani, he'd be arrested and sent to New Cranwell—if the soldiers didn't decide to enact their own justice here and now. But what else could they do? It was one thing to allow Ezekiel to take his chances in the woods. They couldn't leave a comatose man outside of the fort walls.

"I'm not going in either," Premislav said. "I don't much like the army's plans for me, and I expect this gallant fellow can use some help."

Jonathan fixed his eyes on Josiah. "And you, young man?"

"I'm stayin' with Ezekiel," Josiah said. "We go find the River People. Help them." For a moment his composure broke, and he shifted his attention to Smith and Sarah. "You won't let them hurt my pa," he said. "Usual he can take care of himself, but—"

"We'll do our best to keep him safe," Sarah said. "We all will. Your pa's a free man. We won't let them treat him any different than they do the rest of us."

They might be empty promises. Jonathan knew it. They all knew it. But it was the best they could do.

Premislav fixed his intense eyes on Smith. "Are you sure you won't stay with us out here?" he asked.

"I'm sure," Smith said. He drew Sarah closer and wrapped his other arm around Lila. "I won't leave my family to face the army alone. Not again. Nor will I leave the rest of them." The corner of his mouth twitched. "I am governor, after all. Anyway, this time we're coming in numbers. They can't throw us all into prison. And this time we have a common enemy to worry about. Things may be different now."

He looked after the rest of the group that was making its way through the trees toward the river. "I suppose our greatest fear should be that they won't let us in at all. I don't like leaving you. Any of you. Come with us. We'll protect you."

But Ezekiel shook his head, and the others did the same. "Nothin' you can do against the law," Ezekiel said. "I'm a runaway; nothin' you can do about that. This boy, now, he should stay with you. But I been tryin' to tell him that for miles. I can't force him to listen."

Slowly, Jonathan pulled away from Letty and approached the stretcher where Jacques lay. He knelt to pick up one end, and Martin Foster took up the other. They hefted the Imitator between them. Jonathan felt that he was taking up the greatest burden of his life. He carried a worthy man's life. He would do all he could to stand by him.

From the woods behind them, a screech arose—some kind of howling, tormented creature giving voice to its torment.

They were nearly out of time.

PART 3
CHANGE

CHAPTER 18

The Midlands, Somewhere in Time—The Old World

Anyone who saw him now would immediately know Herman Melrose had changed since his younger years.

Back then, when he'd returned from years of service in the wars and their aftermath, when he'd gone to seminary already a world-weary and battle-scarred man, he had dressed neatly and simply in the best clothing he could find. He had been usually quiet, often sad. He was a large man, he always had been, yet his expression was gaunt.

Everything was different now.

Now he dressed in black, in the plain, almost threadbare style of the Tremblers. Now, when he spoke, his voice resonated with power and conviction. His eyes no longer looked hungry; now they blazed with passion. He stood straighter, walked more lightly. He was older, but he seemed to have regained his youth.

Jacques observed all this from his vantage point in the small crowd outside a large and wealthy Midlandish kirk. He wove in and out of the crowd, seeing everyone, hearing everything. He exercised his uncanny ability to see without being seen—or rather, without being noticed. Everyone assumed he was there with someone else. He just seemed to belong.

He counted on that. It was an appearance he had carefully cultivated for years.

How else had he followed Joseph Crispin so long without being found out?

Melrose's appearance here, today, was unexpected. Jacques wasn't here for him. But he was glad to see him. He was glad to see that he looked well. He was glad—though perhaps he shouldn't have been; his own commitments inveighed against it—that Crispin's old friend had followed the call of his heart. It certainly seemed to have done him good.

The doors to the kirk opened. The crowd began to file in. Herman hung back a little, entering after most others had already done so. Jacques lingered near the doors until Herman had gone inside and seated himself in one of the hindermost pews. He slid into the same pew, seating himself at the end. Herman didn't look over at him. His eyes were fixed on the man who stood at the front of the kirk.

Joseph Crispin, pastor of this congregation and the recently promoted Elder of the Midlands.

If Herman had grown simpler in his dress and more vital in his bearing, Crispin had done the opposite. His robes and the rings on his fingers were ostentatious. He stood out in the barren setting of the Puritani kirk like a beacon of opulence. Deacons and toadies clustered around him, bowing and scraping almost unconsciously as they spoke to him. His girth had grown, and with it his stature—Jacques could have sworn he had actually grown several inches, even though common sense told him he had not. His face was florid and his manner an equal mix of charm and thinly veiled danger.

Jacques had been watching him for years. Long ago, his superiors had sensed a threat in the soldier turned minister of the kirk, and they'd assigned Jacques to monitor it. So he had watched Crispin grow into this. He had seen him swell with power and pride, even as everyone in his circle seemed to fall under his sway.

Jacques considered it a tragedy.

He hadn't been here all the time, of course. There had been other missions, other causes. Sitting in the pew, he unconsciously tugged at his green gloves. He wasn't used to them, and his hands still gave him pain.

Bells began to ring, calling more of the faithful into the kirk. The toadies dispersed, and a choir sang. Then Crispin made his ponderous way into the pulpit. He preached a strong, fine sermon. His voice carried every point home like marrow and honey: the words were rich, inspiring, enlivening. Even Jacques's heart was stirred. For all else that could be said about Crispin, this much was true: he was easily the most gifted orator Jacques had ever heard.

Several times, Jacques glanced over to the middle of his pew, where Herman Melrose sat, leaning forward so his elbows rested on his knees. He looked perturbed.

When the service ended, Melrose made his way directly to the front. Crispin didn't notice him coming, distracted as he was by others fawning for his attention. But as soon as Herman had broken free of the crowd, everyone else hushed and backed away as though by some unspoken command. Crispin's eyes lit with surprise.

"Old friend!" he said.

"Yes," Herman answered. He took a deep breath. "I'd like to say it's good to see you."

Crispin frowned and raised a hand to shoo the others further away. Jacques, lingering near the altar rail, lowered his eyes but stayed close enough to hear.

"Well, it *is* good to see you. Though I take it you haven't changed company since last we spoke."

"I answered the call in my heart," Herman said. "I wish I could say the same for you."

Crispin flushed. "You can say the same for me. This is my calling, Herman. It has always been my calling."

"And what about the seed?" Herman asked. "I was there when the Fire Within placed it in your hands. I know what he called you to do. How long have you hardened your heart against that call?"

Angry now, Crispin stepped closer to his old friend and lowered his voice. Jacques strained to hear, even as he backed away, further into the shadows at the side of the kirk. He couldn't afford to be noticed now, and Crispin was growing more sensitive to onlookers.

"Did you come here just to berate me?" he said. "Look around you,

Herman. I've made *great* strides. I've done great things. Can you not congratulate me even a little?"

"I can't congratulate you for amassing power at the expense of your soul," Herman said. "You may fool all of these people, Joseph. You can't fool me. You didn't believe a word you spoke today. You treat the Book like a token to help you win. I only wish I knew what game it is you're playing."

"I meant what I said," Crispin answered, "when I said it was good to see you. But that goodness has quickly fled. Are you always this full of love and kindness for your old friends, or has the Fire Within burned all the humanity out of you?"

Herman flinched. "I do think of you kindly, Joseph. But I'm afraid for you."

"What are you doing here?" Crispin asked. The hurt had gone out of his voice, replaced now by coldness. He straightened up and let his voice carry a little more loudly, no longer so afraid of being overheard.

"I came for the seed," Melrose said. "To ask you about it. To urge you to take it to the New World. To get it from you if you won't."

"What makes you think I would trust something so precious to you?" Crispin asked.

"Because it *isn't* precious to you," Herman snapped. "You don't value it at all, or you would have done something with it. You would have *obeyed,* as a minister of the gospel should."

Something flickered in Crispin's eyes. "We're saved by faith, not by works," he said.

"Don't play that game," Herman said. His eyes pleaded. "Do you ever intend to act on what the Fire Within gave you? Or has your heart shut him out completely?"

"I am acting on it," Crispin said. He spread his arms out. "Look at what the Fire Within has given me. This pulpit. This kirk. Authority that increases by the day. Power against our enemies. Do you know, Herman, since I've become elder here, I've uncovered three Sacramenti nests and had them destroyed."

Jacques's carefully schooled features did not flinch, but inwardly his heart ached. What Crispin said was true. There would have been more if

Jacques had not been there to issue warnings, but he had not managed to discover every plan before it was carried out.

"You take pride in routing an already gutted enemy?" Herman said. He sounded less angry now, less personally betrayed—more saddened. "When we left the wars, Crispin, I thought we left them. I thought we were seeking out life, not more death and destruction."

"The pathway to life is through death," Crispin said. "You know that as well as anyone. But you are right, you know. The Sacramenti are nearly gone. Past the point of usefulness. I may need a new enemy soon."

Jacques almost caught his breath at the brazen threat. Herman simply stared at the man who had once been his closest friend. A long time passed, and Herman blinked away tears that had gathered in his eyes.

"Will you give me the seed?" he asked.

"No," Crispin answered.

Herman nodded slowly. He turned to go with ponderous steps. He might have aged ten years in the course of the interaction. Jacques watched him go with pain in his heart.

When Herman left the kirk, Crispin motioned for two men in the shadows to step forward. "Follow him," he said. "Don't let him see you. He will be meeting with a group of dissenters called Tremblers. I want to know who they are and where and when they meet."

The spies nodded. They left the kirk and immediately split up, taking different routes to carry out Crispin's orders. Jacques slipped out a side door and took his time picking up the first man's trail. How many people in this world, he wondered, were occupied with watching their foes? Was this all life was anymore—enemies watching enemies watching enemies?

Jacques followed the spy from the green, oak-shadowed lawns of the kirk into the cobbled city streets and down the twisting alleys where the sun barely reached. As he passed through patches of dappled light and shaded dark, he had a strange sensation of being outside of himself—it was nearly déjà vu, but different. He was present here and present elsewhere at the same time. He was living this moment for the first time, and yet he had the distinct sensation that he was looking back on it, with new knowledge and understanding, and with a strong sense of anticipation—something was about to happen that would change everything. Not only for the men he followed, and for Joseph Crispin, and for the wider world, but for himself.

Far ahead, Herman turned into a narrow alley. The spy Jacques was following stayed back, risking losing him—for now—for the sake of not getting caught. When some time had passed, he cautiously pushed forward.

And Jacques stepped outside of himself.

He didn't know how he did it. Only that his physical form was still hiding, still keeping his own wise distance, but his spirit was walking close on the spy's heels, unseen and unnoticed.

The moment he separated from himself, Jacques knew everything. He knew that he was asleep in the New World, that he'd been poisoned and saved, however temporarily, by the waters discovered by Linette Cole. He knew that he was traveling through time somehow, sometimes reliving his old memories and sometimes going into places he had never been and seeing and hearing things he had never witnessed. He knew that this was one of those moments. In reality, he had been there that day Herman Melrose came to challenge Joseph Crispin, and he had followed Crispin's spies. But he hadn't been able to push forward any further than this—not in this moment. He'd found ways to retrace Melrose's steps later, to discover who he met with and where and why.

So he knew what he was about to see.

In spirit, aware that he was incorporeal and invisible to anyone but himself, he passed through the door Melrose had entered into a large storeroom at the back of a tavern. It was packed with people, spiritual seekers sitting and standing shoulder to shoulder, heart to heart. At the front of the room people had cleared space for a small family. Man and wife; son and daughter. Southerners. They stood out—not only because of their coloring and features, not only because their clothing was finer and more expensive than that of anyone else in the room, not only because everyone was hanging, hushed, on everything they said. They stood out because of the girl.

She was younger by several years, younger and lighter. Her presence was just as riveting as Jacques had ever known it to be—but something was different. He hadn't known it until this moment. He'd never known, when he looked at her, how much fear, suffering, and pain were etched into the passionate lines of her face. He knew it now by its absence. In this place, this *time,* she was bright with hope and glory. She had not yet been hunted. She had not yet been hurt. She had not yet learned to know herself, to define herself, by the demands of martyrdom.

A lump grew in his throat as he realized that he wasn't the only one seeing her for the first time. Crispin's spies were too.

He wanted to warn her.

Or even to greet her.

But he couldn't speak or make himself known.

Still his heart said, *Oh, Serena.*

New Cranwell—The New World

Phinehas Cole sat at his desk of polished walnut and lifted his pen from the page. He reviewed the words again, taking each one carefully. The resolution would not pass easily. It mattered that his words leave as little room as possible for confusion or challenge.

But he'd read them many times before. It was hard to focus this time. He tried, but his mind wandered, as it often did these days.

He was thinking about the Vaquero woman and her Imitator friend.

They could not have appeared in New Cranwell at a worse time for the chief elder of the Puritani kirk of New Cranwell. His support was already growing frayed—diffused by too many competing interests and ideologies. His most important work—this resolution—depended in part on the support of his most unlikely allies, the Tremblers. But it also needed—demanded—the support of the New Cranwell synod. Serena Vaquero had done more than any single individual other than Herman Melrose to create popular sympathy for Tremblers and simultaneously galvanize the most zealous of the Puritani against them. She'd arrived just behind orders from Joseph Crispin: she was to be executed at once. Had Cole obeyed, he would have lost the support of the Tremblers completely, probably forever. He might as well have re-crushed the Son of God.

On the other hand, he couldn't let her go without scandalizing the synod and making enemies of every one of them.

At least with her companion, the issues were simpler. Tremblers and Puritani alike vilified the Imitators. Rather than execute him, Cole had simply given orders to send him back to the Old World to be dealt with there.

Back to Joseph Crispin, who was responsible for placing him in such a bind.

Phinehas Cole had no doubt that Crispin had done this to him deliberately and with full knowledge of the chaos he would cause. The High Elder of the Old World Puritani wanted Cole removed from office. He knew that. Cole wasn't controllable.

He had no love for Serena Vaquero. He'd done his best to intimidate and cow her. He'd declared his intention to put her on trial himself, and execute her only if he actually found her guilty. He'd never intended for things to get that far—somehow, someway, she would have to escape. Likely he would leak news of her arrival and imprisonment to his Trembler contacts, and they would spirit her away before Cole could become guilty of her blood. He would be innocent of wrongdoing or disobedience in the sight of the synod, even if Joseph Crispin would never believe it. And hopefully, he would have threatened Serena effectively enough to ensure she would never come back here to trouble him again.

But then she'd disappeared early, and word of her presence here had reached the wrong people. Somehow the synod knew all about it. They were incensed that she'd escaped. They whispered that Cole had helped her. Her imprisonment and trial hadn't proceeded long enough to prove to anyone that he would do his duty.

He forced his eyes back to the resolution.

… that herewith the institution of Human Chattel Slavery be abolished in all towns and lands under His Majesty's governance in the New World, by all right-thinking men supported and by the full strength of the law enforced.

He sighed and laid the pen down. He'd spent years getting to this point—that his sermons could become a movement, a movement words, words perhaps a law.

The governor himself had asked that Cole put words to the resolution. But it would take a vote to pass it, and that vote would depend heavily on the mood of the people. The city council would not strike down slavery in

New Cranwell unless they believed the people wanted it, and the mood of the people was fickle. Far too often, the clerics spoke for them.

Right now, many of the clerics were casting aspersions on the resolution simply because Cole was involved with it, and Cole had released Serena Vaquero. For faithful Puritani, the taint was enough to make them ask whether some seditious, hidden purpose was concealed within the words Cole wrote.

He rubbed his forehead. He had a headache. No surprise there.

A thought of Linette flitted through his mind.

That *did* surprise him. He'd thought himself too distracted by other, weightier matters to think about his daughter.

But then, she was never really far from his mind.

He had expected her to be home by now—although part of him was relieved that she wasn't. When Principio Premislav, the new commander of Fort Collins, left New Cranwell, Cole had asked him to give her an escort and tell her to return. He wasn't sure why he'd done it. At the time it had felt urgent—a compulsion. He'd acted on it and couldn't take it back. He'd been thinking of her, thinking of their last meeting, wishing he had said and done things differently. He should have worked harder to make her feel hopeful about her life here. He should have tried harder to convey to her that things would get better, that the shame of her sins wouldn't swallow her up forever, that her daughter would be happy and well without her.

He had been angry when she left, but he understood. Part of him did, anyway. She thought she had no place here. He should have worked harder to show her that she was wrong.

It might have been something in her letters that compelled him finally to insist that she come home. He'd been intercepting them for months—it was better that Beth not know about her mother. They were cheerful, newsy, innocent. They said she lived a good life on the frontier. They said the people of Jerusalem Valley were kind and that they all loved each other, Puritani and Trembler alike.

Even now, Cole snorted at the memory. He knew better. He was privy to the synod's correspondence with Jonathan Applegate, the Puritani parson in Jerusalem Valley. He knew trouble was brewing between the factions in

Jerusalem Valley and that its utopia of peace and toleration couldn't last much longer. Only a fool would have thought it would work in the first place.

The same kind of fool, he wondered, glancing down again at the parchment before him with its drying ink, who thought he could pass a law and bring justice to his corner of the world?

Not for the first time, he reflected that he might have more in common with Herman Melrose than he liked to admit. It galled him that for some reason Linette had become so enamored with the Trembler purveyor of political ideals and spiritual teachings. So much so that she'd run off to join Melrose, leaving her own father behind.

Because she didn't understand, he reminded himself. Because she had lost hope. When she arrived, he would make her see that her hopelessness wasn't necessary.

If she arrived.

She was late, and it was probably too late now—the snow would block her way home, and she wouldn't come until the spring.

Maybe she had refused. Maybe she had told Commander Premislav she wouldn't leave.

But that wouldn't last. The fabric of society in Jerusalem Valley would collapse, as had always been inevitable. She would be bereft again. And she would come home.

It was a little satisfying to know how it would all play out. But his heart panged for her anyway.

She'd suffered so much. It was hard to think of her suffering more.

Below his study, he heard the heavy brass knocker on the front door and the sound of muffled voices as his manservant answered. He let the sound draw his attention away—away from Linette, away from the resolution, away from all the threads of his life that had somehow spun out beyond his control.

The conversation was short. It was followed by steady footsteps coming up the stairs, then the expected knock.

"Come," Cole said.

The door opened. His manservant, Parker, neatly dressed and groomed, held out a sealed letter. "Sir."

"What is it?" Cole asked, taking the letter and breaking the seal.

"No good news, I fear," Parker said. "It came from the council."

Cole frowned. He took the letter out and opened it, skimming it quickly. His heart sank.

In light of these concerns, we, a joint committee of the City Council and Clerical Synod of New Cranwell, call upon you to stand before us. Be prepared to give full answer to the charges brought against you.

The letter didn't specify what charges would be brought. But the "concerns" named were clear enough: the civic and kirk leaders had reason to believe Cole was involved with seditious and criminal elements. It ended with the date he was expected to appear—just a few days from now.

Crispin's trap would spring after all—now, at the worst possible time.

"Go," Cole said, waving Parker out the door. When the door had been shut firmly behind him, he leaned over his desk with his head in his hands.

Creator, he prayed, *strengthen me for what lies ahead. Help me. I place all this in your hands—let your justice be done.*

The Wilderness—The New World

Amos Thatcher was terrified.

He berated himself ceaselessly as he searched. Hadn't he come on this journey to protect Linette? Hadn't an angel told him to mind the growing things—to mind her, to mind his love for her? He'd been trying his best, despite her apparent discomfort, trying to care for her and honor her wishes for distance at the same time—though he didn't think he was imagining her growing warmth toward him. And then, in a single moment, a storm had wiped out all his best efforts and Linette was lost.

That he too was lost hardly troubled him. It was immaterial. He'd come out here with a mission, and he'd failed at it.

Unless he could find her again.

Possibilities nagged him as he searched. She might have been killed in the storm—struck down by lightning, felled by a falling tree, buried in the snow. She might have been driven deep into the wilderness and found by the wolves.

She might have been happened upon by unscrupulous soldiers, or worst of all, by Fredrick Almon.

Amos wasn't truly worried about the soldiers. Under Carson's leadership, they all seemed to be decent enough men. Carey had been another story, but Carey was dead, and the others seemed unlikely to follow in his footsteps. But Almon was the most frightening and wretched man Amos had ever met, and not only because he was a Machkigen.

Amos prayed without ceasing as he tried with all his heart to pick up a trail. But there was nothing. No sound, no footsteps. He'd been separated from everyone else in the storm, and he could see no sign of them—not of the army, not of Almon, not of Linette.

He'd come all this way for no reason but to take care of her. And at the first real trouble, he'd failed her.

He had been floundering through the snow for hours. His skin was slick with sweat beneath his winter clothes.

A thundering clatter stopped his heart. He reached for his gun, even as his brain registered what he was seeing and hearing: nothing but a raven taking flight from the branches of a pine, leaving needles and boughs to knock against each other, sending clumps of snow raining down.

He almost laughed with relief, but his hands were shaking.

The moment brought him back to himself. He wasn't going to find anyone charging blindly through the woods like this. He wouldn't be any help to Linette if he found her—*when* he found her—if he didn't get a grip on his emotions and formulate a real plan.

The raven gave him an idea. He was surrounded by the woods, blocked on every side by trees and branches. He needed a higher vantage point.

That shouldn't be at all difficult to find. He was, after all, surrounded by woods.

Strapping his long rifle to his back, Amos picked out a tall, stately pine with sturdy branches studding its length nearly to the height of his shoulders. Grabbing hold, he hoisted himself up and began to climb.

As he gained height, breathing in the stinging fragrance of needles and sap, the landscape opened out before him. Mostly he saw the grey-green and blue-green peaks of coniferous trees, stretching out for miles from west to east and north toward the mountains. Snow lay heavy on their branches, bowing them low and blanketing the forest in a sacred stillness. The mountains rose to the north and west; in the south, the evergreen forest petered out and gave way to the bare, spiked branches of deciduous trees. Beyond them he could just make out the Mescahannec, its waters slow and sluggish but mirroring the pale sunlight like a shining vein of silver ore.

He couldn't see any of his companions, but he didn't let the fear take him again. Instead he closed his eyes for a moment, breathed, stilled his soul. He listened.

Fire Within, he prayed. *Show me the way. Help me find her.*

An inexplicable rush of heat filled him as he prayed, setting his body on fire in protest of the cold. It faded as quickly as it had come.

The stillness pressed on him. Another raven cawed, then took flight from a tree lower down, near the river perhaps a quarter-mile away. Amos noticed it because a cold breeze carried the sound to him, and because the raven's flight was followed by a burst of other birds, a small flock disturbed by something beneath the trees. Amos tightened his grip and tried to sit up a little higher for a clearer view. He thought he caught a flash of red. Soldiers. The breeze carried voices; there was a whole group of them. Perhaps Carson's men had all found each other.

Well and good, if Linette and Almon had joined them too. But what if they were still out here?

It would be simple enough to climb down and head for the river. Having found his bearings, Amos could rejoin the soldiers quickly. But instead he continued to search the landscape for some sign of Linette. He shifted his position in the tree, and snow fell from the needled branches. He realized suddenly how high he was, and closed his eyes against a wave of dizziness.

But it wasn't just the height.

The tree was swaying.

All around and below him, the trees swayed—gently at first, then harder. Branches and trunks began to knock and clack against one another. In the sky, clear and blue just a moment ago, dark clouds were gathering over a central place in the middle of the woods, swirling and spreading outward to cover the sky. The wind grew violent, and the tree lashed to one side and then another. Thunder boomed.

All thought of his mission gone, Amos could do nothing but hang on for his life. His knife, worked loose during his long climb, jarred free from his hip and spiraled down through the boughs. It had grown so dark Amos couldn't even watch it fall. The tree lunged to one side, leaving his heart behind. Thunder shook the world.

Lightning flashed even as the tree collided with another and then lashed back again, and Amos lost his grip and fell away. He was falling. Everything went black, swallowed by the storm, and then another flash of lightning lit the sky and the trees and the ground below—

He saw, in the otherworldly light and the falling snow, beings filling the air like floating leaves. There might have been hundreds—hosts. Some, tall and sylvan, dressed in white. He seemed to know them, to know the sound of their voices—which might, as he fell, have been singing, a song that somehow wove the fabric of reality and which he'd always known though he'd never consciously heard it before. Others, crumpled and hollow, empty-eyed, the mottled grey and brown of death, he knew to be shades.

Amos saw all of this.

It was an impossibly long way to fall.

He did not hit the ground. Instead, an instant before he should have, the sylvan figures bore him up in their arms and set him down gently.

You are not finished, he heard in a whisper. *Do not quit now.*

A moment before the blizzard began again, Linette heard men's voices on the wind. The soldiers. Dark clouds were swirling overhead, but she couldn't afford to lose them again. She gathered up her skirts and pressed toward the voices. Wind began to howl, blasting her. Snow whipped into the air, carried by the wind, whiting out the world around her. Her clothing and hair blew wildly. She threw up an arm to shield her eyes against the stinging snow and lurched forward, hoping she was still going in the right direction. Lightning forked down through the black sky and lit everything in a blinding flash.

An arm wrapped around her neck and hauled her backward, choking her and pulling her up against a hard, warm body. Almon. She struggled against his grip, but he only lowered his arms and encircled her torso, pinning her arms to her sides and dragging her forcefully back. Terror so keen she could taste it filled her. She could see nothing but snow, could hear nothing but the howling wind. She could feel nothing but the knifing cold and the iron of Frederick Almon's arms.

He pulled her back several steps, then turned and shoved her up against something rough and unyielding—a tree trunk, she realized, wide enough to act as a windbreak. Overhead, branches clacked and waved wildly, many breaking and blowing away to litter the snow like a rain of arrows. The clatter was deafening. Turning her back to the trunk, she slid down, making herself small against the tree. Almon placed his hands on the trunk over her head and loomed over her. His body shielded her. Some part of her knew he was saving her life. But he scared her more deeply than the storm. The elements were wild, powerful, maybe even malevolent. But they couldn't be more terrifying to her than this man.

She hated him, she realized. She hated him for what he had done to Sarah and her family, for how he had kept her and Serena and Jacques trapped underground while he lorded his power over the people of Jerusalem Valley. She hated him for pushing Jonathan and the River People into an act of war that might yet bring terrible consequences to the frontier. She hated him for his utter lack of respect for everything she loved, everything she wanted.

He loomed over her like a threat or a savior. She wanted to spit in his face.

Instead she wrapped her arms around her knees, drew herself in as small as she could, and closed her eyes until the storm was over.

She didn't know how long it was. The roar of the wind and the clamor of the trees wiped out any normal sense of time and place: the sound swallowed everything and blurred it together into a single sensation, a single experience of disassociation and fear.

Through it all, Almon never moved.

Creation dissolved around them, until at last the wind died, the snow ceased falling. A hush fell, and the world returned.

Slowly, as though he'd half-frozen and his limbs needed to thaw, Almon straightened and pushed himself away from the tree. He hardly looked human. Snow clung to every inch of his body; ice crystals had formed on his beard and eyebrows. Moving sluggishly, he beat his hands together to knock away some of the snow.

Using the tree for support, Linette pushed herself up. She'd been half-buried, but the broad trunk on one side and Almon on the other shielded her from being blasted directly by the storm. She tore her eyes from Almon and looked in the direction they'd come. Overhead, the sky was still grey— but except for an occasional gust of wind picking up tendrils of snow and blowing them along the top of the crust, visibility was clear. The world had been restored to itself, if deeply transformed.

"They were this way," she said, gesturing in the general direction of where she'd heard voices. She started to move. "With any luck, they're still there."

"No," Almon said.

Something in his tone stopped her. She turned slowly, afraid of what she would see.

He was pointing his pistol at her head.

"No," he repeated. "You're not going back. You're staying with me."

Forcing her voice to stay as steady as possible, she said, "I need to go to New Cranwell."

"Yes," he said. His hand didn't waver. "And I will take you there. Not them." His mouth thinned in a bitter line. "Your father sent word to Fort

Collins to find you and bring you home, and that's what I'm going to do. *Me.* Those soldiers, they think I'm mad. And insubordinate. They want to have me court-martialed. But I'm going to take you to your father. Then you'll tell him how I rescued you, and he'll see that I'm acquitted of any wrongdoing."

"My father doesn't have authority in the army," she said. Her voice was trembling, and she inwardly excoriated herself for it. "He's a cleric. He couldn't even pardon you if you were a civilian."

"He's the most powerful man in New Cranwell," Almon said. His tone was dismissive—it stung. "If he wants to help me, he can. I need you to make sure he wants to help me."

She wanted to scream at him. She wanted to say, *What makes you think I would ever help you?*

But the barrel of his gun stared her down. Her limbs felt frozen in place, and not because of the cold. He could kill her—and if she ran, or tried to defy him, she felt certain he would. If she died, who would help her father? More importantly, who would help Beth?

She'd set out to be a rescuer and become a hostage instead.

With the pistol, he waved in the opposite direction from where she was heading to rejoin the soldiers.

"There's a long way ahead of us," he said. "Let's go."

CHAPTER 19

The Midlands—The Old World

The plan had been for Lucaan and Caterina to take as many leaflets with them as they could carry and then spread them, everywhere they went, *secretly.* When they roomed in an inn, they would leave leaflets behind. When they slept in barns and lean-tos, they would slip leaflets under their hosts' doors. When they did odd jobs to fund their travels and spent their earnings buying dinner in taverns, they would keep their mouths shut, look inconspicuous, and be careful to remain discreet.

But it turned out that discretion fit neither of their personalities.

Lucaan was naturally open, friendly, and sincere. He had a bad habit of telling everyone everything.

Caterina was sick of hiding.

She'd never been a hider by nature. She'd done it out of love for her family, for her brothers. To protect them. But she'd slipped Crispin's noose, and things were different now. Now she had another way to help.

So they did spread the pamphlets Paulo had printed. But they also told the story themselves. And they also shared their own part in it. Caterina, who was red-haired and striking, enraptured audiences and won allies for their cause before she'd even opened her mouth. Most of their listeners were half-drunk when they heard the story, but that only made them more passionately sympathetic. Lucaan called out the best in every last one of them, and by the time they left a place, he had them all promising help and calling down imprecations on plotters and hatemongers—often in song, with arms around one another's shoulders and tankards of ale splashing in time.

Caterina and Lucaan made each other feel invincible.

They were also in love. It took them very little time to admit it to themselves, though neither admitted it to the other. Under the circumstances, it seemed better not to throw fuel on a fire they couldn't righteously allow to burn.

Yet.

Along with their plan to travel quietly and inconspicuously, they had also meant to go directly. Their intention was to cross the Midlands on the shortest course for the sea, then take ship to Angleland. This plan, too, went by the wayside almost immediately. Every time they left one town in a blaze of glory and righteous indignation, they rode for the nearest town no matter what direction it was in—more eager to continue their work than to get where they were supposed to be going. They discovered along the way that some towns had printers, and those printers were capable of printing their own editions of Paulo's explosive pamphlets, albeit a little flimsier and smudgier than the originals. Both of the self-appointed missionaries happily gave up some of their meals to pay for the extension of their message and their mission with it.

Now and again Lucaan told Caterina that he had no house and no money. She understood what he meant. *I love you, but I can't tell you because I can't ask you to marry me. I can't take care of you.* She saw the irony. All he *did* was take care of her. She didn't care that there was no roof to go over her head and no purse to provide for their needs. They were doing fine without those things, weren't they? What would marriage change?

She nearly said so. But she bit her tongue and used every ounce of self-control to douse the longing that burned in her, that flared up constantly, that hummed through every fiber of her when she looked at Lucaan. She talked sternly to herself. Marriage would change things, because marriage might mean children, and they could not do this work with an infant in their arms. And there was more. Lucaan was a faithful layman of the Puritani kirk. He didn't know that Caterina's allegiance lay elsewhere. If he suspected, he did not ask. She refused to tell him without being asked. She refused to open that door. It wasn't only a matter of conviction and loyalty.

It was also the reality of holding differing loyalties in such a bitterly divided world. Say Lucaan did not mind. Say he allowed her to hold her own faith intact and married her anyway. They would be shunned by his people at best, persecuted at worst. Caterina had spent so much of her life on the run. Could she really bring children into *that?* Even for Lucaan? Could she doom Lucaan to it?

He wanted to help, yes. But maybe one day he would want to go home and buy a house and live out his days in quietness. She didn't think that life was possible with her.

So he didn't say "I love you," and she didn't argue with his reasons for staying silent. They loved each other nonetheless, and the flames both tried to contain fueled their work. They made their mission everything. They did not feel that they had any other choice. And it brought them both to life—joyful, exuberant life.

Their mission continued in this energized, rip-roaring fashion until the night Caterina pushed open the door of a tavern and walked right into another woman who stepped into her path.

"Caterina Diego," Bettina demanded. "What on earth do you think you're doing?"

Lucaan, following close on Caterina's heels, made to rush to her rescue—but he stopped short when he saw that Caterina's affronter was a woman, and clearly one who knew her.

"What are you doing here?" Caterina asked.

Bettina held up a leaflet and shook it. "Word travels. These words have been traveling much further and faster than we thought possible, and what do you think? Guest after guest tells us they've heard the story is being spread by a young man and a young woman and—" she lowered her voice in a dramatic stage whisper—"every word must be true because the young woman is none other than Massimo Diego's *sister.*"

Caterina swallowed. She seemed to have shrunk several inches. "We wanted to help."

"Who's *we?*" Bettina demanded. Her eyes darted past Caterina to Lucaan. "Who are you? And what are you doing gallivanting around the Midlands with my little sister?"

"We're going to find Diego," Caterina answered for him. "We're just trying to help. He rescued me from Crispin's men, Bettina. You don't have to look so scandalized; it's not like that."

Lucaan stepped forward and fisted his chest. "I am Lucaan Feeanstra of the Boglands," he said. "I have devoted my life to helping your sister."

Caterina turned scarlet as Bettina glared at her. "It's 'not like that,' eh?"

"We haven't done anything wrong," Caterina insisted. "Some men came after me like Diego said they might. Lucaan helped me escape, and then we found these." She pulled a pamphlet from her pocket, smearing her fingers with ink. She hardly noticed; her hands were near permanently stained by now. "We found what you and Paulo have been doing to make a real difference, and we thought, well, we're going to find Diego because where else am I supposed to go? I don't have a safe place. And on the way we'll help him, and help you."

The red had subsided from her cheeks. "Lucaan is a perfect gentleman. I think you're focusing on the wrong thing here."

Bettina did not look any less scandalized. "Do you love him?"

Caterina lifted her chin. "Bettina, this isn't the place to discuss that."

"Do you want to marry him?"

Caterina glanced behind her and gave Lucaan a shy smile before answering, "Maybe we could talk about it later?"

A small crowd had gathered around them in the doorway, all of them leaning forward with interest. Bettina stepped back, apparently taking Caterina's point—this was a little public for matters of the heart.

A small, dark man stepped forward and bowed his balding head toward Caterina and Lucaan with a gentle smile. "It's good to see you, sister," he said. "We were a little worried."

"Paulo," Caterina said, holding out her hands to grasp her brother-in-law's. The next moment, a gangly boy burst through the crowd and threw himself at Caterina, wrapping both arms around her waist. She kissed the top of his head and laughed. "Jorge! What are you doing here?"

"I went with Diego and Carlos," he explained. He didn't say from where. They couldn't say that out loud, not in the heavily Puritani Midlands. "They left me with Bettina and went to Angleland. I've been helping with the printing press. I'm going to be a printer, like Paulo."

"Good," Caterina said, eyes shining as she pushed her little brother back and filled her eyes with the sight of him. "They do a great deal of good, these printed things." She looked up, meeting Bettina's gaze. "People are reading them everywhere."

Bettina sighed, but she couldn't stop a wry smile from creeping onto her face. "You'll be the death of me, all of you. It was bad enough worrying about you in hiding all the time. Now that you've all come out it's ten times worse." She gave Lucaan a pointed look. "It took us no time at all to find you, once we started looking. This can't continue."

"But since you seem so determined to spread our work, we brought you more leaflets," Paulo piped up. "They're out back."

Caterina laughed. "Well, which is it then? We must stop or we must carry on?"

"First I think we must eat," Paulo said. He eyed his sister-in-law discreetly. "I'll say it so Bettina doesn't have to—you're looking a little gaunt."

Caterina lowered her eyes and smiled. "Tale-telling doesn't pay well."

Paulo had already turned back into the tavern's great room, and he waved at a server behind the bar. "Food for all of us," he called out. Jorge and Bettina fell in, ushering Caterina and Lucaan to a round table they had earlier claimed and apparently held in waiting. Hot drinks sat steaming on the surface, five of them.

Caterina slid into a chair and sighed with pleasure at the sensation of sitting down in a warm, welcoming place—with family, no less. Lucaan took the seat next to her. She gave him a quick glance before turning her eyes back to Bettina, who was eyeing them both with her lips pursed. Bettina had picked up a knife and a spoon; she laid them both down again ceremoniously and announced, "If you want to be married, you should do it. That's all I'm saying. Your story will carry better if you don't ruin your reputations in the process of spreading it."

A server appeared laden with bowls of stew, fragrant with sage. He set one down in front of Bettina, ignoring the conversation.

"Our sister did suggest this conversation might be better held later,"

Paulo said mildly.

Bettina snorted. "It's been held a little long already."

"It hasn't been the right time," Caterina said, pleading. "We've been focused, Bettina, really. On spreading your story."

Paulo leaned forward. "You've been effective. When we decided to print Carlos's tale, we didn't know how far or fast it would spread—or if people would read it at all. But they *are* reading it, and they care. And you two … people talk about you. When Carlos and Diego come back, I think Crispin won't find it so easy to move against them again."

Lucaan smiled fiercely, but Caterina said, "He should have been deposed long ago."

"That is not so easy," Paulo said. "Enough people need to turn against him first."

"Enough *powerful* people," Caterina said. "We are turning the hearts of common people just by telling them the truth. But it's powerful friends who put him where he is, and powerful friends who keep him there. I'm afraid many of them already know the truth. They just don't care."

"Even powerful people need the support of those beneath them," Paulo said. "They may not acknowledge it, but it's true. If word continues to spread, the ground beneath Crispin will eventually fall away."

"If word continues …" Caterina repeated the words slowly as it dawned on her why Paulo was here—and why Bettina was so focused on her relationship with Lucaan. "You don't want me to join Diego."

Her sister and brother-in-law exchanged a look. Paulo answered slowly. "You are very effective," he said. "Here in the Midlands, you're changing things. If you were to go South, into the princedoms around Tempestano, your efforts might turn out to be the key."

"Of course you would need to be very careful," Bettina cut in. She didn't meet Caterina's gaze. "Crispin will send more men after you, if he hasn't already. And you must take care not to discredit your message by discrediting yourselves."

Caterina shifted in her seat and looked at Lucaan, questioning him. To go South—it would change everything. It would be far more than just a daring commitment to spreading their message on the way to somewhere else. It was a wading into the thick of a fight—a choosing to go into battle.

And a choosing to do it together.

A choosing to *stay* together.

He met her gaze with an expression so intense it burned. She couldn't read it. Except that she knew it said *Yes.*

He must have seen the answering *yes* in her eyes. He turned away and leaned toward Bettina and Paulo.

"Tell us what you are thinking," he said.

"We can work together," Paulo said. "There are other printers like me all across the princedoms, people who want to see change and are willing to risk something for it. We can plan routes—several different ones, in case you have to change course. You go to the towns spreading the word; I will work with my fellows to have literature waiting for you so you can constantly replenish your supply."

"Are we the only ones doing this work?" Lucaan asked. "Can you find and enlist others?"

"You are the only ones right now," Paulo said. "But I am adding to the pamphlets we print—a call to action. A call to speak up. I hope that others will join us, especially inspired by you."

To Caterina's surprise, Lucaan reached over and took her hand. She caught her breath at his touch.

"You know I will guard her with my life," he said. "But what you're asking us to do is dangerous."

"It doesn't matter," Caterina said. She tightened her hand in his. "I want to do it. I—thank you." Suddenly overwhelmed, she blinked away tears. The food in front of her, so far ignored, made her aware of being ravenously hungry. "Thank you for not trying to make us stop. I was so tired of hiding. Of being afraid."

Bettina reached across the table and squeezed Caterina's free hand. "I would give anything to know that all my family are safe," she said. "But that cannot be while oppression and injustice masquerade as righteousness. It seems to me we've been chosen to stand up against the lies. Now. Eat. You look ready to faint for hunger."

If it hadn't been for John Worthington, Carlos suspected he'd never have gotten back in for another audience with Henry. At least, not during this season. The new king's court was overrun with guests and regular courtiers alike, all looking to assert their position in the nascent regime. As it was, even with Worthington urging Henry to see them, it was a week and a half before Carlos and Diego were admitted into his presence again.

Thankfully, their way had been prepared. They had given the papers Bure entrusted to them to John Worthington immediately, and he had promised the king would see them and be made to understand their significance.

When they finally entered the king's opulent study an hour before supper on a midweek night, having made themselves perpetually present at court for the last ten days in hopes of admittance, Carlos's hopes were drawn tight.

Henry looked angry. Carlos's stomach churned. He didn't know whether anger was good or bad.

The letters Bure had given them were open and laid out across the king's gleaming mahogany desk, overlapping each other in a damning array. Henry swept a hand across them.

"This," he said. "It's all true?"

Diego cleared his throat. "They were given to us by one of Crispin's righthand men," he said. "It seems even his friends grow tired of this evil."

"Evil?" Henry said, raising an eyebrow. "A strong word."

"I was there when he massacred a tavern full of Tremblers," Diego said quietly. "I helped him depose my own friend, because he threatened my family. What he does is evil, and I will help him no more."

Henry nodded slowly. Behind him, John Worthington leaned against a wall, quietly. His burned-out vines and scarred face made him seem like a watcher from another world.

"I will help you take back Tempestano," Henry announced. The words were so unexpected that Carlos nearly stumbled where he stood.

"I will send troops with you," Henry continued. "Two hundred men. We will hope for a bloodless return, of course—I am merely sending you with a show of force so your neighboring princes will back away, and so that the High Elder will be seen to lose face and therefore some of his power. We will make it public, very public—I want Crispin to know I'm backing you before you even leave here, while he's still in my courts. I don't think he will dare defy me to my face, and I hope that if he can see clearly what cards lie on the table, he will be less likely to try to stop you. The best possible outcome is that you will return to your home, thank those who have kept order in your absence, and resume your earldom without any real opposition."

"How likely do you think that is to happen?" Carlos asked. His heart was pounding with hope. It was happening! The alliance they had come all this way to seek was his, thanks to Adolphus Bure and Crispin's overplaying of his hand.

"This kingdom is a powerful one," Henry said. "My father usually got his way. I have good reason to believe things will go my way as well. And at this moment, my will is that Crispin not continue to consolidate power in the South. I will count on you to be a firm ally to me in return."

Carlos was nodding without even realizing it. "Of course, my liege," he said. "You have always had my family's loyalty."

"Yes," Henry said with a frank gaze and an amused smile. "But I'd like to know I have *yours.*"

"Your generosity is more than I hoped for," Carlos said. "And I believe you give it for righteous reasons. You've earned my loyalty."

"What if things *don't* go smoothly?" Diego asked. "Suppose Tempestano has been overtaken by some neighboring prince who doesn't want to give it up, even faced with Carlos's return?"

"Then my men will fight for you," Henry said. "Captain Diego, I'm placing you in command. You may fight as long as you are confident you can win. If you cannot, you will withdraw to the nearest friendly haven and send word. I will send more men to stand with you."

"You would escalate this into a war?" Diego asked.

"I will do all I can to avoid that, save giving Crispin his way." Henry set a heavy fist on the desk full of papers. "The reports here tell me what Crispin's way is and how he plans to actualize it here, in *my* country, under *my* nose, fomenting unrest among *my* people. As far as I am concerned, he's already committed numerous acts of aggression. Moreover, he deposed the young count here in a most unjust and unscrupulous manner. We will expose all of this. If the Southern princes are still inclined to see him as an ally after that, they are fools, and I will chance them in battle to take back your land. We will make it very clear I am not taking Southern lands for myself—merely aiding a rightful lord in regaining the territory he was born to."

Carlos's head spun as he considered what Henry was saying. This was exactly why he and Diego had come—it was the outcome they had hoped for, not only that Henry would help them, but that it would result in Carlos regaining his territory. Yet, until this moment, he had never really believed it would work. He'd always just been pushing forward in what felt to him like futile hope. But now he could see no reason why it *wouldn't* work. The truth was, in his pride and ambition, Joseph Crispin had taken things much too far. The princes whose lands bordered Tempestano were rapacious graspers to a man, but none of them would openly side with someone whose star was falling.

Afraid to let hope fill him *too* full, Carlos reminded himself that while Henry's open enmity was a terrible thing for any man, Crispin still had near-universal support on the mainland. But how long would that last, with Henry denouncing Crispin's actions and Carlos testifying to having been unjustly removed—nearly murdered?

"Thank you," he stuttered. He didn't know what else to say.

A hand pressed his shoulder. He turned to see John Worthington standing just behind him, leaning on his shepherd's staff. "Fret not yourself because of evildoers, and be not envious of the wicked, for the evil man has no future; the lamp of the wicked will be put out," he said. "So says the psalmist. You did right to come here seeking help, old friend."

"Now," Henry said. "The coronation is over. You have been away a long time. You should prepare to go home. I will see to it that you leave with some splendor."

The preparations took three days. At the end of that time, Carlos stood on the steps of the palace with the king of Angleland by his side, overlooking two hundred men and horses in parade, ready to go. Worthington and Diego stood by them. A large, ornate carriage awaited, and gunners lined the drive, ready to salute the young count of Tempestano as he pulled away.

Courtiers lined the steps in ranks betraying their position. Diego and Carlos's temporary landlord nodded to them with a smile—their accounts were paid up, mostly through Henry's coffers. The man's status had risen too, as he'd been seen to be connected with the young Southern lord who was suddenly such a favorite in the new king's eyes.

Joseph Crispin and his retinue stood near the base of the steps. Crispin's eyes glittered darkly as he watched the pompous sendoff.

"My friend, I bid you farewell," Henry boomed, kissing Carlos on both cheeks in a show of favor that nevertheless felt genuine. He squeezed the younger man's shoulders with his broad, strong hands and smiled. In a quieter voice he said, "You might come back and visit sometime. And keep me and my administration in your prayers. I should like to leave a good mark on this world."

Carlos swallowed an unexpected lump in his throat and smiled. "I can't thank you enough," he said.

Henry waved his remark aside. "You are far too genuine for this profession. Simply take my help as your due, whether it is or it isn't."

Carlos nodded. With a final raise of his hand in farewell, he turned and began to descend the steps toward the carriage. He wore a brilliant blue cloak, thrown back jauntily over one shoulder—a parting gift from John Worthington, whose gaze Carlos felt with every step.

At the base of the stairs, Carlos turned and looked Joseph Crispin in the face.

"I trust to see you in Tempestano one day soon," Carlos said. "Perhaps when you are visiting in the South."

Crispin shook with anger—he all but spit on Carlos's feet. But then he smiled. "I'll be returning to the mainland soon," he said. "I'll give your regards to Caterina Diego."

The smile on Carlos's face faded. He could see in Crispin's eyes that the High Elder spotted his loss of confidence and took satisfaction in it.

Diego came down the steps, pulling on his riding gloves, and nudged Carlos. "Shall we?" he said.

Carlos pulled himself away from Crispin's gloating and steeled his jaw as he continued down the steps. "Diego," he said, "we have to talk."

"Let us be on our way, and we will," Diego said. A line of soldiers saluted him as he reached the base of the stairs, and he saluted them in return. A white horse awaited him; as commander, he was expected to lead. "When we're out of the city, I'll join you."

Carlos nodded, miserable. He didn't want to wait—but there was nothing they could gain by allowing Crispin to disrupt everything now. He proceeded to the carriage, raising his hand to the crowds and the soldiers who stood in smart array.

Inside, he sank into the comfort of cushioned leather. His mind spun as commands and the stamp of feet sounded outside, and the carriage jolted forward, then began to roll steadily as the horses pulled him along the drive. Like thunder, the gun salute went off.

I'll give your regards to Caterina Diego.

Crispin had Diego's sister.

It was Carlos's worst nightmare—Serena all over again.

Outside, people lined the drive to watch the parade. They left the circle in front of the palace and moved onto the bridge into the city, where crowds of common people had turned out to watch. Carlos hardly noticed them. This was all for nothing, anyway. He couldn't go ahead with Henry's plans. They had to call everything off until they could get Caterina out of Crispin's hands.

Or maybe they had to call it off forever.

Maybe trying to take back Tempestano simply cost too much.

Yet, he remembered the massacred Tremblers and wondered—if Crispin wasn't stopped, if he kept amassing more power, then what would the cost be? And who would pay it?

Outside the city, the march slowed a little, and the carriage door swung open. Diego jumped in and seated himself across from Carlos, closing the door behind him.

"Well?" he asked.

"We can't go through with this," Carlos said. "Crispin has Caterina. He told me so on the steps."

Diego blanched, but his expression remained otherwise steady—not what Carlos expected. "Then we can afford to change nothing," Diego said. "Playing into Crispin's hands won't help my family."

"But your sister—"

"Was always at risk," Diego said. "My whole family has been at risk since Crispin decided to use them to control me. That isn't your fault."

"But aren't you worried?" Carlos asked.

"Of course I am," Diego responded. "But we can't change anything. You can't throw away Henry's help, Carlos. You might never get it again. *We* might never get such an opportunity to counter all the evil Crispin has done again."

"And Caterina? She's just going to suffer for what we do?"

"I'll try to find her," Diego said. His voice thickened. "I'll try to rescue her."

"So I'll be doing this without you," Carlos said. He felt petty even as he said it. Of course Diego had to go. But he couldn't imagine going on without his help.

"Maybe," Diego said. "Eventually. For now I'll stay by your side, because where else am I going to go? We don't know where he has her. We don't even know *if* he has her. He might have lied to you."

Carlos nodded, harried by his own thoughts and memories. "How can I do this?" he said, clasping and unclasping his fingers. "How can I let you go through the same torment I suffered?"

He lifted his eyes hesitantly. Diego was looking at him straight on. "You and Serena suffered for the sake of a greater good. I'm willing to do the same. I can't speak for Caterina, but—but I don't believe she would want you to change course. I'm not sure you've truly grasped it, Carlos—we *cannot* let Crispin win. We especially. We've seen what he does to people; we've been the victims of it. He's on a quest for power, and we have a better chance to set him back than anyone has ever had. We *have to* act on it." Diego sighed—a long sigh, weary and sad. "You can't give up, not even for my sake, not even for Caterina's, or for Serena's for that matter. Because this isn't about you. It isn't about any of us. It's about standing up for the truth and for justice when we have the chance. We might never have it again."

Carlos nodded, slowly. He wasn't convinced. No matter how grand Diego made it sound, wasn't this still just a matter of him trying to go home and reclaim his seat as ruler? Wasn't it just about showing Crispin up and making himself more powerful in the eyes of his neighbors? Hadn't this—all of it; the Trembler alliances and Serena and making Tempestano into a sanctuary—*always* just been about Carlos trying to prove himself?

He balled his hands into fists. He wanted to curse. He'd tried so hard to rise above himself—to become something more, like his sister or John Worthington. A man of principle and faith. A man whose commitments and convictions were real. But deep down, he still felt like an imposter. He could argue, sometimes, that his actions were right. But he didn't trust his own motives, or even his ability to assess them. Whenever he looked at himself in a mirror, he saw an insecure boy looking back at him.

"Carlos," Diego said.

The young conde looked into his friend's face again—Diego's older, more mature, grizzled and lined face. The layers of suffering in his eyes, and the longsuffering in his manner. Diego's was the face of experience and of authenticity.

"Now isn't the time to doubt yourself," he said. "Do what you know is right. Question yourself later."

Carlos nodded, swallowing back all of his protests.

The sea lay ahead.

For better or worse, he was going home.

CHAPTER 20

The Wilderness—The New World

Almon led the way through the snow-covered river valley. He seemed sure of where he was going. Linette followed—once or twice tempted to hang back, just slow down until the distance between them grew great enough for her to slip away. But then what? She wouldn't survive out here alone, and he could easily follow her tracks. If he did, he would likely be angry when he found her.

Better to stay with him.

She didn't trust him, of course. The light began to fade in the late afternoon as the sun swung lower, and Almon found a slightly sheltered hollow where they could camp. He threw down the small bundle of possessions he carried and started scrounging for wood.

"Help me, woman," he said. "We need a fire to keep warm."

Moving slowly, she edged closer to the bundle. His back was turned. Feigning that she was scanning the ground for wood, she spotted what she was looking for—a carved ivory knife handle. She darted forward and grabbed the knife, her sudden movement drawing his attention. He spun around.

"What are you doing?" he demanded.

She held the knife up where he could see it. "Protecting myself," she said.

He scowled. "What's that supposed to mean?"

"It means stay away from me," she said.

He all but snarled at her, but to her relief, he gave a short nod. Good. They had some understanding.

Tucking the knife at her waist where she could easily grab it, she turned and began hunting for firewood as he'd suggested. She didn't like helping him, but freezing to death wouldn't help her.

Keeping an ear open to Almon's movements so she wouldn't get lost, she wandered deeper into the woods, following a line of bare elms and picking up newly fallen branches from the top of the snow. The wind had helped in that respect—they weren't stuck picking up firewood that was soaked from lying under the drifts.

As she bent to pick up a large, three-pronged stick, she wondered when she'd stopped praying.

The question came out of the blue. Herman Melrose would have said it was the Fire Within prompting her.

She didn't know if that was true. But she *had* stopped praying. Probably at the same time she had quietly lost her expectation that the Fire Within would speak, either to initiate or to answer.

When? Why?

The answer to both questions was the same. She had stopped praying when she decided to give up the seed. She'd stopped because in giving up the seed, she believed—deep down—that she was turning her back on the task given her by the Fire Within. She'd tried to justify it, telling herself Serena was the better person for the job. And she didn't really feel that she had a choice. She was a mother. Her daughter was in danger. She *had* to go to her.

A question came to mind, this time unmistakably addressed *to* her, unmistakably originating in Another.

Aren't you my daughter?

She blinked back sudden, fierce tears. What did that matter? Yes, the Creator was her father. But she was running away from him, just like she'd run away from Phinehas Cole.

It was her fault she was here, lost in the wilderness with a dangerous enemy as her only ally. She had brought this on herself.

Does that mean I can't help you in it?

She pushed the question away. Pushed the whole conversation away. She hadn't meant to start praying again, or listening again. She'd wanted to be a Trembler, to hear from the Creator for herself. But the burdens of doing so were too great.

The Fire Within asked too much and offered too much. She could neither give nor receive what was required.

She spent a fearful night by the fire, sitting as close as she could for warmth, watching Almon warily as he slumbered on the other side. She was afraid to sleep, knowing that he might also be watching her. Eventually she couldn't help drifting away; she was too tired, too emptied out. But she slept in fits and starts—she woke up more than once clutching the knife handle so hard her fingers ached with the effort.

In the morning he didn't speak to her. He grunted once or twice as he ambled around the camp, kicking dirt into the fire, going off to relieve himself in the trees. There was nothing to eat. Linette tried to ignore the hunger pangs she felt and how heavy and weak her limbs seemed as she got up and brushed away snow that had drifted across her in the night and now clung to her cloak and skirt and boots. She stamped her feet and smacked her hands together to try to get her blood flowing, and she wondered how far they were from New Cranwell and if they would make it there alive. Briefly, when Almon disappeared in the forest, she considered running. But she reached the same conclusion she had the day before. She *could* run— and then what?

At least he was going in the right direction.

They moved closer to the river, and Linette's heart fell a little when Carson wasn't there. There was no sign of red coats in either direction, no sight or sound of the men who had served as their escort. The landscape changed as they went, the riverbanks becoming sharp and clifflike, bluffs that hung over a narrow and icy waterway some thirty feet below. After a while the ground plunged downward, and the ice gave way to tumbling rapids and treacherous rocks. This wasn't the Mescahannec, Linette realized with a sinking feeling. She would have remembered passing through something like that on her journey up the river to Jerusalem Valley when she first ran away. They were on some other river. At least it too must eventually lead to the sea—or more likely, to join the larger Mescahannec in its course.

Around midday, they heard wolves howling again. The sound seemed distant, but it chilled Linette nonetheless, and even Almon stopped for a moment, still, head raised as though he were scenting the woods. After a few minutes like that, he moved forward again.

Linette followed, not sure if his animal-like behavior made her feel safer or more vulnerable.

In the end, it wasn't wolves that attacked them. It was a cat.

Unlike the wolves, whose eerie, mournful howls alerted them at all times to the fact of their presence, the mountain cat was silent and completely unseen. It was not there, and then it was, bounding across the snow straight at Linette, lithe and powerful, its ears lying back and its dark eyes gleaming. There was no time to react.

Linette had fallen behind; Almon was several yards away. She fumbled for her knife and dropped instinctively into a crouch, bracing herself.

The cat slammed into her. Claws sank into her shoulders as its weight bowled her over. She struck out wildly with the knife, plunging it into the cat's foreleg again and again, blinded by pain and fear. It screamed, but she didn't know whether the sound meant pain or triumph. It didn't matter. Her neck was exposed and she knew she was about to die.

Something roared.

The weight of the cat lifted off her; the claws tore away from her flesh. She opened her eyes to see that Almon had pulled the mountain lion away and now held it in the air as it writhed and screamed at him, trying to twist itself around so it could tear out his face. But Almon, preternaturally tall, preternaturally strong—*transformed* into something inhuman—broke the cat's back and flung it away.

He turned and snarled at Linette.

She'd been here before, lying in the snow, menaced by a Machkigen, but last time it was Jonathan and he wasn't like *this*.

Almon's transformation was … more, somehow. Hideous black ichor pulsed through his vines, spiderwebbing across the sides of his neck and face. His eyes were yellow; his muscles bulged. He barred long, snakelike fangs and hissed at her.

Eyes wide, she tried to scramble away.

He was going to attack her.

"No!" she shouted and raised both her hands, calling up the energy she hadn't used in what seemed like ages. It burst out of her, light surging like the sun itself.

It knocked him back several feet. He roared and tried to block her light with his massive, clawed hands.

The brighter her light shone, the dimmer their surroundings seemed to grow. And she saw them again. The other things. The beings that were always there. Almon was surrounded by the shriveled, dead kind, the wraith-like creatures called demons or shades. They were all over him, climbing on him, whispering in his ears, tugging at him, tormenting him, laughing at him.

It was terrifying.

Yet in that moment he seemed less a monster than a frightened, victimized child.

She rose unsteadily to her feet, hands still out, the light fairly pulsing from her. She could hardly see, blinded by her own light and by the busy, crowded dimness of the otherworld, but she pushed him backward, and he staggered away from her and roared again.

Too late she recognized that the rushing in her ears wasn't just her own blood pounding in fear. It was the sound of the river.

Frederick Almon lost his footing and toppled backward, over the bluff to the rocks and water below. He cried out as he fell.

This time the cry sounded human.

Linette stood blinking at the empty spot where he had disappeared as a gust of wind blew a flurry of snow across the top of the bluff. Light was still pulsing, pounding through her. It made her head ache and her eyes throb.

Further downriver, she could see a cleft in the bluff and a path to the water. She ran for it. The light faded from her vines, but she could still feel its heat. The pain in her shoulders was less where the lion's claws had dug in; perhaps the heat had partially cauterized the wounds, as had happened before.

Then, of course, she'd had Sarah's help. Now she was alone.

Not alone, a voice reminded her as she pelted toward the opening in the bluff.

She half-slid, half-ran down the path, barely keeping her feet in the slide of mud and snow. She stopped and hurriedly scanned the water—there he was. Facedown in the river, alternately caught amid the rocks and ice and pushed forward by the violent rush of the current. She was further downriver than he was; she could catch him.

She didn't know why she was trying to save him.

It just didn't feel like she had any choice.

Almon had surrendered to the madness, and now it had swallowed him whole.

Always before, when the madness came, it came with heat. He'd thought it would burn him alive.

This time it was cold. Cold, violent, battering, numbing, *freezing.*

It rushed in his ears and filled his nose and his mouth; he swallowed it and coughed and thrashed.

But it was going to kill him this time, and all the shades were laughing at him.

He should have known better than to think he could master or control it. He loved the strength it gave him and the promises of vengeance. He loved what it promised to make him and how it made other people afraid. But deep down he'd always known he was lying to himself. That it would not make him great and powerful, but turn him into a mewling, squalling, helpless thing; a fetus floating in the cold; a child born to a mother who hates.

His mother was there.

He could see her through the transparent sheen of madness. He recognized the shape of her; the color of her red-blonde hair. She was overhead, balanced on something—*a log, reaching out over the water*—reaching for him.

He hated her.

It was all her fault, this cold, this madness, this death he would face too soon.

He reached back so he could grab her hand and pull, force her down into the cold and dark with him, make her succumb.

The madness shoved him forward and his head slammed into something hard.

Everything went dark.

Clinging with her legs to the fallen tree, Linette grabbed Almon's hand with one hand and the shoulder of his coat with the other and hauled.

He had been conscious a moment ago, had even reached for her. But his head slammed into a rock and he went slack, his body dead weight, sodden and heavier than ever. At least, as he lost consciousness, he seemed to shrink—some of his unnatural size atrophying back to more human proportions.

She was now lying fully across the tree, holding on to him with both hands as the current pushed against his body and the weight tried to drag him down. She would never be able to pull him up and out of the water. But she might be able to inch her way back and drag him along with her.

It was long, slow, torturous work, and as she did it, feeling as though her arms would be torn off or she would be crushed against the tree; as its wet, rough surface scraped the skin of her face and neck, she more than once asked herself why she didn't just drop him and be done with it.

It wouldn't be her fault if he died, would it? He'd fallen into the river. He'd drowned. She was just one woman. No one could expect her to save him—to be strong enough, or determined enough, or brave enough.

This man had hurt her.

He had hurt her friends.

He was a monster.

She paused in her tugging and her slow, backward crawl to breathe, to raise herself slightly off the tree so she could get air in her lungs. How was she even conscious? Using her light the way she had usually drained her faster than this.

How. Why. What in the world did she think she was doing.

You remind me of my mother, he'd told her once.

She cursed out loud.

Moving a foot took a small eternity. Moving another foot took a slightly shorter one. Another foot, maybe another—who really knew how far she had to go? She couldn't twist to look back with her half-numb hands clinging so determinedly to this man—and suddenly it wasn't water below them anymore; it was the sandy, snow-covered riverbank. Linette gave the mightiest heave she could and was satisfied to see Almon come partially out of the water; his head and part of his shoulders resting on the bank. The water was shallow here and the rapids less urgent, not pushing the rest of him so hard. She dared let go with one hand so she could slide down from the tree, stand on the bank, and grab on to the other shoulder of his coat. She pulled, putting her whole weight into it. He came free from the water.

With her whole body aching and almost numb, she wrestled him across the sand and into a sitting position against the bluff, in as sheltered a spot as she could find. His skin was blue with cold, but he was breathing. His eyes were closed and his head lolled to one side. Blood ran from a wound near his temple; other scratches seeped blood, and his lip was split.

His clothes and hair were soaked, of course.

She realized with a sinking heart that she might have saved him from drowning, but she couldn't stop him from freezing to death.

Could she?

Deep within herself, she felt a hard determination set in. A pragmatic, no-nonsense resolution; a mother's determination.

She would not give up until she knew she had been beaten. And she would not know she was beaten until he was dead.

Maybe not even then. If he died, she could still pray, and sometimes, miracles happened.

While a part of her continued to marvel at her own ability to stay conscious, move, and make decisions after pouring out so much light, a more *present* part of her went to work. Steeling herself, she began stripping off the lieutenant's wet clothes, one item at a time until he was down to his skin. Then she pulled off her cloak, coat, hat, and gloves and wrapped him in them.

Fire next. Their campfire from the night before wasn't far. Almon had cursorily put it out, but hopefully she could still find a live ember or two. Fuel would not be a problem, and she didn't even have to go hunting for it—the bluff sheltered piles of deadfall that had been pushed there at some point when the river was higher.

Leaving Almon, she clambered up the path and held up her hand against the bright reflection of the sun on the snow. Without thinking, she thanked the Creator that the sun was out—that they had some warmth, finally, to help in this bid to save a life.

Following her own tracks, she made her way back to their little campsite. Along the way, the dead cat lay in the snow, staining it red with blood. She stood and stared at it for a moment, then nodded.

Fire first.

As she'd hoped, she found still-burning embers without much trouble, beneath a pile of ash where Almon's dirt-kicking hadn't quite reached. The lieutenant's little bundle of belongings included a small metal pan; she put the embers inside it and added a little moss from the night before for extra fuel. The moss began to smoke and smolder, and she carefully carried the pan back down the bank.

Almon hadn't moved.

Grateful again for the sunshine that warmed her as she moved, she gingerly set her little fire aside while she built up a pile of dry deadfall, branches arranged to allow air to get in and the fire to build quickly. She prayed again, once more in thanks—this time for the settlers who had shown her how to do things like this, who had helped her grow beyond her citified ways. It was Samuel Foster, she remembered with a quick smile, who had first helped her build a fire.

The pile built, she carefully maneuvered her little flame beneath it and watched with satisfaction as it began to catch and burn.

Still the sun shone down on her; still the sun kept her warm.

She turned to look at her patient. He sat slumped forward, unmoving. Perhaps he was dead. But no, she saw the slight rise and fall of his breath. With a sigh to fortify herself against expending yet more effort, she tromped over the ground to his side, got her hands beneath his arms, and wrestled him over to the fire. She dropped him to the ground near it, arranged her cloak over him so it would catch as much of the heat and direct it to his body as possible—he was still dangerously wet—and left him there.

Knife in hand, she climbed the bluff again and looked over at the golden shape in the snow and the bloody aureole around it.

Another deep breath. Here we go.

Once or twice, she had been invited over to a settler's home for a butchering. She hadn't wanted to go, but she wouldn't admit that to them. Just because she'd never had to kill her own meat didn't mean she didn't know that life came from death, that girls who lived in beautiful homes in the city ate their fine dinners because someone else got blood on their hands. She had chosen to move to the frontier. Let her be a frontier woman.

They had involved her, taught her what to do, handed her the knife.

Without skill, but possessing knowledge and experience enough, and grimacing all the while, she skinned the cat.

The body was still warm. She didn't have time to properly clean the skin, but she used her knife to scrape off the worst bits of flesh and fat still clinging to it. The whole process took forever, and she kept wondering if Almon had died, or worse, if he'd returned to consciousness while she worked to save him.

She did not bother to prosecute her feelings about that. She *did* want him to die. And she couldn't let him—not without doing everything she could to save his life. Both were true, and that was simply the way it was.

With the skin removed and as clean as she could make it in a hurry, she rolled it up and carried it down to the man who was warming by the fire.

His eyes were open. They were glassy and didn't see her. He moaned, but wordlessly.

Once again she stripped away some of his clothes—*her* clothes—removing what had grown damp in contact with him. Then she sat him up, propped against a rock, and wrapped his shoulders around with the cougar skin. She left his legs bare; he was seated close enough to the fire to be warmed by it, and the sun was still shining—*on the evil and on the good,* she heard Sarah's voice say.

Or maybe it was her father's voice, or Jonathan Applegate's, preaching in a Puritani kirk sometime in her past.

With Frederick Almon as comfortable as she could make him, Linette hunted for his soaked clothes and spread them out on branches near the fire to dry. She did the same with her own cloak and coat, though she pulled her gloves and hat back on—they weren't too wet, and she was beginning to feel the winter cold too deeply herself, in spite of the sun.

Finally, everything urgent was done. He was as safe and warm as she could make him. He would live or die, but it wouldn't be her fault if he died.

She was aching and hungry.

She sighed again, deeply, and began trudging back toward the path. She was hungry, and she knew where to get meat.

It felt wrong to even consider eating a cougar. Predators were not meat. But there it was, and she was willing to consider that they could starve out here. She didn't think she was capable of hunting or fishing, or otherwise finding food in this frozen waste. So cougar it was.

She gripped the knife tightly again. She'd stolen it with entirely different purposes in mind.

As she flayed the cat, she remembered that Almon had saved her life. In his monster form no less.

It was another thought she didn't prosecute.

All of her work took a long time, and the day was short. By the time she had cut away meat, bundled it up and carried it down to the water, cooked it, and eaten—and then tried to feed some of it (unsuccessfully) to the man who still sat there, limp and battered, it was growing dark.

Almon's clothes weren't dry enough yet, and the catskin didn't cover him well enough. With the sun sinking away, the air grew bitterly cold. He began to shiver, even sitting close to the fire.

She stared over at him, studying his battered and bleeding face, his damp hair, his bruised and bare feet near the fire. His clothes, stretched out on their makeshift racks, were tattered in the darkness. He was a handsome man, and young.

She stood and went to him, seating herself a little behind him. She leaned him back against her so his head rested on her shoulder, and she spread her cloak around them both.

Today she had prayed for the first time in ages. Several times, in fact. Every one a prayer of gratitude. It didn't make her feel more free to pray now, and if she'd been pressed to request something, she didn't know what she would ask for. But she did feel that whatever separation had prevailed between her and her Creator, it was over. Or at least, it was better.

My daughter, she heard a voice say. *Do you know that you look like your father?*

As darkness fell, Linette Cole cradled her worst enemy, and she sang a lullaby as she rocked him by the fire.

In the morning, Amos Thatcher found them. Hours later, so did Thomas Carson.

CHAPTER 21

The Wilderness Outside Fort Collins—The New World

When Serena learned that Jacques was inside the walls of Fort Collins, she nodded and tried to ignore the huge lump in her throat and the sudden, devouring ache in her heart.

She was alone now.

That was the way it had to be.

Premislav told them what had happened. With the Machkigen bursting out of the woods behind them, Anderson had opened the gates to the settlers and let them in while his men, high on the walls, held the creatures back with volleys of musket fire. In the clouds of gun smoke and the howls of the enemy, they had disappeared inside the high log walls.

They knew nothing more: whether the settlers had been received as enemies or friends, whether they were free or imprisoned. At least they were behind walls where the Machkigen could not easily reach them.

Serena didn't ask about Jacques—she couldn't bear to—but Premislav told her that he was inside with them, and that Jonathan had personally promised to guard him with his life.

She tried to smile at that. She tried to attach some kind of hope to it. But in truth she didn't even feel worry for Jacques. She couldn't. All she could feel was the pain of separation.

She loved Jacques. It wasn't romantic love. Not on her part, and not on his. They both knew the other was separated from marriage and romance, that they lived a different mystery and were attuned to different concerns. But it was love nonetheless, deep and intense and vital. And she had not, for a very long time, felt so much need for another human being, or grieved with such intensity over being apart. From the moment they met, he had watched over her, cared for her, protected her. She had tried to give the same gift back when he needed it.

But it was over now. He was out of her hands. She was alone again, vulnerable and afraid in this great howling wasteland.

Fire Within, she thought. She meant to pray. But she couldn't get past those two words to a prayer.

Maybe it was just presence she was praying for.

Driven back by the soldiers' defense, the Machkigen had for now withdrawn. Premislav and his companions, Ezekiel and Josiah, had slipped away to a sheltered place in the woods under cover of fire. When Serena found them—or more accurately, when the band of River People on whom she now depended for life and limb and everything found them—they were hiding without a fire. Josiah was in constant motion, a bundle of nervous energy, charged up on adrenaline and the promise of a real adventure. He might also be relieved to be free of his father, Serena thought; there was nothing he could do for Eben, and knowing that Eben was safe in the fort might feel like freedom.

She tried to feel that for herself, to find a silver lining to the loss of Jacques, but she couldn't.

Ezekiel, on the other hand, had a look of residual terror in his eyes, and his old hands shook. He nevertheless managed to smile when he saw Serena and assured her, twice, that everything was going to be all right.

She marveled that he'd chosen to stay out here, that he valued freedom more than life.

Premislav had found a good hiding place, but the River People conferred with one another and told him, bluntly, that they were moving on and he would be wise to go with them. If they had found him easily, their enemies could too. Anyway he couldn't just stay here. The Jerusalem Valley settlement offered no real protection, and to remain in the wilderness on his own—with just a boy and an old man for protection—would be the height of foolishness.

He didn't like it, but he agreed.

And so they began moving.

Serena had regained some strength over the course of the day. After the short battle in the woods she had found she could stand and walk a little, though the warriors took turns picking her up and carrying her on their backs. It was awkward and she felt guilty and foolish, but that was her own doing—they did nothing to make her think they saw her as a burden. On the contrary, they treated her like one of their own and said not a word of complaint about the extra effort it took to move her.

Even so, they also put her down now and again and let her walk as much as she was able, and once she had begun to regain strength, the process seemed to speed up. Whatever she had spent from inside herself, it was regenerating, growing back. She felt her vines growing stronger and more alive, saw them growing a deeper red in color. By nightfall she felt nearly back to normal, and that meant she had to carry herself on her own two feet.

This she did, despite the darkness and the punishing pace the River People set.

The warriors spelled each other off in leading, but all kept up the same near-run through the night. She kept from tripping or getting lost only by staying close enough to the person in front of her to reach out and touch him. No one spoke. She could hear labored breathing in the darkness; she knew it was mostly her and the other outsiders who were struggling—Premislav, Josiah, Ezekiel. None of them were conditioned for this.

But none of them complained, and no one fell behind.

How the warriors knew where to go in the dark, she couldn't imagine. There was moonlight, brightened by its reflection off the snow, only occasionally occluded behind drifting clouds.

Without a word, without asking, one of the warriors pulled Ezekiel onto his back and kept going.

A little while later, another did the same for Josiah.

Shortly after, they stopped.

At first, Serena thought they did this because she was about to collapse. Not far from her, Premislav was bent double, hands on his knees, dry heaving into the snow. She was drenched in sweat, heart pounding, and trembling from head to toe.

But no, they hadn't stopped for them. The world, after all, did not revolve around Serena Vaquero. Instead, the warriors coalesced around what looked like a thicket and began moving it. This confused her in the darkness; they appeared to be picking up trees and walking off with them, and beyond them was not more forest but a deep, yawning hole in the world.

It took her a few minutes to realize she was looking at the mouth of a cave, and they were moving away brush that had been placed there to conceal it.

With the men all working together, it didn't take more than a few minutes. Then Wetëndeis reached out, took Serena's hand, and led her into the darkness.

Inside the cave, the air was utterly still.

The moment she stepped inside, the sounds of the others who were still busily at work, and of Premislav who was still gasping for air, fell to a muffled murmur. The moonlight winked out. Wetëndeis led her further, then stopped and released her hand. Serena heard faint sounds as Wetëndeis brushed the side of the cave wall, knelt. Then there came the striking of a flint and a bright spark, followed by the comforting roar and flood of light as a torch was lit. Wetëndeis lifted the torch high. It reflected off her red cloak, the scarlet feathers in her dark hair.

Others came shuffling into the cave behind them. Josiah was wide-eyed, looking all around him in wonder. He inspired Serena to do the same.

They stood in a narrow tunnel, barely wide enough for one person to file through at a time. But its ceiling was high, barely visible in the shadows. Serena hadn't really noticed their surroundings in the woods and it had seemed, to her, that they were stepping into a hole in the ground or perhaps into the side of a great boulder. She realized now they had been at the foot of a cliff and had stepped inside a mountain.

The tunnel led far ahead of them, far longer than the light could illuminate. Serena pressed forward as more of the band came inside, and then

Machcopoiken, at the very back, nodded. Wetëndeis nodded in return and began leading the travelers deeper into the cave. At the entrance, Machcopoiken slipped back outside with two of the others.

Serena didn't ask, but Wetëndeis said, "They will cover the cave door and make our tracks disappear. They will catch up."

Serena didn't envy them—how, and how far back, would they have to go to cover their trail? They had been running over snowy ground; they must have left tracks for miles. Surely they wouldn't try to retrace their steps all that way.

She didn't ask, but she did send up a silent prayer for new snowfall. And for the safety of the men outside. And for Jacques, because she was praying, and he would never not be on her mind.

Wetëndeis must have led them a mile inside the mountain. The stone beneath their feet was unyielding. Relieved not to be running anymore, Serena nevertheless began to wince with every step she took. She hadn't realized her feet were blistered and raw while her lungs were screaming for attention. Now she most certainly did.

Their trek came to an end finally in a large, round cavern. The walls were painted, intricate scenes of people, animals, and woodlands, and geometric figures Serena couldn't interpret. It seemed to her that these paintings were ancient. There was a store of good, dry kindling here, and Wetëndeis quickly started a fire while the warriors disappeared into various dark nooks and came out with piles of animal skins and furs in their arms. This was a well-used shelter, a safe haven well stocked. It was naturally vented in some way, because the flames drew well and the smoke rose and did not fill the chamber. Serena sat down by the fire and almost cried with gratitude when Anasan put a soft, warm cloak of white rabbit skins around her shoulders. One by one, the warriors were seated and began to pass around strips of dried meat—sustenance that must have been stored here as well. They ate, talked quietly, and then curled up and went promptly to sleep.

Josiah, who sat down next to Serena, leaned on her, then slumped over, head in her lap, sound asleep. Premislav began to snore.

It took Serena longer. She stared at the dancing fire, stared up at the rows of paintings rising up the walls, the two-dimensional memories of distant generations. She settled her spirit in a place deeper than prayer, letting the fire without remind her of the Fire Within and simply resting in the presence, here, of the Creator of all things. She soaked up the warmth of the flames and the warmth of the rabbit skins enveloping her and the warmth of Josiah and the warmth of good men and women committed to caring for one another, protecting one another. She let herself feel just a tiny touch of hope at the thought that Jacques was somewhere the Machkigen couldn't easily reach him, and that although he was surrounded by enemies, he was surrounded too by friends. The people of Jerusalem Valley, Herman Melrose's people, had taken him in and made him their own.

She thought of Joseph Crispin.

She didn't know why. But there in the firelit cavern, deep within a mountain in the wilderness of the New World, she remembered him and the first time they met.

She'd been so young then. Not more than fifteen—but already a leader. She hadn't chosen that role, hadn't wanted it, really. It just came over her, like a mantle. When the Tremblers met together, the Fire Within filled her and overflowed. She spoke words that weren't hers. She perceived with senses that transcended eyes and ears. She trembled with power and with love. And everyone else, even her own mother and father, made room for her with awe.

In those days Tremblers were not yet truly persecuted. They were generally disdained and held in great suspicion. People accused their meetings of being a cover for some kind of conspiracy, most likely driven by the Sacramenti. Some of their neighbors would break up their meetings or throw dirt and detritus at them in the streets. All of this paled in comparison to the glory of meeting together in the heat of heaven, so they soldiered on.

Real persecution was something different. Real persecution meant making enemies in seats of power, not just provoking local bullies.

Serena was there when it began.

Sometimes, she thought she was the reason for it.

They had been holding meetings in the Midlands. Herman Melrose was there—he was the keystone of the local Trembler community, as he was of many such communities, viewed by Luminari all over the continent as a modern-day apostle. He had invited the Vaqueros to travel with him. His influence and authority opened doors for her, and everywhere they went, people responded.

It wasn't some message that she preached that moved people, although she did preach messages—she could remember very little about any of them. It was just that she carried a presence. People came near her and fire seared them. It left them changed. It wasn't her doing. She knew that.

Later, her messages *did* become more central to her work, and also more clearly defined: she preached the power of faith and hope and love to stand up under persecution; she preached the need to resist the enemy so as not to become like him.

In that first meeting, though, she didn't remember speaking much at all. There was prayer and weeping. They had been singing when the authorities burst in. The people tried to scatter but there was nowhere to go; they were packed into the storeroom at the back of a tavern. It had two exits, and one was blocked by the police. The other, leading into the tavern itself, didn't allow for quick enough escape for the hundred or so Tremblers all standing in each other's way.

The police ordered everyone to freeze, and Serena saw eyes looking to her.

She was only fifteen.

But she nodded and held out her hand as though to say, *Stay.* And the people stayed, fearful but not panicked, willing to trust and to stand still.

The authorities arrested Herman Melrose and a few other men who sat near him. They also arrested Serena and her parents. Carlos was left behind.

Melrose asked why they were being detained, and on whose authority. The police answered that they'd been sent by the Elder of the Midlands, Joseph Crispin, and they were simply wanted for questioning. Melrose pushed but was given no more.

They were put in shackles and marched into the street, where the police made a grand show of forcing them into the back of a prison wagon, caged and barred but not hidden from view. "For questioning" was also, clearly, meant to warn anyone watching not to associate freely with Tremblers.

Crispin was waiting for them in a sparsely furnished room above the jail. The wooden floor was dusty and creaked as they entered. He stood to meet them. Tall, broad-shouldered, imposing, and stern.

Serena looked in his eyes and was nearly borne backward by an over-powering flood of *love*—the pulsating, world-rending love of the Creator for this man.

She had almost forgotten that.

The sensation was so consuming that she barely heard the questions he barked at Melrose, or the cold tone with which he questioned her parents about the Sacramenti in the South, about their ancestry, their roots, their connections. She barely comprehended that he was trying to ferret out the old loyalties, which were, of course, far more prevalent in the country beneath the Midlands. There was something deliberate, too, in the way he spoke to Melrose—something mocking in his coldness, like this conversation was a parody of a past relationship. She remembered thinking that at the time—being sure these men knew each other, but something had gone wrong between them. It was one of the few coherent observations she could remember making. Everything else was consumed by her overwhelming awareness of the Creator's love.

Finally Crispin turned to her and asked her a question. She didn't hear it, or couldn't answer it. She locked on to his gaze and held it, and he stared back.

After an interminably long time he flushed, and began to tremble.

With his voice on the verge of breaking, he ordered the police to remove them from the room. He said he needed a minute.

Two hours later, he called her back in.

She was alone this time—alone, that is, as far as the Tremblers were concerned. Her parents and Melrose and the others were left in a cell while she went up to be questioned without them. But they weren't *alone;* Crispin had packed the room with police, with a kirkman or two, with secretaries to take notes.

This time he didn't ask about the Sacramenti. He asked her about the Fire Within. He asked her about things she knew and how she knew them. She knew, as she tried to answer, that her words were being twisted into something else.

She and the others were released that night. But soon new rumors started to spread. Now they didn't say the Tremblers were Sacramenti in disguise. Now they said that what happened in Trembler meetings came from hell itself, that they called upon demons, that Serena Vaquero was a witch.

A week later, the real persecution began.

The Midlands, Somewhere in Time—The Old World

Crispin could not stop the trembling. He only hid it, letting his long robes fall over his hands, pacing back and forth as he questioned the girl, flinging out his hands in grand gestures for the benefit of everyone seated there to witness.

Inside, he still shook. He shook as he had that day years before, when he abased himself on the floor of a Trembler meeting and fell so far he nearly lost everything, all for the sake of some strange inexplicable *feeling* he called God.

He had come so far, and accomplished so much since that night, that he'd almost forgotten what that feeling was like. It remained in the back of his mind as a vague and fearful impression.

He remembered it now. She'd brought it back to him in a moment, with one penetrating look from her glorious brown eyes. The feeling had filled him again, like a flood, like a calling, and he'd begun to shake, and it terrified him.

With all his strength, he resisted it. He rose up in anger and fear and he beat it back. This was not the love of the Creator. It could not be, for the Creator, if he existed at all, cared nothing for the affairs of men. Hadn't Crispin himself proved that, over and over again? The ease with which he manipulated kirks and governments, the power of words to sway men's hearts, turn them against each other, or bend them to his will—the only god Crispin had encountered in all his years of ministry was himself. It had taken him years to admit that, but finally he had—to himself only, of course. If other fools wanted to go on believing, it was all the better for him. There was no God, or God was dead, and so a vacuum remained where men wanted to place their faith. Into that vacuum Joseph Crispin stepped, and he filled it.

But he couldn't stop trembling.

When he went home that night, something was waiting in his room.

He couldn't say *someone*. It was a being, yes, vaguely humanoid, hunched and wrapped in a cloak made of shadows. That was all Crispin could see. The harder he tried to make the thing out, the more it didn't seem to be there at all.

But it was there, for it spoke.

Its voice rustled like dead leaves. It spoke words, and Crispin understood them, but he could never recall them afterward. He didn't know if he was facing a real creature, a being like himself, or if perhaps this *was* himself—a manifestation of his own mind, some dark part of his own soul that possessed knowledge and knew what to do.

It offered him power.

It showed him how to use the Tremblers and promised him that on their blood he would rise to great heights—High Elder of the whole Puritani kirk, but a kirk made greater and more powerful by his own actions, one that would rule men. One that would rule kings.

Crispin would reign supreme one day. He would crush the dissenters who had once brought him low. He would tremble no more.

As he listened, he *saw* it all unfolding before him. This was no mere hope: it was prophecy, history already laid out before him.

He might go even further, the shade whispered to him. He might not merely manipulate men but poison them. He could learn not just to bend them to his whims but to make them actually change—to force them to embrace their own darkness and grow into the creatures of power they could become.

This, Crispin rejected.

Almost.

The shade spun insistent visions of the horror that could be unleashed, but Crispin recoiled from it. It was too much. This couldn't be what his heart was really suggesting—if indeed this creature he thought he saw was his own heart speaking, as it must be. He was not really experiencing this; he was having some kind of waking, revelatory dream.

But its first suggestion, that he use the Tremblers, that he would do. That he must do. Melrose and his ilk had defied him today. They had tried to humble him again. They were in rebellion against the only god he knew, and their self-will cried out to be brought into submission.

What happened to you, Joseph?

The voice belonged to Herman Melrose. Crispin didn't know if he'd really said the words, or when. Perhaps Melrose had pulled him aside during the interrogation today. Had tried to interrogate *him.* Perhaps he remembered that. Or maybe his troubled mind was putting the words in his old friend's mouth.

Your faith was so real once. So filled with hope. What happened to you?

What had happened to him? Reality had happened to him. Study and knowledge had happened to him; power and favor had happened to him.

And these are they which are sown among thorns; such as hear the word, and the cares of this world, and the deceitfulness of riches, and the lusts of other things entering in, choke the word, and it becomes unfruitful.

Seven days later, Joseph Crispin went after the Tremblers.

Serena Vaquero slipped through his earliest nets, but it was only for the best. The longer she was out there, the longer she stirred up trouble and captured the hearts of people with her strange and terrible power, the more the Tremblers would appear to everyone to be a real threat. They would grow up to be a worthy enemy indeed, a new Sacramenti, the ladder Joseph Crispin would climb till he sat in the very heights of heaven.

Nevertheless he looked forward to the day her usefulness would end and he could snuff out her light for good.

Two years after it all began, Herman Melrose came back to the Midlands and stole the seed. How, Crispin never knew. Melrose came, the seed vanished, and shortly thereafter—with the infuriating support of the Angle King—he sailed for the New World.

Crispin remembered what the shade had once told him of poison, of monsters, of how men could be truly turned.

He remembered.

He considered.

Then he arrested Serena Vaquero, and he turned every ounce of his brilliance and strength to the task of burning her at the stake.

CHAPTER 22

Fort Collins—The New World

Jacques de la Croix, Imitator of the Son, opened his eyes.

He was lying on a hard surface—the floor? The bare rafters of a low ceiling loomed above; the air was smoky and close but still held traces of cold and the sharp, fresh smell of snow. Someone must have recently opened a door.

Cold. Snow. Where was he?

When was he?

There were others lying all around him, and in the murky light above, someone moved.

Jacques tried to clear his throat and say something, but that simple action seemed beyond him.

Still, his eyes were open. This was a good start. He wasn't sure why he thought that. Had he been dreaming? Where was Serena?

Serena. Someone meant her great harm. He tried to bound to his feet, suddenly full of the need to defend her, but he couldn't move. Where was she? Did *he* have her?

"Jacques?"

It was a man's voice, low and disbelieving. Jacques blinked again, trying to clear his vision. Someone was bending over him now, but he couldn't see clearly.

He'd been poisoned.

And the man standing over him was Jonathan Applegate.

His vision cleared along with his memory—though he found himself struggling to put together the pieces of the past, as though it was all flooding back at him simultaneously, as if everything that had ever happened to him had *just* happened.

He *had* been dreaming. Or, perhaps, traveling.

"Are you awake? Can you see me?"

Jonathan's face came further into focus—a young face, brown eyes, with golden stubble brushed across his chin and cheeks. His bright yellow-green vines were beautiful—clear and full of life, like spring. Behind him, Jacques could make out a few barrels and pieces of furniture shoved up against walls, and tools and strips of leather hung from the rafters. They were in a workshop.

"Where …" Jacques croaked.

Jonathan dropped his already hushed voice even lower, as though he were afraid someone would overhear. "We're in Fort Collins," he said. "We came here for safety from the Machkigen. We barely made it."

Jacques struggled to understand this. Jonathan went on, "They don't know about you. The fort was attacked too, when we arrived; the soldiers didn't have time to inspect our wounded. We brought you here. We're going to keep you safe."

"Serena?"

"She's outside," Jonathan said. "With the River People looking for allies. I expect Anderson thinks you're with her."

Jacques let out a long breath. As his senses slowly returned to him, he became aware of being incredibly stiff and sore. He turned his head and looked across the wooden floor at another man whose head was turned toward him—Eben Axel. He was asleep.

"What …"

"They're all like that," Jonathan said. "You remember, don't you? We took them to the water beneath Sarah's house, and they fell asleep. The same thing happened to you after Almon attacked you. It seems as though the water holds the malliku off. Only I don't understand how it is that you're awake."

Jonathan was eyeing him warily, and Jacques understood his fear immediately. He tried to shake his head, and pain spiked through it. "Water," he croaked.

Jonathan responded quickly, turned on the heel of his hand and jumping to his feet, then crossing the room to one of the barrels. A moment later he returned with a wooden tumbler full of water in his hands. He reached behind Jacques's shoulders with one strong arm and helped him sit up enough to sip from the cup without choking.

Jacques lay back again. "Thank you," he rasped. "No, I—I don't believe there's any danger."

Jonathan seemed to understand, though he looked skeptical. Jacques could hardly blame him. He *had* been poisoned. Why did he think he was out of danger now?

It had something to do with his dream …

His dream.

Serena.

"Where is Serena?" he croaked again. But wait. Hadn't Jonathan already said—

Jonathan regarded him with an expression that might have been sorrow. "I told you," he said. "She's outside."

The words registered for the first time. "Outside of what? I can see she's not here …"

"She's outside the walls of the fort," Jonathan said. "With the River People and Commander Premislav. They're trying to find help. There are Machkigen everywhere. The mountains are overrun; the valley wasn't safe. We came here to get behind the walls before they attack."

"And Serena's out there," Jacques repeated. Then something else came to him. "With the seed?"

"Come again?"

"Linette's seed," Jacques said. "She gave it to Serena for safekeeping. She still has it?"

"She must," Jonathan said. "How do you know what Linette gave her? You were sleeping when she left."

Jacques groaned and struggled to sit up. He barely made it, and the room spun around him. Yes, he'd been sleeping. Sleeping and yet walking; unconscious and yet seeing and hearing, dead to the world, and yet learning.

He didn't know what it all meant. But he must have learned what the waters of healing intended him to learn, for they had sent him back—

Just in time to prepare for an attack.

New Cranwell—The New World

Every seat in the council chamber was full, and their shouts and accusations were deafening.

Phinehas Cole's defense had not gone well.

"This man," one of his opponents was shouting, purple-faced and pointing, "*This man* knowingly released an Imitator when he had him in custody! He is colluding with our enemies; we need no other proof!"

Beside him, another cried out, "We demand he step down from his position in the kirk immediately!"

It wasn't the first such demand. The man making it, Josiah Benedict, Esquire, had no right to demand anything of the kirk. He was a councilor, without religious authority. To the left of both of the shouters, William Shaft sat back a little, biding his time. Shaft was a prominent member of the Puritani synod. He'd been the chief correspondent with Jonathan Applegate in Jerusalem Valley and would be the first choice to replace Phinehas Cole if the elder were in fact forced to relinquish his position.

In the gallery, Cole's abolitionist allies sat pale-faced and unhappy. It wasn't only that they could all see his resolution for an end to slavery in New Cranwell fading further and further into oblivion the more the meeting progressed. It was also that the revelations of said meeting had made him look to them like a villain. They had learned, as charges were brought forward, that he had detained and threatened Serena Vaquero. Never mind that he hadn't killed her; never mind that he hadn't even been able to keep her imprisoned. As far as Cole was concerned, he had saved her life. But he could hardly stand up in this meeting, before *this* gathering of authorities, and pretend to be on Serena's side. To the council and synod, Serena was a devil. To the Tremblers, she might have been the virgin mother herself. Cole had tried to form alliances on both sides, and now the sides were collapsing and threatened to crush him to dust.

Gathering breath into his lungs to give his voice power, he boomed, "Gentlemen, these accusations are false! If you will give me the courtesy of making my defense—"

"Why should we give any courtesy to a traitor?" Benedict cried. "What courtesy do we owe to a man who undermines *this city* and *this government* at every turn? What courtesy to a man who betrays his very *church?*"

The chamber erupted once more in a barrage of "hear hears" and outrage. Phinehas strained for the sound of protest, of anything that would signal support for his cause, but if it was there, he couldn't hear it. Beneath the bench where the councilors were seated, a small group of witnesses huddled, looking harassed—with the sole exception of the ship's captain, Jedidiah Jones of the *Ventarrón,* whose testimony had started all this mess. He looked distinctly pleased with himself.

Phinehas Cole, who stood alone and unaided in the witness box, was angry.

He was also afraid. He recognized in all of this more than the unruly ambitions of men. It wasn't opportunism that snapped and worried at him like a dog. There was a higher plan at work, and a more insidious enemy.

In himself, Cole saw the last holdout against Joseph Crispin's bid for power. If he fell, so did New Cranwell. And it was not a fall into deleterious policies he feared, but a fall into real darkness.

At the far end of the chamber, doors leading out into the street were wrested open. There was a flurry as guards tried to stop someone from entering, and then Phinehas and everyone in the chamber jumped as a gun was fired straight up in the air.

In the momentary silence won by the unexpected sound, a voice said, "I'm a witness; I have things to say on his behalf."

A path from the door cleared, and Phineas Cole found himself looking straight down the length of the chamber at his daughter.

Linette looked frightful. She seemed to be wearing a mix of furs and mud-streaked woolen rags; a cougar skin hung around her shoulders and her long cloak was torn. Her hair was half-loose and wild around her face. Some sort of woodsman stood beside her, holding the rifle that had unceremoniously broken the tumult of the room. He was tall and thin, but imposing in fur-lined moccasins, a long black Trembler coat, and a fur hat. The air of the wilderness had blown through the door with them; Phinehas found himself shivering in a sudden draft and a presence like lightning in the room. Their vines stood out bright on their faces: they seemed more alive than anything or anyone else in the room.

Behind them, through the open door that looked out to the cobblestone street, Phinehas glimpsed red coats.

Linette started forward, raising her voice again as Cole hadn't known she was capable of doing, explaining her actions to all onlookers even as she addressed the council. "We heard the charges; they're everywhere in the street," she said. "I can speak to them. I've been in Jerusalem Valley, I've met Serena Vaquero. The charges are false and I will testify to it."

Momentarily shocked into silence by her entrance, the whole chamber now erupted into commotion again. Several Tremblers shouted the name of Serena Vaquero. A senior member of the synod was ranting; no one seemed to be listening to him, but that didn't stop him from keeping up whatever diatribe he had launched. Josiah Benedict fairly quivered with rage and elation.

"You!" he all but shrieked. "We're supposed to take you seriously, Phinehas Cole's own *daughter?* How are we to trust a word you say?"

Linette had nearly reached the witness box. But William Shaft stood, and his cool, clear voice fell over the room like an incantation.

"Yes, she is his daughter," Shaft said. "But she has not been his ally. Do you hear what she says? She's been in Jerusalem Valley, run there or banished there, perhaps Elder Cole knows—ingratiating herself with the Tremblers, and why? Because she could not remain in a city that talks of her dubious virtue everywhere."

The room stilled. Linette stopped. A whisper could have been clearly heard.

Shaft went on. "Don't pretend to be shocked, my friends, we all know the truth. Does she not have a daughter hidden somewhere in this city?"

Phinehas Cole pounded his fist on the podium and shouted, "Enough!"

All eyes turned to him. Some looked stunned, a few ashamed—like children whose game had suddenly gotten out of hand. Shaft took a step back. He looked smug.

"I was called here," Cole said, breathing hard, "to answer charges made against me in a private hearing. I came, I have answered, and as there is no judge here and no jury, *your* task has been to listen and discern, not to pass condemnation. If my fellow kirkmen wish to charge me with wrong, I expect they will do so. If the city council wants to charge me with a crime— treason or otherwise—I expect it to be done properly. But I will not stand here and allow you to tear at a woman's honor like a pack of lowborn dogs."

He turned his back on the council bench, facing the doors. He didn't look down at Linette, who still paused near the base of the witness stand. "As I am a free man," he announced loudly, "I will take my leave. When any of you with authority wish to pursue these matters further, you know where to find me."

He stepped stiffly down the steps of the witness box to the floor. He considered taking his daughter's arm—whether to escort her or pull her along he wasn't really sure—but shied away from the wild mass she presented. Instead he said in a low, tight voice, "Let's go."

She fell in step behind him. Near the doors, the woodsman she'd come in with nodded to her and followed them both out. Phinehas considered ordering him to leave. He shuddered at the thought that this man might be married to his daughter, and he shuddered at the thought that he might not be, yet they had been traveling alone. So much for the moral fiber of Trembler society.

Not knowing who the man was or why he was here, he decided against giving him orders one way or the other.

As he'd observed before, the street was full of soldiers. There were half a dozen, dressed in red but tattered and dirty, clearly exhausted and worse for wear. To Phinehas's surprise they too nodded at Linette when she exited, and one stood at alert—he nearly saluted to her.

"It's all right, Paul," she told him. She sounded deeply weary. "I'm going home with my father. Amos will accompany me."

The young man nodded. "Take care of yourself, Miss," he said. "You call on us if you need us anymore."

Phinehas was at a loss to make sense of any of this, but at least it told him two things—that his daughter wasn't married, and that the woodsman hadn't been her only companion. Evidently they'd had an escort. It struck him blindsided that he had, after all, sent orders with the army to bring her home. Was this sudden and wild appearing simply the manifestation of his own express wishes?

Phinehas had not brought his own coach to the council meeting. He hailed a cab and resisted the urge to hold his nose when Linette and her companion climbed inside with him. He glowered at them the whole way back and said not a word to either. Linette and the man—Amos?—exchanged glances once or twice, but they did not choose to speak first. Phinehas grew angry at the easy intimacy between them and at the fact that this man knew what Linette was doing here and he, her own father, did not. He was angry too at the long rifle in the man's hands and the protective way he leaned forward slightly, as though shielding Linette or warning Phinehas to remain subdued. He was angry at the way they both stank of woodsmoke and animal hair and too many nights and days without a bath. He thought he smelled blood on them, and it made his skin crawl.

By the time they reached the stately manor where Phinehas Cole had raised his daughter, he was ready to stand up and throw the other man bodily out of the cab.

He did not. For the sake of all present, and for the sake of perhaps having fewer regrets after he'd cooled down, he instead opened the door and motioned for Amos and Linette to get out first.

They did, the frontiersman leading the way and giving his hand to Linette as she took the step. Landing squarely on the pavement behind them, Phinehas paid the driver and turned to Amos.

"The servants' quarters are around the back," he said. "You may report there. My man will show you the way to a room and a bath."

Amos inclined his head slightly, but his eyes worried at Linette.

"I'm all right," she told him. She tried a smile. "I'm home."

Phinehas paused, unsure whether to offer her his arm as he escorted her to the front door. She didn't leave him the option, sweeping forward and pushing the door open herself. His man, Parker, stood in waiting, clearly startled by her bursting in on him. Phinehas doffed his hat and gloves and handed them over while he removed his coat. The air in the house was pleasantly warm.

Linette had frozen in place, looking unsure of what to do—how or whether to unwrap the barbarian things she was wearing. Slowly, she reached up and pulled the cougar skin away from her neck and shoulders.

Dried blood flaked the side of her neck, contrasting against faint green bruises. Phinehas felt something inside him contract.

He reached out and took the fur from her. It stank—it hadn't been properly cleaned or treated. Wordlessly, he gave it to Parker and then helped Linette slip off her coat.

"Go upstairs," he said quietly. "You need a bath. We'll speak afterward."

She simply nodded, and went.

CHAPTER 23

Home.

She'd told Amos she was home.

That was what this place was—or was supposed to be.

It held memories like a home should. Vague memories of her mother, long ago, before she died. The dark wooden curve of the bannisters was intimately familiar; she knew the faint creak of the steps. The long porcelain tub was second nature as she sat next to it in a wicker chair, gazing at it, waiting for the servants to finish filling it with steaming water. She knew the scent of the soap and the gleaming brass frame of the mirror on the wall. She knew how many steps to take to reach the stairs; or, in the other direction, her room.

She'd been a child here, been lonely and scared and silly here.

She'd given birth here, on a bed moved into this very room.

That had been brave of her father. Most fathers—especially most men of the cloth—would have banished her from New Cranwell to expect her child elsewhere and deliver her in secret. The baby would have been bundled away to some waiting family without Phinehas ever seeing her. But Phinehas had allowed Linette to stay home. He had suffered her shame with her.

She had wanted to keep the baby. As nine months passed, it seemed more and more unthinkable with every day that they should ever be parted.

But *that,* Phinehas would not allow. Not even after he held his granddaughter and smiled at her, and named her Elizabeth.

Beth, Linette had said, receiving the child back into her own arms. She was happy to keep the name her father had chosen. She liked it. She liked how he said it.

They had stayed together a while. A long while, compared to what Linette had any right to expect. She nursed her own baby for six months, while her father ignored gossip and came to sit beside her and play with Beth every afternoon.

It was only because he hadn't found a suitable family, he explained to Linette one evening while she broke down in tears. She'd dared hope—dared express—that it might stay this way.

He wasn't going to send Beth away to just anyone, but no, she couldn't stay here. What kind of life would she have, with everyone knowing? What kind of life would *Linette* have?

"You think they're going to forget?" she had asked bitterly, through her tears and her running nose. *"If we send her away, everyone in this town will just pretend she never existed?"*

"Don't bait bulls, Linette," Phinehas said. *"Of course they won't forget. No more than you will. But if you don't flaunt your sins, they'll stop talking about them."*

So Beth had gone, and Linette had spent another eighteen months in New Cranwell, unable to see her daughter or hold her or pretend. She couldn't pretend anything. She couldn't pretend she wasn't a mother. She couldn't pretend she was still innocent. She couldn't pretend Phinehas Cole hadn't sent her child away.

Steam rolled off the water in the tub and the servant woman nodded. "Finished, Miss," she said. Linette didn't know her name—she hadn't been here a year ago.

The servant left, and Linette stared at the white porcelain and the clean, beckoning water, and fought back an irrational urge not to get in. She felt like if she did, she would wash Jerusalem Valley away. The soap and hot water would soften her skin and her bones with it; they would take away the year of labor, grief, friendship, and hard-won independence of soul.

No, she told herself. Nothing can take all of that away. And you're filthy. Just get in and wash.

She forced herself in. The water was hot and soothing. While she bathed, the servant came back and took her clothes away. She left a simple grey dress behind, one of Linette's, from her old life. Again she fought back an unreasonable urge to insist that the servant girl drop the cougar skin, the stained and torn woolen dress, the petticoats ruined with mud and snow-melt and blood. She knew she couldn't just put them back on. But they were *hers*. They belonged to her; they were the proud regalia of her savage new existence, and she felt a fierce attachment to them.

Bathed, dried, dressed in the grey clothes that belonged to a younger version of herself who no longer really existed, Linette followed the scent of roasted chicken downstairs and ate dinner alone. She sat at the dining room table at the servant's urging and dined on chicken, potatoes, and leeks. She wondered where her father was, where Amos was. She thought of trying to engage the servant girl in conversation, but she seemed skittish, and Linette didn't have the energy.

After dinner she retired to the parlor and sat by the fire, like a guest. Her father entered shortly after and called for a pot of tea. He never drank alcohol and didn't offer it to guests.

The tea hadn't arrived yet when he turned abruptly, hands clasped be-hind his back, and said, "What were you thinking bursting in like that? Exposing yourself to ridicule?"

Linette flushed. "I was thinking that you were in trouble and could use help."

"You should have left it to me to handle." He appraised her for a mo-ment, and she couldn't read him. His expression softened a little. "You look better. I'm glad to see you're well."

She ignored the backhanded compliment. "I'm as well as I can be. I just crossed a wilderness in the dead of the winter."

"That was foolish," he said, frowning. "I don't know why the army al-lowed it, though at least you had their help."

"*You* called me back here!" she burst out, unable to contain herself. She thought of the terrifying storm and the agonizing hours alone with Fred-erick Almon; she thought of pulling the half-dead man from the river and skinning a cougar to keep him alive. She thought even further back, to leading the men of Jerusalem Valley through a mountain pass at night, using her light to help them find Jonathan; she thought of tearing a hole in the floor of the Trembler meeting house and of uncovering the pool beneath the Fosters' farm; she thought of facing the army with Serena and the children in a desperate bid to save the valley from the grip of evil. And she thought that her father didn't know her at all.

He didn't know her, he knew nothing of her life or of the community where she lived, and yet he'd sent word for the army to bring her home to New Cranwell immediately. As though he had any right. And it was Frederick Almon who had seized on those orders and used them to wreak havoc and terror and starvation in Jerusalem Valley.

Her father had no idea of the damage he'd caused. Linette didn't know how to begin to tell him. But she blamed him for it anyway.

"You should never have sent for me," Linette said, trembling.

"I'm your father."

"I chose to go west. I have a home there."

"It was a scandal that you left; I shouldn't have let you." He appraised her again and this time didn't soften. "I thought some time away would do you good, but there are limits, Linette."

"I left," Linette said. "I left forever."

"Then what are you doing here?" He lifted his chin, jutted out his jaw like a child.

"I came back to help you," she said. "And to save Beth. She's in danger."

"Nonsense."

"It's not nonsense!" She'd been sitting all this time, clutching the arms of the chair by the fire, but she found herself on her feet now, almost flying in his face. "I came here because I got word that you and Beth were in trouble. I come back and find you on trial for sedition and one of your accusers names *my daughter* to the whole court."

"It wasn't a trial, and that wasn't a threat," Cole says.

"You're in danger of losing your position."

He didn't answer that.

She went on. "Who was that man? The one who mentioned Beth?"

He gave an aggravated sigh and took a step closer to the fire, angling away from her and toward the flame as though his burdens had suddenly become heavier. "William Shaft," he said. "He's a member of the synod. He'll take my place if he can."

"He's a Crispin pawn," Linette said. She knew it was true in her bones, though she didn't know Shaft—she remembered him, vaguely, but her father's work had always seemed very separate from her, and she didn't know the men he worked with. She waited for her father to contradict her, but he didn't.

"It was a *threat,*" she repeated. "He didn't bring up Beth just to get at me. He did it to make sure *you* know that he knows where she is."

He stayed silent, jaw still rigid, staring at the fire. A long moment passed. "I'll check on her," he said. "I'll make sure she's safe. But you need to stay away."

He turned to her, and his eyes flashed. "You can have nothing to do with her, Linette. Do you understand that? I thought you did—but all your letters, all your—"

"How do you know about my letters?" she interjected, her face growing red and hot. "And how dare you intimate to Serena that I was reporting to you about the settlers in Jerusalem Valley? That I was some kind of traitor to them? Do you know how much trouble you nearly caused me? Do you know how much trouble you *did* cause all of us? I am here, trying to intervene on your behalf, because I love my daughter and so help me, I even love you. But your interference, and the meddling of the synod in the valley's affairs, have done immeasurable damage. People were hurt; children were threated."

She thought of Herman Melrose, and Cleveland Moss, and her eyes filled with tears. "Men are *dead.* Crispin sent monsters among us. *You* sent monsters among us. And you dare stand there and look at me like I'm something you're ashamed to be seen with."

He stared at her. She saw the old, flinty hardness in his eyes, the indication that he wasn't really hearing a word she said.

"Where's Amos?" she asked.

"Who is he?"

"He's a friend," Linette said. "He's Governor Melrose's secretary, and right now he's the only man in this city I fully trust. Where did you send him?"

"We don't have room for him here."

"Nonsense," she snapped. "We have plenty of room. *You* have plenty of room. If there's no place for Amos to stay, then I'll be leaving too."

She almost thought he would explode at that—Lord knew she was pushing him hard enough—but instead his jaw worked and he said, "He's rooming over the stable, with the groom."

Linette wanted to reach for her coat and furs, but had no idea where they were. She contented herself with standing up taller. "Then I'll find a bed in the servants' quarters."

"Don't be ridiculous," Phinehas snapped. "I don't know where this is coming from, all this—emotion. You didn't used to be so angry."

"I was always angry!" Her eyes flashed and she felt heat growing in her vines. She fancied she could see a matching glow in his. Phosphorescence ran in her family—it was an inheritance from her father, along with her red hair and her bright green vines. "I was always angry, I was always alone, and now I'm here, and I'm changed, and you don't know me. Amos has been my guardian angel since I entered Jerusalem Valley. If you won't welcome him here, that's up to you, but I won't stay here without him."

She looked away, trying to calm herself. Another long silence filled the gap between them. Finally Phinehas said "I'll send for him. He can stay. And I'll check on Beth. But you have to stay away from her. She doesn't know about you. It's better that way."

"How did you know about my letters?" she asked.

"Beth's family gave them to me. They thought it was better she didn't see them. I don't know how *you* knew where to send them."

"Do you honestly think I just let you send Beth away and didn't find out who she was going to?"

His voice was quieter when he answered. "I thought you trusted me to find her a good family. I love Beth."

Her voice quieted to match his. "I know. And I did trust you. But I still had to know. I couldn't leave without that."

"Linette—"

She dared look up. His face had softened. He wasn't looking at her—he was speaking into the fire, letting the flames dance across his face, shadows playing in his fire-colored beard. "I know these years haven't been easy on you," he said. "And maybe I wasn't there for you like I—like I should have been."

"I left," she repeated. "I chose a new life. I still choose it. I came here to help you, and to help Beth, but I'm going back. I *can't* not go back."

He nodded.

The next morning, Linette slipped out of her father's house and took Amos's arm in the crisp, cold air on the street. It was a twenty-minute walk to the Trembler meeting house, and the sea-smell of salt mingled with the scents of mud and horses and citified snow, mixed with dirt and gravel. Amos wore respectable Trembler black, including a pair of boots. His leathers and furs were gone, and he looked more like the old, gangly secretary she remembered than he had in—well, in quite some time.

They set off quietly together, and she ventured a look up at him. She could still see faint bruising on his face from the beating he'd taken back in Jerusalem Valley, when Almon ruled.

She wanted to say, *What are we doing here, Amos?*

But she knew the only fair way for him to answer that question was to turn it back to her. He had only followed. She was the one who had insisted she come.

Their path took them near the harbor. Gulls winged in a low circle nearby, calling to each other raucously. Kirk bells rang, and families on their way to services nodded to one another in greeting as carriage wheels churned through the mix of mud and snow and manure in the unpaved side streets and clattered across the cobbles of the main thoroughfare. Amos's arm under Linette's hand was strong and comforting. She felt like she was leaning her whole weight on him somehow, even though she knew she wasn't.

He had declined to stay with the Coles last night, even after her father issued the invitation personally. In talking with passersby on the street he had learned that neighbors two doors down were Tremblers. He was staying with them. He told Linette this apologetically, but she knew he was doing it, in part, for her. His presence in the house made things more difficult with her father.

She didn't tell him that she *wanted* things to be difficult with Phinehas Cole. She needed him to know that a firm line existed between him and the life she had chosen, and that one was not subject to the other. But she didn't really know how to explain her family or her heart, so she let the matter rest and contented herself with the knowledge that Cole *had* offered. She'd won that part of their argument at least.

"How much trouble is your father in?" Amos asked, surprising her.

"I don't know," she said. "You heard as much as I did yesterday."

"True," he said. "But I think you understand the politics here better than I do."

She nodded, conceding the point. "He may be in a great deal of trouble," she said. "If he's formally charged with aiding an Imitator, he'll be removed from his position as elder and possibly accused of treason. How far they take that—well, it depends on how far they think his aid went. Being an Imitator is a capital crime. Helping an Imitator can be."

"And if they don't formally charge him?"

"It may be bad enough that he helped Serena," Linette said. "But they won't have to *prove* that. Helping Tremblers isn't a crime, just a very bad move for anyone who wants to retain power within the kirk. The synod will remove him if they can. That man, the one who said things about me—" she swallowed. "His name is William Shaft. He wants my father's position. And he's the one who was writing to Jonathan, urging him to overthrow the Tremblers in Jerusalem Valley."

"He works for Crispin?"

"I fear so."

"Everything comes back to that. One man, on the other side of the world, doing so much to uproot us." Amos's eyes twinkled, and he smiled down at Linette. "Who would imagine we could be so important?"

That *we* filled Linette with a warmth so deep she nearly began to weep right there on the street. She'd been afraid that when she reached New Cranwell, she would cease to be a Jerusalem Valley Trembler in anyone's eyes, including her own. But it wasn't true. She was what she had chosen to be.

Nothing could change that.

They reached the Trembler meeting house, a plain, square, simple building of whitewashed boards set up on squat brick piers. It was surprisingly similar to the meeting house in Jerusalem Valley, though larger and with several doors for entry. The doors stood open and the sound of singing already flowed out from within. Amos and Linette separated as they entered, going to the men's and women's sides of the room. As at home, benches were arranged in a square around an open space in the middle, where a stout man stood and led the singing. Linette settled on a bench near the back and let the warmth of human bodies around her, the shining emotion on their faces, and the reverberation of their voices be like a soothing oil to her soul.

The meeting lasted for hours, as Trembler meetings often did. The greater numbers here—there were easily two hundred people gathered—lengthened it. Linette did not rise to speak, grateful that she had no burning messages restive in her soul. She listened and received and enjoyed.

After the meeting women and men clustered around Linette to introduce themselves and bid her welcome. Some spoke with a familiarity that indicated they knew who she was, but she sensed no judgment or animosity from them. Others seemed to regard her as a newcomer to town. She introduced herself simply as "Linette"—Tremblers did not stand on ceremony and were happy to use first names. On the other side of the building, Amos was similarly surrounded. She saw him edging in her direction and smiled.

Before he reached her, a tall gentleman with wispy white hair approached. Three others crowded behind him. Their expressions were kindly and familiar—where had she seen them?

She knew as soon as the first one said, "It was a great shame how you were treated in the council chamber, Miss, but you stood up bravely for your father." They had been seated in the gallery, off to the left, when she burst into the council chamber to rescue her father. Why? Had they been there to speak up on Serena's behalf?

She said "thank you," a little bewildered, as the man shook her hand. He continued to hold it as he said, "Don't give up on that father of yours. He can be hard, but he's a better man than it may seem sometimes."

Amos reached her just then. He reached out and shook the man's hand, who introduced himself as "Quilby, Josiah Quilby." Others reached out and gave their names as well; Linette stepped back and let Amos do most of the small talking. Questions about Jerusalem Valley, Herman Melrose, and Serena Vaquero hung thick as storm clouds in the air, but no one voiced them. This, Linette thought, was a feat of self-control almost superhuman in its scope. But perhaps these people understood the stakes. With a man as powerful as Phinehas Cole practically arraigned for his recent involvement with Serena and the valley settlement, it was clear that whatever was happening in the west, it was not the kind of thing to be spoken of lightly in a public place, even one as nonconformist as a Trembler meeting house.

Without anyone demanding her specific attention, Linette let herself sink back into the general collegiality of the atmosphere. As she did, she became aware of something that had been with her from the moment she stepped through the door—indeed, that had been with her out in the street, and in her father's house, and in the wilderness all the way here. It had been with her without ceasing, as ever-present as her own breath, but she had not allowed herself to acknowledge it until now. She didn't understand why now—what had changed in the course of sitting quietly amid people who worshipped in the same way that she did, sitting as one among many whose worship was to listen, hear, and tremble.

She had not felt any message burning in her bones during the meeting. But as she and Amos at last said goodbye to their new friends and stepped back into the cold, damp morning, she told him, "I still feel it. The seed is still pulling me."

He nodded. He was pleasingly tall beside her. She'd always thought of him as awkward, like he'd never quite mastered his own growth spurt as a young man, but he didn't seem so now. She wished he would say something.

"Well?" she asked. "Don't you think that's strange? I gave the seed up."

"Did you?" he asked. "*Can* you? You didn't choose it. It chose you."

"It wasn't like that," she said, unconvincing even in her own ears. "I was just there."

"You were led there, Linette," Amos said. "You and no one else. You found the spring; you found the seed. It wasn't an accident."

A surge of emotion welled up inside her, coupled with the incessant pulling she felt inside—the always-there tug of the seed. She didn't even know what she felt. Anger, maybe. Anger that the Creator would choose *her* instead of someone else.

"It's like a tide," she said. "It's always pulling at me. The whole way here—even now that we are here—and I should be thinking about my daughter. About my father. I came here to help them, and yet everything in me wants to turn and run for the west. Isn't that wrong, Amos? Shouldn't I care more about what's happening here? Who do I think I am, that I can somehow claim to be called to carry on Herman's work?"

He answered slowly, his jaw working first like he was chewing on his words. "It seems to me that if Herman were here, he would say it isn't who *you* think you are, but who the Creator thinks you are. We don't make ourselves. We receive ourselves. We submit to what the Creator has made us and how he calls us. That's what he would say, and it seems to me he would be right."

She looked at him curiously, struck both by the wisdom of his words and the unspoken stories behind them. "How do you know he would say that?"

Amos shrugged and gave her a half-smile. "It's what he always told me."

"You didn't really feel like you fit in out there, did you?" She was prying. She knew it. But this was a side to Amos she hadn't ever seen before, probably because she hadn't bothered to look.

He spread his hands out in a wide shrug. "Amos Thatcher, secretary. The bookish boy on the frontier. I got sick every winter for years. Couldn't handle the cold. Mother Moss always called me 'that poor boy.' Jonathan's father, old Reverend Applegate, used to ask my father when he was going to send me to the city where I belonged. He would say I deserved to grow up among my own kind. When Herman snatched me up to help him with writing and ledgers and the office side of governing it was the greatest mercy he could have given me. I finally belonged. But I never wanted to leave. I never thought Reverend Applegate was right—that I 'belonged' back here. I wanted to be in the valley. I believed in it. I still do."

He looked at her shyly. "When you came, I saw that in you. To come to the valley, a woman alone like that, leaving a past behind, starting over with no help from anyone—you had to really believe. And you had to let the Creator tell you who you were, not anyone else. You did that. Keep doing it. If who you are is a woman called to carry that seed, then do it. It doesn't matter what your father or anybody else says to you."

He'd grown a little flushed. She was touched to recognize that he was angry on her behalf. He'd been hiding it well. But it did her good to see it.

"Did you know, when I first came? What kind of past I had to be fleeing?"

"I saw your letter to Herman," Amos said. "You didn't say everything exactly. But you said enough."

"But you—" She couldn't say "you've been interested in me anyway." She still wasn't sure when that had happened, or why. And she couldn't bring herself to acknowledge it out loud and deal with how her own feelings might be changing. Right now, Amos was her only connection with Jerusalem Valley, her *home*, and she drew enormous strength and comfort from his presence because of it. If she also drew strength and comfort from him for some other reason, she wasn't ready to face that yet.

"When you come to a place like Jerusalem Valley, where everything is new, it doesn't matter so much who you used to be. On the frontier you are always asking what will come tomorrow. What will you need to get through the next day? What daily bread will sustain you? You're always facing forward, so people don't bother so much about the past. We all knew you were running from something, Linette. Most of us could guess what. But we judge people on who they are, and who they are becoming, not on who they've been."

She blinked away tears. They washed a world that was already white and grey, clusters of whitewashed buildings wreathed in the pale mist that drifted in off the sea. "What am I doing here, Amos?" she asked. "I came all this way—and now what? I can't help my father—I may have made things worse by trying. And Eben said my daughter was in danger, but I don't know how or …"

He patted her hand where it rested on his arm. "You'll have to do this the Trembler way, as you've done before. Listen for the Fire Within."

"But what if he won't lead me?" she asked. She turned an earnest face to him, for once not afraid to let him see how vulnerable she felt. "I abandoned the mission he gave me to come here. Why should he help me?"

Amos frowned. "Because you're his child and he loves you," he said. "And anyway, I'm not so sure you were wrong to come. Maybe you shouldn't have given up the seed. But the Creator's plans are big enough to include detours."

She looked ahead, up the muddy street, past the clapboard buildings toward the finer, taller structures further inland from the wharf, and thought hard.

"Thank you for coming with me," she said.

"You're welcome."

"Here, I mean—all this way. Not just to the meeting this morning."

He tightened his fingers on her hand again. "I know."

"You won't leave, will you? Before my work here is done?"

She could hear the smile in his voice. "I won't leave. I have a mission too: *mind the growing things.* I can't do that if I go."

She sighed and nodded, surprised at the relief she felt just to hear him say it. She wasn't going to have to do any of this alone. Nor was he going to ask anything of her in return. She knew that, knew it deeply. His being here was an unconditional act of grace, even if he was in love with her, even if she might—*might*—be open to the idea that she was falling in love with him too.

"I don't want to go home yet. Back to my father's, I mean."

Amos hesitated like he had something important to say but wasn't sure how it would be received. Unconsciously, she tightened his grip on her arm—and he patted her fingers again and smiled down at her. "You could show me where your daughter is," he said. "I thought I could keep an eye on her. And it might be good for you? To see her?"

This time tears flooded her eyes, and she took a minute to force them back and call words up. "I can't see her," she said. "She doesn't know about me. My father wants me to stay away and he's right … it wouldn't help her."

"I don't mean you need to introduce yourself. Just go see where she lives. You came here to help her. Doesn't this seem like a reasonable first step?"

She nodded slowly. The gulls over the water sent up a cacophony of calls and flapping wings. She felt the seed tugging in her heart, and she knew she needed to get her work here underway. Amos was right. She needed to take a first step, so that she could learn what needed to be done and do it.

So that she could go home.

So that she could resume her obedience.

Or rather, so that she could continue it. It was hard not to see this interlude as a break from walking with the Fire Within. But maybe Amos was right, and she needed to trust that the Fire would never leave her and might, in some mysterious way, still be leading her even now.

I don't know if I should have come, she silently prayed. *But I'm here now, and I want to hear you, and I want to obey you—here, in this place. I'm sorry for every misstep I've taken. From now on, please lead me right.*

She turned in the street. Beth lived with a family on the opposite outskirt of town. "It's this way," she told Amos.

Beth looked like her mother, which meant that she bore a striking resemblance to her grandfather too.

Phinehas, seated in a stiff wingback chair by the fire and watching his granddaughter play, comforted himself in the knowledge that by the time she was old enough to recognize this, his red hair would have finished its process of going white, and his tall, straight form would have bent and buckled some under the unrelenting pressures of the world. His face, with its strong jaw and clean lines, would have wrinkled and his green eyes grown somewhat dim.

She might never wonder.

Barbara Mason, the childless woman who had agreed to raise Beth as her own, added sage to the pot that hung bubbling over the hearth. It already smelled delicious. Her husband, Richard, was out back tending to Phinehas's horse. Barbara looked up at the sound of voices outside—her husband talking with a passerby. Phinehas, comfortable by the fire and made sleepy and slow by it, didn't look away from Beth.

She was three years old. She had Linette's fine, red-gold hair and green eyes. Her cheeks were dimpled and her hair curled around her ears. Her thin, new vines were bright yellow—the one prominent feature she shared with her father. She was a happy, untroubled child, and she was playing with a doll—carefully dressing and undressing it, brushing its hair, occasionally holding it up to Phinehas for approval.

She was a brave child, he thought. He came to visit about once every two months, so she knew him, but of course he was just introduced as "Elder Cole," and he didn't make himself too familiar with her. He knew himself to be a tall, imposing man with an iron-clad demeanor, the kind who intimidated most small children. She *was* intimidated, but she played near his feet anyway and made an effort to include him in her games, as though he were an awkward child and she felt sorry for him. He recognized that this took courage on her part, and he was glad to honor that in her.

Today—not for the first time—Beth's courage made him think of Linette, who was also brave, who always had been, though her mannerisms were timid and she shied away from confrontation and disapproval. He well knew that beneath that shy exterior lay a disposition just as shot through with iron as his.

He'd seen it yesterday, hidden no longer, visible to all. Not only when she'd taken him to task in their home. Before that, Linette had stepped into the council chamber as savage and strange as any creature of the mountains. She had lifted her voice in defiance of every man in there. He'd thought she looked awful; certainly there was nothing civilized about her in that moment. She was barbaric and she stank.

But she was glorious too.

Barbara puttered around in the kitchen, deliberately leaving him alone with Beth. Beth began the process of undressing her doll for the fifth time in the last fifteen minutes. She looked up at Phinehas and explained, "She's cold. It's time for church!"

He nodded supportively at that non sequitur and settled back a little more deeply in his chair. Barbara had offered to share their dinner, which he would feel badly about if he didn't send them money every month that helped the cobbler and his wife stay fed. He had accepted and therefore was in no rush; in fact, this was the most relaxed he had felt in some time.

This was ironic, he recognized. He had saddled his horse and rushed over here after pondering Linette's warnings and the events of the past few days for the better part of a night. In the morning it had all coalesced and he'd felt suddenly and sharply that he ought not to waste any time, but come here and assure himself that everything was all right—and *put* it right if it wasn't. He'd tried not to alarm Richard and Barbara, who had both assured him that everything was quiet and peaceful as always.

The kitchen door swung open, letting in a draft of damp, chilly air.

"Who was that, dear?" Barbara asked.

"Just a visitor to town, saying hello," Richard answered. "Nice fellow. In from the frontier, he says."

Phinehas looked up and frowned. He wished he'd stirred himself to see who was out there after all—was it that Trembler who had followed Linette? Why was he here? Was *she* here? Alarmed, he got up. "Is he still out there?" he asked.

"He's gone his way, but he may still be in the road," Richard answered. The couple regarded Phinehas curiously, but he didn't see any reason to explain. He took his coat from the hook near the door and excused himself. "I won't be long," he told Barbara. "I wouldn't keep your wonderful stew waiting."

With that attempt at congeniality out of the way, he pushed out into the cobbler's yard. They lived in a simple frame house next to Richard's shop, with a large walnut tree that shaded the front steps in summer and now, in winter, cast its skeletal shadow across the remnants of snow. A split-rail fence hemmed the house and shop in a neat yard, with a small stable in the back. This far from the center of town, their street was little more than a muddy lane, with neighbors on either side a fair distance away.

There was no sign of Amos or Linette in the road. Someone else, a tall man with shoulder-length yellow hair, was meandering along the lane toward town, his back to Phinehas and the cobbler's shop. Was that who had stopped to talk? If so, Phinehas had been right the first time—it was no one in particular, just a passerby.

Still, he stood frowning after the man and considered calling out to him. He was a good hundred yards away, though, and clearly wasn't Amos. *Just in from the frontier …* he might be one of the soldiers who had come with them, off-duty. He carried himself like a soldier. Or he might be some trapper or woodsman with business in town.

He could be anyone, really. Phinehas had no reason to stop him.

He turned and went inside.

Major Thomas Carson expected that Frederick Almon would be escorted to the court-martial by armed guards. He would be shackled and closely secured. When he instead walked into the regimental headquarters dressed in a long coat and hat, with mud on his boots and the smell of fresh air in his clothes like he had just come from taking in the sights, Carson found himself on his feet and objecting before his adversary had even found his seat.

"Why is this man free?" he demanded, aware that he was out of line but unable to stop himself. "I delivered him to you in chains!"

"You did," Colonel Wilhelm Regis said with a deep frown, "and we determined that such a condition was unwarranted before this court had any opportunity to hear charges. We released him on the understanding that he would return and so, here he is. Sit down, Major. You're out of order."

Sputtering, Carson sat. Had his superiors listened to *nothing* he said when he delivered Almon to them? Had they dismissed his authority to intervene without even hearing him out?

He'd known that Almon had connections in New Cranwell. He'd not thought they would supersede the army's commitment to justice or good sense.

At the head of the room, six men sat behind a long table. The colonel sat in the center with his aide next to him. The others were army officials of significant rank. Off to the side, in an ornate chair and positioned with honor, sat a kirkman Carson did not recognize. His presence here disturbed him. This was a court-martial; there was no reason for any man of the cloth to be involved.

Frederick Almon sat in the chair closest to the table. He crossed one leg over his knee, sitting with an ease that indicated he thought himself guest of honor. Carson was one of two dozen or so assembled witnesses, including all of his men, seated in rows of chairs behind Almon. The rest of the room was crammed with officers and men who had come to stand and watch.

Colonel Regis rose to his feet. "I call this court to order," he said. "We are gathered to hear charges against this man, Captain Frederick Almon, and secondarily to consider charges against *this* man, Major Thomas Carson, whom we know to have been insubordinate to the extreme, though perhaps not without reason. We know of no other way to explain the coming of a superior officer to us in chains, being brought here under great duress by his inferior and a band of willing accomplices."

Under a deliberately calm exterior, Carson seethed. Why was this matter being introduced this way? Who had already gotten to the colonel, and why? Still, he'd known he was taking a chance—many chances—in acting the way he had. And the colonel's opening salvo *had* recognized that Carson's actions might have been justified. He would have to trust that some form of reason would prevail.

"Major Carson, we call you to the witness stand," the colonel said. "Tell your story. Leave nothing out."

Gratified, Carson stood. The room fell utterly silent as he launched into his tale, the only sounds being the occasional grunts and words of encouragement from his men, who remembered every minute of it and felt just as he did about what had happened. He told them everything: the orders that had been sent with Commander Premislav, the discovery that Premislav was a secret devotee of the Sacramenti and the deposition of him by his men on that entirely lawful basis—no Sacramenti could serve in the king's army, no matter how far removed he might be from the Old World. He told them about Almon coming downriver from Fort Collins and taking over the ship and Premislav's command. And then, with his face growing hard, he told them of Almon's crimes and his madness. His attempts to starve good people; his threats on Sarah Foster's home and children. His illness and insanity and the cold-blooded murder of Matthias Carey on the way here.

He finished his story, paused, and determined to push all the way through. "Every witness here will attest that what I say is true. This man is insane, dangerous, and wicked. I call on you to impose the maximum penalties you feel are just, and above all, to remove his freedom to move in society. No one is safe while this man is free."

The colonel frowned at him, and the other officials leaned over and whispered to one another. Carson heard the word "insubordinate" from one, a man who couldn't help booming even at a whisper; another said the word "dangerous." Another kept shaking his head and saying to himself, "Irregular, that's what this is."

Almon, still relaxed, turned and looked at Carson and the rest of the men before languorously facing the court-martial once more. "Am I to be allowed to speak for myself?" he asked.

"We've heard you," the colonel barked. "You gave your testimony in writing last night and we've all read it. Do you have something new to add?"

"Well, it just seems funny, me being here on trial when all I've done is battle the enemies of this fine colony. Sacramenti renegades, Trembler traitors—that's the word the synod used in their orders. Elder Cole himself said it: Melrose was to be brought in for treason."

Almon stood and dramatically held out his arms in appeal. He was a finely handsome man, much worse for the wear, with a natural charisma that unsettled Carson deeply. "I bear the marks of the good fight on my own body, don't I? And all for following orders!"

Darkness flickered in the colonel's eyes. "Sit down, Captain," he said. "By your own admission you killed Matthias Carey in cold blood. Don't think I'm going to forget that."

Smirking, Almon took his seat. Thomas Carson reflected that though he had seen Almon in a monstrous, half-transformed state, he was never quite as frightening as when he wore the aspect he did now—strange, smug assurance; fascinating charm; hints of confident insanity and a deep and total lack of conscience. When the edges of Almon's true nature showed, he was more terrifying than anything that roamed the western wilderness.

"Nevertheless we have reached a verdict," Colonel Regis continued. Carson's stomach sank. What did he mean—they had reached a verdict? They hadn't even discussed Carson's testimony, much less called for corroboration or heard anyone else. The men seated around him began to murmur.

The colonel's chair legs scraped the floor as he stood and cleared his throat. "Thomas Carson, you have acted in an unprecedented and ill-advised way against a senior officer. We have decided not to prosecute you fully if you will agree to maintain confidentiality about the events that have taken place here and on the frontier. That goes for everyone who abetted you in your act of insurrection."

He glared at the men in the room, who one and all looked as shocked as Carson felt. "You will, however, be sent to a new post south of here, where you will be demoted to the rank of private until such time as you earn back the trust necessary to be promoted again … as I trust you will. Frederick Almon will pay a fine of three hundred pounds sterling to this court, to be meted in equal shares to the king's treasury and to the family of Matthias Carey. Other than that, he is acquitted of wrongdoing. We do, however, consider that he is not fit to serve in any regular capacity with the Army of the Colonies until time has passed enough to put this ugly business behind us. By special request he will be assigned to the personal bodyguard of the very Reverend William Shaft, here present."

Shaft nodded. Almon folded his arms and leaned back, oozing satisfaction. Carson's men burst out in protest, some getting to their feet, some shouting.

Carson simply stood where he was, in shock.

"Order!" the colonel commanded. When there was no instant response, he shouted it again. The room gradually fell quiet. "You are dismissed," he told them. "This matter—this *entire* matter—is to be laid to rest. Anyone caught discussing it will be hauled up on charges of his own. I suggest you all remember how serious a crime you are guilty of, and do nothing to recall it to the minds of myself or any other superior in this town. Now go."

Stunned into quiet, the men began to filter out. Almon stood, stretched, and strutted to the side of William Shaft, who welcomed him with words too low for Carson to hear. The colonel's aide gathered his papers and slipped out, and the colonel himself started for the door.

"Carson, come with me," he said.

Thomas Carson fell in with the colonel's stride, and they stepped into the cold damp outside the barracks.

"I imagine there are many things you would like to say to me," Colonel Regis said, "and you are free to say none of them. I want you to understand: I am not sending you away to punish you. *None* of this is to punish you. I am sending you away for your protection and your family's. Take your wife and children and leave, today if you can. I believe everything you said about Frederick Almon. I examined him myself last night and am profoundly disturbed by everything I saw and heard. I believe he may go after you for revenge, and I do not want him to find you or anyone you love. Am I clear?"

Carson nodded, at a total loss for words. "But, sir—"

"You don't understand. Of course you don't. I barely understand. Why am I not using my power to remove Almon from his position and from the streets, as you requested? Why have I handed him over to a preacher whose word and intentions I profoundly mistrust? I ask myself these questions, and I wonder if I can call myself a man."

He stopped and put a hand on Thomas's shoulder. His eyes, which were watery and grey and older, somehow, than the rest of him, pierced the younger man's soul. "I am under orders myself," he said. "I'm choosing to carry them out. For now. To avoid what might be a greater evil. I wish to God old Principio Premislav were here, and his secret still uncovered, for he might be able to show me a way forward. No one else has been able to. But know, from me, how profoundly I admire your courage and your clarity. You did what you had to do."

"I—thank you." Carson swallowed hard, a mass of bitterness and anger in his throat. "But why say all of this to me, out here? Why not say it inside, where it would have mattered? Why not pass the judgment you believe in, rather than one for which you despise yourself?"

The colonel's eyes glittered. "We are far from home, Thomas Carson, and loyalties are not what they once were. The Army of the Colonies is not the Army of the King in anything but name. I have given the judgment I have given because I am under orders, and if I were to do differently, I might find myself suddenly not under orders any longer—or I might die in my sleep. Do you hear what I'm telling you? Take your family, get out of New Cranwell, go to your new post, and be careful what you say and whom you befriend."

Carson stared at the colonel. He felt as though the ground had just fallen away beneath his feet, revealing a yawning chasm where solid earth used to be. His mind raced, sorting through the scenes of the past days and weeks.

"Phinehas Cole is in trouble," he said.

Light sparked in the colonel's eyes. "Yes."

"He has enemies who will try to remove him."

"Indeed."

"Does that have something to do with all this?"

The colonel tried to hide his smile, but he did not entirely succeed. He pushed Thomas's shoulder lightly. "Go south," he said. "Choose your friends carefully. Earn your promotion and earn it quickly. We will need you."

Carson nodded slowly. With sorrow, he turned away from the older man. He would do nearly everything the colonel urged. Certainly, he would get his family away from here—immediately, tonight, if he could help it. Frederick Almon was free and empowered, and Carson would not play games with time. But for that reason, he would do one thing the colonel had told him *not* to—at least, had officially ordered him not to.

He would talk. He had warnings to issue. His men needed to hear what he'd just heard, to be affirmed in what they had seen with their own eyes— the Army was not its own; it had been overrun somehow. And Linette Cole needed to know that she had been right. Her father was in danger. Her family was in danger. Somehow, she needed to get them away.

Or else she needed to find a way to fight.

CHAPTER 24

The Midlands—The Old World

After the unexpected arrival of Paulo and Bettina, Lucaan and Caterina were loaded down with new literature to spread everywhere. In receiving their new commission, both committed to staying together. They didn't talk to each other about it. Bettina continually insisted that they would have to get married, and though Lucaan had not yet convinced himself to ask Caterina, he thought more and more that Bettina was right. It was, of course, all he wanted. He'd not offered himself because he had so little *to* offer, but he saw the sense in Bettina's words. Sure, Caterina would say yes. He had seen that in her eyes and her smile when Bettina first demanded to know what was going on between them. He still wrestled with the rightness or wrongness of it, taking a woman to be his wife when he could give her nothing but the open road and his own heart and body and mind.

But then, he asked himself, did she want anything else from him?

When he thought about this, and knew that the answer was *no,* he felt that he was the richest man on earth. He was alive and free, in love, and up to his neck in a meaningful adventure: how could anything possibly improve?

But then it did, for his brother Leeanaert shouted his name from the street outside the tavern at the bright hour of midday, and his adventure gained the one thing it had been sorely lacking.

He ran into the street the moment he heard the voice, not even needing his eyes to confirm it. He and his brother grabbed one another about the neck and embraced, forehead against forehead, laughing and slapping one another on the arms.

"You look well, Lucaan!" Leeanaert declared. His eyes shone with pride and wonder. In an instant, Lucaan saw himself through his brother's eyes, and he made his decision. He would ask Caterina to marry him before the day was out.

"I'm getting married, brother!" Lucaan declared.

Leeanaert flushed with pleasure. "And that *is* well! Where is she? Where is the girl who captured my little brother's heart?"

Pulling out of the embrace and wrapping his arm around his brother's broad shoulders, Lucaan steered him toward the tavern, assuring him that Caterina was inside.

At that very moment, a knife hummed swiftly through the air, and Lucaan's ear buzzed and stung. He reached up and felt blood, and Leeanaert pulled him down to the street and shouted, "Stay down!"

Ignoring his own advice, Lucaan's brother shot to his feet and bounded forward like a panther, straight toward the hidden thrower. Lucaan rolled back to his own feet, his fingers sticky with blood, and balled his fists as men converged on him from both sides. He'd never seen them before, but there was nothing ambiguous about the way they moved in. They were coming for a fight.

He swung for the first two men, slightly distracted at the sight of Leeanaert tackling someone to the ground near the door of the tavern. Knuckles and noses crunched; Leeanaert whooped with what might have been joy. Both brothers loved a good fight. But this was different; this time Lucaan felt desperation and fear as he swung, ducked, and knocked the legs out from beneath one of his attackers with a sweep of his own. More were coming, and now he could see the figures lurking all around the tavern, inside and out. There were a lot of men, and they weren't ultimately here for him.

They were here for Caterina.

This time, he wasn't sure he could save her.

Caterina heard the fight before she saw it. Something stirred in the tavern as she came down the stairs from her room, an undercurrent of tension as people peered out the windows and a few began to ask questions. Shouts came next, reactions from people in the streets. A brawl was underway. It was no surprise, really—the last few days, the town had been filling up with outliers who came for the annual winter trade fair. Many were rough around the edges, bringing lumber or fur or leather from wilder places in the north or the Boglands. Some were sly and smooth-talking, as expert in the art of the con as they were in the selling of wares. Tinkers and vagabonds came in wagons and on foot. They had all provided a new and exciting audience for the stories Lucaan and Caterina told, and Paulo and Bettina stayed in town to pass out leaflets and add their voices to the churn of rumor and truth. But anyone could have expected that altercations would break out.

This was different, though. The initial curiosity and tension in the tavern grew quickly into real alarm. That was when she caught sight of Lucaan in the street, buried under a pile of attackers. She took an anxious step forward, ready to rush out the door, and stopped, every instinct suddenly screaming at her.

The tavern was full of strangers.

Many of them had turned to look at her, with expressions that were unfriendly and full of intention. She knew it all at once: this attack was about her. They were here for her.

She almost snarled as the realization hit her and she tensed for confrontation. Last time, she'd been nothing but a pawn—a victim targeted for someone else's sake, hiding away. This time, she was proud to be their enemy. She knew that she and Lucaan had become a real danger to Crispin and his aspirations. Knowing it made her fierce.

Three men converged on her. She ducked and slipped out from beneath their arms, running for the door. Lucaan's hair flashed golden in the street as he popped up again and then went back down. Someone behind her demanded, "What's going on here?" A general din rose in the room as townsfolk protested the newcomers. She barely heard it, too focused on escaping to truly hear.

She reached the door, grabbed the handle, yanked. Strong hands grabbed her arms and she tried to shake them off, but a pall fell over the room behind her, and she felt herself go involuntarily rigid as cold metal pressed against her neck.

"Better come quietly," a cruel voice said, and pulled her away from the door.

She turned slowly, unwillingly. The large man who had grabbed her held her arm in a vice grip with one hand while he pushed the end of a pistol beneath her ear with the other. The whole room had stilled. To a man, the newcomers had drawn weapons. Pale-faced townsfolk stood angry but helpless. At the base of the stairs, Bettina stood aghast, face white and large hands trembling.

The man shoved Caterina forward, and two others grabbed her, each holding an arm. The door swung open and a bloodied Lucaan was kicked inside.

He looked up at her, blue eyes full of concern. His eye was swelling and blood poured from his nose and down his split lip. His knuckles were cracked and bleeding.

Across the room, someone whimpered. Jorge. She wanted to look at him, to tell him with her eyes that everything would be all right, but she needed him to stay unnoticed.

One of the thugs who had brought Lucaan inside reached down, grabbed him by the hair, and pulled him up on his knees. Lucaan winced as another man reached down and shackled his wrists behind him. Caterina closed her eyes as her captors pulled her arms behind her and did the same. She couldn't fight back, or they would hurt Lucaan. He couldn't struggle, for fear of what they might do to her.

How love binds us, she thought. How it makes us weak.

But not *too* weak. If it did that, she and Lucaan wouldn't be there at all. They would never have made an enemy of the most powerful man in the world. And they couldn't have done it alone. They'd been fueling each other in their revolution from the first day they met, the first day he gave her strength to be more than a victim.

So maybe, she thought as her captors shoved her into a chair and the large one stalked around to leer down at her, just maybe love made them *strong.*

She ventured a glance up. The man in charge was well over six feet, broad, swarthy, with a bulbous nose and black, shoulder-length hair. His vines were brown and unusually thick, branch-like in places. His eyes were a particularly bright blue. He gave the impression of being all muscle, a living, lowering oak.

"Who is working with you?" the man demanded.

Caterina just looked at him. He chuckled—and backhanded her across the face.

The villagers, held at bay by the gunmen, gasped and protested.

"Who prints your papers?"

She didn't answer. He hit her again, and for a moment her vision went dark. She could feel her lip splitting and taste blood. Several of the women in the room let out strangled sobs; she thought Bettina was one of them.

The giant turned to Lucaan, still kneeling on the floor with enemies surrounding him. "Are you just going to let me beat her until the answers come? Who do you work with?"

"We work alone," Lucaan croaked. Caterina felt a flood of emotion at the sound of his voice. Love and concern and relief and fear all knotted up together. She didn't want him to talk. But she was afraid, of everything these men might do to her and of the unknown limits of her own endurance.

The giant responded to Lucaan's answer by balling his hand into a fist and punching Caterina in the side of the face. The skin across her cheekbone split and she heard herself crying out as the blow drove her out of the chair. One of the other men caught her and pushed her back. The world spun.

"Stop," Lucaan croaked. "Please stop."

"Who works with you?" the giant repeated. Lucaan closed his lips in a thin white line.

Bettina, Caterina prayed, *say nothing.* Drawing on all her strength, she gasped out, "They need me alive."

The giant turned and looked at her with a horrible gleam in his eyes. "Yes," he said, "we do. Nothing stopping us from hurting you, mind—but we won't kill you. This boy, on the other hand, what is he? Just a bit of mud from the Boglands. Are you willing to let *him* die, girl?"

He signaled someone, and one of the men kicked Lucaan in the chin. His head snapped back with a sickening sound and he reeled to the side. Before he could even fall, another man cracked the butt of his gun against Lucaan's temple. He slumped to the floor, unconscious.

"Stop it," Caterina said, tears pouring down her face and stinging in the open, bleeding cuts. She was terrified—for Lucaan, of herself. If it wasn't for Bettina and Jorge standing in this very room, looking on, in terrible danger if these men had *any idea* who they were, she might have told them what they wanted to know and prayed the consequences wouldn't be too terrible. She loved Lucaan, but she loved her sister and brother too—and Paulo, and Diego, and what they stood for.

She loved them, and love made her strong even as it filled her with a pain and apprehension worse than anything she had ever felt before.

The giant leaned down and put his hands on the arms of her chair, his broad face only inches from hers. His breath was hot. "Do you know what we're going to do?" he said. "We're going to string that boy up in the market tomorrow so everyone in this little town can remember who has the power here. We're going to hang him until he's dead, and you're going to watch. Then we're going to take you away with us like we've been ordered to. Nothing you do can change that last part. But if you'll give us names and information, just maybe we can see fit to cut him down early and run him out of town with a little breath left in him, hmm?"

He stood and nodded at the men standing over Lucaan. "Get him out of here. Lock him up and keep him guarded." He turned and regarded the cowering townspeople. "I am here on the authority of your prince and the express orders of High Elder Joseph Crispin. I'm commandeering this tavern until further notice. My men and I expect to be fed. You'll be recompensed for your troubles. Are there any objections?"

The innkeeper, a middle-aged woman about Bettina's height and weight, quavered, "How long do you intend to stay?"

"Just until our business here is done," the giant smirked. He nodded at Caterina and spoke to two of his associates. "Take her upstairs and let her think a while. We'll talk again soon."

The men pulled Caterina to her feet. To her dismay, she had trouble standing and needed their help walking to the stairs. She passed Bettina on the way and deliberately cast her eyes down. She couldn't look at her sister. She didn't know what she would do if she saw the expression on her face.

As the men took her upstairs, her heart ached for Lucaan, and she felt the regret of all their unspoken dreams.

She didn't know if she would have said yes. But it pained her now that he'd never asked her to marry him.

Leeanaert Feeanstra the Younger watched with keen displeasure as armed men dragged his unconscious brother between them down the street. They were headed for the local gaol, which they would no doubt pretend to own just as they pretended to own this entire town, where they did not belong and had no rights above any other man.

After he'd taken down the man who threw a knife at his brother, Leeanaert had of course joined in the fight, just as a few other young men had done. But the elder of the Feeanstra brothers had a keen eye and a quick wit, and he realized almost immediately that something was deeply amiss. This was no mere friendly street brawl. There were many of the men, they were armed, and they were on a mission.

Judging discretion to be the better part of valor, and recognizing that his brother was helplessly overwhelmed, Leeanaert had chosen to withdraw from the fight before he drew undue attention to himself. The knife-wielder would probably know him to see him again, but he wouldn't necessarily have reason to think Leeanaert was anything more than an interfering passerby.

Well, except for his striking resemblance to his brother, and the fact that they had been warmly embracing in the street moments before the knife was thrown.

Wedged uncomfortably in the upper loft of a public stable with a view of the street, Leeanaert cursed gently. Maybe the man just wasn't very sharp. Or maybe Leeanaert had hit him hard enough to drive away any clear memory of the brothers' interaction.

In any case, he couldn't worry too much about that now. The bigger problem was clearly getting Lucaan out of his enemies' hands before they carried out whatever designs they had for him.

The gaol was not far. Leeanaert watched the men take his brother there and disappear inside, behind solid stone walls. There didn't appear to be any windows, just a slight gap between the stone and the roof for air flow. Several more men, clearly and ostentatiously armed, stood guard in the street outside. The men seemed to be everywhere—a small army.

Deciding there was nothing more to be seen, Leeanaert pushed away from the rectangular loft window and shuffled back through the straw. The loft was barely big enough to crawl in, and he felt his way with his feet until he reached the open trapdoor and ladder he'd used to get up.

When he dropped to the ground floor of the stable, four men were waiting for him.

Leeanaert fell into a fighter's stance immediately, but the men, sweating and looking from side to side, held up their hands and shushed him.

"It's not like that, it's not like that," one of them said. He was a short, portly man, wearing a clean butcher's apron. "We're on your side. Or at least we think we are. Whose side are you on?"

Leeanaert relaxed—mostly. "My brother's side," he said. "Lucaan's."

The men nodded with evident relief. "We knew it!" the spokesman said. "We don't know who these outsiders are or where they came from, but they're no friends of ours nor we of theirs. Now your brother and that girl of his have become somewhat like legends in this town—heroes, you see. We're surely on *their* side."

Another of the men, a taller, more angular fellow, spoke with a faint accent that indicated he came originally from the South. "We believe the stories they've been spreading, of the evil done by the man who calls himself High Elder. We want it to stop. And now it's here. We want it to stop *here.*"

"What we're saying is," said the third man, a nondescript fellow with mud on his boots, "we want to help you. To help you help them, that is."

"Good," Leeanaert said, nodding. "Good." Without a plan, he didn't know what else to say. But sure, this was an unexpected blessing. "How many of you are there?" he thought to ask. "Just you three?"

"Lord, no," said the portly man. "I'd say the whole town's on our side. There is many an outlier in these environs too, come for the market—I can't say about them. But Lucaan and Caterina have been here some weeks now, before the market began, and we're with them. Wholly with them. It makes my blood boil to think of these interlopers taking them prisoner in *our* town."

A pale-faced lad slipped into the stable right then and approached the group without hesitation. He took in the sight of Leeanaert with appreciation but quickly launched into his tale—he'd been in the tavern. He told them what had happened there, while the men all grew pale and dark and clenched their fists and whispered imprecations on the bloody-minded outsiders and their ever-living gall.

It occurred to Leeanaert that this moment was important. That the willingness of these villagers to take a stand against the reach of Joseph Crispin and to side with Lucaan and Caterina was more than just a show of local courage.

It was, perhaps, more like the turning of a tide.

Leeanaert's desire, of course, was to march into the gaol, crack the heads of anyone who tried to stop him, and break his brother out directly. But this would not work: there were simply too many of the armed intruders. The gaol would be surrounded and the brothers forced to surrender, or perhaps simply shot. Two dead sons of Leeanaert Feeanstra the Older were not better than one. He wished for the presence of their friends, Jaapje and Joric, for Joric had always been the best strategist of them. But Jaapje at least had been badly injured when Crispin sent men to the Midlands to try to arrest them all. The fact that they had never shown up in Tempestano to rescue the Feeanstra brothers made Leeanaert fear they had not ultimately survived the altercation.

So it was he, and he alone, who would have to make this plan.

But no, he realized with a dawning light—he wasn't alone at all. He had an entire *village* on his side, and maybe more besides.

When Leeanaert and Lucaan, Jaapje and Joric had come to the rescue of Diego, Carlos, and Jorge in the Western Lowlands, the fight had been six against nearly a hundred. The brothers were well accustomed to odds like that, and found them acceptable because they four at least were the best brawlers they knew, and the hundred tended to be drunken oafs. In this case there were many enemies, maybe dozens, maybe scores; they were not drunk, oafish, or poorly armed. But they were still on foreign ground, and they were outnumbered by the villagers.

There had to be a way to use those greater numbers to their advantage.

Facts first. "Does anyone know how many of those mercenaries there are?" Leeanaert asked.

"No," said the butcher, "but we can find out."

"Do that, and get a report on their arms as well," Leeanaert said. "Then, how many are with us? Who will take our side in a fight?"

The men looked at one another. "Many of the outliers might," the farmer said. "I hear them talking in the market. They're no friends to the High Elder or his bullies."

"And all the village is with you," said the Southerner. "We are four hundred men, and women and children. But what can we do?"

Leeanaert's eyes were beginning to gleam. "My father taught us, Lucaan and me, that evil triumphs only because good men do not tackle it down to the ground. If you will all help us, we can stop it from having its way here."

His mind raced with ideas, problems, counterpoints. If all the men, women, and children of the town simply joined hands and converged on the gaol and the tavern, they could overwhelm the mercenaries and force them to lay down their arms. But no doubt the mercenaries would fire into the crowd. People would die. Likewise, if the men of the village armed themselves and simply went into battle, people would die.

He knew there might be no way around that. But he wanted to find a way that did not cost lives. Lucaan would not want anyone to die for him.

Leeanaert chewed his bottom lip. "First we should find out how many friends we have among the outliers," he said. "We need to know before tomorrow morning—before the hanging."

The Southerner nodded. "Everyone wants to help," he said. "Word is already spreading all over the village. We can recruit talkers to find out how many allies we have."

"It has to be done carefully," Leeanaert said. "If anyone sells us out to the mercenaries, we will have trouble."

The Southerner nodded again. There was a dangerous light in his eyes. "We will be discreet."

"Then we need a plan," Leeanaert continued. "But I don't know what that should be. Everything I can think of ends with everyone being shot."

The butcher laid his heavy hand on Leeanaert's shoulder. "Let us find our facts," he said. "Perhaps the plan will come to us."

Two hours later, Leeanaert sat safely ensconced in the tack room at one end of a long, narrow barn on the outskirts of town. The Southerner, it seemed, was a dairyman and a brewer with an unusually industrial operation; among other things, he employed a surprisingly large fleet of delivery boys who routinely ran milk, cream, and beer all over town—and who were adept at being both quick and discreet. They had been brewing for weeks in preparation for the influx of marketgoers and now had customers throughout the outlier camps. Called together and given new instructions by their boss, the boys set out to the camps and began to return in short order, bearing lists of names.

Most were on their side. To four hundred villagers would be added nearly as many outliers who were willing to force the mercenaries into submission somehow. Among the market people and the peddlers were many who dissented in some way from established norms, and very many who had been personally affronted by Crispin somehow.

Also, many had read Paulo's papers and grown convinced that the High Elder was a threat to the freedom and justice of the world they knew.

Amid this flood of good news, the plan found Leeanaert as well.

It was an old tinker woman who suggested it—and provided the means. The Southerner's delivery boys and the village's several tavernkeepers would do the rest. It meant—Leeanaert *sincerely* hoped—that no one would die.

It meant that good people were going to take a stand.

The chief mercenary's name was Roderick Rih. His first name meant "famous king" and his last name simply "king," and though he ruled over nothing and lived only for money and the pleasure gained through brutality and control, few men in the whole of Kepos Gé carried themselves with more assurance of their own innate right to lord power over others.

Roderick Rih set up court in the tavern where his men had arrested Caterina and Lucaan. He commandeered the kitchen and the taps with vague promises that Crispin would send payment for expenses incurred, and brooked no argument from any of the staff who might have protested that they did not want to cook, serve, and clean up after the mercenaries till all hours of the night and day. They were, so Roderick felt, here for the purpose of serving, and that was what they would do.

As though he expected his subjects to come before him with requests and favors to bestow, he set up a large chair in the middle of the dining room and sat there, facing the door, with his men arrayed around him. A roaring fire in the great stone hearth cast orange light upon him and his retinue. Others stood guard at the base of the stairs and still others outside the door to Caterina's room on the second floor. Still more men patrolled the street outside. They were all heavily armed and well trained—a hundred fifty men, Roderick's own small army.

As though they'd been summoned, a delegation of townsmen appeared in the street outside and demanded to be let in. Roderick sat drumming his fingers on the arm of his chair while he waited for his men to make the usual threats and refusals and finally let them in—having well cowed them first.

Five villagers entered together. They looked properly browbeaten and nervous, but there was a steel in their eyes too that surprised Roderick.

The man who seemed to be their leader was a butcher, or at least his apron and large hands indicated as much. Halfway across the dining room he must have realized the intimidation outside had left its mark, because he straightened perceptibly and set his jaw before taking a wide-legged stance in front of Roderick.

"I speak for the village," he said. "We don't want you here."

Roderick grunted and shifted in his chair. "We won't be here long," he said. "We've a hanging to carry out and a prisoner to take away with us, and you'll be nicely rid of our company."

"We don't want a hanging," the butcher answered.

"That's good then," Roderick said, lifting a huge mug of beer to his lips and taking a deep draught. He wiped his mustache and beard with the back of his hand. "You don't have to do it."

"We want you to release your prisoners and get out of town," the butcher went on. "Tonight."

Roderick leaned forward at that. "You've come here to throw us out?" he said. "Might I assume you've got an army to stand behind that demand?"

"We've got nothing but our rights," the butcher said. "This is our village. The man and woman you took are our guests. We don't want trouble, but we won't stand for what you're doing."

"So you've made clear," Roderick said. "But I'm afraid we won't go willingly, and unless you are hiding a hundred armed men somewhere, you can't make us. I believe you know we come backed by the power of the Puritani kirk. We're on duty for the High Elder. You're just going to have to tolerate our presence until we finish with our business and leave of our own accord." His dark eyes glittered. "Of course, you could make us want to stay. You could get in the way of carrying out the High Elder's orders and force us to subdue you. We would enjoy that, but I don't think you would."

The butcher's lips tightened in a thin line—but the steel didn't fade from his eyes. Roderick was impressed. He'd overrun quite a few villages in his day, and most did their best to hurry him on. Few would actually send men to stand up to him.

"We've seen well enough how you operate," the butcher said. "Beating helpless women. Hanging innocent men. If that's what gives you joy, we can't be rid of you fast enough."

"Be careful," Roderick said. "Or we might hang a few more innocent men. Maybe even beat a few more helpless women."

The butcher gave a short, defined nod. "I've heard all I care to hear," he said. "You said yourself, we're no match for you in a fight. But don't think your sins won't find you out."

Roderick raised his eyebrows. "Are you threatening me with judgment?" he said. "Do you think yourself a prophet, or maybe an angel? We're doing God's own work, man. Threaten yourself, if that's how you're feeling."

His tone mocked, and he knew his eyes showed nothing but confidence. But he felt just the smallest bit uneasy, facing this wide-mouthed butcher. He had the smallest feeling there might actually be trouble before the hanging tomorrow.

That was fine. He would put his men on high alert. How much trouble could one small village cause?

CHAPTER 25

New Cranwell—The New World

Phinehas Cole had never liked Frederick Almon.

He had known him as a young man—hardly more than a boy, really. Almon had been sly and conniving, and cruel in a way that marked him as a coward. He'd also seemed *off* in some way that was hard to define—Cole knew the rumors about the boy's mother and tried not to let them color his perception too much, but it was hard to ignore the boy's own strange behaviors and violent temper.

Almon joined the army as soon as he was old enough, a move that Phinehas Cole, looking on from the distance of his pulpit, approved. It did indeed seem the best thing for him. Discipline, hard work, and a forced equality with his fellow soldiers brought stability and calm to his life, or so the boy's harried father told Cole in confidence. Years passed and he earned an officer's commission and a post in the west. His spotted past seemed behind him.

Even so, when Cole sent orders with Principio Premislav to have Linette escorted home, he hadn't imagined those orders would end up in Frederick Almon's hands. Knowing that they had, and that Almon had done damage to the community Linette had chosen to make her home, piqued his conscience in a way he found greatly uncomfortable.

Now, as he watched Frederick Almon saunter up the cobblestone street to the Coles' front door, Phinehas felt that twinge of conscience more strongly than ever.

It was possible that in his self-confidence as elder of New Cranwell and Linette's father, he had missed some important elements of the bigger picture.

Parker showed up at the study door. "Captain Almon, sir," he said. "He insists on seeing you." His tone was shaped by a grimace he didn't bother to conceal.

"Let him come up," Cole said. He turned slowly in his chair, away from the window, facing the door. He wouldn't rise.

Almon stepped inside still wearing his coat and doffed his hat ceremoniously. "Elder," he said.

"Frederick," Phinehas answered. "I hope you don't mind me calling you that. I doubt that it's 'Captain' anymore, after all. From what I've heard, I confess I'm surprised to see you roaming free."

Almon went straight to the chair across from Phinehas and sat down, sitting tall with his hands on his knees. He met the elder's gaze without a hint of trepidation, and the light in his eyes was terrifying.

"Whom do you serve, Elder?" Almon said.

Cole frowned at the unexpected question. "I serve the Creator," he said. "And his kirk."

Almon wagged a long finger at him. "But there you are wrong. You've been told, I'm sure, that I'm mad. That I see and hear things that *aren't there*. But it isn't true. I've had time to think, and I've realized it isn't true. Look at me, Elder! You see a battered, bruised man, harrowed by exposure and the violence of the wilderness, and yet I am alive, after having been stabbed by my own man; I am alive, and strong, and on my own two feet, after being nearly drowned and frozen to death. Do you know who saved me? Do you know who pulled me from the river and held me in her own arms, who rocked me and kept me warm?" His eyes glimmered. "Your daughter did. Think on that, and ask what responsibility you have to me. But she didn't give me this strength back. If I am just a crazy man, a loon who sees things that aren't real, why am I not in bed, making my slow recovery like mortal men? Why do I heal and grow strong, why do I have insight and power like a god? It is because the things I see and serve *are* real. Their power flows through these very vines and gives me life divine."

Almon held out his arms, forearms up, displaying the yellow vines that outlined strong, sinewy muscle. "The life I live is more real than yours, and I know more than you do. So I know what I will tell you: you don't serve the Creator. Not anymore. You serve the one whose image first came to me and made me what I am: the High Elder of the Puritani, Joseph Crispin." Almon stood and leaned over the desk toward Phinehas, grinning wolfishly. "And I know what he wants from you."

With anger slowly rising, Phinehas stood in response and put his palms on his desk. He brought his face close to Almon's. "I do not serve Crispin," he said. "I have never served Crispin."

"And that's why he's removing you," Almon said. "Because *you* won't submit to the unavoidable truth. You say you serve the kirk. Crispin *is* the kirk. He will remove you from your position and then you will die." He grinned. "I'll probably be the one to kill you. But it doesn't have to be that way. I want to save you. For old time's sake. For Linette's sake."

"It would be better," said Phinehas, his voice low, "if you didn't bring Linette up to me again."

"You can be saved," Almon went on, leaning closer, eyes blazing, "if you give up your attempts at reform and surrender to your master's agenda. End Jerusalem Valley. Go after the Tremblers here in the city like you should have done years ago. Kill Serena Vaquero. Do all that, and you'll be back in Crispin's good graces. You don't even have to do it yourself. You can send me. Do you understand what I'm offering you? You're right—I'm not with the army just now. They acquitted me, *fully,* you understand—Colonel Regis knows whom he serves—but I've been asked to take a place in the personal bodyguard of William Shaft."

Almon nodded, pleased, as the light of understanding rose in Phinehas's eyes. "I am Shaft's man, so I am supposed to help bring you down and replace you. But I'm offering to help *you* instead. I'll double-cross Shaft, because I know who the master really is and what he really wants. He won't care if it's you or Shaft who does the work. In fact, if it's you, he'll be more pleased than ever because it means you've seen the light and ended your rebellion. Do away with Shaft and show that you're the stronger man, the better man. Crispin will embrace you with pleasure."

Every muscle in Phinehas's body was taut, nearly trembling with anger.

"If you think for one minute that I would go along with you in this—would even *entertain the idea* of helping you—you are more insane than I imagined."

"Your daughter saved me," Almon said. He dropped his voice to a near-whisper. "Deep down, she knows the truth too. She knows who has to be served. She'll help me once she's not distracted anymore. There are too many distractions right now, but I'll take care of them, and she'll be free to stay with me."

Phinehas exploded. He grabbed the young man by both his shoulders and shoved him down so his head hit the desk, and he leaned over him, pressing his face into the polished wood with an elbow in the back of his neck. "I told you," he seethed, "not to mention my daughter again."

Phinehas Cole was the older man by thirty years or more. But his body was made of iron, and his soul was a foundry. There wasn't a young man in New Cranwell whom Phinehas Cole couldn't have pounded into a pulp if he wished to. There wasn't one who, face-down on a desk with the elder pinning him down with all his weight and his anger, could have gotten free.

But Almon roared like an animal and threw Cole off. He grabbed the elder by his shirt, hefted him over his head, and flung him across the room.

Cole slammed into the wall and slid to the floor, heart pounding and head spinning. Eyes wide, he stared back at the young man who had become a monster.

Almon had grown several feet. His shoulders were broader, his neck and arms thicker. Black ichor pulsed through the vines on his arms and neck and face; his eyes had lost their features and become black as pitch. He roared again, and his teeth were fangs.

Cole didn't understand what he was seeing, but he knew he had been wrong about several things. Almon had been telling the truth. He wasn't—exactly—insane. And whatever was happening here, it was more than political wrangling and fights over the freedom to dissent. Crispin was playing a bigger game, and they were all pawns in it.

Almon snatched up a chair and held it aloft, advancing on Phinehas with it. He was going to bring it down on his head and kill him.

But Phinehas couldn't die.

Distractions, Almon had said. He meant *him,* Phinehas. And he meant

Beth. It was Almon Phinehas had seen in the road outside the Masons' house, he was sure of it. He hadn't connected the dots then because he'd assumed Almon was in a barracks jail awaiting trial. Now that seemed unlikely. When he finished here, Almon would go after Beth, and when he'd *taken care of her,* he would kill the young Trembler Amos Thatcher too—and then he would try to claim Linette.

Almon swung the chair for Phinehas's head, and Phinehas lunged forward and wrapped his iron arms around the younger man's knees. His momentum carried them both backward, Almon stumbling but somehow not falling. He roared again and slashed a massive, clawed hand across the side of Phinehas's face. Pain like fire burst through Phinehas Cole. He let go of Almon's legs and threw himself away, rolling back to his feet near the fire. He grabbed a poker and fell into a defensive stance, wary, watching Almon for an opening.

The young man growled. The sound sent a shiver down Phinehas's spine. Pounding footsteps came up the stairs—Parker, some of the other servants perhaps. "Stay away!" he shouted. "Go for help!"

Almon glanced over his shoulder for a bare second, distracted by the sound, and Phinehas leapt forward and swung. The poker should have caught Almon just below the ribs, but instead he moved with superhuman speed and caught it mid-swing. With impossible strength he wrenched it out of Phinehas's hands.

The elder man stared at the younger and realized he was facing his own death.

But *no.*

If he couldn't stop Almon, he could at least reach Beth and Linette before he did.

Never taking his eyes off Almon, who was grinning with menace, Phinehas danced a little closer to the fire again and snatched up another tool, a heavy iron coal shovel. He hefted it in his hands, feeling its weight. Almon raised the poker like a sword. Phinehas crouched, back in his defensive stance, daring the one-time soldier to advance.

Sweat poured from Phinehas's forehead. His face was a bloody rag, gashed and burning. Almon moved slowly, like a man savoring the moment. It was murder Phinehas saw in his eyes.

Almon lunged. So did Phinehas. But not toward his attacker—instead, he turned and ran to the side. He vaulted the chair Almon had tipped over, jumped onto his desk, and rammed the coal shovel through the window pane. The glass cracked and splintered.

Somehow, Phinehas found time to say a prayer.

Then he dove headlong out of the window into the night.

The air was cold, the fall so fast he could do nothing but react to it. Pieces of glass seemed to float in the air beside him. He'd had time enough inside—just a few split seconds—to think it through and decide his chances of surviving a second-story fall were better than his chances of surviving Frederick Almon. He knew enough to reach for the eaves of the house and slow his fall, and to maneuver in the air so he would land on the balls of his feet and not his head.

He landed—feet first. Pain jolted up his legs and he stumbled forward, catching himself on his hands. He tried to push himself back to his feet and found that he could. He could move. He could *run*.

He ran.

Behind him, he heard and almost felt the impact of Almon hitting the ground—he'd leapt out after him. Screams sounded as Phinehas charged into the shadows across the street, dodging a passing carriage and causing its horse to rear back in alarm. Good. The more people who reacted and raised the alarm, the better the chances that Almon would be slowed in his pursuit. He prayed the soldier would not kill anyone as he gave chase. He hoped with all his heart that his servants would be all right. He thanked the Creator that as far as he knew, Linette had not yet come home.

Funny. Just hours ago he'd been resenting her Trembler connections and her choice to stay away from home all day. It had angered him, because he felt deeply that if she would just come home and stay home, they would find a way to talk out whatever hurts and resentments she still felt. There could be no healing if she refused even to spend time around him. But now he had never felt so thankful for distance. If staying away from him could keep Linette safe, he would give up every claim to her for the rest of his life.

Between the cold wind blowing past him, the pounding of his heart in his ears, and the clatter of the city sinking into evening, Phinehas couldn't hear if Almon was behind him. Surprised shouts and the whinnying of horses indicated he was. He didn't turn to look. He just kept weaving, dodging and doubling back, using every inch of knowledge he possessed to trace a path through the city that would be difficult to follow. A long-time insomniac, Phinehas had spent hours upon hours wandering the streets and alleys of New Cranwell in the dark. He could never have imagined that the resulting map that lived in his mind and muscle memory would save his life.

He reached the wharf and the warehouses and shops that lined it. City lights gleamed off the half-frozen water. He ducked inside a blacksmith's shop—one with three back ways out—and let himself stand still and listen.

Nothing but the clink and slap of water and ice lapping against the break wall, and the low voices of a few dock workers who were still out at this hour. He waited—still nothing.

He'd lost him.

He took a moment to calm his breath and think through the task ahead. If Almon had given up his pursuit, he might have gone after someone else immediately. Phinehas knew the terrible racking of a choice made in ignorance—he didn't know where Almon would go first. If Phinehas chose to protect one, he might be condemning the other.

Beth.

He had to go to Beth. Linette had at least a prayer of protecting herself.

In that moment, standing in the still-warm darkness of the forge, he thought the choice might kill him.

Still, he made it.

He stepped out onto the wharf again, and Almon was there with a pistol pointed straight at his face.

"You should have listened," he said.

Before he could pull the trigger, Phinehas Cole lit his vines with years' worth of sun and blinded Almon with the light.

The younger man yelped like a dog in pain and dropped the gun in his haste to cover his face. He backed away, the poisonous substance in his vines visibly churning as he did. He convulsed, and Phinehas kept flooding him with light, pouring it out of him, gathering every ounce of energy and strength he had and pounding Frederick Almon with it. He reached out his hands, willing all the light to flow in a single direction, and fell as his knees buckled. Black spots merged in his eyes. Still he poured out the light.

Roaring with pain and anger, Almon fled.

Kneeling on the dock behind him, Phinehas Cole wavered a moment before he collapsed.

Linette and Amos realized something was wrong when they were still half a block away. A crowd had gathered in the street outside the Coles' house. Linette hurried, then ran, until she burst through the crowd and saw glass scattered across the cobblestones from a broken window on the second floor—her father's study. The young servant girl from the other day was sobbing while a kind passerby tried to comfort her. Parker, her father's man-servant, stood in the midst of things looking bewildered and chagrined.

"What's going on? What happened here?" Linette asked, rushing up to him.

"The young captain came to see him," Parker said. He sounded like a man begging for a pardon. "He told me to send him up, and next thing I knew there were sounds of a fight. I ran to help but the master shouted for me to stay away and get help. Before I could go for anyone, he'd leaped out the window above and the man was chasing him. But he was—he was—"

"Changed," Linette said wearily. "Monstrous."

Parker looked sharply at her, brought back to his wits immediately by the appearance of duty. "You know something about this, young miss?"

"More than I ever wanted to know. Where did they go?"

Parker pointed. "Your father disappeared into the alley there. The captain jumped out of the window after him and followed, but your father had a good lead. I've already told the police everything."

Linette nodded, trying to sort everything through in her mind. Almon had been here. He'd attacked her father. Now the police would be after him—that was good news—

"Linette."

An unexpected hand on her shoulder made her jump, and she turned, wide-eyed, to find herself facing Thomas Carson.

She didn't recognize him immediately. He wore the simple clothing of a civilian, and his face was darkened by his hat and the lamp-cast shadows of evening in the street.

"What are you—"

"I came to warn you." He looked over his shoulder like he thought he was being followed. The small crowd gathered in the street was largely ignoring them—their attention was on the broken house, the sobbing servant, the swelling gossip held and spread by the neighbor next to them. Parker was close enough to overhear, but he nodded and stepped back. Carson surveyed the scene and understood.

"He's been here already," he said flatly.

"Who?" Linette asked.

"Almon."

"He attacked my father." She knotted her hands. "The police are after him."

"It may not do any good." He met her gaze with firm blue eyes. His was a face that inspired confidence, trust. She wished she could have known him under different circumstances.

"The army acquitted him," Carson said. "They know he's guilty, and dangerous. They did it because they're under Joseph Crispin's control. The same may be true of the civic powers here. The police may save your father, but they may not. And even if they do, they may still leave Almon free."

Her hands were shaking. Amos had let her break away from him to rush into the crowd, but he approached now—silent, stoic, attentive. "Why are you telling me this?" she asked.

"I'm leaving town," Carson said. "You and your family need to find a way to do the same. I'm sorry I didn't get word to you before … whatever happened here. But maybe it's not too late. Don't try to fight him with the law. The powers that be have turned on us. They're on Almon's side."

Your family. Of course she hadn't told Carson why she wanted to return to New Cranwell. That wasn't the sort of conversation you sat down and had with an army official you barely knew. But he was perceptive, and he cared. Deep down, she was gratified to know that.

She and Amos had gone to the home where Beth lived. They'd seen Phinehas Cole arrive and watched him receive familiar greetings at the door and be ushered inside. They'd stood side by side on the other side of the wide country road, and Linette had ached to go inside, to see the green eyes and the sweet face and the dimpled hands of her daughter.

For one breathtaking moment she'd caught a glimpse of red hair through the front window, as a little child skipped past.

She hadn't known what to do or how to help. She was glad her father was there—she could only assume he was acting on her warning somehow. Maybe putting Richard and Barbara Mason on alert.

She wasn't needed and couldn't stay. So she had turned away, refusing to cry, and said, "Let's go, Amos. There's nothing for me to do here."

But now there was. Now she knew what had to be done. It wasn't complicated at all—she had to go and tell her daughter's family to run for their lives.

She half-turned, then remembered Carson. "Thank you," she said.

He nodded.

She looked up at Amos, who filled her eyes like hope. Her heart leaped. For a moment, she hardly knew why.

But then she did, and she knew that it was good.

She and Amos could talk about that later.

"We have to get Beth away," she said.

He nodded. He already knew. He was poised like a buck about to bound into flight—with her. Her mission was his. He would be here until the end.

It broke over her like a wave on the sea that she was not alone.

She nearly reached out and took his hand. But it would have slowed them down. She turned to run instead, and he grabbed her arm and stopped her. He pointed to the stables behind the house.

"Horses," he said. "We can beat him there."

CHAPTER

26

The Midlands—The Old World

Late at night, sitting by the fire in the great room of the tavern with his feet propped up on a barrel, Roderick Rih read one of the pamphlets Lucaan and Caterina had been spreading all over the Midlands.

He'd come across them before. They were the primary way he and his men had tracked the couple. But it had been a while since he'd had this kind of luxury—the downtime that came with already having won, with having everyone and everything under his thumb.

He read it with amusement. It was written well. He savored the pride of literacy, of being able to read for himself something that many of the people of this backwater town had likely needed to be read to them. It did not name the writer, but other names it gave freely, along with charges of crime and malfeasance and calls to demand justice. It was not so much a revolutionary piece of writing as it was a cry for accountability. It called for no princes to be overthrown, but it demanded that princes step in and stop the overreach of power by the Puritani kirk under Joseph Crispin. It called for no violent uprisings, but it denounced the blind eyes and apathetic responses of the law, from local magistrates to chief judges.

The tavernkeeper offered him a drink. He waved it away.

The crimes listed in the pamphlet were crimson and named explicitly. Crispin had unlawfully deposed Carlos Vaquero, lawful count of Tempestano, and ordered him executed. He had controlled Carlos's righthand man, Massimo Diego, by blackmailing him with threats against his family—for years, and for no purpose but control. Long before, he had hounded Serena Vaquero nearly to her death—stopping only when it became clear that he would lose popular support if he killed her. He had massacred innocent men and women and children for no crime but dissent. He had hounded and chased and slaughtered doves and sheep in an unholy sacrifice meant to empower his own arm at any cost; he had undermined governments and sown distrust and fear between neighbors. It was all allowed only because no one stopped it. The people of Kepos Gé, said the writer, had let the scars of the old wars grow so thickly in their hearts that there was nowhere now for peace to take root.

Let us clear the ground, the pamphlet said. *Let us till the soil and soften it again. Let us make room for peace and for courage, and uproot these pernicious seeds of fear, and envy, and bigotry. If we do not, they will overrun and destroy us. If we do, we may transform our world.*

It took on, for a moment, a preacherly tone. *Does not the Book—with which we all agree—warn us that a root of bitterness will defile many? Does it not warn us that our enemy prowls among us, seeking to destroy and to drown us all in a sea of debt? Can we not choose a higher ground?*

Roderick finished his reading, held the pamphlet in his fingers for a few reflective minutes, then flicked it over into the fire. The pages browned and curled as the flames licked them up, reducing them quickly to ashes.

He lowered his feet from the barrel, pushed back his throne-like chair, and nodded to the men who stood watch at the doors. He went up to the heavily guarded bedroom on the second floor and waited while the guards unlocked it for him. He pushed his way inside.

Caterina sat in a chair by the window, looking out on the darkness. Her captors had freed her hands, and they rested lightly on the arms of her chair. Her thick red hair hung over one shoulder, recently braided. Bruises and cuts marred her face. She didn't turn to look at him, or even flinch. She gave no sign that she'd heard him enter at all.

"He's in the jail," Roderick announced. "More heavily guarded even than you are. Never mind that we hit him so hard he's probably not even awake. He has no hope except you."

She continued to stare out the window and said nothing.

"Those people out there think you're some kind of heroine," Roderick said. "Such a romantic young couple. So inspiring. And you're not even going to save him?"

She reacted, finally—if only a little, lowering her gaze slightly. Then she turned and looked at him.

"Do you know what the worst part was, during all the years we were in hiding?" she asked.

He hadn't expected the question—any question—and he didn't make himself look stupid by trying to answer it. She would go on even if he didn't, he was sure.

She didn't disappoint him. "It was knowing that my brother was being blackmailed into helping Joseph Crispin. We were safe—year after year, we were safe. But I wished we weren't. When he sent word and said to vanish again, because the danger had become suddenly so real—it was a terrible day, and a good one, all at once."

She looked back out the window, at the people passing by in the dim street and the lights of encampments beyond the town. "Joseph Crispin plays us all against each other, and do you know why it works? It works because righteous men believe they can use power to purify others. It works because they trust in their own righteousness and superiority to others. So superior that they are justified in forcing repentance at the end of a sword. For generations upon generations, we have all thought to defeat our enemies by becoming them. And so we all learn to hate and fear each other, and we all learn to abuse power."

She looked hard at him, like she was willing him to understand. "I'm not afraid of failing to be a hero," she said. "I'm afraid of becoming another villain. If you kill us, you kill us. If you kill Lucaan and drag me off to some prison somewhere, so be it."

Her voice trembled a little—she did have wits enough to be afraid, and to grieve. But she wasn't done. "*We* were never going to win this fight. We're counting on truth to do that. Truth, and compassion, which has been too dull for too long. So I'm not going to tell you anything. I'm not going to give you names, or places, or anything you ask for. I'm not going to help you because Crispin has been helped enough, and it's time we all stopped and realized who our real enemies are. *We're* the enemy. When we know that, we can end all this. Not before."

He stared at her. He'd come up the stairs to intimidate her, to gloat. He'd expected fear, maybe some pleading for Lucaan's life. Not this.

For a wild moment he considered letting her go. Letting them both go, and telling Crispin they'd slipped away again. If they were free in the world, he could hunt them down again. They would be more careful, harder to track down and capture. A challenge worth having would exist in the world.

A challenge worth losing.

But Roderick Rih wasn't a man who lost, and he wasn't a man who went to Crispin cringing and apologizing like everyone else in the world.

After all, truth would have to win this fight without their help.

He didn't want to leave her thinking she had won this encounter, so he sneered at her. He pulled an hourglass from his pocket and thunked it loudly down on the bedside table next to her. "Eight hours," he said. "When you change your mind, call for the guards. They'll bring you to me."

He left. He knew she wouldn't call.

For some reason, that made him glad.

At eight o'clock in the morning, the sun shone pale but hopeful all across the Midlands. It blanched barren streets and fields, here and there dusted with snow. Roderick Rih sent his drummer to stand in the street by the gallows and beat a baleful sound, calling his men to form ranks and the village to come and see the cost of opposing those in power—rightfully or not.

He did beat his drum, and the villagers did appear—in great numbers, far more than Rih had expected. He realized many were outliers, merchants and tinkers and traders of all kinds who had come for the market. They'd left their encampments in the frozen dawn and moved silently into the streets.

But the mercenaries did not form ranks.

At first, the drum meant to call them together beat in vain. Then a few began to stagger out, their uniforms in sad disarray. They took their place, leaving wide gaps where others should be. There were a dozen men where there ought to be twoscore already. Roderick grabbed a latecomer by the scruff of the neck.

"What's happening?" he barked. "Where are the men?"

"I don't know," the frightened young man gasped out. "They wouldn't wake. I barely woke myself, sir. Feels like I'm fighting through a fog just to keep to my feet, sir."

Roderick released him. The man stumbled like he'd lost all muscle tone in his legs.

The drummer kept beating his drum. The crowds waited. They were watching the few mercenaries with bright eyes. Too bright. Too expectant. A few turned and looked toward the inn's stables, as though they knew what Roderick's orders had been: the stable doors were to open and his mounted mercenaries ride out in an impressive parade.

He already knew it wasn't going to happen. Shoving the young mercenary toward the pitiful line, he charged toward the back of the stable, keeping out of sight of the curious villagers and calling down curses as he went.

Roderick burst into the stable's dim confines. A horse whinnied loudly as he entered. Only three of his men were inside—three to a dozen horses— and none were mounted. The horses weren't even saddled. One man was inside a stall, crouched beside a horse, trying to calm it as it shivered and shied away. Its legs were tied with thick rope in thicker knots, not in one place but in three.

"What in hoary hell is happening here?" Roderick demanded.

"Somebody hobbled all the horses," one of his men explained, panicky. "We're trying to get them free, sir, but we can't possibly make it out on time."

"Where are the others?" Roderick roared. He didn't wait for an answer, even though the man stammered it at him. As he charged back out, into the inn that served as a barracks, the words "wouldn't wake up" followed him.

He knew what had happened. He knew it before he burst into the first room where his men were sleeping in rows and kicked and pulled at them.

Some did not stir at all, even when he pulled them out of their cots and dropped them on the hardwood floor. One or two were up, but on their knees—not even able to see straight. The majority groaned and tried to open their eyes but didn't seem able to move.

I'm commandeering this tavern, Roderick had said last night. *My men and I expect to be fed.* They had been. They'd eaten well. They'd drunk well. All except Roderick, who tended not to eat much or drink much the night before a mission, and a few of his men who'd been on watch or who had similar habits—or perhaps some of his men just had better constitutions, and were able to sleep off whatever powerful soporifics the townsfolk had slipped into their food and their ale. How in damnation had they acquired so *much* of the stuff?

But he knew the answer to that too. The market. Traveling herbalists would have rolled in here with enough of every herb and potion to supply multiple villages for a year.

The pressure of the moment stretched Roderick's face in a garish, skeletal grin. He glanced out the window at his men—maybe eighteen had managed to form up. They were heavily armed and glaring at the villagers and their guests. They understood that things were not going as they should, that something was wrong and they were no longer in control. Somehow, they had already been made fools of, and they didn't like it.

Roderick stepped back into the street. Eighteen men, and himself.

There were nearly a thousand people in the street.

If these people were cowed, if they were sheep, if they were merely here to observe, there would be no danger in this. But they were not, and the danger was real.

If they hanged Lucaan, Roderick Rih and his men might not live to see another day.

Understanding this electrified Roderick. He'd been given a task, not even a difficult one, and in a single night it had become a contest for life and death. Himself against these villagers. Himself against the girl upstairs.

Himself against truth.

He drew a pistol from his belt and held it high so that as he slowly walked forward, cutting a path through the crowd and approaching his men, everyone could see that he was uncowed.

The villagers backed away. His men saluted.

He cleared his throat, then slowly turned and faced the sea of faces—dangerous, waiting faces.

He stared them down. Near the front of the crowd, he noticed a couple from the tavern the night before—a short, dark man and a tall, broad woman who must be his wife. They glared back at him with a vehemence that was personal. Something about the broad woman seemed familiar—it wasn't just that he'd seen her the night before. It struck him suddenly that she bore a slight resemblance to Caterina Diego. Behind them both, a teenage boy skulked, restless, hands clenched in fists. They were interesting, and if Roderick survived the day, he would find out more about them.

It was a large "if."

He raised his voice and ordered, "Bring the prisoner out!"

The crowd swelled and murmured as the jail doors burst open and Lucaan was hauled out. He was battered, bloody, and in chains. He could barely stand. The guards hustled him to the base of the gallows and paused there.

"I gave Caterina Diego the opportunity to save this man's life," Roderick announced. His voice carried over the crowd like a booming storm wind across waves. "She would not take it. So I offer it to you. All I ask are names. This man, and that woman, are guilty of conspiring against the lawful powers of kirk and state."

This drew a loud protest, a rise of whispers and complaints and shouts that rose all together from a thousand throats.

"If you don't also wish to be found guilty of conspiring and hung as traitors, you can help us," Roderick said. "Names. Names, and we will grant this man leniency."

A large man near the front of the crowd—a trader, by the looks of him, and carrying a sizable axe—stepped forward. "Found guilty?" he said, shouting the words so everyone could hear them. "Found guilty like this man? Without a trial, without a magistrate? Who here is conspiring against the lawful powers of the state? When did the kirk begin to hire mercenaries? When did the Creator enforce his will with lead ball and sword? We appeal to the prince! We appeal to the law!" He shook his axe in Roderick's direction. "And we will have no more of this sacrilege in our streets!"

Roderick grinned again—the same rictus that had disfigured his face before. He took a step back and nodded at his men. They shoved Lucaan toward the gallows.

And the crowd surged forward.

Eighteen armed men. A thousand people in the street. From the tavern, a few more of Roderick's mercenaries came staggering out. They saw immediately what was happening, and opened fire from the back at the same time as the eighteen fired into the charging crowd.

The foremost men fired off their pistols and then drew their swords, rushing to meet the oncomers. Behind them, several of the men jumped up to the gallows and fired from there, reloading their pistols as quickly as they could while their neighbors kept up fire. Villagers dropped, women screamed. But they kept coming.

Roderick drew his sword and brandished his pistol in the other hand. He slashed at a man barreling straight for him and kicked him away as he screamed in agony, his face and chest streaming blood. Roderick whirled and fired point-blank into the chest of another. He could fight here, alongside his men, take as many of these untrained curs down with him as he could before being finally overwhelmed—for he *would* be finally overwhelmed. The numbers alone dictated this. His back was to the gallows so he could not be surrounded, and peripherally, he caught sight of Lucaan, still in chains but fighting—driving both fists up into the chin of one of his men, pounding him as they fell together, rolling away. He caught sight of another Lucaan—taller, broader, but nearly a mirror image—dodging lead balls and smoke and ramming straight into the guard nearest the younger man. Roderick's grin broadened impossibly far. Lucaan and his lookalike would beat the guards. The other mercenaries were already overwhelmed and could not help.

The young man would live.

He could die with his men. Or he could return to the tavern, get out using Caterina as a shield, and be the one to stand before Crispin and tell him how the tide had turned.

Roderick Rih was a king of kings. He had won many victories by his own hand and witnessed many more. But Joseph Crispin's loss of face was a victory he'd never thought to see.

Stepping on a woman's body, Roderick vaulted further into the crowd. He cut and slashed his way deeper into the melee. His pistol was out of shot, and he threw it away. There was no time to reload it here. As he pushed his way back toward the inn, he ripped off his dark coat and let it fall. He threw his hat away. Finally he dropped his sword. He kept moving.

Then no one tried to stop him. He hunched, turned so that he was facing the gallows like the rest of them, but pushed backward against the press. He'd divested himself of his identity, and no one was looking closely enough to know who he was. The fight was up front, not back here in this chaos. Closer to the inn, more of his men were firing into the crowd, and people were being trampled.

It was a costly war these people had chosen to fight.

Looking behind him and seeing an opening, Roderick made a dash for the tavern doors.

He didn't get there.

One of his own men saw him coming, failed to recognize him, and fired a pistol ball right through his spine.

Upstairs, the guards were nervous.

There were four of them. They'd known quickly that things weren't going as planned. Standing in the hall outside Caterina's door, they could hear the drum beating, calling the mercenaries to form ranks. But the sounds that followed weren't right. There was no silence as the crowd fell still, no clear, stentorian voice as Roderick Rih made himself king. There were no horns blowing as the horses paraded down the street. Moreover, they should have heard the men downstairs, marching together over the tavern's polished wooden floors and into the street. Instead they heard only disorganized banging and the occasional shout, scuffling footsteps and cursing.

Something had gone wrong. Or everything had.

The narrow hallway had a window at the end, but it looked out on an alley and not on the street. They couldn't see anything, but one of them kept going to check anyway. The sounds outside got louder. Shouts. Screams. Pistol shots. The scout at the window shouted, "They're spilling into the alley! It's some kind of fight!"

From the other side of the door, there came the sound of a window being pushed open and a breathless shout.

The guards shoved the door open and rushed in. Caterina was leaning halfway out the window, waving at someone in the alley below. One of the men, Groos, grabbed her around the waist and hauled her backward. She struggled.

"Enough of that, enough!" Holtz shouted at her. He drew his broad dagger and wrestled it around her throat. She stopped fighting. Groos quickly bound her hands behind her again. The other two men, Schuster and Silva, waited nervously by the door. They all knew what they were doing. They didn't know how the tide had turned against them, but it clearly had. There would be no show of power this morning, only a rush to save their own skins.

This girl was the best way they had to do that. And if they returned to Joseph Crispin with her in hand, they might be able to win praise for themselves while blaming whatever had gone wrong on Roderick Rih.

Rather than charging into the street, they took Caterina out the back way. No one saw or tried to stop them. Just as they made it out the back door, the front doors of the tavern burst open and the screaming, ashen crowd spilled inside.

Leeanaert bent low over his brother and unlocked the chains with the keys he'd taken off a dead guard. The worst of the fight raged around them, but a ring of villagers surrounded them, forming a human wall that kept them from being attacked. Their leader was the big man who had spoken up against the chief mercenary. Leeanaert felt they were in good hands.

The chains loosed, he shoved them away and tried to help Lucaan up, but his brother could barely stand. Leeanaert got him up just enough to hobble back toward the jail, where he could put Lucaan safely behind walls until the fight was over. Screams and agonized cries sounded all around them as the last few mercenaries kept fighting with all the skill they possessed, and the crowd opposed them relentlessly with the weight of their bodies, the edges of their few weapons and tools, their refusal to back down.

"Caterina," Lucaan croaked as they crossed the threshold into the jail's cold, stinking darkness.

"She'll be all right," Leeanaert said.

Lucaan shook his head. "Make sure."

There was a rough wooden bench along one wall of the jail. Leeanaert helped his brother lie down on it. His brow crinkling with concern, he hesitated a moment and then pulled off his red wool cloak, covering Lucaan with it.

A figure appeared in the door, holding a cleaver in each hand—Leeanaert relaxed as he recognized the butcher. "Take care of him," Leeanaert said. "I'm going after the girl."

The butcher nodded. His face was bloodied and grim. Leeanaert saw tears in his eyes. He wondered at the cost this man and the others had paid for this day.

There was no time to ask. He cast a last worried glance at his brother and flew out the door.

Caterina's heart beat wild notes of fear and wonder and hope as two guards shoved her ahead of them while two others led the way, ducking and peering around corners, then rushing her through scant crowds that had spilled off the main street into the alleys and byways of the town. The air was a ringing cacophony, anguish and pain and exultation. She had hoped their efforts would change things on a grassroots level. She hadn't expected to see the change so soon.

Soon enough to save Lucaan's life. With all of her being, she hoped for it.

Just before the men hurried into the darkness of a stable, she caught sight of Bettina across the street and opened her mouth to call out to her. She didn't have time—a guard shoved her and knocked an incoherent cry from her mouth. But her sister's eyes widened with recognition, and Caterina went into the darkness knowing she'd been seen.

In the dim light, confusion reigned. Horses whinnied in terror and pain. Several hit the sides of their stalls again and again. The foremost guards scattered, looking from stall to stall and cursing more and more loudly as they went. Finally they gave up and ran back. One of them glared at Caterina with so much hatred it nearly took her breath away.

"They hobbled the horses," he spat. "Too tight; they lamed at least half of them. What kind of animals would do that?"

"Never mind that, Groos," said the guard with his grip on Caterina's arm and his knife at the ready. It wasn't at her throat anymore, but he kept it close enough that she didn't dare try to get away. "We'll go on foot."

"Out the back, come on!" said another, waving the others with him. They spilled out the door into an empty yard. Groos pointed toward the outskirts of town. "The traders have horses," he said. "Come on."

The men broke into a run. Caterina considered lagging, or falling, but instead yelped as her personal guard picked her up and threw her over his shoulder. The motion and the sight of the rushing ground made her sick, and she closed her eyes tight.

There was no one to stop them. It seemed that everyone had gathered in the town, and now everyone was part of the riot; the market encampments on the outskirts might not have existed. They had been arranged in a surprisingly orderly patchwork of tents and tinker wagons. Horses and mules were tethered everywhere, along with the occasional milk cow. Goats wandered freely, searching out tufts of grass in the warming winter muck.

The man set her down and stuck his knife point against her side while the other three quickly untethered four horses and threw saddles on their backs. They worked quickly and precisely. Caterina's heart sank as her captor lifted her onto the horse and then climbed up behind her. He wrapped an arm tightly around her waist.

They were going to get away. The riot had changed things—she hoped it had changed everything—but it hadn't set her free.

At least she would get the chance to look Joseph Crispin in the eye herself and tell him what she'd told the mercenary captain the night before. No matter what else happened, he was going to lose.

The men kicked the horses into a gallop. Caterina lowered her head against the stinging wind.

For some reason, she thought of Amelia—the little girl she'd nannied back in the village by the sea. Amelia had always been so frightened of bullies.

Caterina wouldn't want the little girl to see or hear about anything that had happened to her in the last few days. It would wound her childish soul to know how cruel and violent people could be. But she would grow up, and be stronger. And when she did, Caterina hoped that maybe she would hear about her and Lucaan, and be inspired.

Someday, maybe, Amelia would be a grown woman in a world that had changed, and she would be proud that she had once known Caterina and held her hand.

Sweeping off across the countryside in the hands of her enemies, galloping toward a destiny at the hands of the worst bully of them all, Caterina smiled.

And for some reason, she looked back.

Peering around the mercenary at the road behind, she caught sight of someone riding after them, faster than it seemed any man should be able to ride. His hair gleamed golden in the pale morning light. Her heart nearly stopped. Lucaan!

It *couldn't* be Lucaan. He couldn't ride like that after being beaten by the mercenaries, not even to save her. Besides, Lucaan was a boatman, not a horseman. He could barely ride at all.

Nevertheless, she knew two things. That this man or angel, who looked like Lucaan and must have been sent by him, because nothing else was possible in this economy of grace, was coming to save her. And second, that this task would be made immeasurably harder as long as the mercenaries could hold a knife to her throat and use her against him.

She looked back again. He was gaining on them incredibly quickly.

So she threw herself off the horse.

She might be killing herself, she thought in the heartbeat between fall-ing and hitting the ground. One good blow to the head, one rock in the wrong place, one miscalculated trajectory so that she ended up under a horse's hooves, and it was over.

But she didn't think she was going to die.

She hit the ground and rolled through a patch of dead grass, gathering mud and thorns on her way. It jarred and hurt every bone in her body, but she felt mostly elation. She wasn't dead, she was free, and the horseman was almost upon them.

When her guard shouted in anger and surprise, the others turned. They all stopped and wheeled their horses around. Caterina tried to sit up in the grass, a difficult task with her head spinning and her hands tied behind her back. Her skirts had wrapped themselves so tightly around her legs that she couldn't move without unwinding herself first. She said a fervent prayer for the man of grace, the rescue she did not expect and hardly deserved.

The horseman—it *was* Lucaan, but it wasn't—brandished a shining sword in the air. He didn't slow down. The mercenaries were still fum-bling for their pistols when he was upon them. He cut down the tall man who had been guarding Caterina, sending him reeling from his saddle. He whirled and charged straight for Groos, who had his flintlock in his hand. The other two mercenaries turned their horses and fled.

Groos pointed his pistol at Caterina and fired.

She blinked in shock, missing the moment that the rescuer cut Groos out of his saddle as well. She saw him going down.

She couldn't breathe.

The rescuer leaped down from his saddle and ran to her, falling on his knees in the mud. He circled her back with a strong arm, holding her up. Now that he was so close, she could see that he wasn't Lucaan—he was older, taller, more mature in the lines of his face. The blue of his eyes and the bright red of his vines were just a slightly different shade.

"Leeanaert?" she asked.

He seemed too shaken and afraid to respond. "He shot you—are you—"

She shook her head. "I'm all right. He missed. He must have missed." She smiled. "I'm Caterina."

He pulled his hand away from her back. It was covered in blood. The world, she realized, was getting dark. And fluid, somehow. It didn't want to hold her up.

"I just need to lay down," she told him. "Thank you for coming to get me."

Caterina Diego closed her eyes and slumped against Leeanaert's chest. He held her for a broken, shocked heartbeat, and then he howled with bitter grief.

Three miles away, eighteen armed men had fallen, and with them thirty-six men, nineteen women, and nine children who were pistol-shot, mortally wounded by sword or dagger or arrow, or trampled to death in the riot. The farmer and the Southern dairyman were among the dead. The tavern-keeper's wife tended to the wounded for hours before succumbing, quite suddenly, to a wound of her own that no one knew had been bleeding steadily for hours. She couldn't be revived.

Bettina and Paulo made their way to the jail in the aftermath, and Bettina wrapped her arms around Lucaan—one around his shoulders, one around his head—and rocked him as though he were a child, as much for her benefit as for his. Jorge stood in the doorway, fretting. Paulo sat beside Bettina and Lucaan on the bench, patting each of them gently in turn, until he finally rose and looked out on the bloody street from Jorge's side.

"It is a great story," he said quietly, "with a high price."

From the other end of the street, he saw Leeanaert coming toward them. Caterina was limp in his arms.

He closed his eyes. Behind him, Bettina saw them too—and began to wail.

"She's alive!" Leeanaert called out, his precious burden held close to his heart. His arms were bloodied. "Call a doctor; she's alive!"

Two hours later, a new tinker wagon arrived on the outskirts of the village. It brought word. Carlos Vaquero had landed in Auguste-on-the-Sea with a company of soldiers under Henry of Angleland. He was going back to Tempestano. He would take control of his land again.

He would only be the first, the rumors said. When Carlos Vaquero took back what was his, the whole world would begin to be put right.

CHAPTER 27

New Cranwell—The New World

Linette and Amos rode for the edge of town like a high wind chasing the snow. They clattered into the yard of the cobbler's shop and house. Everything was dark and still. Smoky remnants rose from the chimney, smudgy against the clear moonlit sky. The family might be in bed.

Linette pulled her horse to a stop, threw the reins aside, and dismounted at a run for the front door.

It was open—off the latch and swinging just slightly as a cold wind kicked up.

With dread, Linette pushed it in. It didn't creak as it opened onto the small but cozy living space just off the kitchen, where the last embers of a fire smoldered in the hearth. In their dim light Linette could just make out the shadows of home: a large rug on the wooden floor, a rocking chair, a table. There was no sign of anyone, least of all Almon. She breathed a little easier.

But Amos, entering behind her and pausing for a long moment, said, "Linette."

She turned. He lit a match and lifted it so that she could clearly see the latch was not just open but broken—fractured and splintered out of shape. Worse, a dark spray of something formed a large blot on the wall next to the door, dripping down in long, viscous lines—blood. Amos fingered a hole in the wall near the top and dug out a lead ball that dropped to the floor and rolled with a loud ringing sound.

She turned to look at the room again. With her eyes adjusting to the darkness, she could see signs of disarray where she hadn't before—the rug was turned up along one edge; a stool near the rocking chair was tipped on its side. She imagined Richard Mason standing in front of the hearth, firing at Almon as he came through the door. Her eyes lifted to the back door off the kitchen. Barbara and Beth would have fled that way.

Amos was way ahead of her, already crossing the floor in a jog toward the back of the kitchen. This door was properly closed, but he pulled it open and dashed out into the yard. A moment later he called her name.

She shook herself out of her fear and joined him. He'd crossed half the yard and stood near the stables, pointing at the ground. "They rode out," he said. He turned and faced away from New Cranwell, out toward the interior and the wilderness. "That way."

She couldn't imagine why they would have made for the woods when the city was so close by, with its open streets and its safety in numbers. Maybe Richard hoped to lose Almon in the trees. Or maybe Almon had been so close on their heels that *he* had chosen their path, driving them away from the town like a wolf culling a herd. Linette had seen him in his thorn-state often enough to know that a gunshot wound was unlikely to slow him—if indeed it was Almon who had been shot, and not someone else.

It was, she told herself. If it had been anyone else, Almon would have finished them off and left the body behind. If it had been anyone else, this pursuit would already be over.

She refused to think about the bodies that might have been left behind. She was here to save Beth, and she could not allow herself to imagine any alternative to salvation, or fear would destroy her ability to keep going.

Once again Amos was ahead of her, collecting their horses while she was lost in thought. She shook her head. She had to stop losing herself like that.

Amos handed her the reins to her horse and mounted beside her. He was grim but not defeated, and she took strength from his focus. He pushed his horse into a canter and led the way after the hoofprints in the thin layer of snow. Linette gave thanks for the bright moon overhead and for Amos's long experience of reading the ground in the wilderness. He was not a tracker, not a hunter, just a man who had grown into manhood far from civilization and knew a few things because of it.

Linette hung slightly behind Amos as they moved as far as they could without losing the trail, but even she could make out the signs of others passing. They were following at least two horses. Almon, she suspected, was on foot—but hardly disadvantaged for that. She wondered if he was actually capable of running down a horse.

They left the edges of town behind and entered the woods, where the tracks followed a well-worn trail through barren trees and fragrant evergreens. She considered lighting her vines to help Amos see, but he still seemed confident of the way without her help, and she didn't want to weaken herself before—before whatever would happen when they caught up. She imagined her daughter, frightened and clinging to a horse's mane while her adoptive parents drove deeper and deeper into the woods. She imagined Almon, running after them, covering the ground in impossibly long, loping strides.

Unexpectedly, she thought of Jonathan. Her friend. Letty's beloved. The young preacher of Jerusalem Valley. What if he hadn't been saved? What if he had been lost to the madness like Almon seemed to be, and it was he they hunted through the woods?

She shivered and urged her horse to go faster.

Some long-ago memory stirred as they rode, and she realized where they were heading just moments before they got there. The trees abruptly thinned, then cleared, and they rode onto a strange landscape, eerie and alien in the moonlight.

The colonists called it The Rocks—a plain miles wide and miles deep where the forest opened onto a landscape at once shattered and fortified. Here, soil gave way to gently rolling slabs of rock, slippery with ice. Miles distant, a long, low ridge hung on the horizon. Peaceful as it seemed, Linette knew from memory how treacherous the land here truly was. Clefts in the rock and enormous black boulders and other rock formations had carved the terrain with numerous hollows, caves, and ravines. More dangerous were pits where settlers and tribal people had quarried limestone and granite. Some of these were filled with water, now covered over with a thin layer of ice and snow. Only a few brave and hardy trees, mostly small conifers with sinewy, twisted trunks, grew here.

It was a perfect place to hide, but a terrible place to be lost, or backed into a corner. Linette's heart sank at the thought of Beth here, somewhere, scared.

For a moment The Rocks shone, the moonlight glinting off the snow and highlighting plates of limestone and sparkling veins of quartz. Then clouds drifted across the light, and a wash like charcoal covered the plain. All was still. Amos and Linette had stopped, unable to see tracks here and unwilling to charge into the open.

Hundreds of feet out amid the rolling slabs of rock, a light began to shine.

It was warm, orange, a glowing beacon. It was a man, Linette realized, standing on a high black boulder.

It was her father.

"Almon!" Phinehas shouted. A wind picked up his voice and carried it, making him sound closer than he was. Linette understood things from the sound. She understood her father's resolution to fight. She understood that he was in pain and exhausted to the bone. And she knew that he would not go down out here unless he took Frederick Almon with him.

"Almon," he called again, "come and face me, coward! Come and finish what you started!"

Amid a broken cluster of rocky plates a hundred feet from Phinehas, something moved. A tall, hunched shape stepped out from a ravine and stood outlined against the sky. It was so dark Linette could hardly make him out; he was a silhouette amid silhouettes, shadowed and indistinct. But she saw him and knew it was Almon.

Where were Beth and the Masons? Had Almon killed them already— were they lying in the hollows of the rocks behind him?

She shook the thought out of her head. She couldn't think it. Couldn't picture it.

"Come on," Phinehas said. His tone was wearier now, the challenge directed straight toward the figure who faced him. "Don't keep me waiting."

Amos slid down from his saddle and held out a hand to Linette. She didn't know what they were going to do, but his wisdom struck her immediately. The horses couldn't cross this landscape without risking grave injury. She took his hand and jumped down, and together they began to make their way onto the rolling slabs toward the two.

Almon howled. It wasn't the sound of a man. It was the sound of an animal. It rent Linette's heart. Almon bounded forward into a run, closing the gap between him and Linette's father. Phinehas slid down from the boulder where he'd taken his stand, readying himself on wider ground below, still glowing, both fists balled and a halo of light shining from each of them. Linette too began to run, straight after them, and Amos after her—

And then somewhere behind them, toward the southwest and the moon, a child screamed and began to cry.

Linette whirled around, eyes aflame with fear, and found Amos right behind her.

"Amos, please!" she said.

He knew what she meant. He hesitated, and she saw the battle in his eyes. He wanted to stay with *her*. He wanted to help her, to protect her, to fight by her side.

"Please," she repeated.

He nodded, curtly, and turned. He ran for the sound of the child crying, and Linette turned back to the battle.

Almon had reached Phinehas. They were locked in a hand-to-hand struggle. Even with Almon's enhanced height and weight, Phinehas Cole was nearly as big as he was—and shining like the sun. Almon snarled and screamed with pain as the light burrowed into and through him, but he did not fall away. As Linette barreled toward them, slipping across the surface of the rocks, Almon picked her father up and hurled him against the great black boulder where he'd stood. The light went out. Her eyes filled with tears, blinding her. Still she kept going.

Amos, save my daughter, she prayed.

And then: *Creator, help me save my father.*

Her father's light flickered on again; he pushed himself up, using the rock to brace himself. He held out his hands and for a moment Almon seemed unable to push forward and attack.

It seemed to Linette that the ground beneath her feet buckled. It seemed that it heaved with power and desire, that under her, in the roots of the world, was something yearning to well up and break free.

She felt the seed tugging at her, deep in the core of her, calling her west.

Justice is the healing of the world, she heard.

She slipped and went down, catching herself on her hands as she skidded three feet off to the side, struggling to find purchase on the icy rock. She could feel something beneath, pulsing, pounding.

I am here, Linette, a voice said, a voice from memory, a voice that she had been silencing all this time but knew now would never leave her, was woven into the core of who she was. Once it had said, *Underneath the floorboards. Remember.*

Remember.

She found her footing again and charged forward, and her father's eyes locked on hers and widened in recognition a second before Almon charged into him.

"Light up, Linette!" Phinehas screamed. "Use your light!"

But it wasn't her light that she needed. Nor was the light, her phosphorescence, her inheritance from her father, the only thing she had.

Almon's clawed hands were around her father's throat. Phinehas struggled. She heard him gasping as his light flickered. Almon let go with one hand and slashed wicked claws across her father's torso again and again, tearing clothing and drawing blood. He was going to eviscerate Phinehas where they stood.

Linette fell to her knees, laid her hands on the rocks, and felt the energy beneath the surface.

"Almon!" she cried out. "Frederick Almon, look at me!"

He turned. He flung her father aside, and his eyes locked on her. They blazed yellow and black. Almon was gone—or nearly gone. It was something else that looked through him.

But she had to try, didn't she?

"Get out," she said, her voice cracked and trembling. "Creatures of the dark, by the power of Father, Son, and Fire Within, get out and leave this man alone."

The ground rolled beneath her. The sky went darker, the moon entirely gone. The air split like film separating from a kernel, and she saw in it shades and angels, the powers that exist beyond perception, the world above and behind the world. But the shades did not release the man, and they grinned down at her with Almon's face.

"He doesn't want us to go," they said.

"Go anyway!" she screamed. "Get out! Get out and *let me save him!*" She hammered the ground with her fists. "By the Father! By the Son! By the Fire Within!"

Almon threw back his head and screamed. He fell to his knees, shaking and bucking. She couldn't see the shades anymore—the world had reunited—but she knew they tore away from him, that they left him. He seemed to shrink down. He curled in on himself, and he looked up at her with human eyes—eyes hungry with desire and hatred, eyes burning with fear and with pride.

"You've come," he said. "You're mine."

"I want to help you," she said.

"I don't need help."

He pushed himself onto his feet with evident effort. His eyes were devouring her. She saw the moment the shades came back—the moment he invited them. He grew and stretched again; his muscles gained new power, his eyes changed.

He wasn't Jonathan.

And she couldn't save him.

She bowed her head with her palms on the rocks. "All right," she said. *"Let justice roll like a river, and righteousness like a ever-flowing stream."*

The rocks split. From the depths, a raging flood welled up. The roar filled her ears. Spray drenched her from head to foot, soaking her woolen dress and cloak and gloves. It rose from fractures in the rock behind and before her and on every side, surging up from the deeps. It shoved Almon away from her, carrying him back with unspeakable force and rolling over him. The water shone with light; the glory of God covered the earth as the waters cover the sea. It swept over and around her; she could not breathe and yet she could; and the water was warm. It lifted her and spun her around like a father dancing with his child. A wave carried her up and above the surface, and as the water curved in and shone around and below her, she saw that it was flooding the entire plain, covering the Rocks, answering the silver of the moonlight with an inner golden glow.

The wave raised her as high as the ridge in the distance. She was cold and soaked and shivering; she was warm and full of light. The deeps rose to meet the sky and she was there in between, held in suspension like a star.

In that high, clear place, she heard the seed calling to her from the west, and it said, *Grace is the coming of a new creation.*

The water roared like thunder as the wave crashed back to the flooded plain. Spray surged up against the highest rocks. The force of the water pulled Linette under, and in the light beneath the surface she saw Frederick Almon suspended in the flood.

Whether she would live or die, she didn't know. Whether her daughter and her father and Amos, dear and strong Amos, would live or die she didn't know. It didn't seem to matter, for there would be justice either way. But Almon was dead. His eyes were open. They were not the saturated eyes of his monstrous form, but neither were they really human—they seemed hollow, as though they'd never belonged to a living man; as though they had been perfectly formed and yet had never seen anything.

She reached for him. She swam through the waters, grabbed on to his sinking form, and kicked toward the surface, pulling him along. Somehow she knew where to go. She reached a large, glimmering rock formation and pulled Almon up, above the waters. She laid his broken body on the surface and allowed herself a moment to sit back, hands on her knees, and look out on the shimmering sea. The water, she realized, was shallow in most places. She and Almon had fallen down into one of the deep quarry pits. Her father was lying still on a swell of granite above the surface; and far away, Amos was wading toward her with a man and a woman on either side.

A lump formed in Linette's throat as she watched them coming in the moonlight. As they drew nearer she could see them more clearly. She could see the little girl in Barbara Mason's arms, clinging to her and looking shyly out over the warm, softly glowing waters toward Linette.

They drew near. Linette had no words to say. She looked mutely at her daughter, her beautiful face, her shining eyes. Beth snuggled a little closer to Barbara, shy and perhaps a little afraid.

"See," Barbara said, turning Beth out just a little, "this is the pretty lady who was lifted on the water."

Beth smiled, glanced up at Barbara for reassurance, and tightened her fist in her adoptive mother's hair. But she met Linette's gaze and said, "I saw you! You looked like a star."

Then she turned and snuggled deeply into Barbara again, and Barbara nodded and stroked her hair and met Linette's eyes without a word, only giving thanks, only offering herself, only silent and apologetic and pleading. And Linette understood. She understood all of it.

"You and your father saved our lives," Richard Mason said. "I can't tell you how grateful we are."

Amos nodded as though satisfied. He lifted his eyes to where Phinehas lay beyond them all and began to wade toward him—pausing a moment to look down on Almon's stiff, battered form.

"He's dead," Linette said. Barbara and Richard had already turned away. They were already walking off. Beth was curled so tightly into Barbara's arms that Linette was sure she couldn't hear. She looked back at Almon again, trying to parse her feelings, and trying to feel anything at all. She didn't know how it was possible to feel everything and nothing at the same time.

"It was his own choice," Amos said.

She didn't know how he knew that. But it was true. Amos took a step away and Linette reached out and grabbed his arm. "Not that way," she said. "There's a pit—you'll—"

She didn't finish, because he took her arms in return and then pulled her off the rock to him, and then he kissed her and she kissed him back, standing there waist-deep in the shimmering waters of justice and of grace.

Anywhere else, anytime else, they would both have been so flustered and confused by his impulsive move that they would have broken apart in a rush of apologies and stammering, blushing, needless awkwardness.

But that would have been out of place here. So when they were done, he stood and gazed down into her eyes for a moment, and then she stood on her tiptoes and they kissed one another again.

Epilogue

Joseph Crispin left Angleland afraid, so he banished Bure to some tedious paperwork position in the Midlands and went back to Tempestano alone. He arrived in style, of course, with pomp and with power, and invited himself to pay a visit to Alvise of Cortello, Tempestano's neighboring prince and the opportunist Crispin had counted on to sweep in and take over once Carlos Vaquero was gone.

Alvise had certainly made inroads. He'd sent some of his courtiers and personal guard to Tempestano to keep an eye on things and "help maintain peace." But he had yet to declare himself prince and was still acting largely on Carlos's behalf, at least in name.

Crispin intended to change that.

He was ushered into Alvise's lavish private audience chamber overlooking the misty green hills of Cortello by a pair of men in sharp purple livery. The young prince, dripping decadence in every line of his clothing and the cut of his hair, stood looking out with a glass of wine in his hand. A decanter sat on an ornately carved table along with a spread of cheeses, dried meats, and hothouse-grown citrus fruit. Alvise waved his slender hand at the board to indicate Crispin should help himself, which he gladly did.

They exchanged insipid pleasantries and no small amount of flattery, mostly on Crispin's part—he wanted the young man pliable, after all, and as he seemed more than slightly inebriated, he wouldn't grow suspicious if the High Elder was more effusive than usual.

Unsteadily, Alvise sat down in a stuffed, high-backed chair embroidered with green and gold thread and waved for Crispin to take a seat in a slightly less ostentatious version of the same.

"I'll get down to business," Crispin said, holding his glass of wine carefully as he sat. He smoothed out his satin cassock over his knees. "I am surprised to see you haven't taken full control of Tempestano. You must know it needs you."

"Sometimes it behooves one to move slowly," Alvise answered, slurring slightly.

"But sometimes a quicker, bolder approach is needed. Tempestano has been under the unfortunate dominion of the Vaqueros for so long, it is desperately in need of a stronger, more competent hand. And you must know it would benefit you. It's a small province, but well located—close to the sea, and with such vineyards! You are not a great lord, Alvise, but you could be, with another such a gem in your pocket."

"Are you in such a rush because Carlos Vaquero is coming back?"

Crispin nearly spat out his wine. "You've heard that, have you?"

Alvise waved a bejeweled hand in the air. "They say he's coming with soldiers like he expects some kind of war to break out—like he thinks his neighbors will have taken over in his absence."

Alvise fixed his eyes on Crispin, and there was a keener light there than the elder expected. "I don't want a war," the young prince said.

"No war is necessary," Crispin said. "Carlos Vaquero is returning, it's true, but there are serious charges against him. And he has only one small company of men, a bodyguard, really. If they arrive and find another prince in power, they will have to change their approach. Vaquero is a Trembler— and a weakling besides. He won't have the stomach for bloodshed."

Alvise's mouth quirked, and Crispin thought he saw something there— a point of connection, a shared cynicism and a sense of irony about power and politics on which he could capitalize. "You don't talk much like a kirkman," Alvise said. "Shouldn't you be pressing me to abandon my sins, not urging me to invade my neighbor?"

Leaning into the promise of that smile and that cynicism, Crispin bent forward and lowered his voice conspiratorially. "Come now, my prince," he said. "You and I are men of the world. We know what real power is. Let others talk of God and religion. We must talk about the true stuff of life—of strength and intellect and will."

He thought he had him. But to his surprise, Alvise frowned slightly and leaned away. He looked at Crispin as though he were regarding some new and not entirely appealing specimen.

"Are you confessing yourself irreligious?" Alvise asked. "You, the head of the Puritani kirk?"

"I have been a man of the cloth for many long years, and I was a soldier before that. I saw men kill each other over religion, and then I watched them use it to climb the ladders of power and prestige. I know where real power lies, Alvise. When it comes to God, I am rather more agnostic."

He thought the confidence would bind his ally fast. But instead Alvise looked at him soberly—truly soberly, as though he'd burned off all his wine in an instant.

"I confess," Alvise said, "that rather disturbs me."

He stood abruptly and turned his back. "I have other business to attend to," he said. "You look hungry. Feel free to stay. Finish my wine. You may find it helps you believe a little more fastly."

Alvise of Cortello made no moves on Tempestano, except to alert his men there that Carlos Vaquero was expected back soon.

Three days later, Carlos arrived—and everywhere, people who had read Paulo's pamphlets said that the remaking of the world had begun.

The End

Web: www.rachelstarrthomson.com
Facebook: www.facebook.com/RachelStarrThomsonWriter
Twitter: @writerstarr

THE SEVENTH WORLD TRILOGY

Worlds Unseen Burning Light Coming Day

For five hundred years the Seventh World has been ruled by a tyrannical empire—and the mysterious Order of the Spider that hides in its shadow. History and truth are deliberately buried, the beauty and treachery of the past remembered only by wandering Gypsies, persecuted scholars, and a few unusual seekers. But the past matters, as Maggie Sheffield soon finds out. It matters because its forces will soon return and claim lordship over her world, for good or evil.

The Seventh World Trilogy is an epic fantasy, beautiful, terrifying, pointing to the realities just beyond the world we see.

"An excellent read, solidly recommended for fantasy readers."
– Midwest Book Review

"A wonderfully realistic fantasy world. Recommended."
– Jill Williamson, Christy-Award-Winning Author
of *By Darkness Hid*

"Epic, beautiful, well-written fantasy
that sings of Christian truth."
– Rael, reader

Available everywhere online or special order from your local bookstore.

THE ONENESS CYCLE

EXILE HIVE ATTACK RENEGADE RISE

**The supernatural entity called the Oneness
holds the world together. What happens if it falls apart?**

In a world where the Oneness exists, nothing looks the same. Dead men walk. Demons prowl the air. Old friends peel back their mundane masks and prove as supernatural as angels. But after centuries of battling demons and the corrupting powers of the world, the Oneness is under a new threat—its greatest threat. Because this time, the threat comes from within.

Fast-paced contemporary fantasy.

"Plot twists and lots of edge-of-your-seat action,
I had a hard time putting it down!"
—Alexis

"Finally! The kind of fiction I've been waiting for my whole life!"
—Mercy Hope, FaithTalks.com

"I sped through this short, fast-paced novel, pleased by the well-drawn characters and the surprising plot. Thomson has done a great job of portraying difficult emotional journeys . . . Read it!"
—Phyllis Wheeler, The Christian Fantasy Review

Available everywhere online or special order from your local bookstore.

THE PROPHET TRILOGY

ABADDON'S EVE   COMES THE DRAGON   BELOVED

**A prophet and his apprentice.
A runaway and a wealthy widow marked as an outcast.**

They alone can see the terrible judgment
marching on their land.

But can they do anything to stop it?

**The Prophet Trilogy is a fantasy set in a near-historical world
of deserts, temples, and spiritual forces that vie
for the hearts of men.**

Available everywhere online or special order from your local bookstore.

REAP THE WHIRLWIND

Beren is a city in constant unrest: ruled by a ruthless upper class and harried by a band of rebels who want change. Its one certainty is that the two sides do not, and will not, meet.

But children know little of sides or politics, and Anna and Kyara—a princess and a peasant girl—let their chance meeting grow into a deep friendship. Until the day Kyara's family is slaughtered by Anna's people, and the friendship comes to an abrupt end.

Years later, Kyara is a rebel—bitter, hard, and violent. Anna's efforts to fight the political system she belongs to avail little. Neither is a child anymore—but neither has ever forgotten the power of their long-ago friendship. When a secret plot brings the rebellion to a fiery head, both young women know it is too late to save the land they love.

But is it too late to save each other?

Available everywhere online.

TAERITH

When he rescues a young woman named Lilia from bandits, Taerith Romany is caught in a web of loyalties: Lilia is the future queen of a spoiled king, and though Taerith is not allowed to love her, neither he can bring himself to leave her without a friend. Their lives soon intertwine with the fiercely proud slave girl, Mirian, whose tragic past and wild beauty make her the target of the king's unscrupulous brother.

The king's rule is only a knife's edge from slipping—and when it does, all three will be put to the ultimate test. In a land of fog and fens, unicorns and wild men, Taerith stands at the crossroads of good and evil, where men are vanquished by their own obsessions or saved by faith in higher things.

"Devastatingly beautiful . . . I am amazed at every chapter
how deeply you've caused us to care for these characters."
—Gabi

"Deeply satisfying."
—Kapezia

"Rachel Starr Thomson is an artist, and every chapter
of Taerith is like a painting . . . beautiful."
—Brittany Simmons

Available everywhere online or special order from your local bookstore.

ANGEL IN THE WOODS

Hawk is a would-be hero in search of a giant to kill or a maiden to save. The trouble is, when he finds them, there are forty-some maidens—and they call their giant "the Angel." Before he knows what's happening, Hawk is swept into the heart of a patchwork family and all of its mysteries, carried away by their camaraderie—and falling quickly in love.

But the outside world cannot be kept at bay forever. Suspecting the Giant of hiding a treasure, the wealthy and influential Widow Brawnlyn sets out to tear the family apart and bring the Giant to destruction any way she can. And her two principle weapons are Hawk—and the truth.

Caught between the terrible truths he discovers about the family's past and the unalterable fact that he has come to love them, Hawk must face his fears and overcome his flaws if he is to rescue the Angel in the woods.

> "A beautiful tale of finding oneself, honor and heroism;
> a story I will not soon forget."
> — Szoch

> "The more I think about it, the more truth and beauty
> I find in the story."
> —H. A. Titus

Available everywhere online or special order from your local bookstore.

LADY MOON

When Celine meets Tomas, they are in a cavern on the moon where she has been languishing for thirty days after being banished by her evil uncle for throwing a scrub brush at his head. Tomas is a charming and eccentric Immortal, hanging out on the moon because he's procrastinating his destiny—meeting, and defeating, Celine's uncle.

A pair of magic rings send them back to earth, where Celine insists on returning home and is promptly thrown into the dungeon. Her uncle, Ignus Umbria, is up to no good, and his latest caper threatens to devour the whole countryside. He doesn't want Celine getting in the way. More than that, he wants to force Tomas into a confrontation—and Tomas, who has fallen in love with Celine, cannot procrastinate any longer.

Lady Moon is a fast-paced, humorous adventure in a world populated by mad magicians, walking rosebushes, thieving scullery maids, and other improbable things. And of course, the most improbable—and magical—thing of all: true love.

"Celine's sarcastic 'languishing' immediately put me in mind
of Patricia C. Wrede's Dealing with Dragons series
—a fairy tale that gently makes fun of the usual fairy tale tropes.
And once again, Rachel Starr Thomson doesn't disappoint."
— H. A. Titus

"Funny and quirky fantasy."

Available everywhere online.

SHORT FICTION
BY RACHEL STARR THOMSON

Butterflies Dancing

Fallen Star

Of Men and Bones

Ogres Is

Journey

Magdalene

The City Came Creeping

Wayfarer's Dream

War With the Muse

Shields of the Earth

And more!

Available as downloads for Kindle, Kobo, Nook, iPad, and more!